AGE OF MENETHON

THE CHOSEN

A M THOMSON

First published in 2021 by Immortalise

contact: info@immortalise.com.au

ISBN   - print: 978-0-6450377-8-4

         - ebook: 978-0-6450377-9-1

Cover design by:Amber Withers
Map by A M Thomson
Typeset by: Ben Morton

For the keeper of my heart.

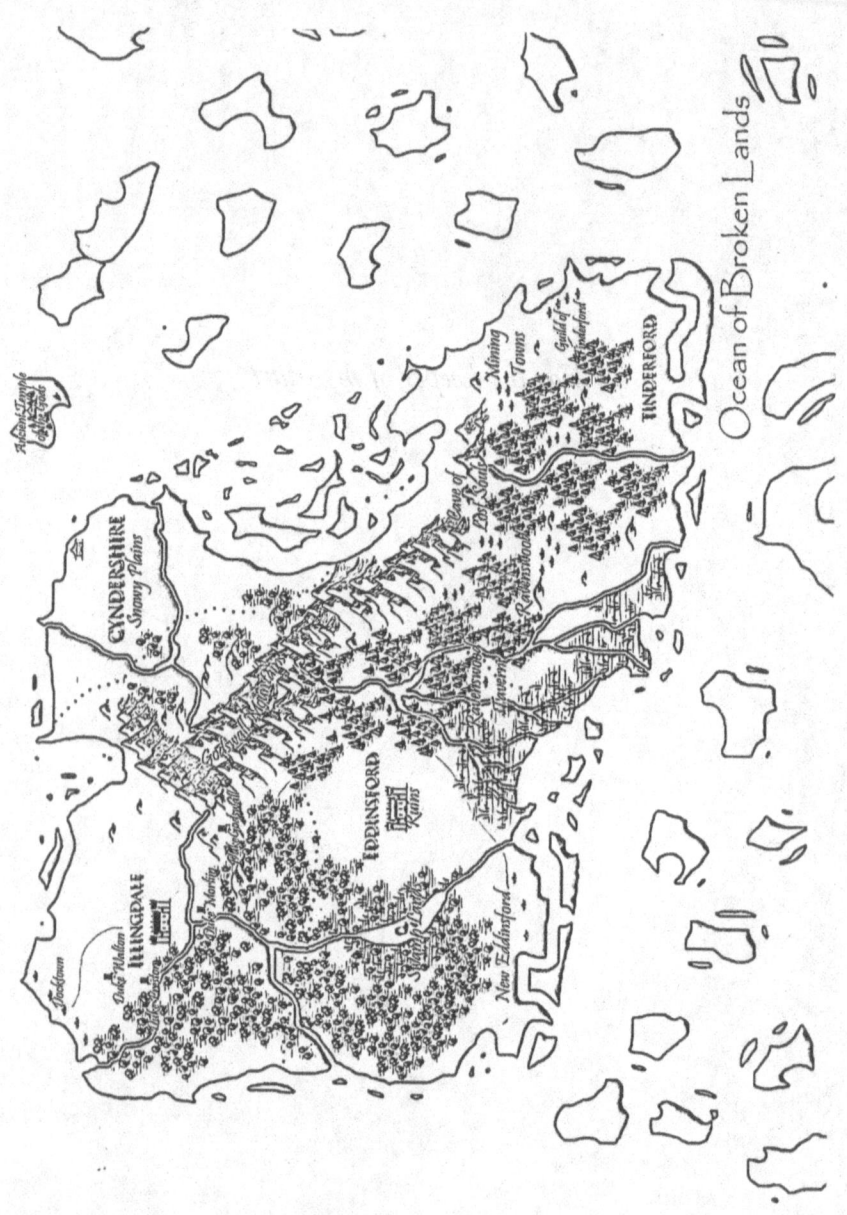

Ocean of Broken Lands

CYNDERSHIRE
Snowy Plains

TINDERFORD

Mining
Towns

RHINGDALE

EDDINSFORD
Ruins

New Eddinsford

PROLOGUE

Randal, Ĭdućhii iife Ĭgodiiwaŀ, Ĭŀiiŋgdale.[1]

Drip… drip.

'Intolerable, simply intolerable.' Randal turned to the small window beside his writing desk and glowered at the raindrops, his lower lip thrust out with annoyance. The drops slid down the dirty glass pane in a chaotic mass, as if they had somewhere important to be.

Drip.

'Menethon be damned for this blasted rain!' He said, throwing his quill down in frustration.

The duchy of Godswall was nestled in at the base of the Godswall Mountains and blanketed by conical pine trees so

---

[1]Translation: *Ĭdućhii iife Ĭgodiiwaŀ, Ĭŀiiŋgdale.* Randal, Duchy of Godswall, Illingdale.

1

dense the winter snow could only get within four metres of the dirt by way of stealth and agility. Today was no exception. The rain had continued all morning and the constant drip falling in perfect rhythm above him had begun to echo in his mind. It was not until the doors to his study flew open unannounced…again, that he gave up, chucking his hands in the air and launching from his chair. 'Damn that man!' The reports would just have to wait. The interloper, a servant, strode in stopping inches away from Randal, his lips pursed, and his eyes squint, giving him the appearance of a man who habitually sucked unripened lemons.

'My lord, I present to you, General Balor Mallory of Illingdale!' He said, his absurdly erect figure holding position inches from Randal's face, oblivious to Randal's obvious discomfort.

Randal squared his shoulders and took a step back. "You might wait to be permitted, Tandus." He said, hoping the boy would at least apologise. He did not. Tandus may have smelled of freshly pressed linen, but he had the manners of a hot iron.

'I knocked, sir.' He replied, his face as blank as new parchment.

Randal pinched the bridge of his nose, his mouth scrunching up to consider the point further when he realised the boy had already left. Randal had time to shake his head at the retreating figure when the General swept in. He was a capable looking man with a kind, angular face. He looked well into his fiftieth year but still had the occasional tendril of colour in his short wavy white hair. He stopped in front of the Duke and offered a swift, but not discourteous bow, his temples furrowed tightly with concern.

'Sorry to impose, Duke.' The great General must have been desperate to come all this way from Illingdale alone.

Randal waved him off, intrigued. 'Please, be seated... shall I ring for some refreshment?' He motioned to the sitting area by the fire. The winters were growing crueller as his age advanced and so he was sure the warmth would ease the General's mood, if not his own. His mind flashed again to the absurd, yet efficient servant he kept, wondering if he was the cause of his frequent headaches.

'No, thank you, Duke.' He said, shaking his head.

'Please General no formalities, just Randal.' He motioned for the General to sit.

'Randal,' Balor settled down and took a deep breath, studying his hands; he was nervous. 'I have no doubt that by now you are aware I have quarrelled with the king regarding his advisor, Lord Gelraen.'

Randal gave one deep nod of accent and then joined him in the seat opposite. 'I have heard the rumour... you had some concerns?'

3

'To put it lightly,' Balor remarked, and then waited for a moment, fishing for the right way to start. 'I need to be frank with you, Randal. Others may label you as eccentric, but I know you to be a man of honour, so I have risked the King's additional wrath to ask for your help.' He waited, his plea hovering in the air like a desperate fly.

Randal nodded and then took a deep breath of his own, careful to keep his face passive. 'What service can I offer Illingdale's favourite General?'

Balor relaxed back into his chair. '18 years ago, I was charged, as you will remember to escort the Queen safely to Mespar so she could deliver the prince, or princess, as it were… my report to the king concluded that our vessel was set upon by mercenaries, and that the shock caused complications with Queen Nemelliia, resulting in early labour.'

Randal took another deep, controlled breath 'Go on …'

'We were not far out from the coast when our ship was fired on. They came out of nowhere Randal, damaged my ship beyond repair, and killed all my men, good men.' He paused for a moment, reflecting on the painful memory. 'The Queen was moved in secret, so I knew it had to be someone close to the crown who betrayed us. I also knew the move was a cover to transport something of great value. Why else would they attack a random envoy unprovoked? … I ordered Nemelliia to take the raft to shore, and let me stay to distract them, but she refused to leave. She said it was her they were wanted and ordered me to get the princess to safety. Were it not for the sake of protecting the infant, I would never have listened!' He lowered his gaze to the floor, 'The last time I saw her, she was staring out at the advancing ship, right up until flames engulfed our vessel.' Balor shifted uncomfortably, snapping himself out of the growing melancholy. 'I have heard from a reliable source that, Lord Gelraen was behind the attack, and I believe he is still looking for the lost item.' A tiny, but perceivable weight lifted from him.

Randal slowly dug a fingernail into the leather of his chair. 'Do you think he knows where it is?'

Balor frowned. 'The item? ... I don't know. But recently, he has begun turning his attention to the princess. Maybe he thinks it has been recovered since and passed on to her…in any case I can no longer ignore the situation … something has to be done.'

Randal removed his now bloodless finger from the leather of the chair and placed it against his mouth to think. 'Is it not possible that, Lord Gelraen simply wants the throne?'

Balor threw his hands in the air, frustrated, 'Then why just attack the ship?' He said, slamming them onto the arm rest again. 'Had he been after the throne he would have followed us as well, not pursued the ship, and then why would the Queen sacrifice her life? No, he coveted whatever it was, she was hiding.'

Randal stood and walked to the blazing hearth, allowing a moment to digest the General's words. *What to tell him, what to tell him*' 'What exactly have you discussed with the King?' He turned back to face the General, half lit by the fire.

Balor adopted a pained look, scratching the back of his head. 'Cailem keeps talking about some war he thinks is coming, and he intends to announce a betrothal between, Gelraen and the Princess. It's a tactical alliance, meant to guarantee, Gelraen's troops. I advised him, if we uphold the treaty, Mespar will never be a threat. I also strongly advised against the marriage, on the grounds that I believed, Lord Gelraen to be distrust worthy.' Balor shifted in his seat. 'I could not tell my old friend the whole truth because I have been lying to him for the last 18 years.'

'Indeed.' Randal's face remained controlled as he stared into the fire.

'Randal, the King is besotted with the man, he has made that abundantly clear. I have already failed the Queen; I cannot allow her daughter to come to harm.' Balor puffed out his chest, full of conviction. There was no deterring him.

'What are you proposing?' Randal asked, walking back and sitting opposite the General, and rubbing his temple to ease the headache that grew stronger.

A spark of warm confidence filled Balor's face; he had been anticipating cooperation from the Duchy, 'I plan to make sure the situation is resolved permanently.'

Randal contemplated the General long and hard. 'Assassinate, Gelraen?'

Balor was intent, his arms crossed in concentration. '... What I need from you is an assurance.'

Randal paused, chewing the idea over. 'What kind of assurance?'

'Whether the item was recovered or not is of little consequence, Lord Gelraen has wormed his way into the King's graces and waited 18 years in the hopes of another chance. I cannot take the risk that he is the only one who knows of its existence, whatever it is. The princess could still be in danger; I need someone I trust to guarantee her protection.'

Randal lowered his eyes, 'Your proposal is treason, for both of us!'

Balor's face was steady, but his shoulders slumped against the weight on his conscience. He was a man who had reached his last resort, whether he wanted to or not. 'I know. But since the king won't listen, I see no other way. Do you?'

Randal left the question unanswered, drumming his fingers on the arm of the chair, 'What do you know of the princess's involvement?'

Balor frowned 'As far as I am aware, she has none. I cannot see how this item, whatever it was, could have been passed to her. Thankfully, she does not share the same favour for the man, which is something at least. Cailem is having a hard time getting her to agree to the alliance.'

Randal stood and walked slowly back to the fire, covering his busy expression from view. 'It just so happens I have noticed something strange in the reports from Mespar. It has been only three years since Lord Gelraen's return from that accursed land but, since then, my spies have been growing concerned.'

'Concerned, how?' Balor sat forward; his eyes boring into Randal's back.

'As you know, Mesparian soldiers patrol the Isle of the Forgotten to stop Malagara from escaping.'

Balor nodded. 'I am aware.'

'Well, I have noticed inconsistencies that started around the time of, Gelraen's return that could be related.'

'What kind of inconsistencies? And why am I only being told about this now?' Balor was becoming agitated now, shifting in his chair as if it was made of stone.

'Because my official reports from Mespar obtained no news about the Isle of the forgotten. Just, usual trade talk, and weather reports.' Randal turned, selecting his words, more from the pain in his head than the need to think. 'But my spies report that soldiers have gone missing, only to be found days later, miles away from their post with no memories of what happened.'

'Are you suggesting, Gelraen is somehow interfering with the official reports?'

He ignored the question. 'It was a small issue at first, so I dismissed it. But lately the inconsistencies have increased, so I have sent someone I trust to investigate.'

'Would you care to elaborate on whom?' Balor sat back in his chair and crossed his arms, he disapproved of matters being taken out of his control.

'Suffice to say I have the situation in hand for now, Illingdale need not concern itself just yet. Lord Gelraen however, is another concern entirely.'

Balor scratched his beard, like it would dislodge some of the secrets that were determined to evade him. 'If this is true, and Gelraen is connected to these disappearances somehow, I need to act now!'

Randal rapped his fingers on the oaken mantel of the fireplace automatically, his mind far away. 'Do nothing for the moment; the princess is in no *immediate* trouble. She is stubborn and that will keep her out of danger. Go back to Illingdale and keep a watchful eye on Gelraen; let me know of anything you find. I will do some more digging here.'

Balor stood looking relieved. 'Thank you, I must confess this is more help than I had hoped for.'

Randal nodded. 'Will you allow me to see you rested?'

Balor shook his head. 'No, thank you.' His voice cracked, 'I must be on the road immediately or I risk raising the king's suspicions further.'

Randal stood, 'I understand, good speed to you General!' He watched as Balor swept from the room, leaving behind a score of concerns to be turned over in his aching head. The longer the princess went without knowing who she was, the more danger she was in. Randal considered telling Balor the truth, that the princess was chosen. But deep down, he knew a man like that would never see her as anything but a despised Malagara, a heretic. No, the General could never know, and so Randal walked back to his rain-covered window and stared back out, regretting the knowledge that there was more in play than simple truths; Balor was now riding the wheel of fate, in a dangerous game he didn't understand.

CHAPTER ONE

Isyllia, City of Illingdale.

"He's dead! Our king is dead!" Coldness permeated the ornate room, having nothing at all to do with the fireless hearth that stood awaiting food. It took a moment for the small doctor to gather his wits, stepping back from the corpse and then mopping his brow in disbelief. He cast a nervous eye at Isyllia, she remained still, never taking her eyes off her lifeless father's face.

"Check again!" The voice came from the doctor's back, muffled as though filtered through teeth. He turned to find a tall man with long dark hair and proud angular features glaring back. The man tightened his already rigid shoulders, his face alive and tensing against the spreading red stain in his cheeks, not even the heavens could abide such a glare. The doctor fell backwards, grabbing onto the bedpost for dear life and dropping his damp handkerchief in the process. For a moment, he fumbled on the

11

ground, unwilling to take his eyes off the towering lord, and careful to hide the spreading wet stain on his groin he managed to at last deposit the square of cloth into the sleeve of his alabaster jacket. He placed his other hand in front of him, with the vague notion that it would stop the livid man reaching him. "Lord Gelraen, his majesty's heart has ceased to beat. He grows cold; there is nothing more I can do!"

Lord Gelraen grabbed the man's shirt and thrust him against the bedpost, "Check. Him. *Again!*"

"Enough, Lord Gelraen. You heard the man, he's gone." Isyllia stood and walked away from the bed, stopping before one man, who until now had remained silent at the back of the room. His head was down, and it was clear, unlike Gelraen, this man was devastated. "How could you let this happen?" Her voice was thick and full of pain, causing the recipient to step forward.

"I." General Balor paused to swallow back his emotion and stop his voice from cracking, "I'm sorry." He looked like he wanted to say more, but it was clear there was nothing more to say.

Isyllia drew herself up, still concentrating her amber glare on the forlorn man. Balor came from a long line of Generals; it was unusual to see him so broken and unsure of himself. For a moment she felt herself soften, "What will we do now?"

Balor took a deep, unsettled breath. 'Justice, majesty.' Balor said, letting his shoulders slump. The princess stood close now, mirror images of each other. He exhaled, and then turned to leave, forgetting to bow.

'I will first hear your intentions!' Lord Gelraen had discarded the doctor, who took the opportunity to flee, and instead directed his cold wrath at Balor.

Balor clenched his jaw and faced the man, undaunted by his physical presence. 'I will discuss nothing with you.'

Gelraen stopped almost nose to nose, but Balor refused to flinch, challenging each other with a glare thick enough with hatred to render words pointless.

'Enough!' Isyllia breathed deep for a moment to compose herself, her words slow and deliberate. 'You will seal the gates; *no one* will leave this city.'

Balor hesitated. 'We also need to place you under heavier guard, Princess. We have to assume the culprit aims is to seize the throne, making you the next logical target.'

What little colour remained in her silken cheeks drained, leaving a mask of white behind. 'I understand, I shall now take my leave. Lord Gelraen, you will take charge.'

Balor went rigid, his face a dangerous shade of red, 'That is unwise, Majesty.'

She ignored him. 'See that William is brought to my chambers. I will trust my safety to no one else. You are dismissed.'

Balor bowed and swept from the room, thundering his heavy footsteps out the room like a storm cloud looking for a victim.

Lord Gelraen looked to the floor as Balor left, hiding what looked like a small note of victory, then changing to concern as his face narrowed like he had a headache. 'With respect, Princess, Balor is correct. Right now, the best approach would be to show some fortitude and take your father's seat. The attacker can no longer move freely, a show of strength could weaken his resolve.'

Isyllia slumped a little, knowing she could not keep up the façade of indifference much longer. 'I'm not my father, Lord Gelraen. I will fool no one, least of all myself. I will be ordering a transfer of authority right away, and as our military advisor, I trust you to make the right decisions. It cannot be a coincidence that this has occurred right when my marriage contract was being negotiated.'

Lord Gelraen scratched his creased forehead, 'You suspect Illingdale's having obtained the last duchy is a motivating factor?'

'I'm not sure, but it does seal the final point in our city's defences.'

'I agree. What do you suggest?' Lord Gelraen waited.

Isyllia took a deep breath, though it was not enough to quell the bile that tried to force the words back down. 'I suggest we finalise the arrangements, as soon as possible. I will have the contract drawn and ready to sign at once. It will then be announced at the feast. It looks like, Father may have been right, war is coming.'

Lord Gelraen lowered himself into a majestic bow. 'I am honoured.'

She ignored the gesture, turning back to face the cold remains of her father. 'Ensure our King is prepared for his Honour-Giving, spare no expense.'

'Of course, I shall make the necessary arrangements.' Gelraen's voice was quiet, yet filled with a sudden, tremendous confidence.

There was no emotion left on the dead man's face, save the shock of life being taken too soon. Isyllia drank in every detail, the clench in her stomach building to a new crescendo, knowing this would be the last time. *I need to leave.*' The thought took control of her body, directing her to the door and away from the pain. 'Send for me when the transfer of authority is ready.' She didn't look back to see if he had heard, she no longer cared.

'Guards, escort our new Queen. Arrest anyone who disturbs her, besides William!'

The halls were not deserted, but she knew they would not be. Isyllia strode ahead, pulling her shoulders into herself to avoid the sea of never-ending faces that swam with her the whole way. All distraught. All begging for news of the king. Isyllia walked in a daze, pretenders, all of them. Instead, she focused on the clacking of her shoes down the marble halls. William, she needed William. He would already be waiting. Her pace quickened; unaware of the guards still forming around her, who were trying their best to shoo well-wishers with their spears. When at last she did reach her rooms, she burst through the door and swung it closed with an audible thud.

'Thank goodness you're safe!' He was *always* there. William crossed the room in a second, throwing his arms around her, his face filled with anguish.

Could she tell him?

'What happened?' He pulled away, smoothing his blonde ponytail and searching her face for answers.

Isyllia walked to the window and sat with her head against the cool windowpane, unable to look him in the eyes. 'He was poisoned.'

'Poisoned!'

She nodded then began depositing hairpins on the frosty white surface, shaking her long brown hair loose, 'Your father believes I remain a target.'

William gave a long sigh and then sat on a chair next to her. 'The General is right.' He said, curling his face like he had just eaten something sour. 'It wouldn't make sense to kill the king yet leave an heir.' He picked up one of the pins and tossed it across the room, not watching to see where it landed. 'I just don't understand how this could happen in the first place.'

'I asked him the same question.' She said, frowning, her concentration on her fingers tracing patterns in the misty window.

William kept talking, almost to himself. 'It was most likely a cook... bribed or tricked to slip something in the food.'

Isyllia shot back around, 'Surely not!'

'I doubt they would have known it was poison.'

Isyllia blanched, 'I can't think about this right now. Please!' She pounded her fist against the window frame, watching as tiny droplets hurried toward the ground.

'I know, I know.' William touched her on the shoulder, "I'm sorry, I just thought it might help to have some idea on their possible methods.' William took a deep breath and then looked at her, resetting himself ... 'How are you doing?'

Numerous emotions surged at once, leaving Isyllia lightheaded. She took a deep breath. 'I feel like my world has been turned upside down. I'm not ready for this. I don't want to walk out there and smile and laugh and pretend everything is fine.' Isyllia leaned into his hand, soaking in the comfort... 'I don't want to be strong.'

'I know. Just take it one day at a time, that is all you can do. And if things get bad, we can always throw grapes at the nobles, that always worked in the past.'

Isyllia laughed despite herself, 'We were kids then, we're too old for that now, Will!'

William stood, bracing one arm at his abdomen, his fist clenched in protest. 'Never!'

The spark of mirth left her as quickly as it had ignited, her mouth giving way. 'Will, be serious.'

William deflated, his pale blue eyes taking on a look of concentration. 'Being serious. We are going to need to make some changes.'

Isyllia straightened, 'What kind of changes?'

William exhaled, puffing out his cheeks in the process. 'Well, all your usual staff will need to be dismissed, and all your food will need to be tasted – most important. We cannot take any kind of risks, big or small.'

Isyllia's mouth tightened, 'I'll consent to a reduction in staff, but I must have at least one, and I'm not having someone taste my food.'

'Issy, you wanted to be serious.'

'I know, I just can't handle the idea of someone else dying that way.' She said, shaking the thought out.

'Better them than you.'

She glared, her jaw open in shock, 'That's disgusting, Will.'

'It's reality, you *are* the queen.'

Isyllia turned herself away, her nose raised in defiance, 'It's barbaric.'

William sighed, 'Fine, I will think of something. In the meantime, I would also suggest keeping public engagements to a minimum. It's harder to control crowds.'

Isyllia swallowed, trying to ignore the belief that the room was closing in on her. 'That at least won't be a problem.'

'Why?' William asked, his temples creasing in confusion.

'Because I have taken my leave. Lord Gelraen will now be regent until the crisis has passed... This situation is forcing me to accept his marriage contract.' The words sounded wrong; she knew it too late. All she could do now was brace for his response. It was not going to be good.

The blood drained from William's face, and he swallowed hard, gripping onto the side of a chair for support. 'I thought you hated Lord Gelraen. I thought you told your father no!'

'I did. But now … How I feel is immaterial, Will. Father wanted his duchy to ensure the protection of the city.'

'There has to be *other* options?' He said, pleading.

Isyllia sat forward, her back hunched from the pressure. 'It's what father wanted!' She regarded her friend, he needed to understand. 'Will, I'm not ready to rule a Kingdom - he is. As much as I despise him, I need him right now… and his men.'

William was unconvinced, the agitation dragging him back and forth over the same spot, pacing. 'He's a Duke of the Realm, isn't he already duty bound to provide men and service if needed? You don't need to marry him for that!'

'Yes, but father didn't want an alliance abroad, so he chose Gelraen because he's a military man, a tactician. Plus, the Duke of Morliin is not a Bellamy, he's not kin. Father needed to *guarantee* his allegiance.'

William stood and began pacing the room.

'Father agreed to give him my hand William, it would be a dishonour to his memory if I didn't abide by his last wish… I cannot continue to refuse him now, as much as I want to.' Isyllia looked on, helpless. 'Will.'

'No.' He started for the door.

'Will, please.'

William stopped for a moment, but did not turn around, 'I will see to your ladies.' And then he stormed out, not sparing a single glance back, or bothering to close the door. Isyllia continued to regard the vacated space, half hoping she had never said anything, and half knowing she had, had no other choice. The emptiness of sleep was what called her now. She contemplated the bed, deciding to stumble over one step at a time and fall into its welcoming embrace like a new lover's kiss, soft and full of promise. Not at all caring about the chaos on the other side of her open door, or the pain that William had left behind. Closing her eyes, she allowed her consciousness instead to fall into a deep and empty chasm of sleep.

Three-dull-thuds. She knew that knock, it sounded morning after morning.

'Curse of the gods go away! … get your own cakes!' She buried her head under a free pillow.

He ignored her and came in; she had expected nothing less. 'I have your maid.'

Isyllia frowned, did he sound angry? She sat up and eyed him, William was rigid, he walked across the floor without making eye contact, that was unlike him. 'What are you babbling about?' She said, concluding she was in no mood for his tantrum, whatever it was about.

He sensed her confusion and took a mental step back. 'I appointed someone to see to your needs!' He spoke slowly, shooing the hovering Petra in the opposite direction. 'You will need to get out of bed, Lord Gelraen is asking for you!'

'Lord Gelraen…Why?' Then it hit her, vaulting into her stomach with a force that could have broken her ribs as well as her heart. 'Father!' She remembered someone had slain the king. But it was not just her father, William was tense, like he would rather be anywhere else. Isyllia felt the panic begin to take over, a burning sensation growing in her throat. She took a deep breath, *'I can't lose it, he will see. I have to calm down.'*

His face softened, 'I'm here.'

Her muscles felt like they had doubled in weight, causing her to drag herself to the edge of the bed, wishing instead she could hibernate until the whole ordeal passed. The thought brought her an alluring comfort, making the journey to the end of the mattress slow and unbearable. 'I thought you were angry with me?'

William sat next to her, staring at the wall in front of him. 'I'm sorry, my reaction was unfair. Now isn't the time.'

She sighed, 'No, *I'm* sorry … I don't *want* to do this, you know!'

William swallowed and then retreated inward, hiding from his own emotions. 'I know.'

Isyllia tried a smile; it felt forced, but she knew in the circumstances he would understand. 'I don't want to fight, not now.' She rested on his shoulder, knowing deep down it was wrong, knowing she should let him go, but she craved the comfort he brought, she always had, like an ant to honey.

William placed his arm around her and then rested his head on hers, a kind of peace drifting over his face. 'I miss this.'

'So, do I. I don't know what I would do without you.'

He shifted his shoulder out from under her, walking several paces away. 'You do plenty without me.' He said, his voice taking on a dangerous tone again.

'I don't understand.' Isyllia felt her anxiety blossom again like tiny contagious flowers, forcing her to place a hand over her abdomen to trap them spreading under her palm.

'I'm sorry, I know now is a bad time, but unlike you, I can't pretend. I told myself that being your friend, being the one you trusted was enough. I thought maybe one day you might change your mind.'

Isyllia cut in, 'I'm not free to make my own choices, Will! You know that!'

William nodded, 'Were it just that, I would understand. But it isn't. I know you have secrets that you won't share with me, and it's pushing us apart.' He pointed to her; she had begun shaking her head without knowing. 'You can shake your head, but there is no point in dancing around it anymore.'

'All girls have secrets, Will. It's nothing, I swear!' She said, but the tremor in her voice suggested otherwise.

'Not us… We used to always sneak out to the rose garden and talk until the moon rose, now you won't even go there alone with me. You're always nervous, you faint all the time.'

Isyllia tried to slow her breathing, but the panic was feeding off his pain and she knew it. 'It's nothing, Will, I swear it's nothing.'

He ignored her, 'Then you lied to me… I think that's the worst part.'

I'm scared! But that was not what she said. Instead, she continued to shake her head, 'I'm not lying Will, there are no secrets. I'm just unwell, it's all the pressure. I don't want this life; you know I don't!' She said, her voice rising several octaves.

Now William shook his head, 'I just don't believe you anymore.' He started for the door.

She felt her heart begin to pound in protest. 'Wait! I know things are not perfect right now, and I know marrying Gelraen isn't helping, but I still need you, I've always needed you.'

He sighed, unconvinced. 'Your actions say otherwise!'

She shifted away slightly so she could face him better. He stared out the window, not making eye contact. He had closed off. 'I'm the same person I've always been.' The words were a lie. She knew it but most of all, he knew it.

'I'll find someone suitable to replace me.' He continued to the door.

'Will! I can't do this alone, please.' She reached out and clutched his arm in desperation, anything to stop him walking out again.

William stopped for a moment, creasing his mouth like her touch caused him pain. But it didn't deter him. Still he dislodged her, thrusting open the door and then pausing for a moment. 'You're not alone, you have Gelraen now.' This time the door closed over in slow motion. In silence except for the thud it left behind. The final moment. Isyllia breathed fast and short, each exhalation a new emotion flying outward from her body, and then straight back in again. Leaving her paralysed from the unbreakable repetition.

'Majesty-' Petra edged her way over, placing a timid hand on the distraught girl's shoulder.

Isyllia threw the maid's arm off, 'Don't call me that!' She said, regretting the outburst and dissolving into tears.

The maid dropped her bundle on the floor where she stood and taking Williams place on the bed, she cradled the crying queen. 'Shush now child, it will all come about, shush.' Petra had been the favourite lady in waiting to Isyllia's mother, and so it was only proper for her to continue and care for Isyllia. For many years, Petra had been like a mother to her. She was also the only person who knew about Isyllias condition. Even above her own father. 'You must dress child.' Petra's eyes were red, she had also been crying.

Dejected, Isyllia moved to her dressing mirror like she was hollow, an empty puppet. She didn't bother to wipe the last-minute tears that hurried down her face, nor did she care what happened around her. Oblivious to Petra bustling about, gathering things and giving her a reassuring pat on the shoulder. It was some minutes later when she stepped forward in a familiar gown of plain navy velvet, one of her favourites, not realising it had ever been fitted.

'Thank you.' She said, the words finding their way out of their own accord.

Petra craned her neck to the side, taking on some of the girl's sorrow. 'Think nothing of it, child.'

Isyllia looked to the floor, again filled with shame for having snapped at the ageing woman. Petra placed a hand under Isyllias chin, 'You have your fathers' strength, and your mothers grace. I know right now things are tough, but it will turn out, I promise.'

Isyllia launched forward and wrapped her arms around the woman.

'Careful, my bones aren't what they used to be.' She said, returning the girls' needs. Isyllia soaked up the warmth, somehow finding the strength to tear herself away and put her dress right. A replacement guard already waited, and it wasn't William. 'Keep up.' She shot, picking fault with the way he walked, stood, anything and everything that gave her someone else to focus her pain on for the short distance to the council chambers. Isyllia threw open the heavy oak doors, having no intention of waiting for the harried soldier and strode inside. The room was filled with men, all dressed in black, all except one. Lord Gelraen stood on the dais, tall and imposing in his crimson jerkin. He always wore red. The image made her cringe, but deciding now was not the time, she walked to the front and stood next to him, positioning herself as far away as she could manage. The men waited, some with looks of pity on their faces. She ignored them.

'Good day gentlemen.' She waited a moment; men nodded their encouragement. Gelraen looked to the floor, the picture of decorum. It was an odd sight. 'It is our honoured general's view that this attack on our beloved king could in fact also be directed at me. Therefore I have decided to accept the marriage contract set forward by Lord Gelraen Pennerly and my father, and appoint him regent until the crisis passes.'

Some of the men frowned, a small portly man among them. 'Majesty?' He stood, 'If indeed these attacks are to continue as you suggest, it would be best to show your strength. They will think twice about another assault.'

'Lord Gelraen agrees with you Imaar.' She nodded to Lord Gelraen, who still eyed the floor. '... But I am inexperienced in the ways of government, and a golden throne will not hide that. I believe that a unity between House Bellamy and House Morliin, will give our enemies a tactical show of strength. We cannot rule out that war is a possibility.'

The men nodded in unison. 'Unlikely though it is, you are right. All possibilities must be heeded. I support your proposal Majesty' Imaar sat back down.

'Is there a second?'

One of the men at the back raised his hand 'Second!'

'Good. The support of the people was important to my father, I intend to continue this tradition.' There was a murmur of approval throughout the room. She turned to Lord Gelraen, 'Have the documents been drafted?'

He nodded, and then motioned to a scribe standing hidden at the back of the room. 'They have majesty.' The scribe brought the rolled-up parchments forward, laying them out on the table in the centre of the room. She glanced through the words to be satisfied they were in order, and then picked up the quill that had been set beside her, dipping it in ink. She scrawled her name, not taking the usual care or attention to the way she looped the letters, thrusting the quill to Lord Gelraen. He took it, his face unreadable, and signed his name.

'It is done. Thank you, gentlemen, I now take my leave.' Isyllia turned and walked from the room, not even tempted a little to look back and see the man she loathed sitting in the golden throne that used to be her father's. A chair connected with so many memories, and now holding a future, from which there was no escape.

CHAPTER TWO

Ember, Seaside Docktown, Illingdale.

It was a slow night. To most, the fear of being blown into the sea proved to be greater than the desire to drown the senses in ale. A few brave sailors occupied the bar beside Ember, and they sat in a corner in companionable silence, not showing the slightest desire to move anytime soon, except to reunite ale with lips. Ember however, sat alone. He always sat alone.

'Want another one?'

Ember shook his head deliberately, his eyes unfocused. His concentration was elsewhere. 'Not tonight Phil, just the one.' He said, snapping back into focus.

'Somewhere to be?' The barman asked, his eyebrows raised with anticipation.

Ember cracked the ghost of a smile, the corner of his mouth lifting with amusement. 'Never let up do you, Phil!'

Phil, slapped the bar and then stood up straight, grabbing another tankard and attacking it with a rag that was tucked into his apron. 'Well there's plenty of young girls around the town that'll have you, you're a sturdy looking lad, and you make a decent living. Not getting any younger you know!'

'Maybe.' Ember tucked his shoulder length brown hair behind his ears, and then reached into his pouch for some coins, his eyes unfocused again.

Phil sighed. 'My wife says I'm a tough nut to crack.' He threw down his cleaning linen and put the now polished tankard on the bar, ready for its next victim, if one was brave enough to make it there. 'Where are you off to tonight then?'

'Got someone to see!'

Phil's face lit up with approval, his hands saluting the air. 'See now that's more like it, what's her name?' He leaned forward, like if the act would enable him to perceive the answer a notable timeframe earlier.

On the other hand, Ember wanted to remain serious, but the man's excitement got the better of him, leaving a grin to spread despite his better judgment. He shook his head. 'Just a chat Phil.'

'So that's what they call it nowadays!' It was clear this was the most exciting news Phil had heard in some time.

'That's generally how it starts.' Ember said.

'Don't waste time courting laddie, snap her up and then bed her good and proper.'

Ember cocked another grin, tossing some silver coins onto the bar. 'Why would I need a wife, when I have you!' He said.

Phil took the coin and returned the grin, 'King keep ya safe lad!'

Ember nodded, and then turned into the waiting storm. A heavy wind greeted him the moment he stepped outside and then did its best to push him on an unknown journey. Ember frowned, wrapping his cloak tight around himself and trudged forward through the enthusiastic weather with purpose. He stopped on occasion, allowing the gale to steer him a little off course, and then once righted made sure to misstep an appropriate amount of times down a deserted alleyway. There were no houses, save one at the end. A solitary light could be seen burning in the distance, but there was no movement. It was perfect. Ember concealed himself against the wall with his cloak and waited. A shadowy figure turned down the darkened lane. He had one unsteady hand out in front of him. Like he knew he was walking into a trap, but not where his assailant would strike. The man kept walking, his eyes darting to and fro with each crackle and whistle of the night. He had just passed the place where Ember crouched, waiting, when he gasped. Ember's blade pressed tight against his throat.

'You have one chance to answer: Why are you following me?'

The man swallowed against the blade, then tried to speak. Ember loosened his grip on the man's mouth, 'I bring a message, that's all I swear, I'm just a messenger, please don't kill me!'

'Then why not make yourself known?' He pressed in deeper, not at all convinced.

'Because I was told to ensure you were the right person before I came forward. Check me for weapons if you don't believe me, you'll find nothing!'

'And who do you think I am?' He already knew the man was unarmed.

'You are, Ember Clae are you not?' He asked, his hands raised in surrender.

Ember stepped back and sheathed his dagger. 'Not around here I'm not!'

The man turned to face Ember, rubbing his throat theatrically and then stepped back a little further. Like the extra distance would protect him from a repeat onslaught. 'Yes, I am familiar with Illingdale's Laws, what should I call you then?'

'Call me, Anton.'

'Anton it is, and as I said; I bring a *message*.' The man thrust a folded-up slip of paper to Ember with the unmistakable air of someone wanting to be *anywhere* else.

Ember nodded to the man, ignoring the not-so cryptic complaint, and then turned the envelope over to examine the red seal which held no indication of its sender. 'Whose seal is this?'

The man nodded to the letter, 'Read.'

Ember obeyed, tearing the wax away to reveal a short note;

Ember

I apologise for the method in which I call upon you champion, but things grow desperate. You must travel to Illingdale tonight, remove her by any means necessary, and take her to Godswall. You will find a woman named Adella at the Dale Inn who can introduce you to Balor. He will help you get her out of the city. It is time for you to be who you were born to be.

Gods protect you champion; her life depends on it.

Guardian.

'I took the liberty of preparing your horse; you will find supplies already waiting.'

Ember nodded, noting that the man had been confident enough to prepare the right horse. He decided against mentioning it. 'Is this from, Randal of Godswall?'

'I am unaware who the sender is, I follow instructions on behalf of a mutual correspondent. The letter could have come from anywhere for all I know.' He said, sensing Embers continued scepticism, the man then turned on his heels and strode in the opposite direction. Not at all looking back to offer any further form of explanation.

Ember waited until the man disappeared and then looked at the paper again. Instinct told him to take some time and study the situation, an answering jolt in his abdomen acting to reinforce the idea. Instead, he stuffed the note into his shirt, deciding not to stop at the workshop and leave a note for his apprentice, he would send a bird from the Wentworth birder. Instead he took a direct path to the stables and the danger promised, swallowing the regret that sailed in. Ember walked away from the life he had built, wondering, if he would ever return.

Illingdale was often referred to as the gloomy alternative to the godly city of Mespar. It sat nestled somewhat next to the Godswall mountains, its many pointed buildings reaching to the sky like they were slowly being sucked up by the surrounding clouds. It was often cold here, and this year's winter was no exception, the bad weather travelled with Ember all the way from Docktown, determined to inconvenience as many people as possible. With apprehension he rode forward and tried not to think of the letter stashed in his wet shirt or what was left of it by now. Instead, he focused on finding somewhere to stable Perrin. He remembered one place on the poorer side of town; a place free of the kinds of people who like to ask questions. Ember set Perrin into a trot, arriving minutes later, and handed the boy a double fee, instructing him to wash and give his horse extra food. The boy thanked him repeatedly, almost backing into a hay bale in the process and falling over backwards. Ember shook his head and looked back outside; it was still raining. He stood for a moment, taking a deep breath, and then plunging for the damp streets once more, his boots sloshing as he walked up the narrow merchant's quarter. It was different from how he last remembered it. The street was deserted, no shoppers bustled about among the various, boarded up windows. Only one sign was left hanging among the stretch, the Dale Inn. He stood for a moment, hesitating but knowing he was left with little choice if he wanted to know what was transpiring inside the castle. He had no choice. Ember sighed, and then stretched out his fingers to push open the grimy door. Assaulted by a pungent smell of vomit and intoxication, testing his will to step forward and cross the threshold, and not abandon the whole idea. Instead, he clenched his jaw, and walked in, shaking out his cloak and taking in the scene around him. Prostitutes danced to jeering patrons, their sumptuous breasts trying to poke out of their clothes. Some had gone as far as satisfying their customers where they sat. It was not an enjoyable sight. Looking away in disgust, he made his way to the bar, an old man with vacant eyes smiled at him, toothless but for one stubborn yellow-brown fang sitting at the top of his mouth.

'Ale?' the man slurred, and then spat into the tankard he was cleaning.

Ember nodded, eyebrows furrowed and a clenching in his stomach that protested the idea of his drinking anything. He placed some coins on the bar and nodded his thanks, taking a reluctant mouthful. The liquid was cool and satisfying on his parched throat, despite his previous trepidation. He was even less enthusiastic about sitting down. The chair was sticky from spilt beer and stank of what he hoped was old yeast, but still he sat with an inward shudder and began to observe the patrons. One by one he studied them, stopping when he came to a woman in her 40's, one of the older whores. She was attractive despite her obvious advance in age and compared to the girls around her. The whore had wiry blonde hair and held herself with a confidence unbefitting of her role. Looking closer, he noticed how making certain gestures with her hand, the other girls followed her lead, heeding otherwise secret instructions. She drank and laughed with the drunken men, flashing her breasts in their faces but the laughter did not reach her eyes. What seemed like a group of simple, filthy peasant women, was in fact an elaborate robbery. Their prey, the disorderly men who threw what little coin they possessed at the promise of flesh. She had to be Adella.

He made eye contact with her, then looked back to his tankard. She sauntered over to his booth, taking a seat next to him and placing her filthy hand on his leg. 'Looking for a good time handsome?'

'You don't get married for a good time, that's for sure.' He took another swig.

The whore cackled, 'Trouble at home? ... Cera can make you forget!' She moved her hand further up his thigh with the clear intent of being seductive.

Ember flinched and fought the impulse to push her off. Instead he looked up and studied her for a moment, then placed a gold dale on the table in front of her. 'I think I could use what you've got to offer.'

She smiled, a knowing glint in her eye. 'Thata' boy' Then stood, indicating to a door at the back centre of the room.

Ember closed his eyes for a moment and concentrated. A drunk lay in a puddle of his own vomit a few streets away but apart from that, the streets outside were deserted.

'This way.' She prompted again, but this time with a more serious note.

Ember followed, exiting the Inn with caution and then noticing a slight movement on the pavement floor. The drunk had turned in his sleep, cradling an empty bottle to his chest. The whore was unmoved by the unconscious man and his glass lover, perhaps witnessing the unusual union a little more than even she could stomach. The alleys stretched and wound, each one indistinguishable from the next with no distinct indication of coming to an end. Eventually she stopped in front of a shabby, half broken door and motioned for him to follow her inside. Ember hesitated a moment, deciding it was safe despite the dagger in the woman's right sleeve, but nursing the hilt of his sword while he ducked inside, just in case. Cera had crossed to the opposite side of the room, and bent to light a single candle, its insignificant orange glow offering emotional comfort only. For a moment she continued to remain hunched over, her slight movements indistinguishable. Or they would have been for anyone else. Within the blink of an eye, the woman named Cera turned, flinging a dagger with expert precision toward Ember's face. It would have hit anyone else, but Ember was ready, the pulse in his stomach forcing him to move aside with alarm and unsheathed his sword, pointing it at the now unarmed woman. Cera stood with her arms in the air, a smile stretching up one side of her face. 'Had to be sure.'

The explanation did not in any way tempt Ember to lower his sword.

'You must understand I cannot take risks, even now. Had you been someone else, the consequences would be fatal. For us all.'

'Do you know Randal?' His thoughts fell to the letter he had been instructed to burn, tucked away safe in his shirt, if a little wet by now.

Cera lowered her hands, 'I am acquainted with many people!'

The movement caused Ember to inch closer, his sword closing more space between them while he concentrated on the area around her, she had used her one and only trick, he relaxed his concentration. A headache was beginning to set in, and he still had a long night ahead. Best rely on old fashioned senses for now. 'What has happened in the castle?' He sheathed his sword.

'...You mean aside from the King being slain?' She raised her eyebrows. 'Where did you say you came from?'

He ignored the question. 'How did he die? And is the princess safe?'

'I have heard she is being well guarded by Lord Gelraens men; perhaps a little too well. He has ordered anyone who approaches her to be arrested on the spot, even Captain Mallory.'

He nodded, 'And who is Captain Mallory?'

'He's the General's son, and her personal guard. Among other things.' She smiled, not elaborating.

Ember could feel himself growing impatient, 'And what about the King?'

'Rumour has it that he was poisoned.'

Ember swore, 'Are there any suspects?'

'The General believes Lord Gelraen is behind the attack, though he lacks proof currently.'

'Why would Gelraen kill the king only to protect his heir?'

Cera cocked her head to the side, 'Can you think of no reason?'

Ember pushed his mouth to the side of his face, chewing on the thought. 'Regardless of who is responsible, I need to get the princess out of the city. Tonight. Do you think you can convince the General to cooperate?'

Cera smiled, 'Wait back at the bar.'

An hour later, the door creaked open again. An attractive noble woman with tied back blonde hair looked around, squinting until she spotted Ember. It took a moment for him to realise that it was the same woman who had left an hour earlier. Smiling, she slinked over to the bar where he sat, her tight-fitting dress of grey blue velvet accentuating her hips. 'Try to keep up.' She said, turning back toward the door. '... Coming?'

Ember downed the last of his ale, indicating to the barman that he had finished and then left it, starting toward the door. The woman did not make conversation on the way, for which he was grateful. The never-ending dark clouds that still loomed above, promised no immediate end to their tirade over the city. Ember tightened his cloak around himself automatically, he hated getting his mail shirt wet.

'You knew it was me!' She said, turning a mock frown in his direction. 'I'm a little disappointed.'

Ember picked up his pace until he was walking side by side with her. He looked her up and down, noting the considerable effort she had taken to transform herself down to the last nail. 'I can see I was not meant to!'

'It's usually one of my talents. It helps with discretion, you understand.' She said, accentuating each word.

'*One* of your talents?' His eyes creased, wishing he could take the question back.

'Would you like to find out the rest?' She said, giving the impression that something of the whore remained true, despite her effort in portraying two different people.

43

Ember frowned, decided it was wise to change the subject, 'The General has agreed to meet then?'

She let out a small chuckle, 'At his home, you can talk privately there. It's just ahead!' She motioned to a small forlorn looking wooden door at the end of the narrow street. They had only arrived mere seconds when an elderly housekeeper greeted them and led them into a large, dimly lit room. General Balor Mallory waited, resting his hands behind his back, while he gazed at the smouldering fire.

'General, may I introduce...' She motioned to Ember and then paused with an amused expression on her face, realising he had not given her his name.

'Anton.' He answered.

Balor turned, looking Ember up and down. His eyes were red, whether from lack of sleep or crying, you could not tell. 'Who are you?' His voice was flat, like all the life had been sucked out of him.

It took a moment for Ember to respond, the General's despair hit him like a blow to the stomach. 'I come on behalf of Duke Randal Bellamy of Godswall.'

Balor frowned, 'Indeed?'

'I see I am expected!' Ember asked, studying the General.

CHAPTER TWO

'Perhaps!' Balor agreed, but an air of suspicion laced his words.

Ember thought for a moment, deciding it was best to be as honest as possible. 'He has expressed his concern for the princess' continued safety in the capital at this time and wishes her moved to him in Godswall. I come to ensure it happens.'

Balor chewed his lip for a moment, then turned to his sister in law, 'Adella, can you give us a few minutes.'

Ember couldn't help smirking, wondering just how much Balor knew about the woman's leisure activities.

Adella brushed past his arm, and returned the smirk, but took any further comment she had with her into the next room, leaving Ember alone with the General.

Balor waited for a moment to ensure she was gone, and then turned back to Ember. 'I was told to expect a visitor. But how, I ask, could you have arrived from the Duke so fast, he is a week's ride away. The King was poisoned two days ago.'

Ember nodded, 'I did not come from the Duchy, I came from Docktown. I was informed via correspondent. The instructions were to bring her to him in Godswall with all haste. I thought it best I did not delay.'

'Indeed.' Balor said, his face going slack and then turning to face the fire.

'I need to know what happened, why is the princess in danger?'

'It's a bloody mess.' He did not turn around, 'Two months ago I met with Randal to ask for his help. I believed Lord Gelraen was a threat to the princess, and the plan was to deal with him. Somehow he must have found out the plan and taken matters into his own hands.'

'Why would you think, Gelraen is a threat, he is the King's military advisor, not to mention a Duke of the realm!' Ember's eyes narrowed.

Balor turned and regarded Ember. 'Because he has already killed a monarch, he killed the Queen.'

Ember sucked in a breath, the confession catching him off guard. 'If that is true, why would he go unpunished all this time? If he wanted the throne, killing the Queen would be counterproductive, I would think?'

Balor sniggered, 'He was never convicted because Cailem never knew … It's a long story.' He finished. 'Suffice to say I told Randal it was over an item she carried, and that, Gelraen believes the princess now has come into possession of it. I lied. The item is gone, sunk with the ship that day. There is no way that it could have been recovered. No, the princess is … special.'

'Special how?' Ember asked.

'It's best I don't give you the details, plausible deniability.' He paused for a moment. 'I used to trust him, he was arrogant, but I never saw him capable of what he did. I was wrong. I have no idea what the Queen carried that day, why it was worth dying for, and I know less about its connection to her daughter. All I know is Gelraen has his obsessive eyes on her, and if he gets too close, if he finds out her secret.' He looked Ember in the eyes. 'It would be death for her.'

Ember took a long breath, digesting the Generals words one at a time. 'I don't understand why he would murder the King, they are the actions of a desperate man, not a military advisor!'

Balor slumped, holding onto the mantle for support, 'That, was my doing.'

Ember tensed, 'You said, Gelraen murdered the king!'

'I believe so, but it might as well have been me.' He was silent for a long moment, 'It should have been him. This is not how things were meant to turn out.'

'Do you think war is a possibility? It could explain his actions!'

Balor sucked in another breath, 'No. Sure, Cailem was talking about it, but there was no evidence to support the suggestion... Of course, his sudden death has fuelled that rumour now.'

Ember wanted to press further but didn't. 'I can smuggle the princess to Duke Randal, but what will you do to keep Gelraen in the dark? Will the Queen retire for her safety and hand authority to the military?'

Balor's face tensed, a sheet of red filling his cheeks. 'Isyllia has already made Gelraen regent; my hands are tied on that one. My hope is that Randal will be able to knock some sense into her. She is stubborn, but she is not stupid, and she has no love for that man.'

Ember nodded, knowing what she believed now was of little consequence. 'Will you be able to open the city gates without raising suspicion?'

'Not for a couple of peasants, no. But if I send my sister-in-law with you, Adella. I can inform the guard she is leaving on urgent business for me, related to the situation at hand. She will accompany you to Godswall, then go her own way.'

Ember nodded.

'It is risky, but I will also send my son with you, Captain Mallory.'

'... A party of four!' Ember clenched, his mouth forming a crinkled point of frustration. The only visible sign that his faith in the plan was waning by the second.

The General picked up on his frustration, his eyes narrowing, one hand poised in the air. 'I won't take chances with her safety, even if it compromises his. William is a skilled fighter and he would die for her if needed, would you?'

Ember didn't respond.

'It's best she be moved tonight, but I warn you it won't be easy. Since the Queen handed over regency to Lord Gelraen he has moved his own troops in. Isyllia has been confined to her quarters, not even her maids can get in to see her.' He moved over to the back of a sitting chair, clutching the back with his hands. 'Now, she will be at the feast tonight, with Lord Gelraen, and most of society. They will be drunk and distracted... but I still don't see how it is possible to get her out without getting caught. I can ensure my men are elsewhere, but I can do nothing about the Duke's men. William has already tried to get past the guard's numerous times but has not succeeded. I don't see how you will have better luck when he knows the castle like the back of his hand.'

Ember thought for a moment, knowing he could not tell this man the truth. 'The way I see it is, you lose nothing if I get caught.'

His eyes narrowed like he was weighing the idea, then, chewing his thoughts further he looked to some invisible object on the floor. 'Wait for her to be returned to her rooms. I will have William and Adella waiting at the stables.'

Ember nodded.

The General thought for a moment, turning something on his finger, the golden item flashing in the firelight. Sighing, Balor removed a ring, and held it out to Ember. 'Take this with you, give it to Isyllia. Then she will trust you.'

Ember frowned at the golden signet ring glinting in his outstretched palm. A blazing sun sat framing a single silver sword. The Generals ring, that was not a good omen.

'Adella!' The General turned toward the delicate but determined footsteps that answered.

'Brother.' She smiled, her eyes sparkling with seeming innocence.

'Anton is going to be taking the princess to Godswall for the time being, for her safety. I would like you to accompany them, they leave tonight.'

'Of course, brother.' She curtseyed.

'There is one more thing General. Someone will need to retrieve my horse if I am to get the princess out of the castle.'

'Leave it to me.' She turned her smile on Ember.

'He is stabled near the Dale Inn, Perrin.'

She gave a slight nod, and then left the room again.

Ember waited until she had left, and then inclined his head to the General. He turned to leave, his body trying to make the journey, but his mind halted, tugging at his muscles in protest. 'General.'

Balor made a small noise of acknowledgment, his face resigned.

'I could just turn her in!' He said, not altogether sure why the General would trust him with her secret.

Balor exhaled, then pointed to Ember's tanned arm with one pale, bony finger. 'You are Tinderfordean are you not? … Under the circumstances, I believe my instinct is my best option.'

Ember tucked his almost shoulder length brown hair behind his ears and then turned to leave once more with the uneasy feeling continuing to rage in his stomach. More was happening here than he could see, and he did not like it, he did not like it one bit.

CHAPTER THREE

Isyllia, City of Illingdale.

The floorboards outside Isyllia's door announced the languid arrival of a pair of boots that could only belong to one person. They were followed by an equally lazy knock, causing Isyllia to sit on a chair, and swallow hard. It had been a day since she had handed regency to Gelraen, and in that time, he had managed to flood the city with his men. Petra, her faithful maid had disappeared, and Isyllia was forced to wear the same creased excuse for an outfit. To make matters worse, William too, could not be found. She had questioned Gelraen and his unhelpful guards to no avail. Now he was here to escort her to the temple. He knocked one more time and then entered the room. Isyllia did not stand. 'Where is William. And why can I not prepare my father's shroud. You have no right to deny him his honour giving!' She said, throwing the words at him like poisoned darts.

Lord Gelraen was unmoved, flicking his fingernails, and then moving further into the room. 'Until the threat on your life is passed, I will have no risks. It is a mercy that I let you out at all!' He stared at her for a moment longer, turning some un-uttered thought over in his mind, 'You have no idea how much of a risk you are to this city.'

Isyllia clutched the chair, her knuckles white. 'I don't know what you mean.'

'Relax.' He said, laughing at the mirror on the far side of the main room, straightening his pristine vest. Leaving the impression that the occupation was more an excuse to admire himself. Once satisfied, he turned back to face her. 'Consider yourself fortunate.'

'You cannot just lock me in here like a prisoner!'

Lord Gelraen laughed again, shaking his head with amusement at her indignation. 'Hardly. I would remind you; it is you who appointed me regent. Do what you think is best, is that not correct?'

Isyllia looked away, her face camouflaging with the windowpane. 'Yes.'

He nodded, satisfied, 'Yes. And it is my pleasure that you remain confined from all contact. You will eat what I tell you. You will wear what I tell you. And you will sleep when I tell you... for your protection, you understand.'

Isyllia looked at the creased dress she was wearing, close to tears. 'At least let me see William!'

Lord Gelraen stomped off to the closet and rustled around for a moment, coming back with a burgundy garment. He threw it onto the nearest chair and then turned a glare on her. 'I won't have my future wife involved in further scandal. It's for your own good.' He said, thrusting a finger at the dress, 'Put this on.' He made no move to leave.

Isyllia looked at the velvet dress, then back to Gelraen, squinting in confusion. 'Now?'

Lord Gelraen was losing his patience, he stepped forward and grabbed her by the arm, hauling her over to the chair. 'Yes, now.' He stepped behind her, one hand braced over the stitches at the back of her dress, 'Or I could do it for you.' His voice dropped an octave.

Isyllia paled, folding her arms to cover the thought of her nakedness. 'No. Please, just allow me a few minutes. I have never dressed myself.'

Lord Gelraen walked back around and stopped close to her face. For a moment, she was not sure what he intended to do. 'I won't always be leaving the room.' The comment made him smirk, which he carried all the way to the door, closing it behind him. Isyllia could feel him standing guard, waiting. She placed a hand over her heart, calming her nerves, then moved over to the dress that waited.

The arrival at the ceremonial temple came quicker than she had thought it would. Thousands of faces already waited, all clambered together to look at the young queen, all wearing the same expression. Isyllia fixed her eyes ahead, unable to bear the pity and the whispers that assaulted her like gnats. They swam around her face in endless numbers, and she shooed them off, one by one, holding her head high to better pretend they were not there. She braced her jaw, wishing she could also just unplug her arm from Gelraen, and leave it behind.

It was some years since he returned from Mespar, an expedition still surrounded in uncertainty. Officially, it was said he travelled under the king's command, conducting a routine tour to ensure the ancient agreement between the two nations was still being upheld. But there were still those who, like her, believed differently. There was a darkness that followed Gelraen after his return, swallowing the once jovial young lord. Most never noticed the change in his behaviour, blaming it on the unexpected death of his father. Isyllia had noticed. But it didn't matter now, nothing mattered now.

'My Queen' Isyllia startled, not realising everyone had been staring at her. The shroud was already covered in flowers, when had they sat down?

'Would you say the words?' The temple curator was patient, motioning to her waiting father.

'Indeed.' She said, treading over to his waiting corpse. Each face was silent with anticipation, the only sounds the echo of her shoes against stone. Like they were being magnified. The temple was decorated with carved marble scenery, the only surviving stories of the gods, warning people of their trickery, and some celebrating their liberation from the ancient ways. Today, they too stared. Could they hear the nervous way she placed her feet? Did they see the waning strength that held her neck high? Did they know that she just wanted to scream? Isyllia exhaled and brushed a strand of hair from her eye. With her other hand, she reached down and touched the shroud where the once great king's face should be. 'I have washed you and clad you with honour. May you now face the darkness with the love of your kin, the strength of your people, and the wisdom of your years.' She said, her words bouncing off the carved marble walls behind. The curator drew in his lips, passing over the torch for her to take. Isyllia did not respond, her mind had frozen in panic. She reached out for the waiting flame, stopping midway to examine the sudden blur of her fingers, like a half-remembered dream. 'I can't... I have to sit.' A familiar fog spread through her mind, bringing with it a heat she also knew so well. It dragged at her strength, each step back to her seat taking longer than the last. She clenched her teeth and pushed on, determined to ignore the panic that mocked her futile journey. Like the effort would create some invisible barrier to keep the heat from spreading. *'Not now, please not now, hold it in!'*

'With this fire, my King, you protect your people, once more.' She could hear the puzzled curator say the words she was meant to say. And the chant that followed, filling the room with a monotonous, yet deafening sound while the flame began to lick the cloth.

[2]*'Diieṇ ṇedaṇ ee tasa, diieṇ ṇedaṇ pospuṇ.'* She closed her eyes, letting the sound meant to be heard by the gods carry her down, unconscious on the floor below.

It was evening when she at last woke to silence, or so she thought. Opening her eyes, she began to sit up, a sharp pounding in her head again. 'This is becoming an unfortunate habit.' It was then that she noticed one of the guards standing in the corner by the door. He wore Morliin garb. Isyllia sighed, throwing blankets out of her way in annoyance, and stumbled over to her dressing table, landing heavily on the chair. A quick glance out the window told her it was in fact evening, she had been out for hours. The feast would have started without her. She sighed and turned to study the reflection staring back at her. Her hair was a mess and she would need to fix it. Dark circles framed her soft green eyes, once filled with passion and tenderness, now they were lifeless,

---

[2] Translation: Diieṇ ṇedaṇ ee tasa, diieṇ ṇedaṇ pospuṇ. Gods never take thee, gods never prosper.

like her spirit had left with her fathers. She barely recognised the person looking back at her.

Isyllia dropped the last of the pins on the floor and bent down to pick them up. A small section of brown birthmark flashed out of the corner of her eye. Isyllia froze. The glove she was wearing to hide it had moved down, exposing the star shaped mark she hid at all costs, even from William. Taking a deep breath to steady a sure-to-rouse panic, she pulled the glove back over the mark, and rose, taking a deep breath to calm her nerves, then started for the door. The guard that was stationed placed his spear in front of her, blocking her path. 'Move your weapon, or you will wear it.'

The guard was unmoved by her bluff, stepping backward slightly to reach the door, while still holding his spear firmly in place. He knocked twice, then moved back to his original position. The door opened to reveal more guards, also wearing Morliin garb. Her spirits sank and she inclined her head, beginning the long walk to the banquet hall, all the while doing her best to ignore the patrol escorting her. But it was hard to ignore the spears that covered every angle. If she ran, picked up her skirts and fled, would they be able to catch her? The thought held promise for a moment until she remembered that Gelraen had stationed guards everywhere. It was unlikely there was anywhere she could hide. Sighing, she finished the last stretch to the hall door and halted, the men remaining behind. *There is that at least.'* She thought, as laughter pierced its way through the large doors, causing Isyllia to scrunch up her nose, fighting the urge to stand aside, away from the unwelcome sound. It should have been familiar and comforting. But tonight, it was different. Tonight, it pierced her ears like the screech of a hungry crow. But it would not do well to dwell, and nodding to the doorman, she braced herself while he entered the room to announce her arrival.

'Ladies and Gentlemen, please rise for her majesty, Queen Isyllia Mae Bellamy.'

It was done. *'Now let this be over.'* She thought again, trying to walk casually even though her heartbeat protested in panic. Scanning the room, she saw Lord Gelraen had been sitting next to the king's chair. She contemplated the reason for not finding him situated in it, dismissing it again when she realised the answer would require needless conversation with the Lord. Who stood, motioning the room bow, and then indicated to the empty space. Isyllia scowled, moving forward one step at a time. Yesterday, it was just a chair, today it was fear, a dungeon. Deciding to put the visuals that fought for space in her mind with the anxiety out where it could no longer bother her, she took Lord Gelraen's hand, curtsied, and turned to face the waiting crowd. She knew people would question her supplication to a Lord, but she did not care today, nothing mattered, least of all, what they thought.

'May I compliment you on your dress, majesty.' His words were slurred, and his breath stank of wine.

Isyllia kept her face forward, resisting the urge to retch. 'Thank you, my Lord Gelraen.' She motioned to the rest of the room. 'Please, be seated…Tonight, we celebrate my father, Cailem Bellamy… some of you may know, it was my father's dearest wish that I marry. Tonight, in honour of that wish, I announce an alliance between House Pennerly, the Duke of Morliin and, Bellamy.' She motioned to Gelraen; surprised cheers erupted around the room. Isyllia drew her mouth up into a smile, the weight on her muscles dragging with the involuntary act, and then placed a hand up, indicating quiet. 'My father was a good king; he loved his people. And here before all of you, I pledge to honour his vision, for an even greater Illingdale…' More cheers erupted, but she put her hand up again, this would take all night! 'But tonight, let memories guide our way. May joy see our tankards ever filled!' This time, she let them have their mirth, deciding to sit away from the murder of laughing crows. That would have to do.

'May I formally offer my condolences majesty. The kingdom grieves the loss of such a magnanimous king.'

Isyllia shifted in her seat, she knew that greasy voice. 'Thank you, Duke Walton, your kind words will help to ease our suffering at this time.'

He bowed low.

'May I also congratulate you, on your splendid choice of a husband.' He bowed again, but this time to Lord Gelraen. Duke

61

Walton followed power and held loyalties to no one. He was a short-rounded man, and his long black beard always looked like something dead had been stuck to his face.

Lord Gelraen smiled wide, drinking in every ounce of the compliment.

'I would expect someone of your … calibre to find that notion appealing.' She said, wishing someone would interrupt her obligation to address the slithery Lord. They did not. Gelraen drained his goblet, and then thrust it aside, like something putrid had slipped inside, then nodded to Duke Walton. The slimy Duke inclined his head for a third time and then began to back away, sensing the tension no doubt, which did not at all bother Isyllia.

The people approached in droves, one after the other each offering their condolences. Isyllia smiled and greeted them all, meanwhile making mental notes to lessen the invitation list on all future parities. But they stopped approaching, leaving Isyllia to slump back in her chair and watch. People laughed and drank like nothing had happened, she even half expected her father to enter the room at one point, offering various excuses on how he had been held up. The thought made her want to scream, was she alone in her pain? Did no one care? Taking a second look she noticed Balor was missing, but then he seldom attended functions. William on the other hand, never missed parties. His continued absence bothered her. Two other absences that surprised her were the Duke of Preston and the Duke of Godswall. They could have made it here by now! So, where were they? Had Lord Gelraen sent them the news? Fanning her disappointment, she took a sip of her mead; it was hot with welcome hints of spice and a perfect distraction for her nerves.

'You may drink what I have prepared for you, because it has been pre tasted. You are not however to eat the food, if anyone asks, you are to tell them you are not hungry. One of my guards will bring you food that has been pre sampled.' Lord Gelraen took a swig from his goblet, then signalled for a refill. He didn't need it.

Isyllia fought the urge to move away, her body in absolute rebellion. She had almost forgotten he was there, almost. She put her goblet down, no longer trusting her hands to resist the overpowering temptation to throw its contents onto his pretentious face. Instead, she smiled, taking great pains to extract the barbs that hid under it, 'If you'll excuse me, my Lord, I should see to my guests.'

Lord Gelraen bowed, but he was not satisfied, it was evident he had more to say. Isyllia rose, signalling for some food to be brought to her, and found her way to one of the ladies she did not despise, and busied herself in needless conversation. Sharp whispers darted around the room following the exchange, it had not gone unnoticed then. She clenched her teeth and did her best to ignore the buzzing. Anything to make the night move on and avoid even looking at Lord Gelraen, who grew more and more sullen with each goblet he emptied. She didn't care. Isyllia smiled and clapped for the entertainers that danced and sang to her. No one noticed that the laughter did not reach her eyes. No one cared that inside, she was alone, drowning in a sea of despair. Every inch of her longed to be in bed, and so when the time came for her to excuse herself, she motioned to the master of ceremonies to quiet the room once more. 'I thank you all once more for your support tonight, but now I shall take my leave.'

'I will escort you.' Gelraen stood, and it was not a question.

Her heart sank into her stomach, knowing she could not refuse him further attention. 'Thank you, my Lord.' He held out his arm and she forced herself to take it, dismissing the unwelcomed thought of future duties that would be expected. Her approaching door, which under normal circumstances sparked a sense of comfort in the pit of her stomach, now ignited a sense of nausea. Not at all a welcome feeling, as they approached the solid oak barrier.

Gelraen nodded for the standing guard to leave, then turned his wine-stained teeth and foul breath on her. The stench assaulted her like a blow, and she fought the urge to gag, *I'm done with this tonight.'* She had reached her limit. 'I bid you good evening. Thank you for seeing me back in my chambers.' She said, waiting for his train of thought to be aborted, having no intention of seeing where it otherwise ended up. But Lord Gelraen did not turn to leave, instead he opened the door and dragged the surprised Isyllia inside by the arm, then tossed her into the centre of the room, caring little for how she arrived there. Isyllia fell to the ground, landing hard on her wrists against the wooden floor. Gelraen took no notice, turning back to slam the door behind him. For a moment he just stood with one hand pressed against the door, his head weighted down with indecision. Isyllia edged back up, rubbing her wrists, watching his shoulders heave like he had run a marathon. Hoping he would just go, just open the door, and stride out again. He didn't. Lord Gelraen turned back, stopping again too close to her face. Isyllia could almost taste the pungent silence that preceded his next inevitable onslaught. 'You have crossed a line tonight, Lord Gelraen. Tomorrow I will renounce our alliance, and I never want to see you in this city again.'

Lord Gelraen chewed her words for a moment, then he struck. Sending Isyllia to the floor in shock. All the heat in her body diverted to the side of her aching face, the rest of her, like ice.

'Get up!' He dragged her to her feet.

Isyllia's heart began to quicken in fear. 'How dare you! I agreed to marry you, Gelraen, but I will not endure this treatment.'

'This isn't a joke.' His fingers dug into her skin, making her wince. 'Or should I demand your respect. Is that what it takes?'

'Nothing has changed. I don't want you; I don't need you and I don't like you. Now unhand me or I will have you arrested.' Tears began to distort her voice.

He laughed. 'By Who? My Men! What would you do if I was your fathers' attacker?' He brushed his hand over her hip, 'If I had ideas…Could you fight me off!'

Isyllia swallowed hard, deciding to ignore the question. Instead, she squared her shoulders and stood tall, clenching her jaw like she could impale him with the tension that gathered around her nose. Within moments her strength betrayed her again, deflating her voice into a hollow whisper. 'I said remove your heads from me!'

He stepped back a step, 'Weak… and they say I am unworthy.'

'You disgust me!' She said, almost spitting the statement at him.

'You don't know the first thing about me.' He said, leaping forward, kissing her dispassionately, placing one hand at the back of her head, his fingers almost pulling at her dishevelled hair. When he did let go, Isyllia shot backwards, too appalled to wipe the tears staining her pale face.

'What do you want from me?' She asked, not really wanting him to answer. Gelraen considered her, and then shook his head, deciding against whatever action he had planned. 'You are barely worth the effort.' Isyllia closed her eyes, feeling more powerless than she had ever felt in her life. Lord Gelraen stormed out of the room, slamming the door behind him. Leaving behind a loaded silence that was inescapable. It was broken moments later when footsteps sounded from a deep corner of the room. They were slow and measured, each step reactivating the fear in her gut. Someone else was in her room, someone had seen the whole exchange. 'Petra?' She asked, trying to steady her voice, without success. It was a man that stepped forward into the light, one knuckle white where he had been gripping the hilt of his sword. He had brown hair that fell at random down his neck, framing his furious blue eyes and square face that pierced her even through the darkness. He was a tall and muscular man with broad shoulders, and he wore a well-manicured van Dyke which sat on his olive Tinderfordean complexion, making her fall to her knees. She no longer had the will to fight. 'Please don't kill me. Please.' She cried, desperate tears falling in floods.

'I'm not.' But she cut him off, unable to hear anything but her own mental exhaustion.

'Or do. Please, I can't bear it. I can't wake up every morning to see his face, I can't. Please don't leave me like this.'

This time he spoke louder, 'I'm not here to hurt you. If I had wanted it, you would be dead already.' He knelt, his face filling with concern. The man reached out a hand, clasping her under the elbows and helping her to her feet.

Isyllia hesitated a moment, the act driving her out of self-pity. 'Who are you?' She brushed her arms with her hands, rubbing away the chill that lingered under her skin from shock.

'I am Ember Clae, but please, around others call me Anton.'

She nodded, having no care to question the subterfuge. Ember, Anton, what did it matter? 'Ember.' She tried the name, allowing him to steer her to a chair, but she did not sit. 'Why are you here if not to kill me? And how did you get past Gelraens guards?' She asked, still unconvinced. Ember reached into a pocket, producing a golden signet ring. He glanced at it for a moment, tossing it in his hand. 'I have taken care of the guards that were in the way. Don't worry, they won't wake up for some time.' He placed it in Isyllias hand. 'I am here to escort you to Duke Randal. It is no longer safe for you here.' Isyllia turned the ring over in her hand. A blazing sun sat framing a single sword.

'This is Balors ring.' Alarm spread to her face, forcing her body out of the chair and into an upright position again. 'Why do you have this?'

'I believe he intended a show of trust.'

'But I don't understand, why would he trust a stranger? This is unlike Balor.' She said, inching back.

Ember placed a hand over abdomen, deciding something, then stepped forward and lifted the bottom corner of his linen and mail shirt. 'Because of this.' Isyllia stared at the place he had uncovered, a brown, circular birthmark branded his solar plexus. 'Balor knows, but he didn't want to alarm you, understanding the repercussions if your condition were to become public knowledge.'

Fear flooded her mind. She reached out to the side table, steadying herself with one hand, the other clutching at her covered arm. '*He has it too*' 'You're Malagara!' She said, shrinking back from his advance. 'Who are you? I will scream if you come any closer.' But it would not get that far. Already Isyllia could feel the sensation of heat building in her again. She would have to calm herself now or she would collapse again. The thought sent another twang of dread into her abdomen, the anticipation was almost worse.

Ember slowed his voice, sensing her growing panic and despite her warning, he continued to step closer. 'We are not Malagara. I won't hurt you.' He said, holding out one hand in a calming motion.

Isyllia continued to hold the cupboard for support, powerless to move. Her fear was outweighed by the strangling sensation that took over her chest and throat. It invited the heat to rise again, licking its way through her body with an aggressive hunger. Isyllia barely noticed Ember pry her hand away from the side table, placing it on his chest. There was nothing aggressive in his touch, unlike Gelraen. Ember stood as still as a cat, his hand gentle, his breaths deep and soft. Somewhere amongst the fog of mixed and frenzied emotions, she knew she should have stopped him; at the same time however, she knew she didn't want to. There was something honest in his demeanour, something she craved. '… Feel my breathing. In… Out. In…Out. Don't try to hold it in, because you can't. If it needs to come out, let it come out. Let go… breathe…' He said, each word slowed to a crawl. 'That's it.' The comfort washed over her, easing the tension that threatened to consume and slowly, the heat began to drain again. 'How do you know what to do?' She asked, lightheaded from the over breathing, but renewed with a moderate sense of control.

'I understand you, the true you.' His gaze was steady, and he did not let go of her arm. Isyllia did not protest. 'I know you're frightened, but you cannot go on like this. Let me get you to, Randal. Once we reach him, I promise I will tell you everything you need to know about us… About who you are. All I ask for now, is that you trust me.'

Isyllia still did not pull away, afraid to sever the contact lest the heat come back. She looked at the ring again, clutched in her free hand. 'If Balor trusts you, then so shall I.'

Ember waited a moment longer and stepped back. 'Keep the ring somewhere hidden, the less people know about it, the better. I have packed a bag for you already, but you should change into something more appropriate for travel.'

Isyllia raised her eyebrows despite herself, 'I am Queen, what would you call, appropriate?'

Ember nodded to the room behind her. The maids' quarters.

Isyllia craned her head in the direction he indicated, 'The maids' quarters... you cannot be serious!'

'Please!'

She ignored the remark and turned back to her closet, looking through the rack of pre-prepared outfits for something suitable. Isyllia liked to have ample choice, so her maids often prepared a variety of options.

'Appropriate.' He said, his back turned to her. *Has eyes in the back of his head, great.'* She sighed, meandering over to the maids' quarters and found an outfit that was roughly her size, then set to tearing off the dress she was wearing, discarding it on the floor. It took some time for her to figure out the laces, having dressed herself once. First putting it on backwards, and then getting confused over which way the laces tied. Isyllia arranged the last sleeve of the dress neatly into place, careful to hide the mark on her arm. For a moment she compared the two. Ember's was a perfect round shape, hers a star, many lines all sharing one intersecting point. The thought caused her nerves to plummet, threatening to make her flee in stupidity, so she cleared her mind, taking a deep breath and then finished her ensemble with a simple cloak to hide her face. It had to be madness. Walking back into the room she faced Ember again 'I am ready.'

He nodded 'Good, stay behind me.' Opening the door to her chambers, he closed his eyes for a moment, then nodded. Walking down the halls Isyllia looked at the tapestries and the statues for the last time. Each memory forever frozen, and she found herself wishing she had taken more time to study them, when she had the chance. *When I return.'* The promise felt hollow, could she even be certain of that?

'Wait.' He halted and pulled her into an adjacent room, placing his hand over her mouth from behind. Outraged, and forgetting the need for stealth, she struggled to speak, but he was too quick. Ember turned her with ease, his calming blue eyes pleading for her to be silent. For a moment she forgot where she was, lost in the sudden closeness and his intoxicating smell of musk and steel.

'It's safe now.' Ember let go, but his gaze remained steady and he made no move toward the door.

Isyllia swallowed, 'How will we get out, the city gates are sealed?' Her voice was low and breathy, but he heard. The question snapped Ember into focus, and he moved to the door, 'We will work that out when we come to it.' His tone had shifted, was he agitated?

She adjusted herself and pressed on, deciding to ignore the impertinence. 'And what about the castle? We can't just stroll out the front door!'

'Window.'

'A window... you want me to climb out a window... is that a joke?'

'You'll manage.'

Isyllia resisted the urge to slap him, the briskness in which his entire demeanour switched agitated her irrationally, and so she chose not to ask further questions, provoking no further irritation. Almost anything was better than remaining confined in the horrible reality her life had become. They instead walked down the deserted corridor in silence. Meanwhile, the nerves swallowing her concentration grew stronger with each step into the unknown she took. This was her castle; she could leave if she wanted to! Then she remembered Lord Gelraen and shuddered. In a few more moments he raised his hand for her to halt, 'Here, this room is empty.'

Isyllia walked into the room, feeling her heart evaporate at the threshold. 'Of course, this was my father's office.' Walking over to the large oak desk, she ran her fingers over the surface, leaving a trail in the thin layer of dust that had settled. For once, she allowed the tears to blur her vision. It was just another thing she was leaving behind. Then it caught her attention, still poised in the act of guarding an unfinished letter, his favourite quill. So, he had been writing when she had called him. For a moment she considered reading what was now, his last written words. She decided against it, instead tracing her fingers up the quill's soft, waxy edge for the last time. Then she looked up at Ember, almost forgetting he was in the room. He indicated to the open window, but there was a note of pity on his face. She ignored it.

'I'll go first, so I can help you down. It's not far.' He climbed out, checking again to make sure the path was clear, then motioned for her to come over. Taking a deep breath, Isyllia swung her leg over the windowsill and climbed out. She looked over at the rain glistened rooftops of her country, almost colourless in the dark, the tall points stretching gloomily to the sky above. She stared for a moment, watching endless tendrils of smoke evaporate into the emptiness above. It was another thing she had never taken the time to notice.

I'm going to kill myself, what am I doing!' She ignored her own inner monologue and took a breath to steady her nerves. They were only on the second story, but still the ground was a long way down. *'Concentrate, concentrate.'* Sensing her tension, Ember slowed his descent, placing himself over her, still holding onto the pipe, and slowly they made their way down. When they reached the ground, Ember jumped down and then reached up to lift her. Isyllia felt his hands on her waist and allowed herself to be guided the rest of the way, grateful to be on solid earth again. She resisted the temptation to bend and stroke the gravel, losing herself in the security it provided. 'We are lucky no guards stopped us.' She said looking around. The area was deserted.

'They are patrolling the other side now. They will be back within ten minutes, so we need to move.'

'How do you know that? ... Is that... What you can do? See things.' She squinted.

74

He stopped and was silent for a moment, 'Something like that. Look, I promise I will explain, but not here. Right now, I need to concentrate on the guards.' His mood had not improved.

The stables were large, and open during the day. So, it was hard to conceal intentions. But since it was night, Isyllia found herself having to focus to make out the two figures that waited. This did not hinder her in recognising William who stood with his arms crossed, shifting stones with his foot, he was anxious. She picked up her pace, 'William!' She said, throwing her arms around him.

'Are you hurt?' He asked, pushing her away and holding her at arm's length, like she was covered in dung, 'What are you wearing? Never mind that! Gelraen wouldn't let anyone near you, I've tried and tried. I've been worried sick.'

Isyllia sniffed, not realising she had been crying again, 'He locked me up, right after I signed the document. Not even Petra was there to help. I had no one. I was so frightened William.'

William hugged her again, 'It's ok, I'm here now.'

'And we need to get moving.' Adella said, sounding rather amused. Isyllia stepped back, regaining her composure by straightening her cloak, like it would somehow help.

Ember had paid no attention to the exchange, striding over to his horse and stroking it on the head. Perrin nuzzled into his chest, returning the affection his master offered. 'Once we are out of the city, we will stay off the road. It is unlikely we will encounter people there, but in case we do, we will need a cover story.'

Adella moved toward one of the horses, 'I gave some thought to that. A travelling merchant would be the most logical, but there is nowhere we can get stock from between here and Godswall, and in any case the danger will be greatest near the city.'

Ember considered her, 'I was planning on a similar idea, but I had not planned on company, four will be tougher to explain.'

'You were planning to spirit her out of the city alone?' He asked, but the accusation in his voice was unmistakable. Even in the dark you could see William's pale face was growing red.

Ember ignored him, and directed his answer to Isyllia, 'We don't have time to debate it here, we need to be moving, please, choose a horse.'

'He's right, for now let's say we are business partners, and these.' Adella pointed to William and Isyllia, 'Are my cousins, travelling abroad with their aunt. If guards spot us, they are the ones we need to hide anyway.'

Ember frowned, causing creases to line his face suggesting he wore the expression too often.

'Two ladies travelling with no carriage... doesn't that strike you as odd?' William interrupted.

It was Ember who answered. 'The working class cannot afford carriages.'

William shot a look at Ember, 'I am sorry, I forgot to ask your name?' There was nothing polite in the question.

'Anton.' He said through gritted teeth.

William crossed his arms, his eyes narrowing at Embers' back. 'Anton then, how were you planning to smuggle the Queen out of the city, or had you not noticed, the gates are sealed?'

Ember didn't reply this time, instead he looked at Adella, eyebrows raised.

She laughed. 'You are right. Me.'

William soured, and walked toward one of the horses. Isyllia had never favoured an animal, and so chose the brown one with white spots, Marilla. She looked at the saddle, and blanched. 'My saddle is wrong.'

'You'll manage.' It was Ember.

Isyllia glared, 'I beg your pardon?' She shot. He may be here to help, but enough was enough. Adella sat on her horse then looked down. 'Isyllia, it is simple, why not give it a try?'

Isyllia exhaled in frustration. 'I don't know how!'

'Place one foot in the stirrup, then hold onto the saddle and swing your free leg over the other side, and that is it.' Adella said. The woman smiled her encouragement, but the smile was superficial. Isyllia's stomach dropped, dragging the colour from her cheeks in horror, ready to protect again when she sensed Ember's frustration at the continued delays. So, taking a deep breath, she decided to try. It took a couple of goes until she got the hang of it, eventually swinging her leg triumphantly over the other side, then settling into the saddle. A surge of relief made her smile to herself, 'This is more comfortable.'

Adella smiled again. 'See. Now come.' Isyllia glanced at William; he rolled his eyes, scowling and then waited for Isyllia to move, taking up the rear. Isyllia pulled the cloak further over her face, hoping no one would recognise her. They walked through the night stained city slowly, careful to avoid known patrols. From time to time Isyllia glanced at William, but his bad mood was determined to follow him all the way to the gate, so she did not look again. She hated it when he sulked. Instead, she tried again to calm her breathing, terrified the soldiers would hear her heart thumping. Now William pulled his cloak over his face; this was not going to work. Even if they didn't realise who she was, they would want to check William, and they all knew him. Isyllia tightened her grip on the reins, her knuckles turning white from the tension. How could Balor send his surviving son on a suicide mission, his actions would be high treason, whether she was willing or not.

They approached the gate slowly. Ember prepared to go first, then a soldier spoke. 'Lady Adella, is that you?'

Adella moved forward, pretending to squint with one hand over her eyes to shield from the rain. 'Why, Harliin? What a pleasure!'

'Indeed madam. General said you might be coming through, these your friends?'

She turned and indicated to her companions, 'Indeed, Harliin, and we are in somewhat of a hurry.'

He smirked, turning to the gate and bashing his huge fist on the barrier. Somewhere behind him, another soldier began the long, and arduous process of opening the massive gates. 'That's not like you.'

She returned his smile. 'Indeed, I was otherwise... distracted.' She looked at Ember.

One of the elder soldiers approached, no doubt attracted by the noise of the gate. Isyllia's heart sank. She knew him. He was a commanding officer, and one of Gelraen's men.

'Stand down soldier.' He then turned to Harliin, 'The city has been sealed officer, you have no authorization to open the gates.'

'Keep it moving,' Harliin spat, then turned to the man. 'I got orders to let these people pass.'

Isyllia glanced to the gate, a tiny crack of light had begun to filter through, almost large enough to accommodate a fleeing cat.

'Who's orders?' The older man turned toward Adella. 'Lord Gelraen has stated no one is to be let out under any circumstances.'

Harliin glared, 'I take orders from the General, not the Duke of Morliin. If you don't like it, go fuck yourself.'

For a moment the older guard glared, his face turning an alarming shade of red. Then he pulled his sword and faced it at the offending guard, who stood frozen in shock. 'Wrong answer. First, you will order the doorman to stand down, and search this party. Then, I will take you to Lord Gelraen, with whom you may offer the explanation you gave me.'

Harliin paled but made no movement to stand down. The gate was now a bit smaller than they needed to pass through single file. Almost enough.

The older guard pressed the blade further against Harliin's chest, ensuring his point was clear. Harliin gulped, then turned back to the party, ready to obey. 'Wait, where?' Isyllia looked in his direction. Adella's horse was empty.

'Wait. There was another one? Within moments, Adella materialised behind the older guard and smashed him over the back of the head with a large jug. He dropped to the ground with what was left of the terracotta flask, unconscious. Harliin shot backward, rubbing his chest automatically, 'I'd suggest you go. Soon as he wakes, you'll have soldiers on your tail.'

Adella nodded, a serious expression on her face, then remounted her horse. Ember clicked forward, then the others, a pale William taking up the rear.

Once they were out of the city Ember turned his horse right, toward the living woods. Isyllia could tell William wanted to argue. To mention that they were travelling in the wrong direction, but he said nothing. Instead choosing to continue his sulk.

What remained of the moonlit night disappeared fast somewhere behind the tangled mass of trees. Leaving them to ride through the strange forest in complete darkness. Isyllia tried to stare ahead, too nervous to make conversation. It wasn't until the pangs in her stomach reached an audible crescendo that she decided to stop. Swaying atop her horse, she reined him to a halt, and climbed down. Then without another thought, began plundering the small bags that were attached for food. She had sunk her arm halfway through the first satchel when the others noticed she had stopped.

Ember turned in his saddle, halting the others behind him, 'Is there a problem?'

Isyllia stared. 'I'm hungry and tired. I need to rest.'

He began to move forward, speaking over his shoulder. 'You can rest once daylight comes, it's an hour away.'

William stopped. 'The Queen has ordered you to stop.'

Ember halted, his shoulders turning rigid, and then yanking on the reins, he turned to face the voice, dark with annoyance. 'I say when we stop, and it is not safe here.'

'Who put you in charge?' William shot; his face lit with fury.

'Boys!' Adella interjected. Both the men stopped talking, but continued to glare, hatred blossoming in the air between them. Ember shook his head and then turned away, choosing not to share his thoughts. '20 minutes! I'll scout. Adella, you can scout to the left.'

Adella rolled her eyes. 'William, you stay with the Queen.'

Isyllia ignored them all and continued to rifle, thrown by Embers' continued coldness. It had been mere hours; could she have offended him in some way?

'Here.' Her thoughts were interrupted by William handing her a water skin and some cheese.

She took the water and gulped it down, revelling in the cool, and satisfying feeling it left in her throat. She handed it back and flopped down onto the leaf strewn ground, resting her head against the trunk of the tree, nibbling on the cheese like a mouse.

'Remember when we used to sneak out here? … Father was always furious.' she trailed off.

William sat beside her, 'Mm-hm' He held his hand out for the skin. 'Why did we stop?'

She looked at her best friend, passing him the water. How could she tell him the truth, when now more than ever, she needed him on her side? Having lost everyone in her life, she could not lose him too, not now. 'I'm tired … let's just sit… please.' Isyllia closed her eyes, resting on his shoulder, he sighed, then did the same.

She had started to doze when he spoke again. 'There is something off about him.'

Isyllia sighed and opened her eyes. 'He wouldn't tell me anything, except that your father sent him. Still …besides the attitude he seems decent enough.' The mark on her arm developed a sudden itch, she ignored it.

William shot her a look, dumbstruck. 'Seems decent enough! You were prepared to leave the castle with a stranger, has your father's murder taught you nothing, never mind me!'

Isyllia blushed, 'Under the circumstances, I was willing to take the chance.'

'Mm-Hmm…'

Isyllia sat up and eyed her friend, 'What?'

'You keep looking at him, and you're doing the *face*.'

'What *face*?' Isyllia felt more heat radiate from her cheeks.

'The *face* you do when we get caught stealing from the kitchen.'

They both laughed.

'He *is* attractive.'

William gave her a sidelong glance.

'… But he frowns too much. I could never suffer someone so morose.' She finished.

'At least I can smile.' He gave her a toothy grin.

'William, stop. He might hear you!' She hit him playfully on the shoulder and then laughed despite herself.

He was still chuckling with amusement, 'Hardly.'

Isyllia shook her head and returned to rest on his shoulder. 'You're impossible.' Feeling a familiar comfort drift through her body. For a moment their troubles were forgotten, and they had each other, and the world was so much easier to carry when they were together.

CHAPTER FOUR

Gelraen, Illingdale Castle.

Gelraen woke to the sound of bustling footsteps clacking back and forth across the stone tiles. The feast had been a great success, and he had gone to bed content, considering he went to bed alone. The announcement had been received rather well and Isyllia, although clear in her loathing, had been determined to do her duty to her country. She had none of her father's strength, she was all impulse and stubbornness, like her mother. Gelraen turned the thoughts over in his mind for some time, there was a lot to do, and not enough time to do it, he sighed. Permitting himself to lay for a moment longer, the red dress drifted into his mind, bringing with it the awareness that other parts of him were there and ready to be used, even if he had other ideas. Gelraen shook his head to dislodge the memory, then jumped out of the bed like it was on fire. The door guard started, thrusting his spear out with alarm.

'At ease, soldier!' He said.

The guard gave a brisk bow, and then stowed his spear again.

'I wish to speak with the Lord General and the council. Rouse them and send them to the throne room at once.'

The guard bowed again, then walked off, leaving a servant to shuffle his feet alone in the corner.

Gelraen turned toward the shuffling, just noticing the boy for the first time. 'You will not be needed, get out!' He shot.

The boy bowed, but did not leave the room, instead risking a glance up from under his eyebrows.

Gelraen rounded on the boy, shooting the boy a glare that could kill a cat. 'What is it? Speak!' He roared, his voice echoing around the room.

'My lord, only, the Queen is missing!' He stammered, turning red and shrinking into himself.

'What do you mean, missing? When did this happen? Why was I not woken?' He asked, frozen in shock.

'Guards tasted, and took her breakfast just like you ordered, only she wasn't there. Her bed was empty.' The boy replied, even though it was evident he would rather do anything else.

'She could have taken some air, has a search been organised?' He asked, knowing the question was futile, she could not have escaped his guard!

The soldier nodded vigorously, 'Of course, sire but she is nowhere to be found.'

'I see … where is Captain Mallory?'

The boy deflated, the tiny amount of confidence he had gained, leaving through his ankles. 'No one knows, he is missing too, sire.'

Gelraen looked around, lumbering over to the dresser. For a moment, he stared at his own reflection, deep in thought, then bawling his fists; he pounded down hard onto the surface, pushing everything onto the floor. He took a deep breath, failing to compose himself and instead strode out the room, ignoring the pieces from smashed objects skittering in all directions. Lord Gelraen crunched over the shards, leaving the servant to huddle with fear, the morning had taken a dark turn.

Gelraen blazed through the large oak doors to the throne room minutes later, not caring who got collected on the way. A maid started, running forward to courtesy and dropping her bundle in the process. He looked over to the fireplace, dark and silent. 'You, why are these not lit?'

'They are on their way with wood now my Lord' she curtseyed low.

'I better not see it like this again, do you understand?' The girl nodded, her face red as an apple. 'I also want you to find Lord Walton and bring him here at once.' He waved his shivering hand in dismissal, there was nothing worse than being cold.

It was another twenty minutes until the doors opened again and Balor marched forward, followed by a small assembly of confused councilmen, all huddled together, with twelve faceless soldiers taking up their rear.

'You called my lord?' He asked, his face blank, but Gelraen got the impression he was not oblivious to the summons. Balor's attire was neat, leaving no sign of having dressed in haste. Yes, he was expecting this.

The council took their seats along the side, each using a careful amount of noise to convey their displeasure at being summoned so early. One of the men stood, rubbing sleep from his face. 'My lord, what is this about? Council is normally held at noon.'

Gelraen motioned for his silence. 'The Queen is missing. I want to know what's going on in this castle and why your guards failed to stop, now two attacks on our sovereigns. The queen was seen safe in her quarters last night and was reported missing this morning.' He motioned to Balor, 'Your son was responsible! Or can you explain to me his whereabouts?... Speak?' He shouted; all his anger packed into the one command.

Balor swallowed hard. 'My Lord, I have been made aware of the situation, and I had guards stationed in the sections of the castle remaining to me, in addition to your own men. I do not understand how anyone could have gotten in without being seen. However, no effort will be spared in recovering the Queen. As to my son, I cannot tell you at this time where he may be, though absence on his part is not unusual I assure you.'

Gelraen studied the General, and then turned to the men gathered at the side. 'Honoured council, it is my sworn commitment to deliver justice to our king and Beloved Princess... we must assume there is some higher purpose to these betrayals. This could be an act of war, and we must seek out our allies.'

One of the plump councillors stood 'Rubbish, there has been no conflict since the great war of Eddinsford, the only thing they fight over now, is fish.' There was a murmur of quiet laughter around the room. 'We have honoured trade agreements with both Tinderford and Mespar, nobody knows what is even in Cyndershire, and Nethershire is full of barbarians. I see no reason to panic over war. Our priority needs to be the safe return of our Queen.'

Another stood, he was younger than the last, and nervous like most, 'Is it not also known the... affection the Queen and

Balor's youngest son share, is it not possible he thought to protect her by secreting her to safety?'

Gelraen nodded. 'Indeed, and I intend to discover the truth. In the meantime, however, we must study the possibilities. We have been caught unawares twice now. It will not happen a third time. There will be no secrets from the people of this country... Lord Walton will begin questioning at once. Make no mistake councillors, whatever the purpose of these attacks, whoever is behind them, they will end. I will hang every suspect until our honoured Queen is found, no matter who they are.' He looked at the plump man, who shrunk back in his chair. 'It is done then. I declare our business adjourned, until more is known.'

The men all stood and hurried from the room, eager to return to their beds. General Balor remained, backed by his loyal soldiers who had not moved an inch away from their General. 'Twice now your men have failed to protect our sovereigns. Curious, don't you think?'

Balor did not blink, unphased by the thinly veiled accusation, 'As my men were not allowed near our Queen's quarters, I would tend to agree, curious indeed.'

Gelraen turned red, 'If I find you were behind her disappearance!'

'You'll what? My loyalty is to my Queen, not to you!'

Gelraen grabbed the man's tunic, forcing his will out with his words, 'You will tell me what you have done!'

Still, Balor did not flinch. 'I did not confess to doing anything, Duke!' He stepped back, dislodging the red faced Gelraen and turning back toward his men, 'Until you have evidence of anything useful, I bid you Good Day.' Balor signalled, and strode out the room, his men following protectively behind. Gelraen turned, wishing there was something within reach that he could throw, when the doors opened again, admitting a determined Lord, Walton. 'What?'

Lord Walton halted, his eyebrows furrowing in confusion. 'You called sire? And in any case, I have reports you will want to hear.'

Gelraen sighed, motioning with one resigned hand for the man to continue approaching. 'Yes. Speak!'

He did not wait for further invitation, 'I was just approached by one of your elderly guards, he has a problem he cannot take to the General.'

'Go on!'

'He said he caught the gate warden letting some people out the city last night, but when he tried to disapprove, he was knocked unconscious. It appears the warden disobeyed his order to keep the gate sealed.'

Gelraen tensed further, his complexion a deep shade of red, and his eyes bloodshot, giving the impression that he could implode at any moment. 'Balor?'

Lord Walton spoke with care. 'I believe Mallory may have had her removed already; I can't think of any other person a warden would risk his life for, disobeying an order like that.'

'Did the report describe the company?'

'The soldier said he was at a distance, but thought he saw a man with long hair, and possibly a woman in company.'

Gelraen's face was stripped of all colour, 'What else?'

'He said the man could have worn a mail shirt, but it was dark, and he wore a cloak so could not be certain. Why? Do you know him?'

Gelraen looked around again for something to throw and when he still found nothing, closed his eyes, and took a deep breath to calm his temper. 'Once. A long time ago... Organise a battalion, I want them to split up to scour the countryside. Alert the bird families and ask them to send a notice to each country offering a generous reward for information leading to her being found.'

'You want me to use a bird, sire?' He sounded confused. Gelraen sighed, the Wentworth family birder was the only one that existed in Illingdale. It had been many years since the rivalling families had fought over territories, bird services being the most efficient and lucrative form of communication. Still, Gelraen knew although they operated of their own accord, they were held subject to the crown if needed. He hesitated, he had never been a fan of their brand of politics and so called on them as little as possible. The bird families saw themselves above the crown, and that was not a good thing for anyone. 'I fear we must. I want them to submit all order logs for inspection, record any message carried to and from whom.'

'At once, sire.'

'We must discover his direction!' He said, more to himself.

'Of course, sire.' He said, bowing his way back out the door, each step heavy with purpose.

Gelraen slumped over to the fire, his thoughts on the face that emerged in his mind. It had been years. Years, yet still, a warm feeling of friendship ignited within. [3]'Aiiła theii suuŋa riiseas, aweii iiraii ćhoiiseŋa. Aiiła theii suuna waiiŋs, aweii iiraii oiiŋ.' He lifted his hand, a new memory beginning to take shape. He could almost feel the slice cut his skin anew, and wincing, he studied the scar that sat as a reminder. The last memory he held of a friendship as dead as the king, that left him standing alone, occasionally looking back at the ornate golden chair that loomed behind him. It Framed the cold and almost empty room that tried

---

[3] Translation: As the sun rises, we are chosen. As the sun wanes, we are one.

its best to swallow him. Gelraen closed his eyes, clutching the
illusion of power that he just realised he was holding.

CHAPTER FIVE

Isyllia, Living Woods, Illingdale.

'Time's up!'

Isyllia snapped her eyes open to find a chunk of meat hurling in her direction, not realising she had fallen asleep. She caught the airborne object and then looked up for the source of the insult, it was Ember.

'Eat!' He said, stomping off in the direction of his horse. He was still moody then.

'What about William?' She asked, having a feeling that she already knew the answer.

'I'm not here for him.' He said.

Isyllia looked at the meat and began tearing it in half, offering the bigger portion to William. William sighed, but he didn't take the meat.

'You eat, I'm not hungry.' He said, his eyes salivating despite the remark.

Isyllia sighed, there was no point in protesting, so she climbed back atop her horse while holding the food with her mouth, chomping her frustration into each bite.

They rode for hours, winding their way a step at a time through the Living Woods, a name feared by most. Many people journeyed into the forest and never returned. Isyllia didn't believe the rumours that the trees were alive, they just looked like ordinary trees and like her father she felt the beauty of their presence. Today in particular, the winter sun was pleasant, it filtered down through the tall forest, and brushed over Isyllias face like a mother's tender kiss. She arched her neck backward, basking in every droplet of warmth it had to offer.

William slowed, 'You seem more relaxed?' He said.

She kept her face upward, not yet willing to give up her sunbathing, 'The fresh air, it sounds like the trees are singing.' She said, stealing a glance at her friend. 'They watch as generations of us come and go. There is a sobriety in the thought that I find comforting right now.'

William glanced up, then down shifting uncomfortably, 'My father said trees bring a different kind of comfort.'

Isyllia looked over, smiling. 'Your father is a practical man. That's what makes him a good General.'

'Yes. Practical.' He said, a note of steel in his voice.

Isyllia frowned, William did not like to talk about his troubles, something that frustrated Isyllia. 'He does not hate you, William, he just does not understand you.'

William smiled and then urged his horse to move past hers, Isyllia shook her head, and then dug her heels into the large beast she was riding and continued her questioning.

'So, what do you want?'

He shrugged, 'What I want is irrelevant. I'll get over it.'

Isyllia pondered this for a moment. 'Do you remember a few months ago, I forced you out into the city with me and we returned to the castle late, and when we were caught you took all the blame? … Balor was furious.' Isyllia made her best impression of Balor 'You're so irresponsible, William, the princess could have been hurt, your enduring lack of formality will be the end of this family.' She wagged her finger at him mockingly.

A reluctant grin spread across his face. 'You sound like him!' He teased.

Isyllia pushed him hard on the shoulder, causing William to lean away with a slight grin. 'I never told you, but later that night I overheard him talking to my father about it. The General didn't understand why you did the things you did, and my father let out

97

a hearty laugh and said he remembered a certain Mallory who broke curfew to win the heart of a maiden.' A mixture of happiness and sorrow surged at the thought of her father. 'I think you two are more alike than you realise, perhaps that is what bothers him.' She finished.

'Can we stop talking about my father? I am more concerned with our current situation!' He said, changing the subject.

Isyllia looked toward Ember, he sat up straight, ignoring everyone else, including Adella who rode close behind. William interrupted the thoughts beginning to form.

'We have done no scouting in hours. Sure, patrols from the castle could not have passed us yet, but Lord Gelraen would have alerted the bird families by now, and his own duchy is not far from here, I am not confident this man was the best person to trust your safety to.'

'It is odd, I'll grant you that!'

'... Odd?'

Isyllia sighed, holding her next breath in her throat in annoyance. She knew William was being concerned, and in many ways, she shared his concerns, but the situation was what it was, and the constant bickering between the two was driving her mad, she already had enough to deal with. 'I'm sure he knows what he is doing is all I meant!'

William shook his head, an incredulous look on his face, 'That you would afford me such trust.'

She sighed, 'William…' But what could she say? He was right of course. She could not tell him the truth.

'Save it!' He kicked his horse, spurring it forward and away. She sighed. Bloody stubborn fool! She thought, but it was hollow, she knew he was right to be upset, but still it could change nothing. If he knew, he would be frightened of her. He has the mark too you idiot, the one I can't tell you about! She finished the thought, her mind wandering to the other night when Ember had revealed the circular birthmark on his torso, so like her own strange star-like shaped one. Then the moments fleeing the castle, how he had somehow known where they needed to go, hiding in the room. The memories made her blush. No, it was best to stay focused right now, and so she forced the moments from her mind, and spent the remainder of the morning thinking about happier times. Stolen moments she had spent with William when they were too young to understand the divide life was to throw at them.

'Isyllia!' It was said with a considerable note of frustration, snapping out of her daydream. She looked around for the voice that called her, Ember had stopped his horse and sat with his body craned around to get her attention.

'Right. We will rest for two hours, William can keep the first watch, and then I will take over.'

99

'Two hours!' William shot, indignant.

Ember glared at him. 'Yes, two hours. Soldiers have begun to scout the countryside; we cannot afford to stay still any longer.'

'How could you know that? It has not even been a day, nobody but my father knows we left the city and he would never jeopardise the queen's safety!'

Isyllia narrowed her eyes, 'Didn't you just tell me you wanted to scout?' The question was of course directed at William.

He turned and glared. 'I wasn't asking you!'

A red stain spread across her cheeks; she had said the wrong thing.

Ember levelled at William, unbreakable in his authority, 'Two hours!' He thundered, and then turned to walk away, glancing at Isyllia as he did.

She sighed, looking around for a spot to rest. The area was littered with trees, and the ground was lumpy despite the piles of leaves. She had never slept outdoors, and it was a different experience closing her eyes, birds chatting noisily in the trees above. She tried to ignore the discomfort that was angling up her spine, that it was day, and that her stomach growled for food. She ignored the rushing thoughts and tried to sink into unconsciousness, the wind dislodging more dying leaves to rest on the cluttered forest floor, some of which stopped at her face first. Sighing, she instead looked around. William sat up straight a short distance away, looking off into the distance, his concentration absolute, except for his chin which jutted down in an unmistakable sulk. Adella lay on the ground, already asleep with one hand curled under a pack she used as a pillow, and Ember. Furthest away again, rested against his horse. His eyes were closed but somehow, he did not look peaceful, he looked like he was alert and listening. She regarded him, confused by the conflicting emotions he expressed. Moments later he looked up and locked eyes with her, his stare deep and questioning. Isyllia swallowed hard against the panic that objected to his intrusion on the moment, shutting her eyes tight, and trying to ignore the sensation of being watched, she fell asleep.

Two hours flew by fast, and she woke up grumbling to the gentle shake of a hand on her shoulder. She opened her eyes, the warmth of the golden afternoon sun poked through the twisting trees in shy tendrils of light, darkness eager to creep in and take its place. Isyllia stood, stretching out the rest of the sleep her body still longed for. She had been the last to wake and was walking over to her horse; she searched the pack next to hers for some rations. It was barely enough to feed a mouse, her stomach grumbled as much. Sighing, she set herself astride in the saddle, another thing she was yet to get used to, chewing her way through the thickening trees. William rode behind, deep lines were beginning to settle and sensing her gaze he looked up and smiled, but it did not reach his eyes. His eyes told the same story of one who knew he would never be heard. It hurt her to see him in pain, and deciding to try and distract him, she slowed her horse, hoping he had forgotten his earlier annoyance, but knowing at the same time he would not have. 'Remember when we came out here on the hunt?' She ventured, surely that would pique his interest.

He looked around, 'I remember... though I seem to remember we were the ones who ended up being hunted.'

She continued. 'Never was our thing, was it?'

William looked away.

She was not going to give up that easily. 'Pity they found us to be honest.'

'I'm sick of talking about the past.' He tensed, his mouth widening with regret.

Isyllia shot him a confused glance, 'You've never mentioned that it bothered you, why now?'

'I'm sorry, look. When you are safe, we can talk.'

For a moment, the silence was deafening, and her heart began to thump as if to fill the moment. 'Safety. Can we even be sure of that? Safety is an illusion we fill ourselves with so we can sleep at night. Now is the only guarantee we ever have Will.'

'Why do you keep secrets?' He had said it so fast it surprised her. She almost lost grip on the reins, sputtering her reply 'I don't-'

He cut her off, 'Why do you faint all the time? Where do you go alone? The last time I asked this, you lied to me. If our friendship means so much to you, stop lying, and let's talk. Tell me the truth.'

Tears began to fill her eyes, she knew she had asked him to talk, but foolishly, she had not planned how to respond, 'And I told you then, I'm not lying. Why won't you let it go!'

'You wanted me to talk, fine I'll talk. I live my life in service to a man who despises me for an approval I will never receive; the soldiers hate me because of my time with you. You are all I have, and even you won't tell me the truth anymore. I am sorry your father died, and I am sorry you are in danger, I will die tomorrow to protect you if needed but I can't go on pretending things are like they have always been, because they aren't. When we reach the duchy, I think it's best we go our separate ways.'

Isyllias body went rigid, her breath coming in short wisps. How could he do this now? 'Will, don't do that, please, you're tired, breathe and think about what you are saying!'

'I can't.' He spurred his horse forward, leaving her behind to ride alone. For hours, nobody spoke. Her mind was blank, just repeating the clopping of hooves as they moved through the thickening trees. It was Ember who stopped and walked to Isyllia's horse. Her eyes were slits, hanging somewhere between empty dreams and consciousness. Isyllia was unaware she had started to slide off until it was too late, having no energy left to protest anyway. Instead, she allowed herself to fall, knowing that he was ready to catch her. Smiling as his warm arms spread through her tired, cold body, pulling her at last into a troubled sleep as he placed her on a pile of leaves.

Isyllia woke sometime later to the sounds of night birds bickering above, and a smell of meat cooking on a fire. She sat up, allowing her growling stomach to drive her towards the welcoming scent. All she could see was Ember sitting alone, the flickering fire making him look almost ethereal. Isyllia was spellbound for a moment until he looked up and pointed to the portion smoking on the fire. 'Meat!'

Isyllia took it, a little miffed by his one worded answer, but deciding to leave it behind her. 'What is it?'

'Salted Boar, thought you might prefer something hot.'

'Thank you.' They ate in silence for a moment. 'What is the mark on your chest?' The question hung in the air, Ember stared into the fire, deciding.

He still didn't look up, 'Now is not the time.'

'When will be the time, I just left my home, my people, and my father is dead. If you know something I deserve to know.'

He regarded her for a moment, scratching his chin, then placed his hands over hers. 'I know you are afraid. I know you have grown up too anxious to trust. Terrified of who you are. You have spent your life being lied to by a civilisation that is afraid to let go of its own past.' He looked at his hands, his creased brows etched with concern. 'I know that continuing to keep you in the dark is asking a lot from you, especially when things are falling around you but please, trust me a little longer.' He said, his face etched with concern. 'This is not a burden I want you to carry yet, not until you have someone else to help you carry it.'

Isyllia leant close and brushed the place where his mark sat unseen with her fingers, 'I thought that was why you were here.' She said, intoxicated by the energy that existed between the two of them.

His responding gaze was intense. 'I am.'

Isyllia was breathless and unaware her heart had begun to pound. It was the sharp snap of a twig that broke the moment, followed by footsteps trudging through the leaves, Adella and William had returned carrying two dead rabbits. Isyllia snatched her arm away, busying herself with the meat that had sat forgotten. William's walk was casual, more at ease. The hunt had given him a chance to vent his frustrations. Adella sheathed a dagger under the hem of her dress. Ember turned back toward the fire, scratching his short, messy van dyke uncomfortably then began to eat again, like the moment never happened.

'We are a few miles west of the Duchy of Morliin. By now the surrounding areas will be crawling with soldiers, what's your plan?' Adella's hands shot to her hips, her elbows stuck with the impression that she could stab someone with them. There was no hiding the rigid ire she struggled to contain.

'To be careful' Ember did not look up, unmoved by her obvious frustration.

It was unclear what had bothered her and she did not elaborate, instead she continued drilling her stare at his back. 'And how do you plan to do that if we get stopped by a scouting party, two people cannot fight half a dozen armed soldiers!'

'Two?' William asked, his eyes furrowed in confusion.

'Someone will have to protect the Queen!' She said.

'I don't need pro-'

'It will be fine.' Ember cut her off, 'I will protect the Queen.'

'We need you to fight!' Adella thrust her hands in the air, leaning over from the almost visible weight of her growing frustration.

Ember did not share her angst, he sat still staring into the flames, 'I can fight and protect her, everything is under control.'

Adella's lip curled with the weight of the sarcasm she hurled in his direction, 'Of course! ... We should move, the longer we stay in one place, the greater the chance we will be spotted.'

William shrugged, tethering the rabbits and following Adella.

Isyllia walked toward her horse dragging her feet, he had cut her off and the thought left her heavy, like invisible bricks dragged along behind her. Isyllia carried them for the rest of the evening, until the sun could be seen crawling through the trees. Still, she curled her lips from time to time like she had eaten something sour, the memory intent on taunting her. It was noon when they came across two men sitting on a rock some distance away. Their horses drank from the river some distance aware, undaunted by their master's hearty chuckling to themselves about a joke that could not be heard. Ember lifted his fist, indicating they stopped, they had not made us then.

William looked toward the soldiers and leant forward to whisper, 'How are we going to get past without them seeing? We have to cross the river!'

'They won't stay by the river; they are just getting supplies; we will have to wait it out!' Adella dismounted.

'What if they come this way?' The thought confused Isyllia, running from her own soldiers?

Ember frowned towards the men, forming a plan, 'I agree with Adella, if we wait it out, we may be able to avoid a fight.'

'This is madness!' No sooner had he finished the sentence, Isyllia had spurred her horse into motion. She waded into the water, starting across gingerly, each step placed to hold herself against the current. She had not gone far when the soldiers stood, studying the scene for a moment. Her heart quickened, but she kept moving forward, pretending not to notice them. It had not occurred to Isyllia if the others would follow, nor what she would say if the soldiers were to stop and question her. All she knew was she could not run from her own people, not if she ever hoped to return.

The men started forward, leaving their camp abandoned and drawing closer with slow, edgy steps. Isyllia noticed the crest they wore over their plate; it was the Sigel of Morliin. These were Gelraen's men, not her own. Her heart sank, and she felt tears burn her eyes at her own stupidity.

'Halt, and dismount in the name of the queen!'

She stopped involuntarily, unsure what to say to the men; that she was the Queen they named and to step aside, or a poor girl? But Morliin or not, these were still her soldiers to command, why was she stopping? What was a further dismay was that she could now feel herself dismounting, knowing it was the last thing she should do, but unable to control her own body!

One of the men grabbed the bridle of her horse, the other circled around, eyeing her up and down, they did not recognise her but dread began to flow through her veins, bringing with it a familiar sense of panic trapped deep within her stomach, the same feeling she had housed the night Lord Gelraen had torn her dress. 'Nice … nice!' the man that had been circling stopped, licking his lips.

"I'll thank you to take your hands off her!" A cold voice rumbled from close behind. Then men turned and grinned. 'What do you think Vern, bout time we took some time for ourselves don't you think?'

'Oh yeah." The man named Vern eyed Isyllia, "How's about you hold him first, then we swap.'

'You heard him, we are just passing through, let go of my horse at once, this behaviour is deplorable!'

The men chuckled, 'Mighty fine words there, what, you think you're a noble?' He laughed.

'I am going to ask one last time, let... her... go!' He said, the words coming in ferocious drabs.

The men ignored him, 'I think she wants to be fucked, don't you sweetheart, can see it on her face, clearly not gettin it from him!' They both stopped and laughed, a big mistake. Ember didn't hesitate, seizing the moment they both lost their concentration to pull a hidden blade from his sleeve, plunging it into the first soldier's throat before he even had time to blink. The second man, Vern, had just begun to draw his sword halfway, when Ember decorated his chest with the blade still wearing his partner's blood. Isyllia stood frozen as the men splashed into the river, the pooling water around her now turning a bright shade of red.

To say Ember was livid would be a colossal understatement. There was no human word for the expression that he wore. He wiped his dagger on his jerkin with a deafening silence, leaving the soldiers where they lay in the rushing waters, then tucked the dagger away, turning his dark glare on Isyllia. It assaulted her like a hefty blow, and she had to look away.

'They will send out a search party for these men, any chance we had of sneaking past the Duchy is gone. We will be lucky to make it to Godswall alive... What were you thinking?'

Everything she knew had been turned upside down, and now this, the disappointment on his face, that same look, her father's disappointment shone down at her once again. If she had just stayed put, not been stubborn and crossed the river, it would never have happened. It was frowned upon for royalty to cry, and so she held it in, swallowing the overwhelming sensation like a large portion of food. 'I am sorry. I am so sorry' She couldn't look up, could not meet his eyes.

'Don't do that again.' His voice had softened. Now she did look up, a pain began to break through the panic in his eyes, and once again she found herself captivated by the power of his gaze. Splashing broke the moment yet again and she turned to find William and Adella racing toward them. William was pale, although he could not have heard the exchange between her and the men, she knew he had not needed too. He went to reach out, then stopped himself, instead turning to Ember, 'Thank you!'

Ember nodded; his expression had returned to its resting frown.

'We should hide the bodies.' She said, watching the pools of blood being swept away in lines down the clear river, her thoughts being carried with them.

'No. We need to move; it won't take them long to figure out what has happened whether we hide them or not. I want to get as far away from here as possible.'

For once no one argued, and waiting for no further discussion, Ember took the lead with Isyllia close behind. Adella and William taking up the rear. They wound through the trees at an increased pace, sometimes getting snagged on opposing branches, which whipped back, leaving small cuts in her poor fabric. It wasn't until night that Ember called a halt, 'More soldiers!' He pointed ahead.

'How many?' Adella moved forward, placing a hand over her thigh, taking stock.

Ember frowned, looking off into the distance 'Twelve.'

There was silence for a moment. Isyllia looked to William, she knew her friend well, he had noticed Embers ability to know things he should not, and fear had begun to torture his resolve. She had to divert him from his thoughts.

But it was too late. Drawing his sword, he pointed it to Ember's chest from behind, 'Dismount, now!'

Ember turned to face him, annoyed but making no move away from the weapon.

William's voice rose, fear continuing to overpower him. 'I said dismount. You will travel no further with my Queen.'

'William!' Adella shot, placing herself between William and Ember, 'What on earth has gotten into you?'

'He's Malagara, how else could he know the things he knows? Step aside Adella, it's my duty to take him into custody!'

She did not move, 'William, you need to listen!'

He waited, but his face showed little interest in doing so.

Adella raised her hands in a calming motion, 'He is a spy, he works for the Guild, just like me.'

'You!' His surprise echoed hers. Adella, the unmarried relation favoured travel sure enough, but a spy was not something she would have ever guessed. Then it hit her, all the visits to Balor alone, the rumours. The close relationship with General made a little more sense now.

'There are many things you don't know about me dear boy, most of which you will never know, but I am family, and I need you to trust me, can you do that?'

William looked to Isyllia, imploring her for support. Her stomach dropped, 'Not this time Will.'

He sat for a moment, his wide eyes giving way to a sneer, then sheathing his sword, but leaving his hand as close as he could manage.

She looked over at Ember, but he was not looking at William, his face was turned in another direction. 'We are out of time.' Everyone stopped.

'Can we outrun them? The hills are just ahead!' Adella asked, alarmed.

He shook his head, 'They have archers... and they know this terrain better than us, we would never make it.'

'I am a soldier, perhaps we can trick them?' It was a desperate question, and the anxiety on William's face suggested he knew it.

Ember ignored the question and turned to Isyllia, making sure to take her out of earshot. His expression was pained, 'We cannot win this fight. Not with archers…Not all of us.'

Her heart began to race, she knew what he was going to ask, and the thought terrified her, 'I can't. There must be another way. I am begging you.'

He sighed heavily, not meeting her eyes, 'I know what I am asking you to sacrifice' He looked at William, 'And I can't promise you he will understand… But he would be alive.'

Her heart continued to thump, making her hands tremble, 'I cannot control it. I have always been too afraid to try.'

'I can help you, if you trust me.'

'…Yes' The guilt took no time to swarm through her, wishing she could give the same answer to William.

Ember nodded, his lips pursed and resolute as he moved back toward the others, 'This is what we are going to do. Adella and William, I need you to hide the horses. All of them and hide them well. Ember looked at his horse, it was clear he did not like the idea of leaving the animal alone in a fight. Isyllia and I are going down the hill ahead and we are going to hide. They know we are here, but not our exact location. We will use that to our advantage. Once the forces pass us, I will need the two of you to distract them enough so we can take care of the archers. Once that is done, you will need to draw their attack, their forces should split, trapping them on the slope on their mounts, in the dark. With luck, it should spook the horses.'

William's eyes lit up, 'Of course, it should give us enough of an advantage to take them out.'

Ember dismounted, stroking Periin on the nuzzle then handing the reins to Adella. 'Hide them well!' He stressed the last. 'Wait for my signal.'

William dismounted and walked over to Isyllia. Jumping down from her horse she moved to meet him, thoughts flooding her mind. What should she say? He was about to find out the secret that would tear what was left of their friendship apart forever. She would be damned in his eyes; she had always known deep down, and his reaction to Ember had just strengthened that anxiety.

'You don't have to go with him!' He pleaded, 'We could leave, run away, start a new life somewhere; you know I would take care of you.'

'I thought you wanted to part ways?' She said, but she was unable to look at his face.

William looked down and shrugged, 'I was wrong …'

'…The soldiers.' She shook her head, wishing it had not taken an assault to bring him back. 'You heard Ember, we would be outrun, and you would be arrested for treason.'

'You don't know that; he doesn't know...' He shot, his confidence abandoning him halfway.

Isyllia looked at her friend, the one who had always been there, filling every memory. Both were impulsive, both were dreamers. It had been so easy to get lost in each other's company and she had thought, she would always have that. Neither had recognised the void of reality and expectation plunging toward them, forcing them to walk separate paths, but she saw it now, just like the demented reality she now lived in, and she had no choice but to keep walking forward, with one arm forever stretched behind her. She shook her head, 'Not this time William.'

'Why?' His face was resolved, 'We have spent the last few days running, and for what? You might trust him, but I don't, I know something is not right.'

Isyllia backed away, her body wanting to run with him, but her heart knowing it was the wrong thing to do. Instead she forced herself away, wishing she could reach out and reassure him, reassure herself from the pain that took over with each step that she took. 'It makes no difference; they are risking their lives for us. I will not leave them to die. I'm sorry.' She turned, walking toward Ember, each step was slow, like she had concrete slabs tied to her ankles, the weight trying to drag her back. But she kept going forward, trying to concentrate on the task ahead and use her pain.

The slope was not steep, but she found herself stumbling down like a ragdoll, not in control of her feet. She was grateful when they stopped, Ember signalled for them to crouch behind a bush nearby. 'The archers are right at the back, there are two of them.' He kept his voice low 'Have you learnt to control the wind?'

'I don't know, I could never try!' For a moment she wanted to ask how he knew what she could do, then decided against it, putting it down to another one of his mysterious talents.

'Wind is the easiest element to control, because it is already there, you need only move it. Focus on feeling it around you and moving it where you want it.'

She nodded.

'I need you to plunge these daggers into the archers?'

Isyllia swallowed and held out her hand, concentrating on the gentle brushes of wind through the leaves above, the bushes around them, on her clothes, between her fingers. Pushing out with her energy she pulled it all in, wrapping it around the two daggers held in Ember's hand. Slowly they began to rise off his skin, floating on their own and with a wave of her hand, they began turning in circles on their own. Ember smiled at the rotating objects, 'Perfect. We need them to hit here!' He indicated a spot on the back, behind the heart. 'Drive them deep and true, if you miss...'

She swallowed, 'No pressure!'

Ember's head shot around, and then back again. 'Shh!' His voice dropped to a whisper; they are here... wait till they pass!'

Isyllia tried to calm her breathing and concentrate on the two horses at the back of the small procession. They had bows strapped to their backs and they rode with perfect concentration, waiting for any signal from the captains riding in the front. Ember moved his hands to the hilt of his sword, removing it silently from its scabbard then waited. The soldiers walked a few more paces when he whispered again, 'Now!' Isyllia concentrated on the two metal objects, willing the wind to spin the daggers faster, and faster, then, looking up she squinted at the place Ember had indicated on the two men, just visible next to the quivers they wore in the blackness. Pushing with all of her will she heaved the sharp blades toward the men, slicing through muscle to the heart. It was difficult, but she had done it. Within moments, both men tumbled from their saddles, crashing to the ground, lifeless. 'Stay here. I'll protect you.' They sprung out of the bushes at the same time, leaving the soldiers flanked and confused, the plan had worked, horses fumbled on the slope, thrashing around for any safe exit, and threatening to unseat their riders in the process. Ember wasted no time, thrusting the first of the soldiers in the side. The man screamed in agony, placing his hand over the wound, then tumbled to the floor with the archers. Isyllia began to feel weak, the screams of dying men pulling at her stomach muscles. But she forced herself to keep watching, two more men lay dead, their eyes staring off to the trees they could no longer see. She turned away, trying to put the image out of her mind. She could see William, nervous sweat poured from his face as he concentrated on the man slashing away at his guard. She looked to Adella, fighting with ease, two small blades held in her hand. But something was off. Adella was swinging, but missing her target. Isyllia concentrated harder, the soldier thrust with his right arm, Adella stepped aside, but instead of stepping behind him she stepped back into his front, connecting with his sword again. Adella was missing on purpose, she had to be. They had been led into a trap. Dread began to flood her veins, Why? Why would Adella come along this far to betray them, it made no sense! She had to warn Ember. Taking a deep breath, she stood.

'There she is, get the girl, get the girl!' The surviving captain shouted, locked in battle with William. Ember looked over, panic flooding his face, he had taken his attention off the soldier, and regretted the fatal decision. Isyllia could see the sword swing in slow motion, aimed true at Ember's unguarded stomach. She was going to lose someone else. The thought made her explode, and stretching her hand out to the sword, she willed it to strike him instead. The blade obeyed, recoiling back on its master unnaturally, spikes beginning to grow from the sides. The man uttered a terrifying sound, unable to move away from his own blade as it skewed him, blood spurting from multiple places, taking him to his end like the rest of his comrades. She had saved Ember, but it was not Ember she sought. Tears began to spill from her eyes, blurring her vision. William stood paralysed with fear. For a moment, they stood locked in each other's gaze, unaware of the blade swinging toward him. Adella plunged him in the shoulder from behind, a look of absolute resolve on her face. Williams fell to his knees, first clutching at the dagger and then ripping it from his shoulder. He did not look around to see who had struck him, his eyes were locked on Isyllia. In her mind she wanted to run forward, to strike Adella as the man had tried to strike Ember, but her feet would not move. Shock held her in place like her ankles were fixed into the ground. Isyllia watched the last thing that mattered to her tumble to the ground with the other soldiers, not bothering to look to see if Adella had advanced on her too. Nor did she care when unknown hands seized her around the waist and pulled her up onto a horse with ease.

'I've got you, it's alright, I've got you.' She was unaware she had been crying. How had everything gone so wrong? Why would Adella betray them, and why now? The questions stung at her wounded heart, but she had to know. The trees provided no answers, flying out of her vision one by one as the protective arms around her carried them on an unknown path forward, away from the questions and the pain that was left behind. 'Where are we going?'

'There is a cave ahead. It's well hidden, we should be safe there for the rest of the night.'

Isyllia nodded and concentrated on the colours rushing past her face, trying to quiet her frantic mind, and let time pass by, dragging her along on its mysterious journey.

Even the moon had left them when they reached the cave. Ember led the horse in through the small opening slow and cautious, his other sight directing their steps. Once satisfied, he stopped and rummaged in one of the sacks, producing some oats and dusty carrots. The horse looked at the proffered meal with a sad snort.

'I'm sorry buddy, that's all I have for now.' He let the horse nuzzle into his shoulder affectionately, and then placing the food on the floor began rummaging through some other bags. Isyllia waited for her eyes to adjust, and then watched without a single thought in her mind. He pulled out some salted meat and cheese, offering the larger portions to her.

'Thank you.' She sat with her back against the cave wall, drawing her cloak around her for warmth and started to eat. Her stomach threatened to throw the contents straight back at her, but she chewed anyway, forgetting what else she was supposed to do.

'We will rest here tonight, then make for the duchy tomorrow. If we ride hard, we should reach there by afternoon at the latest.'

'Can your horse carry us both for that long?' She asked, concerned.

Ember looked over at Perrin, his gaze softening; the warhorse was lapping water from a puddle on the floor, unaware of their eyes on him. 'He will be fine.'

'What happened?' The question hung in the air for a moment, neither wanting to relive the events.

Ember shook his head in disgust, 'Adella. I should never have trusted a spy, however under the circumstances, I was given little choice. It is Balor that concerns me, how could he not have known?'

Isyllia shook her head, her throat clenching. 'Why would she do this? Why would she kill her only nephew?'

Ember sighed, 'They are trained that way, to look out for themselves. She may have once been family, but now... Not now.' He was worlds away for a moment, then snapped back into the present.

Isyllia nodded, wishing there was an easy way to ask her next question, 'How did you know what I could do, if I am not Malagara?'

Ember considered her for a moment then instead, asked his own question, 'How much of Illingdale's history do you know?'

'I know it was founded under the first King Medeus the mighty. He saved our people from the destruction of the gods.'

Ember nodded. 'Did you also know that Illingdale was first founded as a world centre, a council?'

Isyllia frowned, 'No, we were just settlers in the time of Medeus, there was no city.'

'Not Illingdale, that's correct. But a council existed, between the leader of the people, Medeus, the four champions of the gods, and a high priestess of Cyndershire.' He took a bite of his food.

Isyllia waited with her hands folded, grateful for the distraction from the emptiness swallowing her inside.

'The four champions of the gods; Kathriin of Abashiina, Semiir of Menethon, Odriid of Caros and Luron, of Nemethiiniia. Together the council existed to keep peace. It comes from the great story of Nemethiiniia, the tender hearted god who longed for sons and daughters, and Caros out of love for his Nemethiiniia, created the animals and presented them each to his beloved, but still, she shook her head, and cried. It wasn't until Caros created man and woman in their exact image that Nemethiiniia at last smiled and gave man and woman powers of their own. So that they might protect their new home. But man was flawed and abused the power they were given.'

123

He paused, taking a swig from a water skin, then offered it to Isyllia who took it with a forced smile, and was careful not to drink too much. 'Caros tried to remove the gift, and for many years, man returned to normal, just like they had once been. Many generations passed, but children began to show signs of the gift once more, and man returned to their evil ways. It was decided that they would leave, letting their children live in the new home they made, each picking a champion among men. Someone of pure heart that would protect ordinary people from Malagara. Each was given a mighty weapon, crafted by the gods themselves, and wieldable only by the champion it was crafted for. Kathriin was the first chosen of Abashiina, it was within her power to control the elements. Her weapon is the Stone of Elements. Semiir of Menethon's gift was power. He had the ability to rally the people, to give them strength. Used unwisely he could control people, bend them to his will. His weapon was the Bow of Power.'

Isyllia frowned 'A bow? Why not a sword, surely a sword would have made more sense?'

'Bows are powerful weapons. A representation of perfect strength and grace. Any common thug can swing a sword and hit a target if they try, training only makes you more effective. It takes true discipline, intelligence, and dedication to wield a bow. These were the kind of qualities Menethon wanted in his champion.'

She nodded, 'Fair enough.'

Ember ignored the comment and continued, 'Odriid of Caros was given the Sphere of Knowledge and Wisdom. The sphere was meant to increase intelligence, heighten his sense of danger, and help increase what the Chosen of Caros can see.'

'See?'

'Yes. The Chosen of Caros can see things others cannot, hidden objects, people.'

'Like you. That is what you can do, is it not?' It was less a question, a slight agitation to her voice.

He nodded, 'It is, but it takes a great deal of energy, so I cannot do it all the time. Only for short periods, or when unavoidable. Not without the Sphere anyway.' Ember settled against the opposite wall then continued, 'With their weapons, the four chosen contained enough power to stand against the magic ones if needed... Semiir was the first to go mad. Over time his advice, turned to direction, which then turned to domination. For a long time Kathriin and Semiir ruled the people together, Odriid and Luron tried to reason with them, but they would listen to no one. Eventually, it was a man who stood up to them, Medeus. He rallied his people against the tyrannical Champions and Semiir was captured and burned. The loss of her loved one drove Kathriin into a vengeful fury, for a week she laid waste to everything in her path, until they tried once more to convince her to give up her anger. This time they succeeded, and overcome with remorse, she gave herself to Medeus and was burned for her crimes alongside her beloved. From that day, Illingdale outlawed the gods and Medeus was hailed a hero and crowned the first king of Illingdale. The Malagara of the gods they are now called, and to this day they are banished to the Isle of the Forgotten. Odriid disappeared and Luron followed the Malagara, never to be seen again.'

'So, what does that have to do with us?' She asked. Deep down, Isyllia knew she was being stubborn but the pain in her heart was so great, it was all she had left to lessen some of the weight.

'The Chosen bear the mark of their god. I have shown you mine... I bare the mark of Caros. You bear the mark of Abashiina... I had hoped to be safe at the duchy when I told you this, not here when you were scared and exhausted...'

'Fairy tales. I bear the mark of the, Malagara, what I am, and what my friend died needlessly believing.' Isyllia turned away, shutting her eyes, willing sleep to come and hoping Ember did not press the matter further, he didn't.

It was dawn when she woke to the sound of rain falling outside the cave. Ember was already awake and eating some stale bread. She stretched, stiff and aching all over. He looked over, nodding to a linen parcel next to her. She reached out and unfolded the cloth to find a hunk of bread and cheese and what was left of the water skin. She ate faster than she thought, her mind still too foggy with sleep to correct her lapse in manners.

Ember didn't notice, and walked over to the mouth of the cave, 'I am going to wash and make sure it is safe to leave.' He indicated the cloth he had wrapped the food in, 'I left that in case you wished to do the same.' And without another word, he left the cave, walking out into the rain, and leaving her alone with the horse. Isyllia finished her food and stood rummaging in the small sack she had with her, the one containing her valuables. Thanking the stars, she had decided to wear it instead of placing it on the horse. She pulled out her last set of fresh clothes, removing the ones she had been wearing and placing them on the cave floor. The water was freezing but she did not care, it did the job. Days of grime washed away, leaving her with a familiar feeling of cleanliness, and lightening some of the weight on her heart. Ember returned wet through and frowning. 'The area is clear. Adella has what she needed, but I want to be gone to be on the safe side.'

'Has what she needed?'

He walked over to his pack, removing his mail shirt. 'Damn rain.'

Isyllia spoke louder. 'Has what she needed?'

Ember removed a dry shirt from his pack, and then turned to face her. 'Information. She has returned to the Duchy, meaning she is working for Gelraen... she has William's body with her.' He removed his wet shirt; it was clear on his face he had agonised over the last bit of information.

Isyllia turned away, blocking out the information. 'What now?'

'Continue to Godswall. We need an ally if we are to find out what Gelraen is planning.'

'Do you believe he murdered my father?'

'I don't know. But I am going to find out. Are you coming?'

She turned, he had re-dressed in his mail shirt, pack slung over one shoulder. She nodded, picking up her own and walked toward the horse. He stopped, pointed to the discarded clothes on the floor.

'What am I meant to do with them?' She asked, confused.

He shook his head 'We are not in a castle anymore; you saw what happened yesterday. Mistakes get you killed. Pick them up.' He turned away and began to fasten his pack to the horse. Isyllia was furious, but she moved over to the clothes and stowed them back in her pack on the way over to the horse.

'I'll get up myself.' She declined his offer of help and settled herself back on the horse.

'I need you to move forward.'

Isyllia turned a bright shade of red, 'Shouldn't I ride behind you?' She asked, shocked.

'I can protect you better like this.' His voice was cold, distant. Isyllia moved forward, desperate to leave the topic behind and gritted her teeth when his cold mail shirt pressed hard against her back. It sent a shiver rippling down her spine, goosebumps finishing off the frigid moment of intimacy along her arms. She tried to ignore it, and the feeling of his arms around her. What would William say if he could see this! Then it hit her again, a painful longing, like a silent scream radiating from her heart, taking her breath away. He was not here. He never would be again. She was sitting on a horse, riding through the rain with a stranger, a soon to be outcast from her own people. She was alone, the careless days of laughter she took for granted were gone, and Williams' familiar smile was dead along with all the dreams she had stowed in her heart. Leaving her with the only reality she had left, the look of fear on his face, the moment she knew she had lost him forever.

CHAPTER SIX

Gelraen, Illingdale Castle.

'Sire, Sire, Adella has passed through the gates. She said it was urgent she saw you.' The guard stopped and bent over to catch his breath, 'She has Lord Mallory with her, I think he is dead.'

Gelraen shot out of his chair like it was on fire, his whisky forgotten. The torture was over in record timing, it did not take long for Lord Walton to extract information from the guard about who was let out of the main gates. Turns out the man did value his own skin more than the General. Though, the ordeal left him with more time than he had planned to sit and wait. It did not sit well, the nervous energy collected in all the wrong places. 'Where is she now.' He did not wait for the man to reply but began striding in the direction of the guest quarters, hoping they had the sense to admit her.

'We saw them in the guest quarters sire.'

He did not turn back to thank the messenger, waving a hand over his shoulder in dismissal. Something must have gone wrong for her to come back here.

'Open the door or be run through!' The door guard flew aside, having no doubt whatsoever that his new King meant every word of the furious threat. Adella was dishevelled, kneeling beside an unconscious figure. She stood, drawing a dagger in alarm. 'Sire!' She sheathed the weapon, offering a hurried courtesy. She had been crying.

'You have me at somewhat of a loss, Adella. Explain.' He nodded to the figure on the bed.

Adella followed his gaze, 'It's a long story sire. Sit, please.' She motioned to a modest sitting area at the side of the room. Gelraen nodded, not wanting to interrupt her flow of thoughts. 'Some days ago, I was asked to help someone escort the queen to safety.'

'Who? And under whose orders'?' Gelraen felt the sweat begin to bead on his brow, he ignored it. He knew the answer already.'

'I received a letter from Duke Randal Bellamy. He offered the queen sanctuary for the time being. He said it was best kept secret so your effort in finding the killer was not disturbed. The man's name is Anton; I was provided his description only. I was told he would find me, and he did.'

CHAPTER SIX

Gelraen inhaled until his chest was puffed out with air, like more oxygen would provide a face to the mysterious name, not the name he expected then. 'Anton you say.' He rolled the name over on his tongue, holding the breath in his lungs for a moment then nodding it out again, 'Go on.'

'I took him to Balor, we needed a way out of the city. I could tell Balor knew something that he wasn't saying. But I didn't take much note of it at the time, I wish I had. It wasn't until.' She turned back to William, fresh tears staining her skin. 'It wasn't until she tried to kill William, that it hit me.'

'What hit you.' Gelraen was breathing in short whips now, each fibre of his being locked onto every word of Adella's painful confession.

'Isyllia. She is Malagara, Gelraen. She tried to kill William. I barely got him out of there, he has been unconscious ever since. That's what Balor knew. He was protecting her for William.'

'The king must have found out!' He said it more to himself, like the pieces of a giant puzzle were coming together one by one.

Adella looked at the floor, 'There is more.'

Gelraen clenched his teeth and ground them against one another, like the tension could be dissolved in his mouth like candy.

'Balor killed the king, I'm sure of it. He asked me to buy him poison, I remember he was agitated at the time… I didn't think anything of it, not until discovering what Isyllia was. Then it all made sense.'

'Does William know? Do you think Randal knew?'
Adella shook her head, 'William did not know about the poison, no, About Isyllia, no, he never knew that either. They quarrelled the whole way, he knew she was keeping secrets, but she wouldn't tell him. He was innocent. Balor knew her secret, and he risked his son's life anyway. As for Randal, I doubt it. We all know he is …eccentric. I think he is just trying to help.'

Gelraen shook his head, 'Can you testify to this?'

'Promise you will help William. Promise you will protect him from her, from himself. I can't lose my only nephew.'

Gelraen nodded, 'The boy is innocent, he is a subject of Illingdale. I will make sure he is safe.'

Adella nodded, satisfied, 'Then I will testify.'

Gelraen stood and walked to the door. 'I will be back with someone to help William. I will call you when the council convenes. I recommend you stay here and say nothing of this to anyone.'

Adella nodded, 'Sire.' Gelraen strode down the hall searching for a guard. But there was no one. The grey marble hall was deserted, 'Where was everyone?' He was almost in his chamber when a boy turned around the corner, striding ahead without seeing Lord Gelraen bearing down on him. He gave a startled whimper when Gelraen accosted him by the vest, almost holding him in the air. 'Fetch Lord Walton to my chambers and tell him to call the council for an hour. Got it?'

The boy hesitated, overcome with nerves. He nodded vigorously and then scampered away the minute the burly Lord had released hold of his attire. Gelraen continued back to his quarters, stopping short of the door which stood ajar. Why was the door open? He placed one hand over the hilt of his sword, and pushed the door open with his free hand, ready to draw if needed. A man dressed in black stood inside by the fireplace, drinking the remaining contents of his whisky glass. The man was tall, and what could be seen of his skin was scarred, like he had been in one too many fights, and lost them all. The man turned, brandishing the now empty glass, 'Thought you wouldn't mind if I helped myself!'

Gelraen loosened his grip on the sword, and reached for another glass, he had the feeling he was going to need it. 'To what do I owe the pleasure, good news I hope.'

The man placed the glass on the mantle and then began to pick his teeth through words, 'Interesting. We haven't found the package yet Duke, but we found something else you might be interested in!'

Gelraen felt his impatience begin to grow, and the volume of his glass to match. 'I haven't got all day, out with it.'

The man grinned, 'We haven't found the package sire, but we found her.'

Gelraen choked, slapping himself on the chest to dislodge the whisky that had tried to take up residence in his lungs by mistake. 'Her! What do you mean you found her?' He said, his voice raspy.

'Hiding in Mespar all this time, temple priestess. I'll take one bet she is guarding the package there.'

Gelraen drained the entire glass, 'That complicates things.'

'So, as you can imagine, my fee has doubled. Retrieving a package is one thing, pillaging the holy temple of Mespar and living to tell the tale, quite another.'

'I'll pay you triple; can it be done?'

The man nodded, despite the scars on his body suggesting he was overconfident, 'Oh it can be done sire, it's more a matter of what you are willing to risk getting it?'

Gelraen sucked in a breath. 'Anything, you have authority to do what you need. But I want no mistakes this time, you are not to kill her. And the package must always remain covered, do you understand.'

The man nodded, 'This isn't my first rodeo, sire!'

'Good, now get out, I'm about to have company.' The man gave him a lazy salute and then disappeared from the room. Leaving Gelraen alone until there was another knock at the door. This time, he knew who to expect. 'Come in Lord Walton.' The greasy Duke entered holding various parchments clutched under his arm. He offered an exorbitant bow, and then waited to be offered a chair. Gelraen did not oblige him. 'What reports do you have from the bird families?'

Lord Walton stumbled with the rolls of parchment, offering one to Gelraen. Gelraen stared for a moment, deciding not to take the parchment. 'Give me the short version.'

Lord Walton inclined his head, 'No trace of the fugitives have been found through the birders sire. However, I did investigate the individual you asked about earlier, and I think you will be interested in what the Clydesdale birder sent back from Tinderford.'

'Yes, go on.' He scratched his chin, half listening. Lord Walton was seldom interesting, but he was loyal, and loyalty always came in handy.

'It appears the Clae Steel merchant has been receiving money from an anonymous source in Docktown. The individual that took the queen may have been watching her for some time.'

'Indeed.' Gelraen bared his discoloured teeth in frustration. *'Under my nose the whole time.'* He poured another glass of whisky, 'Keep looking, I want a NAME. See if you can find a Smithy owned under the name Anton. They are bound to need to communicate with someone sooner or later.'

Lord Walton bowed deep, almost scraping his nose on the floor in the process, 'At once, will that be all Sire?'

Gelraen sat up straight, No. Have you called council?'

'The order has been given sire; they are to be assembled within the hour.'

Gelraen relaxed into his chair, but his back remained rigid. 'I need you to take some guards, Balor is to be arrested under suspicion of treason and brought to the council chambers for questioning.'

Lord Walton paled, 'Sire! Surely there is some mistake!' It was impossible to tell next to his naturally oily complexion if the man had begun to sweat.

'There is no mistake, make sure Adella is summoned to the council. You are dismissed.'

Lord Walton backed out of the room, his eyes wide. Gelraen waited until the Duke had disappeared down the hall and then threw his empty glass at the wall. Not at all sparing a glance back at the broken glass that scattered through the room, some of which that no doubt joined the escaped pieces of earlier. Things were getting out of hand, one thing had to go wrong, and his plan was dust. Gelraen traced his steps, back and forth, back and forth over the creaky wooden planks. Waiting for something to hit him, some way to regain control, he sighed; it would need to wait. Straightening his jerkin in the mirror, he took a measured breath, and then made his way slowly to the throne room.

By the time he arrived, most people were already assembled. They inclined their heads to him as he passed. Adella had also arrived looking sombre. She sat alone, nursing her troubles on her face, but making eye contact with no one. He walked most of the way to the front, stopping short of the throne, he never sat in the throne. 'Gentlemen.' The door opened, revealing Lord Walton, and following close behind was Balor, being led in by armed guards. 'Bring him to the front.' Lord Walton nodded and stepped aside so the guards could pass. Balor had blood trickling down his chin where he had offered resistance. The General locked eyes with Gelraen, his look thunderous.

'Balor Mallory, you have been arrested under suspicion for the murder of our king. What do you say to the charges?'

Balor spat on the ground, a sizable spot of blood now decorating the marble floor beside him. 'It wasn't me who killed the king, but you already know that, don't you Duke.'

Gelraen continued to stare at the man, not allowing the words to anger him, not this time. 'On the contrary, I have evidence that proves you not only bought the poison that murdered our king, but the motive for you to do it. I must say General, we may have had our differences, but of all the people I could have suspected, you were the one person I was hoping I was wrong about.' He shook his head, 'Witness, come give your evidence to the people. There was silence for a moment, everyone waited to see who was responsible for convicting the beloved General. Adella stood, greeted by shocked murmurs echoing around the room. But of all the people whispering their indignation, no one reflected more consternation than Balor. Whatever confidence the General had about his predicament collapsed like a wilted flower as he watched his sister in law approach the front of the room. Adella kept her head down making eye contact with no one.

'Tell the people what you told me.'

Adella nodded once, then faced the council, still not looking at Balor. 'It is with a heavy heart that I confess my knowledge to the court today.' She paused, 'I am sorry for the part I have unwittingly played in the events of recent days. And I beg for forgiveness of my city.' She paused again, 'Some days ago, Balor asked me to purchase poison, which I did. And handed it to him. Council, it is not unusual for a General to purchase poison, but with the events that followed, it soon became clear his motive was not conventional. It started when I was asked to escort our queen to safety at the Duchy of Godswall, accompanied by a stranger, and William Mallory, his own son. I agreed, and all seemed well until we were set upon by soldiers. It was then that I discovered the secret our king had been killed to protect. Our queen, Isyllia, is Malagara. She revealed herself when she struck William. Who lies as we speak unconscious still!'

One member of the council spoke, it was the portly councillor. 'Preposterous, a Malagara could not have remained hidden in such a visible position for so long unnoticed.'

Adella continued, 'I thought so too, but the proof has always been there. The fainting spells, the secrecy, always appearing to withdraw from the public for no reason. Even then I could have excused it, were it not that I saw it with my own eyes. When William began to suspect our companion of his condition, he challenged him, as is proper. As I said, we were set on by guards, so it could not be addressed, but William didn't let it go. He challenged him on the field, and when he was about to strike the man down Isyllia made a blade grow unnaturally, piercing him from behind. She protected her fellow Malagara, at the expense of her best friend.'

The portly councillor dropped down onto his chair, 'This cannot be true.'

Adella looked down, 'Balor murdered our king to protect the love of his son, and then used me to help secret her out of the city so no one could find out. If only he had realised William never knew her secret... I ask you, why would I convict my own family, ruin my own reputation, were I not sure.' Adella now looked to Balor, there was no emotion on her face, just resolve. Balor stood shocked, and it was clear, he was devastated.

'You may sit Adella, thank you for your evidence.' Gelraen scratched his chin, so the man had powers, she had not mentioned that. Gelraen felt his stomach tense, it had to be him, it had to be. Using slow steps, he brought himself back to the present. 'What do you have to say to the charges Balor?'

Balor shook his head, 'It is true, I asked Adella to buy poison, but it was to kill rats. I never killed our king, I would never...I didn't know she was Malagara, that cannot possibly be true. Cailem would never have missed that!' He trailed off. Covering his face in his hands.

Gelraen looked to the council. 'And the people. What have the people to say?'

The council murmured amongst themselves for a moment, then waited as one man hobbled forward, 'The people find Balor guilty, pending search of his premises. If the bottle he claims to have purchased and not used, is indeed still in his possession, then he is to be released.'

Gelraen nodded, 'Balor, can you produce the bottle?'

Balor looked to the floor, broken. 'No. No I cannot.'

Gelraen sighed, disappointed. He shook his head for a moment, taking in the moment and then continued. 'It is then with a heavy heart that I find you guilty of the murder of King Cailem Bellamy. You will be taken to the dungeons and tortured pending your final execution. Do you have any final words for the people of this city, whom you have betrayed?'

Balor continued to stare at the floor, in tears. 'I didn't do it.'

Gelraen frowned, 'The evidence would suggest otherwise. You are required to surrender your ring.'

Balor looked up, 'I don't have it.'

Gelraen clenched his teeth, 'I see. Soldiers, take him away and search his premises.' The men obeyed, dragging Balor from the room, 'Where is my son Adella, where is my boy.' The soldiers struggled with the desperate man who tried with every ounce of strength he had to fight his way back, his eyes locked on Adella's back. She did not turn, allowing him to be carried from the room, his screams carrying down the hall where he could be heard uttering one name over and over, William.

CHAPTER SEVEN

Isyllia, Duke of Godswall, Illingdale.

The ride took forever, hours of endless columns of trees, each one looking the same as the last. Even listening to the various breeds of birds had lost its charm. So when the afternoon sun at last shone golden and strong on the gates to the Duchy of Godswall, their haven, they could have almost forgotten the archers on the walls above who were taking position, arrows nocked and ready. It would only take a single nod from their captain who stalked along the tower to a position where he could better see the riders approaching, and it would all have been for nothing. 'Halt, state your name and purpose, or be shot.'

Ember moved his head to the side so the man could see. 'Ember Clae of Tinderford, I carry a noble lady and we respectfully request an audience with the Duke.' He waited.

The captain signalled for the gates to be opened.

Ember made a clicking sound with his mouth, signalling Perrin to walk forward. The city was small next to Illingdale. A marvellous tiny replica, leaving Isyllia in wonder as people strolled through the township, stopping to look and gossip at the common strangers who were allowed to approach the Duke's residence. They dismounted near the doors. A servant rushed forward to take the horse. Ember hesitated, 'He has had a long ride, please see he is properly rested.' The boy nodded, then trotted away holding the reins clutched in his hands. Ember watched as he left, he did not like giving his horse to strangers, the look of concern on his face said as much. 'We should move!' He said, breaking the uncomfortable silence. Another servant approached, this one older and more confident. 'Please enter!' He stood aside, 'Wait in the parlour please while I fetch the Duke.' They obeyed. Isyllia walked around the room, examining the lavish collection of vases and paintings that were on display. Duke Randall had always been a collector of the old world. 'Hoarder' her father had called him. She smiled at the memory, grateful to be somewhere familiar. A few minutes had passed when the Duke came sweeping into the room, eyes straight to Isyllia, concern etched on his weathered face. He held her out for a moment examining her then pulled her into a hug, 'Thank the gods you are alright!' He stepped back, 'Excuse my informal behaviour, cousin. I have been worried since I received news of your father.'

She smiled, 'In our unfriendly reality, your candour pleases me, Duke. Thank you for receiving us.'

The duke looked over to Ember, who stood tall and patient, the Duke's smile turned formal. 'I owe you thanks for the safe arrival of my cousin.' He bowed.

Isyllia adopted a look of confusion, why was the Duke bowing to a commoner?

'Ember Clae of Tinderford, at your service.' He bowed in return.

'Indeed.' The Duke's words were regretful. 'Tandus, please see our guests to our best chambers, I want all their needs seen to, do you understand.' Tandus bowed to leave, 'One more thing, I wish for their visit to be kept silent. The gates are to be closed; I don't care who knocks on them.'

Tandus bowed once more and signalled for Isyllia and Ember to follow.

'Once you are rested, we shall dine, and talk.' He bowed deep, then to her surprise, he turned, and bowed again to Ember.

'This way!'

They followed through corridors filled with more tapestries and paintings, until their guide stopped without warning, causing them to almost crash into him. He opened a door on the left, 'My Lord Clae, I shall see someone along shortly to see to your needs.

If you have any further questions, please see me, I hope the room is to your liking.' Tandus bowed, bending as little as possible.

'Thank you.' Ember glanced at Isyllia; Questions written on his face. But he did not ask them, instead he walked into the room, and closed the door. Leaving her alone with the servant, who had begun walking once more. She jogged to catch up, when he stopped at another room, not too far up the corridor and opened the door as he had with Embers, Isyllia almost crashed into him a second time.

'I hope you find the lodgings comfortable, my lady. I will send some maids along to see to your needs.'

'Thank you Tandus, could you ensure they bring hot water, I should like a bath.'

Tandus bowed then moved on his way in the same brisk fashion. She shook her head for a moment, amused by the thought of his popularity among the house staff. Shrugging the moment free she walked over to the window, opening the curtains to let in some light. The warmth of the sun was like a kiss on her cold skin. She rubbed her arms, trying to soak it in then decided to look through her pack. She walked over to the bed, it was large and ornate with four columns intricately carved with leaves and trees signifying Ravenswood, and on the head the mountains of Godswall sat proud, framing the crest of Bellamy. Her crest. Isyllia sat tipping the few things she had brought onto the bed. The wet clothes Ember had insisted she collect she threw onto the floor; she had no desire to see them again. She unfastened her mother's locket and placed it next to the sack of Dales she had stowed at the bottom. She was about to pick up the sack when another object caught her eye, the signet ring. The ring of royalty. She picked it up and turned it over in her fingers, wondering if she would ever be able to return, or would Adella betray her as Malagara.

Her thoughts were interrupted by a timid maid, hurrying in with a basket of wood. The girl was young, with a nervous demeanour and the red cheeks to match. She curtsied, and then made her way over to the fireplace, striking the flint with shaking fingers, missing a few times. It was almost cause for celebration when the streak of orange ignited, were it not sure to send the girl tumbling into the fireplace from fright.

'That was quick!' Isyllia asked, amused by the girl's embarrassment and forgetting her own troubles for the moment.

'Thank you, my lady.' The girl rushed a curtsy then began piling wood in one at a time, careful not to smother the small flame licking away at its bounty.

'Not much of a talker?' She moved closer, sitting on the stool and stretched her legs.

'Pardon my lady, we were told not to disturb you.' The girl looked at the floor.

Isyllia smiled, 'On the contrary, I find the distraction refreshing… What's your name?'

The girl chanced a look up, smiling shyly. 'Mariin my lady.'

'Mariin, a lovely name. I thank you for the fire.'

Mariin bowed, then left the room. From then, more people entered, and the bustle of activity reminded her of familiar days, when her largest concern was choosing the correct outfit. Isyllia sat contented for the first time in over a week, watching as everyone went about their business, with practiced precision, and when an elder woman approached holding a measuring tape, with two maids trailing behind she stood, ready. The woman looked at the discarded clothes on the floor, frowning for a moment but not pressing her thoughts. 'My lady, the Duke has asked that I see you dressed for dinner. I do not have time to make you something fresh, but I hope either of these will be to your liking. She held up two dresses. One was deep green velvet with vines of leaves creeping up the flared sleeves. And on the bodice delicate gold flowers scattered from either side of the neck, spilling down the dress, as if they had been thrown. Isyllia took in every detail from the expanse of skirts to the delicate train that trailed behind. The other, was a warm brown, with a rich fur trimmed neckline. There was no choice.

'I'll wear the green!'

The woman nodded, 'If I may measure you lady, we shall make any adjustments required.'

Isyllia nodded and allowed the woman to move forward, humming as the lady prodded here and there.

'My lord Clae has also requested that we arrange you fresh travel clothes, my lady.'

'Indeed.' Did he intend them to be leaving so soon then? 'I have some ideas.'

My lord Clae has issued specific orders on their design, I am sorry, my lady.'
Isyllia pursed her lips, annoyed, 'Did he now!'

'Have I offended you, lady?' The woman stopped what she was doing, but did not look apologetic, more annoyed at the interruption.

'No, you may continue.' Isyllia stopped her humming, already tired of this stranger controlling every facet of her life. She closed her eyes for a moment, taking a deep breath. A bath, a bath was what she needed, and the smell of the steam from the tub dragged at her concentration, impatience threatening to take over. A few more minutes was all, and the woman would be complete.

'The gown should fit you perfectly my lady, only minor alterations needed. I will have it ready for dinner.' The woman bowed and left the room, her maids trailing behind.

Isyllia walked over to the bath, dragging the peasants' clothes off and throwing them in a heap on the floor, eager to never see them again. She stepped in, the hot water creeped up her leg, hugging each of her stiffened muscles., a welcome feeling after days of dirty forest. She had smelt smells, no one person should be responsible for, some, she had even worn. With a sigh, she sat down, the smell of Lavender and Orange relaxing what was left of the stress eating away at her mind. Her life had been a whirlwind of activity since her father had died, grief, and then fear had occupied her every waking moment. Now she was faced with the prospect of being a fugitive, there had been no time to stop. The train of thought brought her to Ember, his puzzling temper, and the story he had told her in the cave. He had not mentioned it again on the ride to the Duchy, for which she had been grateful. She examined her mark, a perfect star shaped birthmark sat, as if burned into her skin. It didn't matter if it was true, in Illingdale, it was forbidden to practice magic. The gods were evil, magic was their way of wiping out the people, her people. It was death to be found guilty, for all but children. Instead, they were sent to the Island of the Forgotten, to banishment. She would have to find a way out of this, but not now, for now she would enjoy the reintroduction of luxury, for as long as it intended to last.

She had been soaking for a good thirty minutes when a maid came in with some fresh linen. Isyllia stepped out, wrapping herself in the sheet the girl held out and sat down on the bed to wait, still lost in her thoughts.

'Ms Pont will be along with the dress shortly; will you be needing anything else madam?'

'Not for the moment.' Her voice was dreamy, and she allowed herself to slump on the soft mattress where she sat, another thing she would never take for granted again.

The maid bowed and moved over to the dresser, 'How would you like to wear your hair?'

Isyllia thought for a moment 'Up will do, something simple.'

Ms Pont walked in a moment later carrying the dress over her arm. 'It is done. If there is nothing else, my lady, I will leave you.'

Isyllia smiled. 'Thank you, Ms Pont, your punctuality is refreshing, you may retire.'

The gave a terse bow then handed the dress over to the servant and exited the room. Isyllia moved forward holding her arms for the corset to be slipped over her head. Laughing to herself at the idea of looking forward to wearing the chest crushing garment she otherwise despised.

'Begging your pardon madam?'

Isyllia opened her eyes and looked to the maid, 'Is something wrong?'

'My Lord Clae has asked that we dress you… lightly.'

Isyllia's face turned red, fury boiling her blood. It took all her strength to hold her emotions together and resist the urge to throw one of the Dukes ornate vases across the room. He had removed her from her home, made her a fugitive, caused her best friend to be killed and now, now he was controlling how she dressed. 'I don't care what he has instructed, I am a lady, not some guttersnipe, I will wear a corset if I so choose, do you understand?' She knew it was wrong to direct her anger at the maid, her coldness had made the girl shake more, if possible, but enough was enough and she intended to make her thoughts known to him as soon as she had the chance. The girl moved to the closet, fumbling with the door and produced a corset, slipping it over Isyllia's head. She thought it best not to disturb the girl further and instead let her work, hoping concentration would calm her nerves.

When the dress was laced, she sat down on the stool in front of the mirror, allowing her hair to be swept up into a two layered bun. The maid was young, but she had a passion for what she did, carefully managing each strand into place, as she wound a wreath of golden flowers delicately through her hair, rounding its way to the top of the bun. It was hard to look at herself in the mirror, she was never certain who was looking back anymore. But tonight, some of the girl she once knew was there, smiling back. Along with another person.

'You look like your mother.'

Isyllia stood abruptly, she had not heard him come in.

'Sorry to startle you child, I came to escort you to dinner… if you are ready?'

Isyllia looked back one last time. Her mother had died when she was born and there were no pictures on the walls, her father had ordered them destroyed in anger. The memory of her face was too painful, and so, Isyllia had assumed she looked more like someone else. 'What was she like Randal?'

He turned to the maid, 'Thank you Patriice, you may go.' He turned back, thoughtful, 'She was kind, but more somehow…. She made a person feel like they could handle anything. And she was strong. The people loved your mother. It was hard when she died.'

Her heart sank, 'I wish she had left some part of herself behind.'

He stepped forward, offering his arm. 'Ah, but she did. You'll see in time.'

They walked to the dining room. It was a long room, with a large mahogany table in the centre. The wall was covered in bookshelves to the right, and armchairs sat in a cozy reading area in front of an open fireplace. Ember was already waiting, he stood near a bookshelf, nose buried deep in its pages. He too had changed out of his dirty clothes, but had worn his own attire, a plain hose and a clean white shirt. The servant had managed to get him to remove his chain vest but had been less successful in depriving him of his sword. Randal frowned down at it.

'Truly Caros is a wonder…I guess it is best to always be prepared for anything in times such as these.'

Ember turned, offering a short bow, 'Duke.' Isyllia waited, her anger still threatening to get the better of her. He looked over to Isyllia. For a moment he stood silent not hiding the trepidation on his face, then remembering himself, he bowed, the resting frown making its way back to the front and centre.

Her annoyance started to get the better of her, 'We have never had the occasion to discuss how I should formally address you in company…Master Clae?'

'Ember.'

She raised an eyebrow, 'I thank you for your service in returning me to my kin. I must confess it is marvellous to be clean and, suitably, attired again.'

His eyes narrowed.

'Shall we sit?' The duke indicated to the table where three place settings had been set out, unaware of the barbs being hurled across the room. Isyllia moved over to the place indicated on the side. Ember sat opposite, with the Duke seating himself at the head of the table. 'I am afraid my chef did not have time to prepare anything suitable for your majesty, but I expect you will like it all the same.' Servants came in with a large silver platter with a roast boar haunch sizzling in the centre. Around the outside simple roast vegetables had been scattered and seasoned with fresh Thyme. Isyllia's mouth began to water, she had a fondness for boar and tonight the meat smelled intoxicating. The days of near starvation drove her lack of manners once again, and it was all she could do to resist pulling the tray toward her and eating like a street urchin.

'Have you received any news from Illingdale Randal?'

'Only the news of your father. I am sorry I could not make it in time for his honour giving child... But I expect you understand my thoughts were to get you here above all else, of that I am certain Cailem would have understood.

'I understand Duke!' She said, some of her disappointment dissolving away back down when it popped out from.

He nodded, 'Did you travel alone? I expected William would be travelling with you also?'

Isyllia swallowed hard, 'There were four of us. We travelled with Adella Bellamy, and William.'

'Ah yes' The Duke sounded wary, adjusting the collar of his neck, 'Her. But I did not see William with you?' The Duke looked around, as if he expected the boy to jump out from behind a pot.

Isyllia looked down, hiding the tears in her eyes. The memory of the shock on his face as the blade pierced him, would haunt her for the rest of her days. 'There was a battle... soldiers...William.' She couldn't finish.

'A battle?' He looked to Ember, hoping for an explanation.

'Adella betrayed us...She killed William, we were forced to flee.' Ember finished for her.

Randal slumped back in his chair, assaulted by the emotion that tore at his niece. 'My dear child. There are no words I can offer to make this right. But know that you are safe, and I am here for you now.'

Isyllia took a deep breath and stuffed the grief back in, where it always hid with the rest of her secrets, 'I will be fine. When I return to the city, he will be honoured as he deserves.'

Randal nodded, 'Whom did you leave in charge of political matters while you are away, the military?'

'I left Lord Pennerly in charge, since my father's death I thought it right that I honour his last wish. A decision I plan to remedy on my return.'

Randal paled considerably. 'You left....-' His words caught in his throat. It was clear this revelation did not please him in any capacity.

Isyllia frowned 'Are you well? Father said he had discussed the proposal at council?'

The Duke set down his fork and took a long draught from his mead, 'He did' The Duke was panicked, 'But I thought you despised Lord Pennerly?'

'I do.'

Randal looked like he had been struck, 'Indeed'

Ember stared at the Duke for a moment. 'What do you know about Gelraen Duke?'

Randal wiped his mouth on a napkin, then looked over to the companion he had almost forgotten was there, 'Before I can answer that, I need proof. You are the Chosen of Caros, are you not?'

Ember nodded, taking a deep breath, then standing as he had with Isyllia back in the castle, he lifted his shirt showing a circular birthmark branded onto his torso.

The Duke started, his eyes lit up with both awe and fear, 'My Word!'

'What have you found out?' Ember asked again, this time more direct.

'Troubling, yes. Troubling' He took another sip from his mead, then continued. 'Lord Pennerly is trying to seize control of Illingdale, why, I am less certain of, but I have seen Malagara here and there, operating in secret for now around the Isles... I feel his plan was to marry into the crown, take it from the inside... Balor tried to take this to the King, but ...Cailem would have none of it.'

'You believe he is working with Malagara?' Ember asked.

The Duke nodded. 'He either needs troops to stop them, or he wants Isyllia out of the way so he can join them... the question I have been unable to answer is why?'

Ember frowned, creases of worry framing his face as he cycled through his thoughts, 'There has to be more to it, Cailem trusted him enough to arrange a betrothal with his heir, it makes no sense for him to kill Cailem.'

Randal shook his head. 'Unless he knew the king would never understand. Gelraen puts his own needs first, you of all people should know that.'

'Duke, sir. I am sorry to interrupt.' A servant came rushing into the room, out of breath. 'A Wentworth Raven has just come urgent; it has the royal crest sir.'

The Duke stood and snatched the letter from the boy, who bowed and left the room as quick as he had entered. He stood for a moment, scanning the contents, his face falling in disappointment. Isyllia became impatient, 'Well, what news!'

The Duke looked over, sorrow on his face. 'The council has been called, they have arrested the person responsible for your father's death and intend to execute him for treason in two days, he will be tortured and then hanged.'

'Who have they arrested?' Isyllia's heart beat hard, the blood hammering through her veins, escalating a cocktail of nerves and panic. For a week she had been desperate to know who her father's killer was, but now that the moment had come, she was terrified.

'The General, Balor Mallory! Convicted by his own sister in law.'

Shock ran through her body joining the now overwhelming procession of panic, 'Balor!' The words came out as a whisper, this could not be, Balor. There had to be a mistake, Balor had saved her, hadn't he? 'That is impossible, they have the wrong man ...I should never have left.' She stood and threw her napkin on the table, intent on marching back to Illingdale on foot if necessary, until she remembered she had a corset on.

'No, my dear, if you had stayed, you could have been next.' Randal placed his hands on her shoulders to calm her.

Ember shook his head, 'When I met him, he was agitated, desperate...he knew Isyllia had powers, but I didn't think he would go that far.'

Randal waved a hand in dismissal, 'Your abilities are incomplete without the sphere, you are not perfect, and you are *not* to blame.'

'What do you mean he knew?' Isyllia shot.

Ember looked to the Duke, 'How much did he know about the Bow of Power?'

The Duke nodded to himself for a moment, 'Enough to panic and do something stupid.'

'Anything of your involvement or mine?'

'No nothing. I revealed nothing to him. Whatever he knows, he knows from the day, Nemelliia died. But as to Isyllias powers, I wager he picked up on it himself. It was always an issue, he was a good General, and with his son always so close... It was the reason Cailem ordered she spend less time with William.'

Ember nodded, 'To keep the secret, but Balor found out.'

Randal nodded. 'And Nemelliia perished because of both secrets, if it is anyone's fault, it's mine.'

Isyllia slammed her chair back into the table. Enough was enough, 'Gentleman if you please, I would like you to stop talking as if I were not here.'

They both looked at each other.

It was Randal who spoke, holding his arm out to her, 'Child, I am sorry. There is so much you do not know.' He trailed off '… Wait' He suddenly walked over to a side table and rang a small gold bell. Within seconds, a servant entered the room and bowed, 'Bring me the gold box from my room.' The servant bowed again then left the room.

'Gold box?'

He nodded. 'I have something that I have kept… promised I would keep for you, when the time was right.'

'What?' she asked curiously.

'Something from your mother… something for both of you.'

Isyllia could not respond, her breath piled like chunks of granite sticking in her throat. Every fibre of her being hungered for something, anything about the one person she knew so little about. Her mother. She looked over at Ember to pass the time, his face was creased with concern.

What felt like hours later, the boy re-entered the room, carrying a small ornate box. Randal dismissed him with a wave of his hand, then placed the box on the table. Clearing his throat. 'For a long time, I wondered if this day would ever come.' He opened the lid, removing two small red pouches. He held up the first, a square object in a velvet pouch, he smiled at the package then handed it to Ember, who took the object and opened it to find an old book with four symbols carved on the front.

'The book is mine, handed down for many years. It is-'

'The journal of Odriid Fenn... have you kept it here all this time?' Ember was awed, unable to take his eyes off the pages.

'It is yours now, by right. May his wisdom guide you.'

'Thank you!' Unable to contain his curiosity, he walked over to the fire, and began to read, oblivious to everything else in the room.

Randal turned his attention to the next object, a small red pouch remained. He stood and contemplated the contents for a long moment, then moved his hand down and picked it up, handing it to Isyllia. He offered no words, burdened with thoughts of his own, and instead carried them over to the fireplace.

Mother' her mind lingered on the words, as she fumbled the lacings of the pouch and removed the contents. A worn letter fell out and wasting no time she unfastened the old seal holding the words of her mother, the woman she had never known.

Dearest Isyllia

If you are reading this, he has found me, and I fear I will not be around to tell you all the things you need to know. You were born a princess, but that is not who you are, your destiny holds a much greater purpose. By now you would be aware of your powers. Of a longing to journey beyond the mountains. You are not Malagara my darling as I know you must fear. If you are reading this, then it is time for you to leave that life behind and become who you were born to be: The chosen of Abashiina the goddess of the earth and all its elements.

Trust Randal, he is the descendent of Odriid the wise, the first chosen of Caros, and guardian of the bow of Power. A dangerous secret our family has carried for years. It is your duty to help him pass it onto its rightful owner, but, if that person be unworthy of its power, you must protect it with your life, as I have done. Gelraen was born chosen of Menethon but he is corrupt, impure. Gelraen covets the weapon and he will stop at nothing to get it, you must protect it, it cannot, must not, fall into his hands. The journal kept by Odriid has clues held in it to the location of all the weapons, you must find this, and retrieve your weapon, without it, you cannot hope to succeed.

Your journey will be hard, little one, you will face trials and loss, but I feel your strength grows inside me as each day passes and I know in my heart that you will be strong, wise, and kind. Have the courage to follow your destiny my little heart, and use your power with wisdom and always, in service of another.

Find the chosen of Caros, he will protect you.

My darling, there are so many things you do not, could not know. I am sorry I was not there to watch you grow, I will never get to see your first steps, or hear you say my name for the first time. But know that you were wanted, and you are loved, with every breath we take together, my heart will always be yours.

Be well my daughter, Abashiina guide you.

Love,

The letter trailed off, unsigned. For a long time Isyllia stared at the page, willing more words to appear. She read, and re read each line until tears burned at her eyes, unwilling to be contained any longer. With regret she tucked the letter into her bodice, beside her heart, and looked up burdened with more questions. Her world had begun to collapse around her and there was so much she didn't understand. 'Did you read the letter?' She looked over at the Duke. He turned and shook his head. 'No child.'

'I feel like my whole world is collapsing around me, I don't even know who I am anymore. I just want my father back; I want William back and I want to go home and wake to find this was all a dream.' She burst into tears. Isyllia let her body pour out every emotion she had held in, every pain, every memory, every moment lost forever in time. So, when Randal came and wrapped his arms around her, she didn't protest, she let him soothe her and be the father that she desperately missed, until there was nothing left. Wiping her face, she pulled away to face the fire, the warmth of the flames calling to her with the soft and dependable comfort they offered. Ember had remained in the same position, rigid, with his nose buried deep in Odriid's Journal, reading the same page over and over.

Randal smiled, then turned his attention to Isyllia 'My dear, would you like to know what happened the day your mother died?'

Isyllia nodded, 'Father would never tell me.'

Randal moved to a chair opposite her. 'That is because, he does not know, none of us did – save Balor.' He paused for a moment, collecting his thoughts. Ember remained where he was, but his face was alert, he was listening. 'Nemellia wished to return to Mepar, to birth her child, as you know, a royal child born within the borders of Mespar is considered in the line of succession to Mespar... at least that's what she told your father.'

'She didn't want to have me in Mespar?'

'She did, but that was not her main reason for going there... Somehow, your mother knew you would be chosen. I do not know how, but she knew. I also could never understand how she knew who I was.' He trailed off for a moment, lost in the memories. Isyllia waited for him to continue, 'Everything got out of hand so fast... she came to me, said she had found Gelraen planning to send mercenaries to attack the duchy, steal the bow. We agreed that it was no longer safe, and she took it, planned to take it to the Temple of Mespar. It was my responsibility, but I trusted it to her... Balor accompanied her, but thought they were just seeing her across, didn't expect trouble, even took little William...' He looked down, unable to bear the shame on his face, 'Gelraen found out, sent the mercenaries. When they realised they would not catch up to your mothers ship in time, they sunk it. Your mother ordered Balor to go, take William, and you, her newborn daughter to safety. She stayed on the ship. Balor said he could see her standing on the deck in the distance, holding the bow and staring out at the boat that perused her...' They were silent for a long moment. 'The bow is indestructible. I guess they thought they would find it in the wreckage, but it was gone. Nothing was found, it has been lost since that day. I have often thought that she would still be alive if I had never given it to her. You would have had a mother, brothers... And now Gelraen wants to marry you, hoping you will lead him to the weapon, so that no one can stand against him.' Randal grabbed her hands, holding them tight, 'Isyllia, you are the greatest hope of stopping him, if he gets to you.' Randall shook his head, releasing her hands, 'There is no knowing what he has planned, but be assured, there is a plan. He always has a plan.'

Ember slammed the book shut, 'That won't happen.' Isyllia looked up at him, his face was serious. 'We will find the weapons first.'

'And then what?' Randal faced him, curious.

'They will be safest in Mespar for now. We will take them there, to the temple.'

'What about Cyndershire?' Randal asked?

'Gelraen can get to Cyndershire, Mespar at least has an army to get through first.'

'Good point… In the meantime, I have sent someone to see if we can't find out how the Malagara came into it.'

'And what about the General, we cannot just leave him?' Isyllia asked, indignant.

'I don't think there is anything we can do for him… although, I guess I could attend the council. By now he would be aware you are coming here, if I go, I could say you never made it, offer to provide men, it would stem suspicion and I could find out what Gelraen is up to. If his plan was to seize the throne, then he has succeeded, and we must know what he plans to do next.'

Isyllia shifted in her chair, nervous. 'Won't that be dangerous? What if it's a trap to lure you out of the Duchy?'

Ember shook his head, 'Gelraen needs him alive, he still wants the Bow of power. Lost or not, he would never give up that easily.'

Isyllia was still unsure but nodded. 'I'm not ready for any of this!'

'None of us were. We were not given a choice!' Ember's words were direct and unsympathetic like barbs deep in her stomach.

'What do you plan to do now?' The question was directed at Ember.

He looked toward the Duke, 'We travel to New Eddinsford, I know a scholar there, and if anyone can help find the weapons, he is the one.'

'What's his name?'

'Thomas O'Brien.'

Randall frowned, 'I have not heard of him.'

'He is young. His father is a merchant, and his studies are mostly private, but he knows more about the old ways than anyone I know.'

'O'Brien, I see. And I will go to Illingdale.' Randal put a soothing hand over Isyllia's. 'I promise I will do all I can for the Balor child, but please be prepared that it is likely I may come too late.'

Isyllia nodded, trying to calm her conflicting emotions.

'Stay as long as you need, I will instruct Tandus to follow your direction. I have also instructed your visit to remain secret, so I will not come to see you off. The less people that grow suspicious, the less chance there is for someone to talk.'

Ember nodded, grateful.

Randal smiled, 'If I should hear anything, I shall send word to Eddinsford directly.' He paused, 'I feel my grandfather would have liked you.' Then he turned to Isyllia and pulled her into a comforting embrace. 'The gods ask too much of you... but they ask all the same. You are strong, and I know you can do this... If I had had a daughter, I would have wished her to be just like you.'

'You talk as if we won't see each other again.'

'That, is in the hands of the gods!' He gave her one last kiss on the forehead, then bowed leaving the room. Isyllia sat back down trying to digest everything she had been told. All her life she had been raised to believe the gods were evil, that magic was evil, so to believe something else was difficult, if not impossible. But what option was there? Deep down, she knew that Adella would have spread her secret and she would be outcast if she went home. Her choice was to leave, live in hiding, poor and friendless until she was found, or to trust the man in front of her. The man who had sworn to protect her, promised her more. She sighed; it was no choice at all. 'This is not easy for me... Everything has changed. But I promise you I will try. I will trust you; I will follow you... and I will learn more about who I am.'

171

Ember nodded; his features set. 'First, you need to learn how to control your powers. Untrained you are a danger, even to yourself... a little sword training wouldn't hurt either.'
'I can use a sword.' Isyllia shot, indignant.

Ember raised an eyebrow, 'Swinging a sword in a training yard, and stabbing someone who is inches away from murdering you are not the same thing Isyllia.'

'Fine.' She frowned, unable to help feeling that she was replacing William. All the memories of days spent practicing swordplay together, his laughing at her clumsy stances, all became hazier as the days passed by. 'I'm going to prepare... I will need clothes.'

'I will talk with your maid.' Ember rose to leave.

'I will organise my own wardrobe this time, thank you.'
He frowned at her gown, 'I think not.'

Isyllia was incredulous, all the forgotten angst from earlier flooding back through her body, 'I said I would try, but I won't be told what to do, I will pick my own wardrobe!'

He ignored her. 'This isn't a palace Isyllia, how many more people have to die until you wake up and realise none of that matters anymore -' He indicated around the room.

'How dare you, I am a Queen-'

'You're a fugitive. And if you expect me to keep you alive, if I say jump you will jump. If I say move, you had better move. You will train when I say train, you will wear peasant's clothes, you will eat gruel and you won't complain, do you know why?'

'Why' She shot the question, her arms folded in defiance.

'Because I can't protect you if you continue to act like a spoiled child.'

Isyllia continued to level a stare at him, not wanting to back down but her eyes burned from

the tears desperate to escape. He was right, she felt broken, stripped naked by the truth of the message behind the words, she had killed her friend. Nobody else, her. If she had never stood and broken their focus, used her powers, maybe he would have seen the blow coming. Maybe he would be standing here with her instead of the cold perplexing man in front of her. But did she wish that?

His shoulders dropped, 'I understand that you are confused, but at what point are you going to realise this is bigger than you.' He looked at her for a moment and let out a frustrated snort, his tone softening further, 'Just one dress, and I'll make sure it is suitable. We leave in the morning.' He left without another word and closed the door behind him. Isyllia did not rise, nor did she watch him go. Instead she faced the flames once more, allowing her mind to wander in the warmth, and without realising she closed her eyes and dreamed of spring days bloated with sunshine and blossoms, under the trees looking at the clouds with William beside her. She remembered his eyes and the way they sparkled with mischief. She lived the adventures they said they would take together, and the promises that they would always be there for one another till the end of their days.

Isyllia jolted awake, her brow was slick with sweat and her body stiff from sleeping many hours in the wrong position. She sat forward and stretched; she had fallen asleep on the chair. The fire had long since burned out; a few lone smouldering Embers lay at the bottom of the hearth; Ember. She sat forward, edging her way off the chair, servants would be rising also, and she had no desire to be in their way. Isyllia tried to retrace her steps back through the hall to her room, distracted by thoughts of the previous evening's conversation. At first, she wandered around, managing to stumble into the washrooms, then excusing herself with apologies. It was not long until familiar tapestries started to emerge, and a door. His door. She stopped thinking, then just as quickly dismissed the urge to knock, and darted down the hallway, not altogether sure he could not sense her standing there. She slowed her pace when she came to her own door, and walked inside, still bleary from the sleep that clung, making her feet feel heavy. The room had begun to catch some of the night chill and for a moment, she considered crawling into the bed and going back to sleep but as she approached, she noticed items had been laid in perfect organisation. Clothes. She let out a sigh, reaching for one of the garments. Four changes of clothes had been prepared, a heavy travelling cloak and a new pair of leather boots. Everything was consistent with earthy browns and greens. Except one, a blue dress. Isyllia frowned at the item and moved to get a closer look. The dress was simple, but the striking electric blue would bring out the hazel of her eyes. It was made of soft silk, with a modest bust line and a small train behind it. She would not be able to wear a corset with it. It was perfect. She supposed Ember had had help with this one, judging from his own dress sense. He was always neat, but dressed plain, favouring no adornments you might expect in society and seldom parting with his mail shirt. Isyllia was convinced in fact that if he had been able to get away with wearing it to dinner the previous evening, he would have. She smiled, tucking it in her pack, along with the other items and put on one of the outfits he had arranged. It itched less with thanks to the cotton shift that she had now been given to wear underneath, and when she was done, she swung the bag over her shoulder, taking one last look around the room. Even though she had never been there, the crest of her house was a connection to her childhood, and a life that was no longer hers. She smiled one last time and made the conscious decision to try and leave the bittersweet memories of her past behind the closed door and focus on her future. She took her time to walk down the hallway, careful to drink in every detail from the ornate tapestries that decorated the halls. Various moments throughout history told their silent tales, that until today she took no notice of, but now she understood their fleeting beauty and found herself wondering if the artist had been there in those great moments, was this how things had been. It was with sorrow when the gallery came to an end and she was faced with the entrance hall again.

Placing her pack on a chair, she decided first to find one of the servants, and wandered in the direction of the faint smell of baking bread, coming across Tandus who was striding around a corner in his uniquely brisk fashion. She almost walked head long into him but managed to dance aside just in time. Tandus stopped, and bowed, not at all perturbed by the near collision, 'My lady, can I offer assistance in any way?'

'Yes, thank you Tandus, I was looking for some provisions?'

'Of course, the kitchen is this way!' Tandus strode back in the opposite direction.

Isyllia had to jog to keep up, she wondered if he was aware how fast he walked, then decided most likely not, and not wishing to offer him embarrassment she decided to keep the observation to herself. 'Has my companion risen?'

Tandus did not stop his pace, speaking over his shoulder. 'Your companion has been in the smithy all evening madam. I shall take you to him once you have dined.' He came to the kitchen and pushed open the double oak doors. Inside servants

176

rushed back and forth preparing food for the day. They stopped when they noticed Isyllia, some of the younger and more inexperienced girls frowning at the mysterious lady's choice of clothing. Isyllia ignored the stares and waited for Tandus to address them. 'Feriin, please prepare the lady some breakfast and some provisions for the road for herself and Master Clae.' He then turned back to Isyllia, 'I will return in five minutes, and take you to the smithy.' He turned to leave.

'The smithy?' She asked, confused.

'Yes, the Duke has a personal smithy' Tandus bowed, and then left the room, allowing the doors to slam behind him.

The servants took a sigh of relief, then Feriin turned to address Isyllia. 'See you met Tandus.' She said.

Isyllia smiled, 'He is rather peculiar.'

'Why the Duke puts up with him, I'll never understand. Anyhow, I got some fresh baked 'honeyed cakes, or I could do you something 'hot?'

Isyllia thought for a moment, 'Some cheese and bread would be nice thank you, and some of the Honey cakes. Please also prepare a portion for master Clae.'

The cook bowed, 'Of course lady.' She turned away, shouting instructions to the younger nervous kitchen hands. They scattered in all directions looking for cheese and fresh bread and came back, avoiding eye contact with Isyllia but depositing the prepared food on two plates then running back into a corner. Isyllia thanked the cook then sat and ate her portion. The cakes were still hot and slid down into her stomach with such a welcome joy that she was forced to sit there dumbfounded. It was willpower alone that stopped her asking for more. Instead, she took long swallows from the goblet, stopping herself short of the bottom, and then placing it back on the table. 'I thank you.' She said, smiling her thanks to the cook and turning to the other portion prepared, along with a goblet for Ember and piled it onto one plate, balancing the sack of provisions over her shoulder. She was about to turn when Tandus came striding in, narrowly missing her again. 'This way my lady and please, allow me to carry those for you.' Tandus took the plate of food and the Goblet of mead from her hands, wobbling it like he had never carried a tray before. He stopped a moment, finding his centre of balance and then strode down the hall, holding it out at an uncomfortable distance from his body. When they reached the entrance hall, she picked up her pack and swung it over her shoulder with the provisions, the weight of the items beginning to make her muscles groan; she had always had people to carry things for her and so never understood how grating the task was. Tandus led her outside into the street. The sun had raised a little higher, bringing more light into the settlement despite the depressing clouds overhead. They had been walking for ten minutes when Tandus stopped and faced Isyllia, 'You will find the Duke's smithy just here.' He handed back the plate of food, and the goblet of mead, 'Is there anything else I can do for my lady?'

'No, thank you Tandus.'

He bowed and strode off. Isyllia stood for a moment, marvelling. Of all the servants she had had in her life, she had never had one like him. But now was not the time to think about the past, she shrugged the thought off, and walked over to the smithy, wondering what kind of tricks the staff must play on him when he was not around.

Isyllia opened the door and began to poke her head through, unprepared for the heat that assaulted her. She took a moment to adjust, shaking her head to remove the sensation, and then moved through the door again, this time a little more prepared. A rhythmic hammering was coming from the other end of the shed, a somewhat free bench standing in between. She placed the food and goblet on the bench and then shook the packs from her shoulder. Arching her back into the sudden freedom of weightlessness. 'Ember?' She said, craning her neck to see what he was working on. He wore a now dirty white shirt with the sleeves pulled up and a heavy leather apron. For the first time, she realised that she knew nothing about this man, and where he had come from. But they were questions for later. Clearing her throat, she tried again, 'Ember!' This time he looked around, surprised and … tired? 'I brought you some food!' She said, craning around to point to the bench where the goblet mead sat waiting.

Ember first washed his hands then looked at the plate on the bench, frowning at the cakes as he walked over. 'What are they for?'

Isyllia looked at the cakes. 'For? To eat... have you never had honey cakes?' She scratched her head in disbelief.

'No use for them.'

She could not believe what she was hearing, 'Try one.' She pushed the plate closer.

Ember picked one up and ate a chunk.

Isyllia waited, 'Well?'

'Well what?' He continued to eat.

'What do you think?'

'It's food, I don't.'

Isyllia flung her arms up like the sudden movement of air would somehow change his point of view. 'Food is not meant to just be about filling your stomach, Ember, it's about pleasure, joy.'

He shrugged, taking a long drink from the mead, 'It's food.' Then picked up the cheese and bread.

She shook her head in defeat, deciding it was best to let it drop, 'I'm sorry about that too.' She nodded to the hot mead he had just put back down on the bench.

'Sorry about what?'

'The hot mead... I didn't realise!' She indicated to the forge.

'It's fine. I don't much notice the heat anymore.'

There was an awkward silence. 'So, you're a smith?' She asked in a feeble attempt at conversation.

'I am.' He continued to eat, not elaborating any further.

Isyllia took the hint, deciding to change the subject, 'Thank you by the way.'

'For what.'

'The dress.'

He didn't answer.

She looked back over to the place where he had been working. From what she could see, it looked as though he had been here all night. 'Did you get much rest?'

'A bit, I don't sleep often. Decided to fix my shirt, just in case.'

'In case of what?'

He looked at her, 'You know there will be more soldiers?'

Isyllia took a deep breath. 'I see' She looked at the floor. 'So, when do we leave?'

'I'll be done in a few minutes.' He turned back to the forge.

'I'll wait outside, it's a bit hot in here for me.' She grabbed the bags and moved toward the door.

'Try to stay covered.'

She paused, 'Stay covered?'

He grabbed his hammer. 'The less people that recognise you, the better. A lot of these people are impoverished and would sell you out in a moment to feed their families.'

Isyllia looked around the almost empty room as if it was crowded with people she had never noticed, 'Surely not?'

He looked sympathetic. 'The world is a different place for the poor Isyllia. They are not bad people; they just need to survive.' His face hardened, 'You have never been hungry!'

Isyllia's face fell, 'I think I understand, I'm sorry.'

He nodded and then returned to the forge, indicating the conversation was at an end. Isyllia sighed, pushing the door to the street open with no distinct urgency.

'Thank you for the food, the cake was good.' He said.

Isyllia swivelled her head in his direction, one hand still poised on the door. His back was still facing her, giving no clear indication if he was aware, she was still there. His entire focus was on the task at hand. Isyllia smiled, there was hope for him yet.

A few minutes passed slower than it ought, giving rise to question Ember's ability to tell time. Isyllia passed it by ogling the busy morning streets, desperate to jump up and chase the faint smell of bread wafting into her nostrils, teasing her. But remembering his warning, she thought better of it, and decided instead to wait by the door with her pack.

Drawn out though the time felt, the opportunity to sit and feel the cool air was a blessing, it kissed her face as it whistled through, bringing none of the sun's warmth that shone through her eyelids, but refreshing all the same. And so, when Ember threw the door open, she started, scrambling to her feet in embarrassment. He wore his now repaired mail shirt and had changed into a clean set of clothes. 'Here.' He pressed a dagger into her hands, it was simple, unremarkable but it was sharp. She stared at it for a moment, then sheathing it, stowed it in her boot, making a mental note to find a better spot for it when she had a chance. 'How many of these do you have?' She asked, mocking.

'I made that one.' He said.

'Oh, thank you!'

He nodded. 'Until you can use your powers you need to be armed, and I recommend not storing it in your boot.'

She looked down at the dagger with a blank expression, like it could answer for itself. 'Why, it's comfortable there?'

'Because if someone tries to stab you, the last thing you want to be doing is bending over to take your shoe off!'

Isyllia blanched. The thought of killing her own soldiers, of being an outlaw sat hard in her throat still. 'Where should I keep it then?'

'In easy reach of your hand, but out of sight. Your cloak has a hidden pocket.'

She felt for a pocket, pausing as a thought struck her. 'What can you see with your powers?'

He frowned, 'What I need to. I asked the maid to put the pocket there.'

'Ah' His wanting to organise her clothes made a lot more sense.

'We should go!'

She picked up her packs and swung them over her back, her muscles peaked, unused to the load.

'Wait!'

Isyllia stopped.

'I'll carry the provisions!' He thrust out his hand.

Isyllia handed over the heavy bag, grateful and began to walk to the stables. As usual Ember took the lead. He walked with purpose, silent and taking no notice of the townspeople as he walked by. At first, his lack of interest in conversation bothered her, but she began to find solace in the quiet. She found herself examining the shops as she passed, careful to hold her head down under the hood of her cloak. Mothers dashed with babe in arms, trying to haggle for their groceries. They would all do their business, then they would go home. And soon enough, fires would rise from the chimneys, stretching to the horizon. All telling the story of families cooking and laughing over the events of the day, then they would go to sleep safe, and warm. Isyllia had nothing. No warm bed to go home to, no loved ones to kiss her goodnight. Nothing. She walked into the stables, glad to be off the street. The stable hand had been expecting them, he shifted on his feet craning his neck back and forth till he could see Ember approach. 'Sir, sir, your horse, this way. Beautiful, right good manners he has. I took good care of him I did, I promise, gave him extra carrots!' He scurried to a stall indicating to the brown warhorse nosing at a bale of hay. Ember thanked the boy and walked up to the creature, the gentle expression on his face returning. Isyllia did not know much about the man she had pledged to trust, but he loved his horse, that much was clear, and

185

enough for her. He stroked its forehead, speaking words she could not make out. It pushed its nose under Ember's arm and snorted affectionately. 'Madam?' Isyllia looked around, surprised, she was unaware she had been staring. 'The duke requested I give this one to you!' The boy walked to another stall, not far ahead. He opened the door, Isyllia walked in; a white mare was standing saddled and gleaming. 'One of the Duke's prized mares my lady!'

'What's her name?' The creature was magnificent.

'Niimorea. She's patient but needs a run every day. Otherwise she gets restless.'

Isyllia nodded and then began to approach with caution, holding out her hand so the animal could smell her. At first, the horse's ears went back a little, wary. It would be a great time to remember any wisdom her father had imparted on the subject. Scanning her brain however, nothing fell out of the deep corners in her memory. So, she stopped and waited, unsure how to proceed. Frightening the mare when they hadn't even met was not a wise idea, she was sure

'Give her some of this!' The boy handed her some apples, 'That'll win her right, trust me, she loves food!'

Isyllia took the apple pieces and held them out to the horse. It took a moment, for the aroma to waft over and steal the horse's attention, but once it did, she began to nudge forward, all

186

wariness forgotten. Isyllia stroked the mare's nose. 'There's a good girl. See, I won't hurt you, you're a beautiful girl aren't you.'

'Have you owned a horse, my lady?' The boy asked.

'No, not my own. But my father used to say; treat your men well, treat your horse better, and unlike your men, he will carry you always!' She said, smiling at herself, she could remember something after all!

'Good advice!' Isyllia spun around. Ember stood outside the stall, reins in hand. 'We should go.' His mood had improved a little, but she dared not test him.

Isyllia nodded and walked to the side of the horse.

The boy panicked, 'Should I get a ladies saddle? Only the Duke did say you be needing a normal saddle?'

'I did not ask your name?'

'Fergus my lady!' He said.
'I will be fine Fergus, but I thank you.'

Fergus opened the stable door, 'Good day my lady!' He looked over to Ember. 'Sir.' Ember nodded back.

'After you.' Isyllia indicated to the door, knowing she should ride out first, but she didn't care under the circumstances.

Ember nodded once and then rode forward, stopping on the road ahead, out of earshot of the stable hand. 'There is something we need to discuss first; I didn't want to say it where we could be overheard.'

'What is it?'' She asked.

'Names.' Ember scratched chin, 'For now, it will be safer if you use a different name. I will say you are my new bride, accompanying me to Eddinsford to inspect new trade opportunities.'

Isyllia nodded, shifting to settle the nerves raging in her stomach. 'Any suggestions?'

He shrugged, 'Whatever you want, just not an Illingdalean name. It might be safer to say you're from Tinderford.'

She nodded, 'Fine... Antonia?'

He waited for a moment, giving the impression that he was clenching his teeth, '*Anything* else!' It was not a question.

Isyllia frowned, knowing his tendency to expeditiously change his disposition, best not to press the matter just now 'Alright ... Marelle?'

'Marelle is fine.' He said, relieved.

'What should I call you?'

'He was silent for a moment. By now Gelraen knows about Anton, but the smithy is less clear. Call me ... Samuel. We own a blacksmithing company called Delmariis Steel.'

Isyllia nodded, 'Delmariis steel. My name is Marelle Delmariis…Ember, what if Gelraen does find out about the smithy?'

Ember chewed the thought for a moment. 'It's inevitable, he could already know. I still think it is safer to use an alias.' He studied her worried expression for a moment, then continued, 'But if it comes to it, I will do the talking.' He said, whistling for Perrin to begin his gentle pace away from the small city. At first, it was slow progress trying to avoid trampling the people that went about their day, oblivious to the large warhorse lumbering over them, but they made it through the main gates and headed back out into the woods, the one place Isyllia did not want to be.

Migrating back was arduous. They were far from the place where William fell, and yet every tree looked the same, each corner held the ghost of his smell, but always one more turn away.

Ember kept a distance between them, somehow able to sense her need for solitude. Isyllia had no energy for conversation, polite or otherwise and so she was grateful. It was almost a shame when he did break the silence, his voice lower down than she had expected. He had dismounted.

'There is a sheltered area just ahead; we will be able to light a fire there.' Isyllia looked around to find that the last of the light had begun to retreat through the top of the trees, leaving darkness and the cold that was never far behind. She couldn't believe the entire day had passed in what felt like the blink of an eye. Less able was she to figure out if that was a good or a bad thing, deciding in the end any day they did not encounter soldiers had to be good. 'You think they are looking this far down?' She did not know where they were, but guessed it to be somewhere near the Tinderfordean border.

'This area is being covered by, Randal's men so we are safe for the moment, however I would expect, Gelraen's soldiers to be around.'

Isyllia frowned, 'Gelraen's men cannot come into Randal's land without authorisation; it would be seen as an act of aggression towards the Duchy.'

'Duke Gelraen wouldn't, but he has crown authority now; he can go wherever he wants.'

Isyllia blushed. 'I was upset, I thought I was doing the right thing!'

'It doesn't matter now; we need to focus on getting out of sight.' Ember turned and steered Perrin into the small path that ran between the looming mountains. Isyllia followed, one cautious step in front of the other. Niimorea flicked her head, jolting the reins Isyllia was holding in protest. 'I don't like it any better than you, but if I have to do it, so do you.' Isyllia felt stupid talking to the horse, she had never owned an animal, could they even understand?

'It's just ahead.' Ember called from somewhere in front. Had he sensed her panic?

Isyllia thought about replying, then decided it best not to talk and instead focus on getting through the small crevice as swiftly as possible. True to his word, it was not far. Isyllia burst into the opening and took a deep breath of air into her lungs and relaxed, Niimorea snorted. The area had little of anything living, except for a tree that stood off to the left-hand side. She started toward it, kicking up dirt with her boots as she walked, it blew around with the breeze then settled back down only to be whisked about again. She sighed; the idea of sleeping here horrified her, not to mention the idea of being filthy again. Isyllia let go of the reins and began to tug accusingly at the straps holding their bags, fuelled by the clouds of dust surrounding them. The horses waited, not even they were in a distinct hurry to be anywhere, since every direction they looked held no immediate source of food. In fact, they were every bit as forlorn about the choice of camp as she was.

'Feed the horses.' Ember turned to leave.

'Where are you going.' The idea of being left alone sat like a sharp lump in her stomach.

'To get some firewood, I won't be gone long.'

'What if there are soldiers around?'

'There isn't, I've already checked.' He said.

'Oh!' Isyllia had forgotten about his strange abilities, 'What do I feed them?'

'There is grain in one of my packs, and a skin. Give half the grain between them and half the skin.'

Isyllia nodded, setting about her task with two left feet. It was not until Ember had left that she had realised she had no idea how to feed them, and swearing, she went back through their bags searching for any dish she could use to put their food in, in the end turning up a bowl and a cooking pot.. They wasted no time shoving their noses into the dishes, the world around them forgotten. Isyllia decided to sit by the tree and watch, she had always liked horses; it was fascinating how easy in one another's company they already were. Niimorea ate greedily at her grain until her portion was smaller than Perrin's then, snorting, she moved over to his, pushing him out the way. Perrin took it well, staring for a moment, then moving over to the food she had abandoned until, unsatisfied again, she repeated the process. When they had finished, Isyllia frowned at her horse. 'Naughty girl!' But as expected Niimorea ignored her, walking in the other direction, no doubt looking for food that she had overlooked. Perrin waited by the tree, sniffing the ground glumly where the food had been. Isyllia got to her feet, brushed the dirt from her clothes, then walked over to where he stood, poured some of the skin in the bowl, and then rifled through the pack of food supplies. Her hand grasped a cool round object, an apple from the kitchens in Godswall. The horses would love that. Smiling, she reached for the blade stowed in her cloak. Perrin needed no prompting, catching the sweet scent of the apple as she sliced it, he turned eagerly toward her, snatching the offered piece and chomping it down with large teeth. Niimorea too smelled the apple, and came trotting straight back, shoving her way in to get a slice. 'What am I going to do with you girl?' Isyllia sighed, continuing to feed slices among them until it was gone. She had been so intent in her focus that she had not noticed Ember had returned, he stood by the stone wall watching her, the customary frown on his face. Perrin, sensing the return of his master who whinnied, trotting over to his side, caused Isyllia to look up. They stared awkwardly for a moment until Ember broke the moment, turning to pat the excited horse on the nose lovingly, and then picking up the wood he had gathered. Isyllia walked over and waited as he began to lay out the wood, ready to make a fire. 'Do you have a flint?' He had gathered everything else, but a way to light the fire.

'I don't need flint; you are going to light it' He did not look up but continued to lay stones around to keep the fire from spreading.

'Me? I can't light the fire' Isyllia was shocked, having no idea how on earth she was going to light it without a flint.

'Yes, you. You are going to use your natural abilities.'

'I've never done that! I can't do that!' She stood and backed away, the urge to run beginning to control her movements like a parasite.

He looked up, 'You have to learn Isyllia, come, sit.' He indicated to a spot on the ground patiently, next to the wood.

She glared at the arid wood, willing it to self-combust. 'History tells you have the power of the elements, and we know you can control the wind to a certain degree. What it does not tell is how your power works. I have been able to theorise, and we will learn more once we reach Eddinsford, but for now, we have to experiment.'

Isyllia sighed. At the end of the day, she knew there was no choice. 'Fine! what do I do?'

'I want you to close your eyes and concentrate.'

She obeyed.

'Now pretend for a minute you want to grow a tree.'

She opened her eyes, 'An entire tree?'

Ember ignored the question. 'In order for a tree to grow, it needs the water and nutrients that it draws from the earth. It also needs light from the sun. So, for you to be able to ... accelerate this process, you must first understand HOW the tree grows in the first place.'

'But how do you grow the tree?' Isyllia was beginning to feel confused.

'Your ability allows you to draw the elements needed, to create the reaction needed. So, in theory, if you were to concentrate on drawing water into the roots, and drawing light from the sun onto the leaves, then drawing the tree higher in your mind, it should grow.'

'I see. So, to create fire I need to think about what fire needs?'

'Yes. For now, I just want you to concentrate on the wood, will the air around it to get hot. See what happens.'

Isyllia looked down at a spot on the nearest log, she had no idea how to make it burst into flames, so she thought about a fireplace and tried to push the thought onto the log. It took thirty minutes for her to give up, the light was rapidly leaving, along with her patience. Ember sat on the opposite side; nose buried in the journal of Odriid. 'I can't do it!' She yelled, picking up one of the smaller bits of twig and throwing it in defiance.

'You just need to concentrate!' He didn't look up.

'If you had been watching, you would have noticed that I have been doing that for the last thirty minutes! I can't do it'

He raised his eyes for a moment, and then looked back down, ignoring her.

Isyllia was infuriated 'Don't ignore me!' But instead of waiting for Ember to reply, she looked down, the log had begun to smoke. She concentrated again, enhancing the heat inside and turning it into fire in her mind. A bright orange light shone through her closed lids, and she snapped them open in shock. It worked. She looked up, Ember had put the book down, and had the ghost of a smile on his face. 'You did that deliberately?'

His smile widened. 'I also theorised that your powers would largely be tied to your emotion. It was said Kathriin was sensitive, I figured there would have been a practical reason.'

Isyllia studied him, somewhat offended, but deciding to let it pass for the moment. He was the company she had, difficult as he was, it was Ember and the horses. 'Fine, but what do I do now?'

'Now, nothing. Tomorrow we will start teaching you to fight.'

'Tomorrow? Why not now. We have nothing better to do!'

Ember turned the question over for a moment, then stood. 'If you are not tired, then draw your dagger.' Isyllia drew the cool metal object she had stowed in her cloak, and held it out, her fingers clumsy around the tiny hilt. Ember drew his own sword, and waited for a moment, shaking his head. 'You need to hold it firm.'

She began to protest when in one fluid movement, Ember knocked the dagger out of her hand with his blade. 'You were saying?' He raised an eyebrow.

Isyllia narrowed, then walked to retrieve her dagger, aware the moment that she bent over that there was now a sword trained on her back. 'What are you doing?'

'An enemy won't wait for you to retrieve your weapon; you must always be ready.' He withdrew the sword and stepped back. Isyllia picked up the dagger and spun around, this time clutching the dagger tighter.

'Again, try to swing at me!' He waited.

Isyllia hesitated, noting the sizable difference in his weapon to hers. 'Your sword is so much bigger; I can't possibly strike you.'

'You think so?' He asked.

Isyllia snorted with frustration, thrusting the pitiful blade in his direction. 'Obviously!'

Ember nodded, his thoughts though unclear, did not give the impression like they were going in a direction that would end well for Isyllia. 'Alright, let's swap. You take the sword; I will take the dagger.'

Isyllia handed over her blade, feeling a little sheepish, and unprepared for the weight of his weapon. It took a moment to remember the things William had taught her, place on foot behind, watch her centre of gravity, ensure your front is always protected, watch the other parts too. 'Right, I think I am ready.' Ember did not wait for her to speak a second time, and in what seemed like a measure of time he made up on his own, Ember dropped to the ground, and in one fluid motion swept behind her, grabbing her sword arm and thrusting his other around her body, dagger trained neatly on her throat.

'You were saying?' He tightened his grip on her arm, until she felt stinging sensations ripple up her arm, forcing her to drop the sword.

'I get it, I get it.'

He stepped back, releasing her and handing the dagger back hilt first. 'One of the greatest mistakes you can make in a fight, is to think you are prepared. People who let their guard down, end up dead.'

'Like the other day. I broke your focus and almost got you killed.' She felt her shoulders drop, taking her energy down with them. 'I am sorry for that. I understand now.'

Ember stood for a moment, considering her, then bent down and picked up his sword. 'We should eat.'

Isyllia decided to allow the change in subject, stowing her dagger and watching as he walked over to get the supply pack, removing some salted ham and cutting two thick slices, then placing them on the fire to cook. She stared at the meat as it fizzed and spat, avoiding his gaze. She had entered a trance like state by the time he removed the meat, snapping her head up again. Ember inspected the food for a moment then passed a slice to Isyllia. For a moment she considered saying she was not hungry, but her stomach growled as the smell wafted closer, betraying its own interest. As much as she wanted to be angry at the situation, she knew she would be angrier at herself if she did not eat. And so, she took the slice and ate it in silence. Ember did the same, having the same amount of interest in sparking a conversation. It was awkward but she did not care. The heat from the food slid down into her belly, bringing the promise of contented sleep and lifting her spirits a little with it. 'Did you know Gelraen was chosen?'

For a moment Ember didn't give any clear indication if he intended to answer the question. Isyllia pouted, returning to the melancholy silence when he spoke.

'I thought I knew him.' He started, putting the book down and poking at the flames which did not need his assistance. 'We were friends, he taught me to fight, and in return, I taught him about the histories. I never knew he was the one who killed your mother. If I had known …'

Isyllia drew her mouth wide in sympathy, 'He knows how to manipulate people Ember, you're a good person. He would have used that…What happened?'

Ember paused for a moment, 'He didn't take the calling seriously. I tried to teach him, but he didn't listen. We were in Mespar, and there was a girl. I told him to leave her, that his destiny was greater.' He was silent for a moment, like the confession caused some pain in finding its way out. 'After he left her, she died… and he blamed me… We went our separate ways from that day.'

Isyllia exhaled, not realising she had been holding her breath. 'It wasn't your fault!'

'It doesn't matter, it's done.' He threw the stick aside. 'You should get some sleep. I will wake you when it's time for your watch.' Isyllia had not noticed her eyelids drooping, an early night might be a good idea since she had no idea what the day would have in store, except that she would need her strength. 'You are right, I need to get some sleep.'

Ember nodded, returning to the pouch he had just closed.

Isyllia stretched for the blanket that lay to her side promising warmth and comfort. She wasted not a second in wrapping it around herself and lying down next to the fire. The floor was hard, and the blanket was much thinner than the thick quilt she was used to, but it would do and within minutes she felt consciousness begin to leave her, plunging her into a deep dreamless sleep.

It is always strange how time seems to keep passing as you sleep. Then you wake and it could have been mere seconds. There is no sense of self in the blackness that overcomes, and while the idea is frightening, like a dance with death each night, somehow, we are never afraid to close our eyes. Somehow, it is peaceful.

So it was that when Ember woke Isyllia, the initial reintroduction to consciousness brought its natural disbelief, she had just closed her eyes! Though trying as she might to convince herself ignoring his prods was a good idea, she knew better and sat with reluctance. Feeling a sudden sharp pain in the lower half of her back. She rubbed the spot that ached, digging her fingers into the muscles as if the gesture would somehow dull the sensation. What she would give for one of her maids, and a hot bath with some lavender and mint oils.

'If you hear anything, wake me. Otherwise we leave at sunrise.'

'Should I put wood on the fire?' She looked at the muted blaze, still somewhat determined to push its warmth into the world.

'You won't need to; the Coals will keep it warm enough.'

Isyllia nodded, wrapping the blanket around her. Ember walked back over to the other side of the blaze and lay down, at last falling asleep. It was strange to see, she could not go a day without sleeping, but Ember seemed able to go days at a time, and not suffer from it. It left her perplexed by how little she knew about him. Did he have a family? Why was he so ill tempered? The questions bounced around in her sleepy head, over and over until light began to spill into the little valley. At first, she thought it was just her eyes adjusting to the darkness, but a tell-tale orange light began to stain the mountaintops, it was already morning, time had flown again and she would need to wake him already.

Throwing off her blanket was difficult, but she got to her feet and walked the short paces over to where he slept. Sitting hours in the same position had done nothing to improve her still stiff back but she ignored its protests and bent down to shake him on the shoulder, he did not respond. Isyllia realised she had partly thought he was pretending, as he often did. She waited for a moment longer, still not altogether convinced then tried again, 'Ember?'

His eyes opened.

'It's dawn.' She said, waiting to ensure the words registered.

Ember prised himself up on one hand, rubbing the sleep from his eyes with the other. 'Good, we should move, we have an arduous journey ahead of us. I will pack up the camp, you just make sure the horses are well fed.'

Isyllia set about her task carefully this time to make sure Niimorea did not steal all the food and scolding her when she nosed her way over to Perrin. Niimorea snorted, walking to the other side of the area alone, unhappy with the turn of events. Isyllia shook her head at the animal, getting Niimorea back was not going to be fun. Perhaps, if she offered her a portion of her own food, it would be enough; it would at least get her to come over here. 'Niim!' She held up the portion of stale bread. The horse lifted her head and sensed if the query was worth her attention. Seeing a food shaped parcel being held out, her ears moved forward, and then at last deciding it was worth investigating, she trotted over. Isyllia grabbed her reins, tying her to the tree so she couldn't run off again.

Niimorea snorted, stamping her feet into the ground with an angry whinny, she had been tricked and she knew it.

'I am sorry Niim, I don't much like it either, but we can't have you running all over the place while we are trying to pack up.'

Niimorea moved her ears back, snapping forward to bite Isyllia hard on the arm. Pain shot upward, causing her to jump back from the animal in alarm.

'Let me see.' Not waiting for an invitation, Ember pulled back the sleeve of her dress. An angry red patch framing a set of large teeth marks, not bleeding, but sure to leave a nasty bruise. 'She didn't cut through; you'll be fine.'

'Doesn't feel like it!'

He shrugged, 'It's a bite.'

Isyllia was incredulous, 'Oh, sure! I feel like I've had my arm torn off.'

'I suggest you get used to it, she is used to getting what she wants, it won't be the last time she bites you.'

'Great!' She looked at the horse, her ears were still back. Ember began to tie the rest of their things back onto the horses, Isyllia watched with mild interest. 'So, what's the plan from here?'

'Get too New Eddinsford.'

She clenched her fists; his directness could be infuriating at times. 'Yes, but are we going to go through Ravenswood?'

'No, that would take too long, the swamp lands would slow us down too much. Eddinsford is the best route.'

She blanched. 'Through Eddinsford? That's out in the open, and New Eddinsford doesn't patrol that far North anymore, so Illingdalean soldiers would venture that far, we could be seen!'

Ember shook his head 'No one will go there, even Illingdalean soldiers try to say clear!'

'Why? It's only a broken-down castle?'

'They fear the voices.'

'Voices?' She was confused 'What kind of voices?'

'Spirits. There are some peculiar stories that have been told over the years about the ruined castle of Eddinsford. People who found themselves there and those who were lucky enough to return have claimed to hear cries for help, and as they got closer to the sounds, they began to feel overwhelmed with sadness, and turned back.'

'Has anyone followed the voices?' She asked, unsure she wanted the answer.

'Many and they were never seen again. Naturally, fear spreads quickly and people are too afraid to go there now, in case they too disappear!'

'So why are we going there!'

'I have a suspicion why the voices are there. If I am right, yes it could be worse for us, but as long as we focus ahead and don't walk toward the castle, we will be safe.'

Isyllia was unconvinced, 'I'm guessing you're not planning to elaborate?' She didn't wait for an answer; instead she mounted Niimorea and did a quick check to make sure that her pack was there. Isyllia had decided to put it on the horse instead of her back; she had no intention of leaving the animal behind, bitter or not.

'It's the only route I can guarantee there will be no patrols, you are not ready to fight yet, last night proved that. And as for the ruins, no. For now, just stay close and do exactly as I say!' He whistled for Perrin to walk forward.

Isyllia did not reply, instead choosing to agree and follow behind Ember. All morning she listened to the twittering reminders of where she was, an orchestra of birds singing the joyful news of another dawn to anyone and everyone that would listen. Unlike Living Woods, Ravenswood had pine trees, giant and as tall as the clouds, spanning as far as the eye could see. There was a kind of peace to be found here, amongst the gentle chatter of the creatures. Not like the eerie darkness of the living woods, and the feeling like the trees were watching. Like the souls of the dead somehow lived on in the branches.

'Ember, why do you think people are frightened of the living woods?'

He did not halt his pace. 'I think it's nothing more than assassins and drunkards with more imagination than is good for them.'

'Assassins?'

'The bird families would do almost anything to ensure their survival in the economy. And most assassins are low life scum who would kill just about anyone for a bit of coin, the woods are a perfect cover.'

Isyllia was troubled, how could there be so much about his own kingdom that her father had not known.

'He didn't want to know!'

The answer startled her, 'Excuse me?'

'Your father didn't want to know, he was a broken man, and the burden of rule taxed him so deeply that often, he passed off too many responsibilities to his governors. Men who are there to serve their own needs, not the crowns.'

Isyllia began to feel annoyed. 'Are you saying he was a bad king? You never met him; how can you know anything about him!'

Ember lowered his voice, speaking softer, 'You forget, every minute you were in Illingdale, you were in danger. You only had to lose control of your powers once, and then what? I had to be near in case it happened. I had to study those around you to make sure they were not a threat to you. Your father was a good man, he just had no desire to be king, and because of that, the kingdom suffered.'

Isyllia found it hard to argue with his reason but hated the reality behind his words. She had never once considered how much like her father she was, but guessed it was perhaps because she had never known her mother.

Isyllia rode in contemplation for the rest of the day. What kind of Queen was she going to make? Was it even right to still consider the possibility, given her circumstances? Her whole life she had fought against what was expected of her and dreamed most of her days away with William. But William was gone, and it was never clearer than it was now; it was a life, she was never meant to live.

'We should stop; we need to rest the horses.'

She looked up, startled. 'Of course,' They had reached the river that led to the swamp lands. Isyllia dismounted and looked around. The river was thin, just coming out from the base of the mountains, but it trickled on its way, promising to become much greater. She turned, and rubbed Niimorea on the nose. The ride had calmed her temper and she nuzzled back, then walked toward the river to drink. Isyllia watched as she trotted away. She had used horses at the castle, usually more than one. But she had never depended on one, so never had the opportunity to form the bond she felt growing with Niimorea. 'We covered good ground; I didn't think we would reach the river today!'

Ember did not look up but continued to untie packs from Perrin, 'That's because we are in easier terrain; we will cover twice the ground. But we still have a way to go. Here.' he chucked a skin to her. 'Drink. I am going to have a quick scout around.' He turned to leave, 'Eat, we are going to ride hard tonight, no fire.' Then he was gone.

Isyllia shook her head. 'I will never understand him!' She looked over to Perrin, half expecting him to reply, instead, Perrin looked blank for a moment, then bucking his head, trotted over to the river to join Niimorea, leaving her on her own. Isyllia decided to sit against the tree and take soft sips from the skin. The afternoon sun was glorious, spilling its golden light onto her face. 'I have missed you!' She spoke the thought, smiling as the warmth spread through her body. *Why didn't I do this more'* she asked herself, and as if in answer to her own question, memories of court life began to flood through her mind again, most containing William. All her memories contained William. But it was time to put aside the pain. With an effort she rose to her feet and walked over to the riverbank. She no longer recognised the soul reflected in the water. She no longer saw the Amber eyed beauty brimming with passion and life. Her eyes had lost their spark, replaced with dark circles from lack of sleep and crying. Her lips were thin and dry, no longer plump and lustrous. And her hair, once long and falling in dark brown tendrils of silk, felt coarse and as empty as she felt. 'I cannot do this anymore, my beloved father, my beloved William, I must move on, I must leave you behind. This cannot become a routine, when you can never hear me. You are gone.' Speaking her thoughts again, she wiped away the tears that had fallen. A new life was calling her, in the form of a surly stranger and although she had no idea where he was leading her, she had decided to trust him. To let go of what she knew. There was nothing left for her in Illingdale, except pain.

As promised, Ember returned, and he was somewhat more relaxed than he had been when he left. 'Did you find anything?' She stood, ringing the water from her hair, then drying her hands on her dress.

'It's clear. We are about a day from the ruins.'

'So, what is our plan?'

'We are going to pass through just far enough in, so we are not followed. But we need to be careful.'

'And you're sure we are not in more danger this way?'
'No, it's not easy to kill a chosen.'

Isyllia frowned, 'What do you mean?'

'Legend says the chosen don't age like regular people. Don't take ill. A chosen can only be slain by weapon, or their own heart.'

'So, the poison that killed my father?'

'Would never have harmed you. It's likely you swallowed it already, but you would never know!' He looked sympathetic.

Too many thoughts threatened to take hold, did she have enemies beside Gelraen? But she could not go down that path, she had to move forward. 'What's done, is done. Let's just get moving.'

'First, we are going to do another lesson, the horses need a rest.'

Isyllia reached into her cloak and closed her fingers around the dagger he had made for her.

'That is not your weapon today.'

She stopped, 'Then why did you give it to me? What am I supposed to use?'

Ember produced a small, smooth stone. 'This!'

Isyllia took the rock, her face dropping with disappointment, 'This, was I that bad! Surely you are kidding!'

Ember showed no sign of laughing, 'I'm not. A rock in my hands is a rock. A rock in your hands is a world of possibilities. You need to learn to control and focus your power. I want you to practice with this rock.'

Isyllia shook her head in disbelief, 'You're mad, but why not!'

'Start by levitating it, and when you have the hang of that, move it just like you did the daggers.'

'But I did that already.'

'Doing something once when you are frightened is not the same as truly mastering something. You need to be able to control your ability without even thinking.'

211

'This is confusing.' Isyllia looked down at the cool, yet offensive stone in her hands. Did it feel heavier?

'Right.' He thought for a moment, 'There are those who live through horror, and fight with fear and instinct, and those that fight with practiced skill, like in a practice yard, but never see true war. Then there are those that have both. To truly master a weapon, it must become like another part of your body. An extension of your arm. You must understand what you are learning to do. You are not learning to swing a sword, you are learning to survive, to defend your life. Under normal circumstances it takes years to learn how to fight with skill, but we don't have that time. You will need to learn to use your power to make up for your disadvantage over regular fighters. I will protect you, but we cannot promise I will always be there.'

'I see.' An hour of effort earned a mild jiggle from the stone, more to mock than obey her. Isyllia sounded her frustration, startling the horses. 'This is absolutely useless!'

Ember scratched his chin, unconcerned, 'It will take time, just keep practicing. We should be moving again anyway.' Ember whistled.

She closed her palm around the cool stone and watched, 'Why does that horse love you so much?' Her tone was dismissive.

He looked over, then back to Perrin 'He was being abused, and I thought he deserved a better life. I guess he is grateful.'

'Abused? What do you mean?

'I came across Perrin when I was travelling, he was tied up and half starved. When I tracked down his owner, I was told he was to be slaughtered and fed to the dogs, like a sack off meal. It shouldn't have been a shock but I couldn't shake the look in his eyes, all the pain and neglect he had suffered, so I just drew my sword, cut him free, and walked him out of his prison and we have been together ever since.'

Isyllia threw her arms around Perrin. 'You poor old thing.' Horses had always been a means of transport, nothing more. But now seeing Ember, and the way Perrin adored him had made her question all she had been taught. Isyllia climbed onto her four-legged companion and stroked her mane, taking in the animal's mortality for the first time. She felt every step the horse trod underneath her, every outtake of breath. Every sneaky nip of grass when she thought Isyllia was not watching. She was real, as real as every breath Isyllia herself took. Niimorea was not a transport; she was a friend who, would ride into danger with her without question. The revelation shook her, and for the first time she felt a kinship growing between her and Niimorea, like the bond between Ember and Perrin, unspoken but true. A tiny spark of hope had begun to burn in her stomach, and she held onto it, with everything she had left.

CHAPTER EIGHT

Gelraen, Illingdale Castle.

It was still early, too early to be arguing with treasurers over money. Gelraen shifted in his seat again, this time thrusting his first onto the table, if he let them go on any longer, he would be here all day. 'Gentlemen, I don't want a history lesson, just tell me if it can be done?'

The men both looked at each other, but only one was game enough to speak, 'Sire, it is not that it cannot be done, the merchants simply will not support a war they think is unnecessary. Without their support we risk bankrupting the crown.'

Gelraen rubbed his temples. There had to be better ways to spend a morning. 'Then I trust you gentlemen can find a way to change their minds, or I will find someone who can.' Gelraen had finally had all he could stomach and stormed out slamming the door behind him. He would need something to cheer him up and hopefully the prostitute he had seen last night was still asleep in his chambers. He had always preferred whores, they were cheaper than maids in the long run, and they didn't gossip. Opening the door, he glanced to the bed where a small shape still lay curled under the vast blankets. *'Good, I may as well use her again'* and pulling off his clothes; he crawled into the bed, sliding his hand over one of her naked breasts.

The harlot smiled. 'Sire!'

'Thought I'd get my money's worth.' He started biting her ear.

The woman rolled onto her back. 'You always get your money's worth!'

Gelraen smiled, 'Turn!'

The doe-eyed woman didn't need further prompting; she turned over and groaned with pleasure, neither taking any notice of the knock at the door; they could damn wait. Some minutes later, Gelraen finished and pushed the panting woman to the side, wiping down with a rag and then walking over to his desk. He rifled for some coins, grabbing a Gold Dale and chucked it at the whore as he began pulling his clothes on, 'I'm in a good mood!'

She snatched at the coin with wide eyes. 'Maybe next time I'll give you one for free!'

He turned to face her, grinning. 'I'll hold you to that!' Then moved to open the door. General Walton waited, his eyes turned to the floor, he knew better than to enter the room until asked. 'Sire!'

Gelraen smiled, 'Ah yes.' He closed the door and motioned down the hall where the two could walk.

'Sire, I have received word back from Docktown.' He looked around for people and when satisfied the hall was deserted, he continued. 'My sources were able to confirm the existence of a smithy as you asked, a Delmariis Steel. The boy running the shop insisted his master was named Anton and had left on business but did not say where.'

Gelraen chewed his lip, 'Indeed. Good work Duke, now what of other matters?'

'Ah, yes, I have received a request to hold the execution for Mallory?'

'Indeed General, indeed. I want to ensure William is well, he would want to be there, I am sure.'

'Indeed wise, sire.' If General Walton was hoping he would elaborate, he did not. The two walked in silence for a moment. 'Also, if I may, the wife of Mallory has come to me this morning. Pleading her husband's innocence. I told her in view of his service prior to his crime, I would grant an audience with the council.'

Gelraen bared his teeth in distaste, 'When have you called the council for?'

Walton hesitated, 'I have not called a time sire, I just asked them to be ready in case they were called on. I wanted to speak with you first!'

Gelraen thought for a moment. 'Call it for noon. We will be done with this mess finally!'

Walton nodded, 'Brilliant sire. I shall make arrangements at once!' Then turning, he bowed and walked off in the opposite direction. Gelraen stood for a moment, contemplating his new general. Then continued his stroll. He had intended to take the morning off but decided instead to try one last time to question Balor. The jailor had suggested torture to loosen his tongue, but Gelraen had never been fond of torture, messy business. No, he would speak, or he would die. Sadly, in the ex-general's case he would still be executed, such is the punishment for regicide. Gelraen walked in, nodding to the jailor who scrambled to open the cell door. 'The general's done stopped eating sire!'

Gelraen ignored the man, almost walking a filthy mass that slept on the floor. He waited for the door to be closed again, then kicked Balor in the back to rouse him, unwilling to bend and touch his soiled clothes. Balor stirred and then turned over; his face scrunched up with pain. The old man sighed when he saw who towered over him.

'I will give you one last chance to confess.' Gelraen gave him an intense glare, 'Speak up traitor, why did you kill your King?'

He was greeted with silence.

Gelraen looked around the cell, stone stained with years of blood and filth. The smell alone was enough to make you lose your stomach. 'Don't you see how selfish your actions are, will you not at least think of your family, don't you think I would like to have something better to tell your wife?'

Balor stared at the ground determined.

He sighed, 'Then you leave me no choice. Balor Mallory, your complete lack of remorse for your actions will see not only you, tortured and executed, but your family title will be stripped, leaving William, if he wakes, with nothing. Your widow will be penniless and without a home, because of your actions.' He paused for a moment. 'Your execution will be carried out tomorrow at sunset, I suggest you use this time, to reflect on what you have done! ... Jailor open the door; I am done here!' Gelraen left the cell disappointed. His hopes had not been high that Balor would speak but he knew he had to try; there was nothing else he could do now but wait for tomorrow.

Gelraen nursed his pounding head all the way to the door, a result of the mead he could still taste from the previous night. It was customary to have dressers, but Gelraen had always felt uncomfortable with the idea of being dressed by someone else and discarded his body staff years ago much to his mother's disapproval. It also meant when he chose to forgo wearing a new outfit for the day, there were no blank stares he had to contend with. Today was one such thankful day. Gelraen strode along to the room Adella was guarding and knocked at the door. It did not take long for a scared maid to answer and step aside so he could enter. Gelraen looked around the room and found Adella sitting beside a now semi-conscious mass on the bed. She looked up, 'Sire' she stood and bowed. He waved her off 'I received your word.'

Adella nodded, 'He woke sometime this morning.'

'Welcome back soldier. You had us worried for a bit there.' Gelraen smiled, baring his teeth in an awkward fashion.

'How do I come to be here?' William asked, nervous.

'The way I understand it is, some days ago you and a party of others spirited our queen out of the city without anyone's knowledge. Arranged by your father who has been charged with the murder of our king. Then, when soldiers set on you, our queen attacked you, using unnatural powers...' He paused for effect, 'You are alive because of your aunt.'

If it were possible William paled further, 'Sir my father just told me it was not safe here for… for *her*, and I had to get her out the city to Godswall…Sir my father could not have. He was devoted to the king. There has to be some mistake!'

'We have evidence…and you are saying you have no knowledge of your father's ultimate plan?'

A tear slid from Williams eyes, 'No! … it's not possible. Why, I don't understand?

'We believe he was protecting the queen. We believe he knew her secret and acted foolishly to protect her. But there is something I must ask, something that will be hard for you to remember. Adella has informed me that Isyllia can use Malagara abilities.'

William swallowed hard and winced against the new offering of torture, like a putrid dish being set in front of him. 'Isyllia.' He stopped for a moment, re-living the memory in his eyes, 'She saved *him*.' William's face turned red, his fists bawled and knuckles white with rage.

'Who? How did she do it?' Gelraen waited, rapt with attention.

'Someone named Anton. She…' He shut his eyes hard, the pain of raw betrayal eating him. 'She made the blade move.'

'She stabbed him?' He frowned, but there was no confusion on his face.

'No… yes. She was meters away from it. It turned on its wielder by itself, and … grew. He was impaled on the shards of metal that she grew from his own sword. She is Malagara sir, an … abomination.' The pain on his face was evident, and Gelraen was sure it had nothing to do with his shoulder.

'Adella says she tried to kill you, that it was Isyllia who moved a blade from behind.'

William shook his head, 'No, I can't believe that!'

This time Adella spoke, 'You said yourself hon, it was like you barely knew each other anymore. Is it so hard to believe? She didn't trust you with her secrets, but she trusted this stranger. Maybe he wasn't a stranger at all? Would you have known?'

William's face darkened, 'No.'

Gelraen nodded to Adella, then looked back to the poor boy lying on the bed, not sure which wound was hurting him more. 'Thank you, that cannot have been easy. I need you to rest now, you have done your country a service today, and for that I am willing to pardon you for your crime, but I am sorry… not even I can save your father now!' He looked sympathetically at William one last time, then turned to leave. He reached the door then stopped and turned back. 'He is to be tortured and executed at sunset, if you wish to attend you will not be stopped. But it might be best, to spare yourself the pain!'

'I will be there!' William set his jaw. Gelraen nodded once then left the room.

He took the long way to the chambers, repeating the morning's revelations in his head. So much of his plan had been altered. Isyllia had slipped through his fingers, but maybe, just maybe he could still turn things in his favour, maybe he could still salvage the plan. He had to try. Picking up his pace he wiped the sweat that had begun to gather on his forehead and took a deep breath, then, opening the door to the royal council hall, walked in to find everyone already assembled. Selina Mallory sat on the side, weeping before the whole room. Gelraen tried to block her out walking to the front of the room with measured steps. He took a moment to stare at the King's chair, then dismissing the moment, turned, and sat elsewhere. One of the council members rose.

'Sire, the widow of Balor Mallory wishes to speak.'

Selina stopped weeping, 'Widow? My husband lives?'

'Enough!' Gelraen was grave, 'You have asked to speak on your husband's behalf?'

Selina edged forward tentatively. 'Sire, my husband is innocent. He has served our king faithfully for his whole life, he is being framed, I beg you!'

'We have an eyewitness that has confessed to buying the drug used to kill the king for your husband.'

Selina began to weep again, her tears filled with anguish.

'I am sorry my lady, but all the evidence points to your husband. I wish it were not the case, but it is, and I am duty bound to protect this realm from treachery, wherever it lies, nobody is above the law. Your husband will be executed as planned, and the city will have justice for their loss … guards, remove her, see that she is seen safe to her home, I will not have her punished for her husband's crimes.'

Gelraen waited for the distressed woman's wailing to grow distant, his eyes creased with annoyance. When he did speak, it was with little patience. 'I have more news for the council, grave news. William Mallory, the surviving son of the convicted, has woken. He was indeed among those who removed our Queen and travelled with her until he was wounded some days ago. It was the plan of Balor Mallory to see her to Randal in Godswall. Gentleman it is with sadness that I report that the Queen, Isyllia Bellamy has left the city of her own free will.'

'Why would she do that?' One of the men shot up, disbelieving of the words he was hearing, 'Our Queen would not abandon her duty to the realm!'

Gelraen took measured breaths, he would not let his temper get the better of him, not today, so much relied on him being calm. 'Indeed. Unless her life depended on it.'

'What are you saying sire?'

'I have received a report that a battle took place some days ago, William Mallory was wounded, but the others escaped, he was left behind. He reported seeing Isyllia use unnatural abilities to save the man she was with. It was also reported that, to hide her secret, she turned her abilities on William.'

'Preposterous! Baseless accusations!'

Gelraen gave the man a cold stare 'I have two eyewitnesses, William being one. Do you suppose he would have reason to lie, knowing the implications'?

The man sat back down disgruntled but having no further argument to offer.

Another councillor stood, 'Even if what you say is true sire, we still do not understand what Balor's motive to slay the king was?'

'I believe he acted out of love for his surviving son. I believe he found out about our young Queen's condition and sought to protect her, slaying the King so he would never have to kill his daughter, and then spirited her away to an ally. What he did not count on, is that his son did not know of her condition, and is loyal to the crown. William acted under official orders from his General to protect his Queen, and as such, will not be punished further.'

'So, what you are saying is, our Queen is Malagara?'

Gelraen nodded gravely, lowering his eyes to the floor. 'I assure you this news wounds me more than anyone can imagine. It was the highlight of my life when our lady accepted my proposal … when she chose me. I had imagined our life would play out differently…' He trailed off, 'But she also entrusted me to protect the realm, even if that means I must now protect it from the Queen herself, our laws are absolute. The people of Illingdale must always come first.'

'Here here!' Some of the men stood and chanted their support. It was as he had hoped.

'Gentlemen, it is with a heavy heart, that I now must pronounce Isyllia Bellamy an enemy of Illingdale, banished under pain of death, should she ever return. Any allies who take her in, will also be declared enemies of the state and suffer execution… Gentlemen, our city is suffering. Let us not falter in our troubles. Now more than ever we must band together and show our strength. Of course, considering this news there comes the question of the throne. Illingdale needs a leader.'

One of the men in the back stood, 'Lord Pennerly's appointment was done by a lawful queen, and he has proven to hold Illingdale's virtues in his heart. I move to make his appointment as King permanent.'

The portly man stood again. 'Duke Preston has more claim to the throne than Pennerly by right of blood, he should be the one appointed'

Gelraen cut him off, 'And where is Duke Preston? Is he here, standing with us now in our time of need?' Gelraen looked around the room. 'As I recall it gentlemen, Duke Preston did not even attend the honour giving for his beloved kin!' Silence fell.

'I second the recommendation of permanency.'

Another stood, then another, then another. The portly councillor remained seated, his face turning an unattractive shade of purple in his rage.

Gelraen smiled wide, 'I thank you for your confidence, I will not let the people down.'

'You mentioned an ally of the former Queen?'

'I did. She was being taken to the Duke of Godswall. He too, will be arrested under suspicion of treason.' There was some murmur of concern around the room. Gelraen could see he did not have everyone convinced in the idea of Randal being a traitor to the throne. 'He will be brought back here for questioning in front of the council. If it proves he has had no part in these allegations, he will receive pardon with our apologies.' There was some more satisfaction with this idea. Gelraen nodded, content that everything had gone well, better than he had hoped, 'Now gentlemen, if there be nothing else, I have other business to attend to.' Gelraen left the room and walked back to his chambers. They were now deserted, no trace of the night's activities, leaving the room with an empty feeling. He rang the little bell on his desk, signalling for the door guard to enter. 'I wish to speak with Lord Walton, and Lady Bellamy… separately.' The guard nodded then turned to leave. Gelraen waited, contemplating the agenda of the day. So many things were happening at once. It was enough to make his head spin, but he could not lose focus, not now. And so, he spent the remainder of the free moments he had with his eyes closed, breathing. He had almost fallen asleep when the guard returned, a swift knock at the door. 'Enter.'

Lord Walton walked in, standing tall but for his short height. 'Sire, I hear congratulations are in order!' He bowed deep, his nose again too near the floor for comfort.

Gelraen stood, he was fond of Lord Walton, he was loyal to their family, but he never could understand his fondness for facial hair. Thick tendrils of oily black hair were trimmed and woven in artful patterns. It was excessive, even in a Duke. 'I want you to take a small battalion to the Duke of Godswall. Randal is to be arrested under suspicion of treason. If the Duchy offers

228

resistance, I give you permission to engage, but bring Randal back here for questioning, and Renn, he is not to be harmed!'

Lord Walton bowed again then breezed from the room on his own bloated self-importance. Another knock sounded. Gelraen waited a moment, taking a deep breath then stood with his hands clasped behind his back, 'Enter.'

Adella Bellamy sauntered into the room. 'How can I be of service Sire?' For a woman, she kept her emotions hidden well. She stopped near the window and waited, always with the heir of a cat stalking prey.

'I need a service of you, it is not something I ask lightly, but it is the only way forward now.'

Adella nodded, 'First, I need to ask you a question. And I expect you to be truthful.'

Gelraen turned, one eyebrow raised, 'Do go on!'

Adella's face darkened, she either missed his moment of humour, or had decided to dismiss it. 'You knew our companion, just like you knew, Isyllia had abilities.'

He considered using sarcasm again, then noted the serious tone her expression had somehow managed to deepen and decided better of it. 'His name isn't Anton, and you are right, I did know him. Once. As to Isyllia, I suspected, but I was never able to confirm it.'

'She isn't Malagara, is she?'

Gelraen felt beads of sweat begin to form on his brow. He was king, he could say what he wanted. But remembering the reputation this woman held, he also knew it was not wise to lie. 'You have your secrets, I have mine.'

It was Adella's turn to raise her eyebrows, 'What secrets do I hold, sire?'

Gelraen scoffed, 'We both know it wasn't Isyllia who stabbed William.' He said, raising an eyebrow.

Adella's eyes took on a darker shade of black.

'Let's suffice to say, right now, we need each other.'

'I see.'

'You won't' He looked at his shoes, wishing there was some other way to ask. 'Because right now, I need you to kill your sister.'

Adella did not speak; she turned to the window and stared. For a moment, she lost some of her composure, her shoulders slumping, and she squeezed her eyes shut tight to prevent the words entering her mind. 'What is the cost?'

Gelraen's voice softened, 'Everything.'

Adella nodded, straightening herself again like the moment had never happened. 'I've heard rumours about the Isle...'

'The rumours are true, and we are running out of time. This is my last option.'

Adella turned, her face was clear, but Gelraen could tell she was still suffering, she loved her sister dearly. Adella curtseyed and swept from the room. Gelraen slumped, a whisky was what was in order now, and sitting he filled his glass a little higher than usual. The dice had been thrown again, he just hoped now, it would be worth it.

◁ ✳ ○ ✳

William, Illingdale Castle.

William woke to the warmth of the afternoon light on his face, and the smell of hot soup awakening the hunger in his belly. He sat with caution, the pain in his shoulder had returned, but not enough to deter him. It would be nightfall soon and he had to be moving. Making short work of the soup, he threw the spoon back into the empty bowel with a clatter, it had been some days since he had had a decent meal. He stood up, aware that he stank and still wore the same clothes he had when they had left the city over a week ago. But he did not care about his appearance right now. He had to find his mother, she would need to know he was safe, and she would need him right now. William set his determination, stumbling groggily through the halls, one foot after another like his feet were being placed at random. All the while looking for a door and finding only a guard walking his way. 'There you are Lord Mallory; your King wishes to speak with you.'

William gritted his teeth, 'Indeed.' He knew he had no choice but to follow the guard. To run would see him hanging next to his father and besides, what did he have left to run to?

They stopped in front of a large oak door. The guard knocked, then without waiting to be admitted went straight in, standing aside so that William could enter. He inclined his head to William, retreating and shutting the door hard behind him. The loud clunk made Gelraen turn. 'Lord Mallory, how are you feeling?'

'I am well sire!' He lied, his shoulder sending pangs of defiance, 'I thank you for your physician, he does remarkable work.'

Gelraen chuckled. 'There is no need for thanks my boy. I wish events could be different but I am about to have your father executed, and it is your duty as a son, to be angry, but I pray in time you can forgive me and we may even become friends.'

William did not reply, unsure how to respond.

'Now let us speak of other unpleasant matters. Please, sit.'

William stared at the chair for a moment, like it was diseased, then shook the thought off and sat, ignoring the protest from his shoulder from the sudden change in position.

'Did you know?'

'Know about what sire?'

'Did you know she had abilities?'

William sighed, a pain he did not want to revisit just yet, 'I did not sire.'

Gelraen waited.

'No. I knew there was something she was hiding, but she would never talk about it. She didn't trust me.' He said the words with utter distaste.

Gelraen sat back, his face a mask, and poured two glasses of whisky, offering one to William. '... And if she had?' There was a moment of silence between the two men, each wondering what the response would be.

'I would do my duty to the realm sire, as my father ...' He stopped. It was like the world had been turned upside down and his head still swam from the aftereffects. William stared at the glass, deciding it best to change the subject, 'Father never let us drink, he would say a soldier's judgement should never be clouded.'

Gelraen pushed it closer to his hand. 'True. But sometimes the best thing for our judgement, is to switch it off from time to time.'

William did not understand what he meant, but fearing further offence took the glass, throwing back the contents in one gulp. The liquid felt thick in his mouth, creating a comforting, and warming sensation as it burned its way down to his stomach. 'Thank you sire.' He offered the glass, but Gelraen smiled.

'Have another!' He refilled the glass

William moved closer, somewhat grateful, but knowing he needed to get moving. He looked at the contents for a moment, this time sipping the beverage for fear it would be refilled again.

Gelraen held his glass, swilling the contents contentedly. 'I do have some good news!'

William looked up, perhaps they had found the real culprit after all. 'Sire?'

'I spoke with the council this morning.' He took a swig, 'It was agreed your acts were an honest mistake, and you will not be tried for treason.' He said.

William's heart lurched; he had forgotten about his own predicament. 'Thank you sire, I assure you the kingdom was always my priority, but if I may sire, as the son of the realm's greatest traitor, why am I not also in chains?'

'Curious isn't it.' Gelraen looked down at his glass, not trying to hide the thoughts on his face, but what, William could not tell. 'It is the duty of a ruler to always put the interests of the realm first. You have been acquitted, but your name is dishonoured, and you no longer have a title. I am willing to let you earn back your position, maybe even take your rightful place as general one day, but only if you agree to help me.'

William looked up at Gelraen, his heart in his throat. 'What do you need from me?'

Gelraen considered him. 'Not now, now I just want you to prove you are willing to be loyal, that you are willing to serve the crown ... but when the time comes, will you stand with me?'

William swallowed the rest of the contents in the glass, the alcohol had begun to dull the pain ever so slightly, and it was a welcome feeling. There were so many different answers he wanted to give to the Question, so many things he wanted to say. But in the end, he knew he had little choice. He had been betrayed by the two people he loved. His father had lied to him, Isyllia had lied to him, but it was her deception that cut the deepest. She had never cared; how could she? If she had never trusted him. William sat thinking about the question and listening to his heart somewhere in the deep recesses of his chest, hammering like a lead weight just barely holding back the agony that threatened to scream its way up his throat. It was the only option left to him. Take this small mercy and try to make a new life. William stood and knelt at the new King's feet, 'Majesty, I pledge to always put the honour of the crown above my own, your life above my own, until death take me.'

Gelraen nodded. 'Stand.'

William obeyed.

'I take no pleasure in what must come, but I am subject to our laws like any other, perhaps more so. Come, stand by your king, show your father that you are well, it is what he would want.'

William nodded, 'Sire, my mother... she would need me now.'

Gelraen nodded. 'Of course, I will have a guard sent to your premises to see your mother is brought here. It is best you do not go alone in the streets today, especially with your injury.' He pointed to William's shoulder.

William felt appeased. 'Thank you sire, your generosity is more than I deserve.' But still, with each step he took toward the ceremonial stage, the place where his father would be executed his legs got heavier and heavier. Until finally, he thought for a moment he would be sick but fought against the urge. He still had not had time to wrap his head around the situation he was in; his father, a disgraced murderer, Isyllia was Malagara. Had Balor truly been trying to protect her? Had he known what the girl's fate would be, and killed the king so he would never find out? There were too many questions unanswered. William turned his head, regarding the new king, unable to fathom why it was that his father had been so frightened of the man.

The executioner slumped, heavy footsteps vibrating on the wooden planks until he stopped in front of a table laden with silver instruments. William looked away, his stomach lurching. He could not bear to contemplate which of the instruments would be used first on his father, whether he had killed the king, or not. The crowd roared, dragging Williams' attention back to the entrance of the stage. Balor had begun a slow and unsteady procession alone to the scaffold. His hands were bound in irons, and he looked half-dead. Like the torture had already been conducted. William swallowed hard, any minute his father would see him standing there injured, what would he do? Would he still care? Did he ever care? William tried to put the thoughts out of his mind, where was his mother? She should have been here by now. He should have gone by the house, scalding himself, he looked around the crowd, hoping to see her, fighting her way through the jeering people to get to the front. But she was nowhere to be seen, neither was Adella. The executioner signalled for Balor to be brought over to the table and turned to face the crowd.

'Any last words scum?'

Balor ignored the man's rudeness, noticing his son for the first time, standing beside Gelraen. For a moment, William thought he could see the alarm on his father's face, but it was gone a moment later. 'I confess freely to the murder of our king. I confess I operated alone, and for my own reasons. My son' He looked at William, 'Is innocent.' He looked down, intending to impart no further information. William felt a lump forming in his throat, there it was, he had confessed.

William set his jaw, his father had made his own choices, he would not fall with him.

The executioner turned to Gelraen, he stepped forward, his face grave. 'You have confessed to the murder of your king, here, in front of your countrymen. You have betrayed the crown. You have betrayed your family. And you have betrayed this city. This grand country that has loved you and nurtured you.' He paused, shaking his head. 'There is only one punishment deserved for such treachery…but … in honour of your sons continued loyalty, I have decided to show you mercy, though you don't deserve it!' The crowd buzzed, hissing and booing from all sides. Mercy was not the favoured option.

William, who had been looking at the floor, unable to look his father in the eyes, shot up, stunned, he could not free his father after confessing to the murder of the king?

Gelraen signalled for quiet. 'Even now, in the face of his father's death, your son stands beside the crown, ready to die in its service. Your honoured wife, weeps broken hearted tears of disbelief for your crimes, and your eldest son, died a hero of

Illingdale. Your family has been like the roses that beautify this grand palace that has nurtured you, cared for you ...' He turned away from the prisoner, facing William for one moment. 'I will not allow one thorn to destroy that legacy ... Balor Mallory for your crimes against the Kingdom of Illingdale, you were sentenced to be hung, quartered, and your name forever displayed on the gates of our great city in shame for all generations to come... I now pronounce you are instead to be beheaded by axe, and your honour giving to take place without shroud... May you now face your eternal destruction alone, and with your eyes open.' He nodded to the executioner then moved back to his place, not looking at William.

William held his breath; the man moved his father over to the block placing his head on the side so that he faced the royal party. William noticed his father had been crying, tears streaked his cheeks, was this remorse? The executioner aimed his axe, raising it in a slow steady motion. William could not breathe, any moment it would come down and it would all be over, the crowd screamed with excitement, happy that the traitor would face his death, some no doubt disappointed that he was no longer to be tortured.

'William don't let...' He said, vehement for his son to hear him. *'Thunk'* But the executioner was swift, not waiting for the desperate man to finish his sentence, freeing the head from the body in one swing. Blood soaked the stage as his father's body fell in a heap on the floor, still jerking its protest at its sudden termination, his last words forever unfinished.

William stood, stunned. What had his father been trying to say?

'Guards, I want to know why lady Mallory was not at her husband's execution. See that she is safe and bring her to Williams quarters at once.'

William had not realised his mother had not shown, lost in the shock of the moment. 'Sire, perhaps I could accompany the guards?'

Gelraen shook his head, anger was reflected on his face. 'No, the people are angry right now, most do not share my ideals of mercy. It is not safe; you will stay at the castle.'

His heart sank, somehow, he had known that was the answer he would be given, but he longed to be alone. William found his way back to the room he had been given in a daze, the empty bowl of soup had been cleared in his absence, and he decided to sit on his bed. The pain was beginning to strengthen in his arm, and he thought resting for a moment would do some good. A new servant entered the room. Her hands were clasped tight together, and she walked with her head down. Never making eye contact. She was nervous. *'Some people do not share my ideals of mercy'* The thought ran through his head again, the maid was one such person. 'Sir, I brought fresh linen for your wound.'

William scowled, 'Fine.'

The girl turned to leave.

'Wait. First, I want a bottle of Whisky and something for the pain.'

She nodded, exiting the room.

William lay down on the bed, trying to not to focus on the pain in his heart. Trying not to imagine her voice, or what she was doing now. He tried not to remember the feel of her and how it made his heart race when she touched him. All the moments they spent together, wishing he had not locked his heart away. Then he remembered the last moment, and the look of shock when she revealed what she could never tell him, had *never* intended to tell him. His world went black, and he fell into the dirt alone. He had tried not to think about those last moments, she had revealed herself to save *him*. Not William, a stranger who she barely knew. William lay on his bed, drowning in the bitterness that ate away at his mourning heart, no longer willing to fight for whatever it was, he had left.

CHAPTER NINE

Isyllia, Eddinsford Plains.

'Ember.... Ember!' Isyllia tried once again to get his attention. Ember sat on his horse, riding at the front. But at times, it was like he was not there. 'EMBER!'

'I'm concentrating,' He said, sounding annoyed.

She did not care. 'I can see the ruins, I thought we weren't going to go this close?'

Ember sighed, reining Perrin to the side. 'We need to stay far enough in to avoid soldiers.'

'Are there soldiers?' She looked around, half expecting them to jump out of the nearest bush.

'Yes, but we are safe now, I am keeping an eye on them' His voice grew more exasperated.

'And what about the spirits?'

'We are fine for now but stay alert.'

Isyllia pouted. She had grown accustomed to his demeanour over the days they had been travelling together, but the lack of conversation had started to niggle at her nerves. She decided instead to glance at the remnants of the splendid lost Kingdom of Eddinsford, even in its state of death. Far away as they were, she could see what was left of the broken architecture, not destroyed in the war. Birds had been carved into the walls bending and weaving their way to the sky, it must have taken years. 'Oh Nim, they never said it was so beautiful!'

'Help' it was close to inaudible, Isyllia looked around in confusion, when it sounded again. *'Help us!'*

'Ignore it!' Ember said, sounding tense.

'No, I beg you, don't leave, please help, I'm frightened!'

Isyllia moved toward the voice, a small girl wearing a white dress stood under an archway in the debris, *'Please!'* The girl walked out of sight. Isyllia moved to follow her, but she felt something grab tight hold of her arm, preventing her from moving. 'You're hurting me!'

'I said, ignore it!' He warned, his eyes dark and commanding. 'It's a spirit!'

'Are you blind? That's not a spirit, it's a girl!' Isyllia shook him off and kicked her horse into a run. She could hear Ember swear somewhere behind her, but she did not look back, instead focusing ahead and finding the girl. The broken bits of walls and buildings that lie forgotten in time were deserted. But she rode on anyway, certain there were people, until she reached the archway and dismounted. *This way, quick, she's hurt bad!'*

Isyllia ran towards the steps of what looked like a broken-down cathedral, noting that she had no experience treating wounds, much less what she was going to treat them with. *Ember will know*, she concluded, and followed as the girl ran inside without looking back. The thought struck her, she could no longer hear Ember, odd, had he decided to wait for her? Or had soldiers found them? She stood for a moment, torn between helping the girl and her friend.

'Please' The voice was urgent, frowning as she walked inside the dark dusty room. 'Hello? Tell me where you are, I've come to help.'

'Why didn't you save them?'

Isyllia started, turning to find the girl behind her, she was crying, blood dripped from her abdomen. 'Save who? Oh, my gosh you're bleeding, hold still!'

'It's too late, they are gone!'

245

'Who is gone, I don't understand?' But Isyllia did not need an answer to the question, sounds of battle began to filter through the doors, 'My friend, he can't fight the soldiers alone, I have to help him, just stay here, you'll be safe!' Isyllia made for the doors, only the doors were no longer there, the church began to disappear and instead, she found herself standing in an open courtyard garden, or what was left of it. Now, it was covered with blood and men lie strewn in unnatural positions, bits of pottery smashed where women and children had been cut down. Most, no longer moving. The sight made her sick, anger raged through every inch of the city, except no one noticed the two figures appear from nowhere.

'It's too late!'

Isyllia crouched to face the girl, grabbing her on the arms, she was real. The blood that had before covered her waist was now gone, her dress was pristine. 'Your wound! It's ...' Isyllia stepped back, her face turning white. 'What is happening, where are we, where is my friend?' She said, breathing herself through the panic that started to bubble deep down.

'The end.'

'The end? The end of what? What does that mean?' Isyllia stood and took in the scene again, think, she had to think. All around her men screamed in pain, swords smashing furious at their opponents. It was a great battle, it had to be, but how was it happening? In her youth, she had been taught about the Great

War between Illingdale and Eddinsford. It was a pointless war over road taxes that had ended in the destruction of the Kingdom of Eddinsford. In the years that followed it had become New Eddinsford, but never had her tutors gone into details about what her people did. Never could she have imagined the leagues of dying men and women that surrounded her. Her feet squelched through blood, impossible to fathom who it used to protect. Hands stretched out toward her, crying for their mothers in their last moments, and somehow, she could feel their pain, all their pain. The burning and the despair tore at her like nothing she had ever experienced. And it was not just the despair; she felt the heat of anger too, of soldiers trying to murder their opponents, the hot hatred and the fear as they thrust at each other. Isyllia kneeled, unable to process the scope of emotion being squashed through her body. A man lay to her left, crying and gargling something she could not hear. She took a shuddering breath, craning her head around to see if there was anything she could do for the man. There was not. The man was too far gone, choking on blood as he tried to hold the delicate parts of his stomach in. Instead she took the man's hand. Knowing it would not help him, hoping it would offer some warmth, the only thing she could do. 'I am here, it will be over soon.' If the man was comforted by her presence, she would never know. Slowly he turned his head to the sky, his face slack, the last of his living pain sliding down his cheek in the form of a solitary tear. Isyllia stared at it for a moment. No one knew. He died alone, forgotten by time. And for what?

'Where is papa?' The voice startled her; she had almost forgotten about the girl. Isyllia stood, if she played along, it was possible she could find a way out of this awful reality, 'I don't know, it is not safe for you here, where is your home?'

The girl pointed to a castle. 'This way!' Then began to run off in that direction.

Isyllia followed her, eager to leave the battlefield and the dead man behind. They ran past a wall, all over its expanse birds were carved, winding and stretching out to the sky. It was the one she had seen earlier only now, it stood in all its splendour, impervious to the destruction being wielded around. Isyllia started, she *had* gone back in time then, but how?

'This way!' The girl's urgency snapped her out of the moment, and she continued, coming to the enormous castle that stood behind the wall of birds. A castle crafted to look like the sky above, taking Isyllias breath away. But why were they going to the castle of Eddinsford? The girl could not live here. But the girl ran inside, and up a vast staircase, leaving Isyllia to run if she intended to keep up.

The girl ran, up and up until they came to a room with soldiers standing guard … Illingdale soldiers. Isyllia stopped, swallowing her automatic surge of panic, and rubbing the sweat off her hands onto her dress. The soldiers had heard them, turning their hungry eyes on the girl. 'You grab that one, I'll take care of her majesty here.'

248

'No!' But it was no use, the soldier grabbed Isyllia, thrusting his blade to her neck so she could not struggle. Isyllia tried to pull the wind, but nothing came. Whether trapped by her fear, or unable to work at all, she did not know. 'You can watch!' He said, dragging her toward the door where the other solder had taken the girl, ripping at the girl's hair to stop her struggling. 'Thought you could get away, did you little rat.'

'Let me go!' The girl did not give up her struggles, despite the man causing her pain. The result of failure reflected on the girl's face, and it tore out what was left of Isyllias thumping heart. 'Bastards! She's a child! Stop hurting her!' She screamed, but the man tightened his blade, 'Wait your turn!' The man dragged the girl into the room to be assaulted by more horror. More death. The girl had been royalty. Her father, the king, lay dead on the floor, his throat already slit. And the mother, still being held down on the bed, had been raped and stabbed, her last moments seeing her daughter being dragged into the room as she choked on air, knowing she could not save her child. Isyllia froze, unable to take in another moment of the terror around her. This had to end. She closed her eyes willing herself to wake, it had to be a dream that was all, she had fallen asleep on her horse and she had to wake now. But when she opened her eyes, the blade was still there, holding her back from saving the girl that had now been stabbed through the stomach. The soldier, not even watching as fresh blood stained her clean white dress. The once beautiful little girl fell to the floor with a hard thud, like she had been nothing. 'You bastards, she was a child, an innocent child!' She cried, no longer trying to fight the man off. The soldier turned, wiping the girl's blood off his sword with a rag. Isyllia felt the blade draw across her neck, falling to her knees with one hand trying to hold the blood in, but there was no blood. 'It's done, order the men to sack the city, leave none alive.'

The other soldiers offered a curt bow then left the room, leaving the man behind to admire his handiwork, then he too left the room. Isyllia felt her neck, still no blood fell, but a warm hard shape dug into her back. She shot to her feet to find a different woman, someone she hadn't noticed earlier lying dead in her place, her throat slit neatly with a blade. It had been the girl's governess. Isyllia knew she should feel relieved, but no consolation swept through her body, only the pain of more loss. Isyllia couldn't take her eyes off the girl, who stared lifeless at the ceiling. Kneeling, she took the princess in her bloodied arms and wept. Not noticing the scene around her begin to change once more, the girl, the mother and the horror around her fading at last. Isyllia held her arms still, mourning the now empty space, then stood, and looked at the empty room around her, had she returned? 'Ember' She began to run for the door, hoping he would hear and get her away from this dreadful place.

'Why did this happen to us?' It was the girl again. Isyllia could tell from the voice. Sunlight burst in through the door ahead and for a moment, she considered ignoring the girl and continuing to run. Guilt however stayed her legs and instead she turned once more to face the girl. 'What was your name?'

'Sarah.'

Isyllia felt as heavy as stone. 'My people were wrong Sarah. I am so sorry. I know that I cannot give you back your life, or your family, but I hope you can rest and know that I will never forget what you have shown me. I will not allow our people to forget your pain again, I promise!'

Sarah didn't respond, instead she pointed out the door. Isyllia looked, a shape had materialised in the frame of light. Isyllia stepped back, looking again for the girl but she was now alone with the silhouetted figure. 'Ember?' It took a moment for her eyes to adjust to the light. She looked at the man, he was much older than Ember, shorter and his expression was kind. She began to weep again, 'Where is Ember, why won't this end?'

'My child, where do you think you are?'

'This was a great battle ... my people caused all this horror!'

'They did.'

'I don't understand why I am here?'

'You don't understand, because you are not meant to. You have your own trial to face.'

She squinted, trying to find a feature that would disclose his identity, 'Who are you?'

'I am who I always have been.' He continued, 'But you may call me Odriid Fenn.'

Isyllia eyes widened, 'Odriid Fenn! I don't understand?'

He chuckled, but there was wisdom in his eyes unlike any, except for one. 'Why did you come here child?'

Isyllia wiped the tears staining her face. 'The girl. I thought she was hurt.' It was useless, more tears began to fall. 'My people did this. Why did they do this? How can people feel so much hate?'

Odriid looked grave, 'It was our responsibility as champions to keep the people safe, and to guide them.' His face darkened, 'Our failure did this, and it is my duty to ensure the next generation of champions, deserve their calling.'

Isyllia frowned, trying to understand. 'So, this was a test?'

'It was, but not yours. This test is for the Chosen of Nemethiiniia.'

'The Chosen of Nemethiiniia, who is that?'

'He will find you when he is ready.'

'He?' If Isyllia was hoping Odriid would elaborate, he did not. Instead he walked over to a desk in the back of the room that had appeared from out of nowhere.

'The weapon of Nemethiiniia lies within this vessel.' He ran his fingers along the ornate polished wooden box, but he did not open it. 'As you are chosen, and you have proven yourself worthy, you may take it and guard it if you wish, but understand, it is not intended for you.'

'I'm confused, how did I prove myself worthy?' She asked.

'Faced with the prospect of mortal peril, you chose to prioritise the safety of another.'

'The girl!' She felt fresh tears sting at her eyes, 'But I did not save her. I couldn't save her.'

Odriid looked sympathetic, 'You were not meant to child, she died thousands of years ago. You were meant to care about her fate, not to change it.' He held out the box.

Isyllia stretched her hand and took the small but magnificent chest. 'How will I know if he is worthy?' She looked up to realise, he was gone. Isyllia looked around confused, and then decided to examine the item he had left behind. A single symbol was carved onto the lid, a diagonal line with two lines crossing through it, like a lopsided 't' with two strokes. She opened the lid; inside lay a quill made from the most magnificent feather. She stroked the soft curve that bent its way up, watching as it shimmered and glowed with her touch. 'Strange weapon.' No sooner had she said it, a nagging feeling began to grow in the pit of her stomach, like a seed, an urge. It needed her; it was as if it was alive and communicating with her. Isyllia listened to the feeling, picking up the quill and the effect was almost instant. She was no longer in control of her hand; it shot over to a piece of paper lying in wait on the desk and began to write by itself, without ink. Isyllia watched as letters began to form, one after the other until, a short message stared back at her. The quill collapsed onto the desk, silent as if nothing had happened. Turning back to the paper she picked it up and began to read the message, at first confusion dominated her features until its meaning sunk in, and her face blanched.

'Isyllia!' It was Ember's voice; she had returned at last. Isyllia stuffed the note into her dress where it would be safe and replaced the quill into the box, happy if she never touched it again. Each step back to where Ember waited with fury and panic on his face was like a trek around the entire world, but she made it, offering him the box, but deciding to keep the note a secret.

Ember looked down at the box but did not take it. 'I am going to say this once, don't ever do that again!'

The look of anger on his face took her breath away, and she felt guilty, knowing she had promised to be more careful. 'I thought she was trapped… I'm so sorry.' She turned to her horse, knowing she had to get off her feet, and fast.

But he was not finished, the panic in his eyes still burning bright, 'The chosen are born for a reason, a purpose, you could have ruined everything with your carelessness!'

Isyllia looked down; her head had begun to spin, a sick feeling spreading like fire in the pit of her stomach. 'I… need to…' She could not finish the sentence, closing her exhausted eyes against her shaking legs. Against the exertion of the weapon she was not meant to receive. It had taken its toll on her and the little amount of energy she had left evaporated like smoke. But again, Ember was there, catching her in his arms. Then, lifting her against his chest he mounted Perrin. Isyllia made no sound as he sped along the Dead Plains, his mind focused, trying not to think about the case still clutched in her lifeless hand, and the overwhelming cost it could carry.

◁ ✳ ○ ✳

Ember, New Eddinsford, Eddinsford.

Ember made his way down the cobbled streets of New Eddinsford as fast as he could get away with. People wandered back and forth, most with a spring in their step. Some tipped their cap in greeting to the evident newcomer. That was the way of New Eddinsford. They were oceanside dwelling folk with chirpy brick buildings lining the streets. Smells of various varieties wafted with Ember as he made his way to his destination. But he dares not stop, on this occasion it was crucial to draw as little attention to them as possible. It had been a long journey, and Isyllia had remained unconscious for two days. As a chosen, she was in no danger of starvation, but he had begun to worry that she would not wake for a long time, time they might not have. He tried to focus ahead, listening to the clack, clack of the hooves and reading the street signs, he knew the house was coming up, but it had been a year. Finally, he saw the street he was looking for and turned down it. The little shop sat out the way of the main street, almost hidden. Ember rode round the back, knowing his friend would be in his workshop, 'Thomas, Thomas!' He called through the door, not having to wait long for a young man to come running out the shop, a magnifying glass stuck out across one of his eyes. He looked up, his pale freckled face carrying a temporary red hue. 'Ember? My word, it's been ages!'

'Tom help me get her down.' Ember looked around, 'Are we alone?'

The man hurried forward supporting Isyllias head. 'Father is away on business.' He motioned to a small cobbled house, much like the rest of the town. 'We can use his room!'

Ember climbed down like she was made of glass and carried her inside, placing her on the bed indicated.

'What happened to her? ... She needs a doctor; I should get a doctor.'

'No doctor.'

Thomas looked concerned but did not argue 'At least tell me who she is?'

256

Ember faced his friend, the magnifying glass almost hitting him in the nose.

'Right.' Thomas took the device off and placed it on a nearby table. 'Drink first, something strong.'

'Whisky.'

Thomas ran off, leaving Ember alone. He stared at her for a moment, the concern beginning to grow again, then deciding it best to let her rest, he walked into the sitting room and looked around, it hadn't changed in a year. Green velvet couches sat in awkward spots, framing shelves laden with books and odd trinkets that Thomas had no doubt made himself. Tom shared a business with his father, a prominent merchant. He was an only son as his mother had died giving birth to him. Mr O'Brien had hoped his son would enter the family business, and Tom stayed close to help him, but knowledge was his true passion. Thomas spent his days with his nose buried deep in lore and his own inventions. In the years that Ember had known Thomas, he had come to respect him. Thomas was kind, and an awkwardness about him made a person want to trust him. Ember sighed and moved over to one of the green velvet chairs. Thomas edged back, balancing a tray with two glasses and a bottle of caramel brown liquid.

Ember squinted at the label on the bottle, 'Tinkerton's Widgets & Things, *old recipe?*'

'I finally perfected it.' He held out a glass with some pride.

Ember took it and sipped the drink; it was strong with a rich caramel taste that lasted well after the mouthful had been swallowed. 'It's excellent!'

Tom turned a delicate shade of red. 'It has been a good seller!' He sat on the edge of the chair, back straighter than was comfortable; taking a sip himself, 'So, who is she?' Then a sudden flash of realisation filled Thomas, 'Wait ...is that the, you know?'

Ember sat opposite, taking another sip, deciding how best to approach the subject. 'Yes, she is the chosen of Abashiina.'

'I can't believe you did it, you got her out!'

Ember nodded once.

Tom scurried to his feet, almost sending the tray flying as he clumsily put it aside and walked over to a desk containing stacks of letters and parchment, 'I have heard news!' He shuffled through piles until he found the one he was looking for. 'Ah!' He walked back with the letter outstretched.

Ember took it and read. It was a copy, addressed to the council of New Eddinsford. He dismissed the impulse to ask his friend how he had gotten it, Tom had a way of finding things out.

Honoured Councillors of New Eddinsford,

It is with sadness that I report news, the King of Illingdale has been slain.

The formal appointment of Lord Gelraen Pennerly has been made as his Successor and a warrant issued for the princess under suspicion of heresy.

We understand, and respect you have different laws with regards to sorcery, however, we would be greatly indebted should you come across the princess,

that you return her to her own country for justice.

Hoping this letter finds you otherwise well,

Secretary in State

Illingdale.

Ember sighed, handing him back the note, 'That didn't take long.'

Thomas returned the note to the desk 'I wondered why they would condemn the heir to the throne, unless she had shown her powers by mistake, or out of grief and run for it.'

He nodded, 'It's a complicated situation. The king was poisoned, the General blamed Gelraen, but I'm not convinced it's that simple.'

'What do you think?'

Ember turned a thoughtful eye towards the bedroom for a moment. 'I think the General knew more than he wanted to let on. He was there when the Queen was slain, so he must have known she was guarding something. He may have found out that Gelraen was behind it, and thought the princess was the most logical target, and sought to protect her.'

'Do you really think the general would go to those lengths…'

'The General's son, William, was in love with her, they were close. I think Balor could have done it for his son's sake, to protect both.'

'And I take it this is where you come in?'

'I met with the General, he helped me get her out of the city but demanded his son, and a woman come with us.'

'Another woman?' Thomas screwed up his face in concentration, 'Who?'

Ember took another sip of his whiskey and his brow furrowed, 'She went by Adella, but that could have been an alias.'

'Adella Bellamy?' Tom's eyes widened.

Ember nodded, 'What do you know?'

'Not much, but more than most, she is a spy and she is good at hiding her tracks. She works for the general, keeping a communication with the Guild, and other affairs of state... She is not someone you want to cross. If he sent her with you, it was not for her safety.'

'We were attacked by Pennerly soldiers, she betrayed us. It seems she works for Gelraen now.'

'And the son you mentioned?'

'Dead. Stabbed by Adella.'

Tom sighed, 'Complicated.'

'Exactly.' Ember drained the rest of his glass.

Tom stood and started to pace. 'This is not good. If she is working for Gelraen now as you say .... what could spook her enough to betray her own family?'

'I wish I knew. Duke Randal said he has found activity of Malagara escaping. It has got to have something to do with that.'

Thomas continued his thought, 'So Adella is working for Gelraen. The king has been slain and Gelraen has now taken the throne and denounced Isyllia. Malagara is escaping the Isle of the Forgotten ... What is going on?' He continued to pace, the riddle sitting painfully on his face. 'What is your plan now?'

261

'I think our priority has to be to get the weapons, without them, we are useless. Isyllia already has the Feather of Nemethiiniia.' Ember frowned again, trying to prevent himself lapsing back into the state he had greeted Isyllia with when she reappeared.

Tom shook his head, 'Feather ... but how?'

'That is why she is unconscious. It drained too much of her energy, she cannot die, but she could sleep, long enough to be too late to stop whatever is about to happen.'

Thomas shook his troubled head, 'It is safe at least, that is something.'

'It is...' Ember sat forward, reaching under his mail shirt to retrieve the cloth bag he never parted with. 'There's something else, Randal gave me this.' Ember pulled out the journal of Odriid. 'It is written in old Daliian, but I believe it holds clues to the location of the other weapons.'

Tom's face lit up with longing, his body beginning to learn forward of its own accord. He was arguably the only person who loved books more than Ember and so when Ember handed it over to his excited friend it left a kind of regret in his stomach.

Tom opened the book delicately, the tips of his fingers just touching the pages. 'Where did she find the feather, was it at Eddinsford?'

'Yes, it appears the 'spirits' were guarding it as suspected.'

'It did make sense.' Tom closed the book and strode over to where he left the magnifying glass, replacing it back onto his head then continuing into another room. Ember followed him, his work room filled with various contraptions strewn about half finished, some piled in a heap and abandoned altogether. Tom walked over to the bookshelf, which spanned the length of one of the walls, filled from floor to ceiling with books. He didn't need long, pulling one thick blue volume then depositing it on his desk along with the Journal of Odriid. Ember stood back, deciding to let his friend work. He had known Tom for a few years and knew better than to interrupt him when he was concentrating. 'Ah, yes...obviously.... Yes!' He flicked back to the journal, continuing to mutter to himself. 'Here it is!'

Ember walked forward, making out the title at the top of the page, Nemethiiniia. 'See here, he says... And the bearer of the feather of Nemethiiniia shall first prove worthiness of their mantle, or forever will it lie, at a place of great suffering.' He repeated the sentence, then continued 'But be warned, death will befall all others who stumble across the weapon, not intended to be its keeper.'

Ember waited a moment, 'Is that all it says?'

'Seems to be.' Tom flicked to the next page, then back again.

'Do you think it has a death curse?'

Tom frowned. 'No, I don't.' He turned back to the volume he had removed from the shelf earlier 'From what I have studied in this book, the death curse refers to only those who are not chosen that try to take one of the weapons. It does not say whether that includes a champion it is not intended for, though I highly doubt it. I believe the weapons are able to be wielded by any chosen, but designed to work with their own chosen, so they may not function at intended capacity with another. The problem is, Illingdale held the only true records from that time, in the council vaults, but that-'

'Was all burned.' Ember sighed.

'Precisely, so nobody knows what they can or can't do. But even the slightest possibility, as you can imagine, is enough to keep gold hunters excited... it does beg the question though, how did Isyllia get it, she is not its keeper?'

Ember shrugged. 'We will be able to confirm more once Isyllia wakes, but for now we need to find the other weapons... Can you work on translating the rest of the texts?'

Tom's eyes lit up with controlled excitement, 'Of course! I will prepare quarters for you... I must ask Em ... Can I see it?' His eyes darted downward like a guilty dog, nervous, but too curious not to ask.

Ember frowned.

'Please... I know I cannot touch it...I just ...you know how much this-'

'All right!' Ember frowned harder

Thomas puffed himself up, thrusting a finger forward in preparation, then stopping short when he realised the answer he had received, was different to the answer he had been expecting, 'Oh... well... Thank you, *thank* you! ... It's got to be safer in here than on your horse!'

Ember raised an eyebrow at his friend.

'What? You leave everything on your horse!' He said, covering the flush of red that spread across his face with a hand.

Ember shook his head, but the ghost of a smile sat on his lips. 'I can feel danger Thomas, it's safe!'

'Still ...'

'They need to be stabled anyway!' Ember turned to leave, poking his head into the room he left Isyllia on the way out, she had not moved. A seed of worry began to grow in his stomach again, *what if she doesn't wake up?* 'No' he forced the thought out of his head, *she will wake up, she just needs rest.* He walked outside and stroked the two disgruntled horses on the nose, Niimorea using the moment to voice her dissatisfaction at being tied to Perrin, by swinging in and biting him, her teeth baring for his arm. Ember however, sensed the horse's intention, and darted neatly out the way. 'Easy girl, you'll get food now!' Niimorea snorted and allowed Ember to steer them away toward the humble stable located at the side of the property. Most residents could not afford to keep their own horses, much less a stable. However, Lewis was a cautious man, and as most of their business was international, he took it upon himself to deliver the stock, and in the long run, it was easier to have your own transport, or so he had said. Tom believed it was more out of a love of the open air, like him, Lewis craved more from life. And he found that something, on the distant roads of the world. Ember settled the horses into their own pens, removing the bags once he was satisfied, they had enough to eat, and Niimorea could not nose in for more food, she had a worrying appetite. He walked back through the house, and into the room, still nothing. It was good in any case, when Isyllia did wake, she would want fresh clothes. She had come a way since he first met her in Illingdale, she was committed to leaving that life behind her, but he found himself shaking his head at her constant need to change clothes. Women!

Ember deposited the bags on the floor next to the sleeping princess, opening one of them and removing the box he had stowed there. He felt the energy pulse within. He had not had time to concentrate on it in the panic, but now that he had it in front of him, he considered it for a moment. It throbbed, seductive and slow, calling to him, yet not. He stood, ignoring its strange call, and walked back into the room where Tom was waiting. He had already started working on translating the journal. Ember placed the box on the desk in front of his strange friend.

Tom shut the book, his eyes now on the box. He extended a hand, slow and unsteady, but determined toward the lid, opening it with trembling fingers like it was made of delicate glass. 'This can't be it! It's just a quill!'

Ember walked around to where Tom stood, looking in the box. The bristles of the feather shimmered and glowed. Ember could feel it calling to him, this time stronger. The urge to stroke it, to hold it was strong, but he resisted. 'Not like any quill I have ever seen, what do you see?' Ember was curious.

'I just see a plain white feather quill, though I know better than to try and touch it.'

'Interesting.'

'Why, what do you see?'

'Not a plain white feather!' He decided to spare his friend the details, its selectiveness would be disappointing enough.

'Well at least we now know those rumours are true, only the chosen can see them for what they really are.'

'It would seem so.' Ember closed the lid again, eager to be away from the captivating drumming. 'I will make myself useful while we are here, you still got a shed?'

Tom looked grateful, 'Yes, we have some mending that could be done, it's all piled in a corner, was going to see the smith up the road, just never found the time.'

'No need, I'll take care of it.'

'What do you want me to do with the weapon?'

'Just make sure it is out of sight. I will know if someone finds it.'

'Right!'

'Oh, and Tom, let me know if she wakes?'

He nodded, then smiled.

Ember left the room, seeing himself to the shed on the back of their property which was located out the back of the main business building. A few short years ago Tom had assembled a basic smithing shed, with the desire to work on his own projects, but soon found although he had the aptitude for inventions, he did not have the necessary skill of a blacksmith. And so, the shed sat now unused and dusty. Ember surveyed the wreck around him. It would be a task to get it into order, but he was grateful for the distraction. Starting off, he threw aside junk, bits and pieces of half-finished and discarded projects that Thomas had tried and failed at. Thomas had a bad habit of discarding things that didn't work out, dumping them in one designated pile and then forgetting them forever. Undeterred, Ember continued, clearing the work benches so he could lay out work tools in a neat line. Then, once he was satisfied it was ready, he decided he should get the forge lit. He scouted around for some wood, not having to look far, and removed a few logs from a large pile at the other side of the yard. For some time, he stared into the flames, beginning at last to feel a sense of comfort.

Once the forge was hot enough, he got to his feet and walked to the pile of bits and pieces he had not moved. Broken goblets, horseshoes and various other household mending lay about gathering dust. He picked up some of the items and took them over to start work, heating them so the damage could be worked out. Once again that familiar clang of hammer on metal rang into his ears, and with each strike he felt the frustration and anger drain from his body. Ember knew Isyllia had faced a lot of changes to her life in a short time, and a part of him felt sorry for her. There was just something about her that drove him mad, aside from the constant recklessness which drove him to utter disdain. So much rested on her shoulders, yet she still ran into the temple and risked their lives. Ember began to feel his anger rise again, so he took a deep breath deciding to focus on the task at hand. He would deal with Isyllia when she woke, if, she woke.

CHAPTER TEN

William, Illingdale Castle.

'It's time William.' Adella stood in the doorway, her eyes were red from crying and she was dressed in her usual navy blue. She leant against the doorframe and waited.

William exhaled long and hard through his nose, his mouth drawn tight. 'Have you.' He paused, almost unable to finish the sentence, 'Have you cleansed mother?' How could she be gone? How could she have left him alone? He thrust his fist into the mirror, leaving nothing but an angry red mark on his hand.

'I have.' Adella said, not commenting further, that she was not one for chit-chat, and he was thankful for once.

'Fine.' William swept from the room, not waiting for the procession, or his aunt. He instead walked straight to the temple.

271

In normal circumstances, a more private ceremony would be conducted for nobility, but as Balor had been executed as a traitor, his Honour-Giving was scheduled to be public. So, the citizens could be reminded, what happened to law breakers, no matter their station. It was Adella who had decided they should be held together. William had offered little. He arrived at the temple early, sitting at the head of the dais, next to the priest. People began to file in, some glared, and others shouting lewd words at the surviving Mallory. Adella filed in some time later, his parents behind her. She glanced up at William, a mixed expression of sadness and annoyance, he did not care. He looked off to the side, refusing to acknowledge her, or the procession. It was not until the priest stood that he accepted he must pay attention, standing to take the torch. William approached the shrouded figure of his mother first. 'I have washed you and clad you with honour. May you now face the darkness with the love of your kin, the strength of your people, and the wisdom of your years.' He lit shroud, and waited as the familiar words were chanted, '*Diieŋ ŋedaŋ ee tasa, diieŋ ŋedaŋ pospuŋ.*' He waited a few minutes, staring into the flames as they consumed his whole world. The priest nudged him, and he walked over to his father. Balor was placed next to his wife, but he wore no shroud. As a traitor guilty of the worst possible offence, he was to be burned without a shroud, so he would face his immortal destruction with his eyes open. There would be no comfort, no words chanted for him. William looked at his father's lifeless body. So many times, they had fought, so many times he had lectured William on duty, for it to end this way. William's lip curled.

'My lord Mallory, would you say the words?' The priest was urging him on again.

William snapped into focus, stowing the bitterness for another day, one in which a glass of whisky accompanied him. 'On this day, you leave us a traitor. You have not been given honour, and you will now face your immortal destruction alone, with your eyes open, so that you may feel the pain you have caused your people.' William lit the shroud, but this time there was no mournful chanting, instead he was forced to listen to the feasting of flame on flesh, until it turned his stomach. William threw the torch on what was left of his father and fled the temple. He needed air, peace. A space he could think and be alone. Somewhere he couldn't hear her voice, or feel the heat of the fire, as it stole his life from him. He sighed, his glance resting on a sign swinging in the distance, The Dale. A smile began to creep onto his face and his feet itched to start without him, *'That will do, that will do fine.'*

Some hours later, Adella found him, drunk and resting on a bottle at the bar. William heard her sigh without needing to turn around, his mother made the same sound. 'What do you want?' His eyes narrowed and his shoulders clenched, sending a pang down his injured arm. Adella sat beside him. 'Got any left?'

The question snapped him into focus, as much as he could focus. 'You drink? I have never seen you drink!'

Adella nodded, producing a small bottle, and downing the contents, then signalling the barman for another glass. 'Today, I do.' She held it up, 'To loss.' She said, not waiting for William to chink and downing the contents.

William scoffed. 'What was in the bottle?'

Adella looked at the bar, turning the empty glass over in her hand, 'Bliss. Blackness, numbness.'

William considered it for a moment, knowing he ought to put it out of his mind, then he pictured her face. 'Got any more?'

Adella smiled, 'I do today.'

◁ ✻ ○ ✳

Isyllia, O'Brien Residence, New Eddinsford.

Consciousness meandered its way back to Isyllia, in no particular hurry. Dappled light filtered in through her closed lids, and a feeling of comfort beneath her confused the process. For a moment, she thought again that it had all been a dream. Any minute her maids would burst in laden with dresses and ribbons, all eager to have their offer for the day picked. Then William would come with his morning check in ... he always stole her cakes, she would have to hide them this morning, he could get his own. William. Another memory, less pleasant than the last, a look of shock and some blood. Then she remembered. William was dead. Sitting up she nursed her pounding head for a moment, then opened her eyes, beginning to remember. She had been in Eddinsford outside a temple when everything had gone black. But now, she was in a strange room, surrounded by various papers, and a portrait of a woman she did not know. Isyllia stood, feeling dizzy for a moment and holding onto the post of the bed for support, then she felt her way out of the room and tried to make sense of where she was, and why she was alone? She did not have to wander long, stumbling across a crack of light from the room with the door ajar, a young red-haired man sitting in deep concentration on a small book. Isyllia cleared her throat, and swung the creaky door open, causing the man to bump his head on a strange contraption above him, 'My word, you're awake!' He said, rubbing the sore.

'Indeed, but I do not know where I am, or the location of the ma ... My husband?' Saying the word made her insides heat up like a burst of unexpected sunshine.

'Right, yes!' He stepped forward and offered his hand. 'Thomas O'Brien, I am a friend of Ember's.'

Isyllia looked at his hand, confused.

'You're supposed to shake it.'

'Why would I shake it?'

'Never mind. Please, sit!' He motioned to a chair behind him.

Isyllia looked behind her and sat, letting the muscles in her body droop into the chair despite her years of deportment training. 'A friend you say?'

'Yes.'

Isyllia looked around the room, captivated by the odd array of trinkets and contraptions whirring and whizzing. Some just lay still, the mystery in their silence. 'What is this place?'

'My workshop. I am a scholar and an inventor... How are you feeling, are you hungry?' He sat in the chair opposite, a worried expression on his face. Thomas had pale skin, and his face was decorated with freckles. He was not tall, though nor was he short, and he wore various versions of blue and grey. And although neat, his idea of style would have been better appreciated some years ago. Isyllia thought for a moment, unsure whether to continue with the false name, and in the end deciding it better to be safe. 'First I need to know where Samuel is?'

Thomas stood straight, cocking his head to the side like a dog with a look of amusement, 'Samuel. That's a new one... It's ok, you can relax. Ember is out back working... He has been for hours, though ... I would not interrupt him yet; I went out a little earlier and… he was a little frustrated still.' He said, a pained look creasing his nose.

'He's always angry!' She said, rolling her eyes. It was one of the things that always embittered her. 'And he always frowns!' She continued.

Thomas' mouth jerked into a smile, then just as quickly returned to its serious expression. 'He carries a lot of weight on his shoulders … you are right though; he does frown too much.'

There was silence for a moment, Isyllia's mouth quirked despite herself.

'Isyllia I know you don't know me, and it is not my place, but I *am* sorry about your father. I can see you are suffering, and I can only imagine what you must have gone through to get here. But I promise, you are safe here and you don't have to face it alone anymore. I am a friend if you need one.'

Isyllia felt her eyes moisten. Travelling with Ember she had become used to his coldness and had begun to lock her feelings away, so it was a surprise to find the warmth and the kindness so freely offered by this kind stranger. 'Thank you. I have not had time to mourn them, but then, I suspect that will take a lifetime.'

'Them?'

'My friend was killed on the road here.' The air grew colder as the words left her mouth, and she shivered into herself, it was hard not to think about him in Adella's clutches.

'Right, yes, I believe Ember mentioned you were betrayed… what happened, would it help to talk?' His voice was gentle and patient.

'His name was William; he was my best friend.' The realisation that she would never see him again hit her and tears filled her eyes. 'I have no memories without him, not even one. And the last thing he saw was me using my power to save Ember.' Fresh tears streamed down her face. 'The last thing he saw was a Malagara who had lied to him for too long.'

Tom was silent for a moment, running one hand through his scruffy short red hair. 'Learning what you are cannot have been easy for you, but I promise you, it is not all darkness. You are called chosen because when Abashiina looked down on the world of man and woman, of all the people that are and ever could be, she chose you to be her champion. You are not an abomination, you are special.'

'I want to believe that, but all I have done is make mistakes. It's hard to entertain any other alternative at this point.'

'Ember believes, so why can't you?'

Isyllia stood, choosing to ignore the question. 'I must see Ember.'

Tom rose, 'No, you sit. I will let him know you are awake, and then I will check supper, I always make extra.' He stood to leave but was stopped by footsteps behind him, heavy and determined, Ember was already there.

Isyllia took a deep breath as he stepped forward, she was nervous. Would he still be angry?

For a moment he stood, his chest heaving as if he had been running and covered from head to toe in black dirt from hours of working. No doubt sensing the tension, he broke the moment by sweeping his rebellious hair behind his ears and sitting in the chair Thomas had just vacated. 'How are you feeling?'

'I have a headache but apart from that I am fine.'

'We need to talk!' He turned and directed the statement at Thomas.

Isyllia watched as Thomas nodded back into his study. It was a small house with a few basic rooms, which left Isyllia wondering if he would be able to hear anyway but decided not to mention the thought. Ember turned back and stared at the floor, measuring his words.

'I am glad you are safe.' A strand of hair freed itself and fell back to the front of his face.

'Thank you.' She said, wiping her cheek to hide her crying.

He didn't notice. Ember did not look up, refusing to make eye contact with her. 'Why didn't you listen? Again! I couldn't get to you; I couldn't do anything.' He said, now looking up. They locked eyes, and his tone shifted. For a moment, she could see it written on his face, the helplessness. It captured his blue eyes like fireworks, then all at once disappeared back down to the place he locked all his emotions, except the tenderness in his voice that lingered on leaving her frozen under his gaze. 'You left me so powerless.'

She swallowed the urge to cry again. 'I'm so sorry.'

There was silence for a moment.

'Tell me what happened, I need to know what you saw!' Ember shifted forward and moved his focus to the floor again, regaining his control.

'I met Odriid!'

'Odriid!' Thomas had snuck back into the room, he leant against the doorframe and eyed Ember speculatively, his arms crossed in front of him. but it was Isyllia that he addressed. 'Did he speak?' Thomas continued, almost thinking out loud 'How is he alive?'

Ember half turned in his chair, raising his eyebrows, 'Alive?'

Thomas shrugged. 'Just a question.'

CHAPTER TEN

'He was a spirit; he was wise and kind. It's strange, he was old, but I could feel a strong energy pulsating from him. He was guarding a weapon. He said it was not meant for me, but I was worthy to pass it onto the chosen of Nemethiiniia, when he was ready to find us.'

Thomas and Ember exchanged a glance, but it was Ember who spoke first, 'He? But I have felt nothing!'

Isyllia shrugged. 'I don't know, I asked who, but he would not tell me anything else. Only that he would find us.'

'You don't think…' Thomas broke off, lost in thought.

Ember weighed the unfinished question, 'Why would he hide that information if it was?'

Thomas nodded. 'Agreed, it was a long shot.'

'Who?' Isyllia tried to ignore her frustration and instead channelled it down to her dress, taking offence in its innocent folds. She hated being ignored.

'Luron Dale.' Ember said.

Isyllia's eyes widened, the dress and its villainous folds forgotten, 'Luron Dale… Wouldn't he be two thousand years old by now? That's not possible!'

Thomas shrugged, 'The chosen don't age… or at least that's what history says, so it is possible, even if unlikely.'

They were silent for a moment. Isyllia's mind had gone blank; she knew Ember had mentioned that the chosen age, differently, as he had put it. But living for thousands of years, did she want that? Did she even have a choice?

'Did he say anything else?' Thomas had sat down now, his arms crossed in concentration.

'Just that I had my own trials to face.'

'He didn't say what they were?' Thomas asked, curious.

'No. But, if what I faced in Eddinsford was any indicator, it is not going to be easy.' Isyllia stood and walked over to the window, she knew they would ask, so decided to relay the events, best to get it over with. 'I saw a girl, she told me she was hurt, so I followed her.' She glanced at Ember again, guilt exercising its cue to rise from the depths of her stomach. 'I thought she had gotten lost... but when I got to the church everything started to change, the girl was covered in blood, and she said I didn't save her. I heard battle sounds coming from outside, I thought it was Ember, and I ran to find him, but he was gone... It was like I was in Eddinsford for the great battle, men lay dying all around me, calling for me, begging me to save them, but I couldn't do anything. I held a dying man's hand, I told him it would be over soon, but I could not help him. Women cried for their sons and husbands, I could feel their pain, all their pain. I kept following the girl, I ignored them all... I figured she had to be the source somehow.' Tears started to fall. She returned to sit on the chair, there was no point in avoiding their gazes. 'The girl ran into the castle, to the throne room where the doors were barred.' They fell heavier now, 'Some soldiers seized her and dragged her in... They murdered the king and raped the mother in front of the girl, and then they stabbed the girl in the chest. She begged me to save her, but I couldn't do anything, she wasn't real, it wasn't real... I felt it as they sliced my neck, but there was no blood, I didn't die.' The words were said with bitterness, 'My people did that. Those soldiers were my men. I murdered that little girl... I was taught about the great battle; minstrels visit the palace and sing of our great victory. But I never knew. I never knew the truth.'

Ember sat stock still; a mixed expression arrested his face.

Thomas took her hand and stroked it, 'I know you feel guilty, and maybe your people were responsible, but the important thing is it's in the past. Odriid said you had your own trials to face, I don't know what the gods have planned for you.' He glanced at Ember for a moment, then back to Isyllia, his own thoughts unreadable. 'But they chose you for a reason. You have a difficult task ahead of you.' He stopped for a moment. 'It's like the old proverb; don't live in the shadow of ghosts, you will only become one.'

Isyllia nodded, drying her eyes, 'You are right. There is nothing I can do for those people. But there are people out there who need me now, and I need to know how to help them.'

Thomas shot out of his chair like it had caught fire, clapping his hands together, 'I for one cannot think on an empty stomach, I prepared far too much broth, first we eat, and then we come up with a plan.' Thomas held out his hand, 'This way if you please, my lady!'

Isyllia smiled at his lively gesture of chivalry, taking his hand and following him into the kitchen. Ember followed behind at a distance, deep thoughts still on his face.

The broth was made of fish, thick and soupy with carrots, potatoes and various spices, none of which matched the food they were decorating. Isyllia felt her stomach churn at the smell, Eddinsford were famed for their cuisine of fish, being an ocean city, and she hated fish. If this were the castle, she could have ordered it taken away, and fired the cook. But it was not, and so she found herself sitting and complimenting him on his efforts, to which Thomas beamed. Each spoonful satisfied her hunger, though threatening to do so for a short time before re-visiting the world. But a life at court teaches you one thing above all else, how to lie.

She reached the bottom, refusing a second bowl and resisting the urge to whoop for joy.

Thomas set his spoon and bowl aside, a happy smile on his face. 'So, one of the artefacts is safe, Gelraen is now in power of Illingdale, this we know... but what about the other chosen?'

Ember threw his spoon down also with a clank, 'Luron was never found. It is said he ventured to the Isle of Forgotten to mentor the surviving Malagara children, but like the others he went mad and when Odriid travelled to the Isle to find his friend, he instead found his weapon. At this point it is safe to assume he died.'

'But you never felt his replacement?' Thomas asked, his eyebrows furrowed in concentration, and one hand bawled in front of his mouth to increase the posture's effectiveness.

Ember shook his head, 'Nothing. Which is strange since, Odriid gives the strong impression that the fourth is among us somewhere.'

'Isyllia was confused. 'Wait you … felt us?'

Ember nodded, 'It is my job to guide and protect the chosen. As such, when your powers came, I was aware. At first, I didn't know it was you, but I was drawn to where you were, it was the same with Gelraen. But I have never felt anything for the Chosen of Nemethiiniia.'

'But you are chosen too?' Isyllia asked, squinting hard against the confusion. It was more complicated than it ought to be.

'Yes, though each of us has a role. Gelraen's role is to rally people, give them strength and courage. Luron's role was to give the people heart, to heal the broken. My role is to see, to protect, and to know.' Ember said, looking anywhere but her direction.

Isyllia tapped her foot, annoyed, but deciding there was no point in mentioning his rudeness. Where would she start? 'And what is my role?'

'You, are the weapon!' Thomas said, his face draining of the little colour it contained in the first place.

Isyllia paled alongside him. Would she ever get used to the idea of fighting? Weapon or no weapon.

'Then there are your actual weapons!' Thomas pointed to the next room.

'Have you found anything about Abashiina's Stone?' Ember sat back in his chair.

'I have my suspicions, but I need to translate the journal more, see what Odriid says specifically. It is hard because some of the pages are worn, it could take some time to make it all out.'

Ember nodded, 'I think for now it is best we lay low anyway, until we know more about what is going on in any case.'

'But what about the Malagara? Shouldn't we do something about them? What if they attack Mespar?' Isyllia hated the thought of waiting when she didn't know what she was waiting for, 'Randal could have learned something new?'

Ember frowned. 'By now Gelraen knows we made it to the Duchy of Godswall, Randal will be as much a fugitive as we are. I doubt he will be able to offer us any further help.'

Isyllia paled, she had not considered she might be putting him in danger.

'He is an intelligent man, he will be fine... and the Malagara, there is not much we can do until we know more. We need to know why they are leaving the Isle.'

Thomas pointed a finger in the air, 'And might I interject, reckless? We Need to deal with the situation appropriately... In any case, while you are here, it would be wise to continue using your other identities; I will draw up some official documents. Just in case.'

Ember frowned at Thomas, confused.

Thomas stood to clear the bowls, 'When Isyllia woke she asked to see her husband, Samuel.'

Ember nodded to Isyllia, 'Well done.'

She felt herself blush.

'I will use the name Samuel. Isyllia will be called Marelle.'

Thomas nodded; his lips pursed in concentration. 'Good. And you have travelled here looking to expand your business into our markets. I will say we are considering a partnership ... but there is one more thing. Ember, she should see the letter.'

Ember sighed, considering, and then nodded. 'You're right.'

'What letter?' Isyllia was struggling to keep up but waited as Thomas moved from the room to retrieve the letter. It was a moment and he was back, handing her a slip of paper then retreated to sit back on his chair frowning. She had not known Thomas long, but unlike Ember, she could tell frowning wasn't something he did often, this could not be good news. She read. A numb cold spread through her body, declared Malagara, by her own country. She resisted the urge to screw up the letter and toss it in the fireplace. 'This is, Adella's work.'

'It is troubling, yes. As loathsome as her reputation can be, it is strange that she would abandon her own family.' Thomas took the letter and set it aside, the frown still persisting.

'Is there any friction between Mespar and Illingdale?' The question was directed at Isyllia.

She turned to face Ember, 'No, nothing out of the ordinary anyway, politically they have reported some strain with crops and requested we send more, father was angry but had planned to comply... nothing that could spark them to retaliate and kill the king, and even if they had thought about it, what would that gain them? ... Is it not possible Gelraen just wanted the power for himself?'

The two men looked at each other but it was Ember who replied. 'Gelraen is not a stupid man, but what he is doing is reckless. Pretending for a moment he was behind the assassination of the king and, Balor was framed. Gelraen has gained the throne, yes. From what I understand though, he stood to gain that anyway. Murdering the king would have put that in jeopardy if anything. Now he has recruited, Adella to his side, declared you Malagara based on no real evidence, what is to stop you walking back into the country and ordering him arrested? You are the rightful heir to the throne, and they don't have any proof of your condition besides the word of a spy! … His actions are desperate, no there is something else going on. And if, Adella is half as resourceful as you say…' Ember shook his head.

'… It is likely she has found something out too.' She finished.

Ember nodded 'Exactly.'

Thomas leaned forward in his chair, drumming his fingers on the table, 'Could he still be looking for the bow? He has already shown a nonchalance in slaying royalty. Having the throne behind him would grant exponentially more resources, if there is something going on, he is as helpless as you are without his weapon.'

A thought struck Isyllia, 'Could he be reacting to the same thing?'

Ember nodded. 'It makes more sense. Randal receives all the official reports, but there must be something the guards are hiding or missing. We need to know more.'

Thomas' eyes widened. 'Mr Fennly!' He shot out of his chair, almost sending half the room flying with him, and then wandered out without another word.

Ember looked confused. 'Who?'

Thomas poked his head back in, bursting with sudden excitement. 'Follow!'

Ember and Isyllia exchanged a look, each as perplexed as the other but each eager to know the cause of the sudden enthusiasm in their friend.

The room Thomas led them into was smaller than his study, she guessed it was his bedroom, certainly it was just as messy as his study. Isyllia blushed, she had never been into another man's bedroom, for a moment she stood behind the door frame, craning her head through and watching as Thomas walked to the window and bent down to retrieve something. He knelt there for a moment cooing and talking softly to something, then he stood, cradling a strange creature in his arms.

'A Fennel? How is a Fennel going to help us?' Ember brushed his hair back behind his ears and shook his head.

'What is a Fennel?' Isyllia asked, no less confused, 'It looks like a fat feathered rat with no tail!'

Thomas smiled down at the jittery little creature flipping in his arms, its fluffy brown and white feathers shining in the catches of light from the window, 'Yes I guess he does have the shape of a rat!'

The creature stopped and squeaked indignantly at Thomas, then made to jump off back to its cosy spot in the light of the window. 'Now Now!' Thomas tried to grab the disgruntled creature, but Mr Fennly would have none of it, 'Ouch!' He bit Thomas hard on the finger, then disappeared back into the windowsill. 'That was an overreaction. I expect you to think about how we behave around guests.'

Isyllia raised her eyebrows, 'You're talking to a rat?'

Thomas winced, then began to suck his finger. 'He is not a rat, come.' He motioned for them to leave the room, closing the door behind them. 'He is a little highly strung.'

'How did you catch a Fennel?' Ember half smiled, amused by the situation.

They walked back to the sitting room. Thomas fell into his chair, 'I didn't exactly catch him. I was in living woods, and came across an abandoned nest. He was a runt, sickly, he just came to me, so I took him home.'

'You still haven't explained what he is, if he is not a rat.'

'He is a Fennel. They are incredibly intelligent creatures, and although they lack the powers of speech, but never get caught short thinking they don't understand you. Over time I have trained him to follow instructions. He is how I infiltrate places for information. Most people don't notice him, and the few who do, would never suspect him of anything but a common rodent. It's perfect.'

'The Mayor's office Birder is not going to have reports from Mespar, at best Clydesdale in Tinderford may have had something come through, but I doubt it. How are you going to get him all the way to Antonio's Birder? He can't run all the way to the Isle of the Forgotten!'

'Would not reports like that be delivered straight to the crown. In Illingdale the Wentworth Birder are not allowed to keep copies.'

Ember shook his head, 'Mespar makes a point of doing things differently, and this concerns the Isle of the Forgotten. The Forgotten guards are instructed to take no chances, on anything.'

'You have been there?' Isyllia found herself sitting forward, intent on his answer.

He shook his head again, 'To Mespar, yes. To the Isle, no. But I was introduced to the guard captain, and he said as much.'

'What has your father told you about the arrangement between Mespar and Illingdale?' Thomas had stopped sucking his finger, but he continued to hold it out at an odd angle. Like it belonged to someone else.

'The arrangement was made hundreds of years ago, they disagreed on Malagara being executed so Mespar sent them to the Isle. We send them supplies in exchange for them managing the situation. Any abnormal activity is supposed to be reported directly to the crown, and from Mespar, to us. Reports are taken by Owl and delivered right to the hand of the king himself. Wentworth is not allowed to see the contents. Father never shared anything with me, he had intended Gelraen to manage those affairs.'

Ember cut in, 'Whether Illingdale received anything or not, that source is a dead end. We have no more allies in the city, and I would put no one at risk.'

'It is as I said, I have an idea! but it is … untested.' Thomas rose to his feet again, 'Wait here.'

Isyllia appreciated any time to sit. The cascade of events tumbling one into the other gave her the feeling like she had to be racing in all directions, and she had no idea where to even look anymore. If she could just find a moment to just rest, to mourn. She had never wanted to be Queen, but she had never seen her life any other way either. Once again, the return of Thomas interrupted her thoughts, he carried a long but small box, another invention? She did not have to wait long for an answer. He knelt on the floor and removed the lid, revealing a tiny set of wings and harness, made from a metal she had never seen.

'I had these made in secrecy. I intended to teach Mr Fennly how to fly.'

'You had someone else smith these?' The hurt on Ember's face was disarming.

Thomas blushed, 'Sorry friend, I could not risk anyone else intercepting the plans, and I knew you had to stay put in Docktown.'

'Sure.' Ember crossed his arms and sat back in his chair, not at all trying to hide his annoyance.

'You are going to attach these to the ra- Fennel?' She corrected; she would need to watch that.

'Teaching Mr Fennly to fly will extend my reach. If I can cover all the main points, nothing will pass my notice.'

'What is it made from? I have never seen this kind of metal!' Thomas took the wings out of their box. It did not take long for the metal to change from a resolute brown to a smoky green, not unlike the wall behind them. It was camouflaging.

'I would think not, Chambrite is Illegal in Illingdale, not to mention incredibly rare.'

CHAPTER TEN

'How did you find it?' Ember's tone piqued her interest against her better judgement, and she gave into the impulse to look over and risk his glance. Some of the indignation still sat on his face, but interest had begun to creep back in, no doubt despite his better efforts. Isyllia didn't know Ember well, but she was convinced he found reasons to be grumpy at times.

'I got lucky.'

Ember didn't buy that and continued to cross his arms, mysteries one of the many things on his long list of dislikes, but if Thomas had planned to elaborate, he did not.

'It will take a couple of weeks to teach him the basics, can you lie low until then?'

'I see no other way.' The idea of sitting around this tiny house, however kind its owner be, burned at her patience like tiny fire ants marching up and down her body in protest. It would be a long two weeks indeed. 'Two weeks it is.'

CHAPTER ELEVEN

Isyllia, O'Brien Residence, New Eddinsford.

'What are you making now?' Isyllia poked her index finger at the strange item with trepidation, like it could jump to life at any moment, and then wrinkled her nose deciding it best to take a step back to be sure.

Ember shook his head, amused by her distaste. 'Just things people need.'

'What people?' Isyllia looked around, half expecting people to pop out from the corners.

'Those people.' He nodded outside and then continued to hammer. At first, he had set himself to completing the piles of repairs Thomas had tossed aside in frustration. But once that was done, Ember had begun crafting his own objects from the scraps. Household trinkets and wares were scattered in all available spaces, ready to be sold in the shop. She believed it was his way of contributing, and although Thomas did not say anything, she had guessed that their presence put strain on his meagre income, so doing something to help felt good, strange as that prospect still was to her. Isyllia had set herself the one task she knew she had the best chance of doing with some variety of success, visiting the markets. She was determined to introduce something other than fish into their diet, cooking skills or none. She thus tried to recreate some of the dishes she was herself fond of, with moderate victory on some occasions, but almost anything at all was better than fish. 'As you wish. I am going to the markets later; would you like to join me?'

Ember stopped hammering, a wide-eyed look of surprise on his face, 'What for?'

Isyllia folded her arms, 'It might actually do you some good to leave this shed on occasion you know, other than to sleep.'

He shrugged, then returned to his hammering, 'I like the shed.'

She eyed the room with distaste, 'Yes I gathered that. Look, people have noticed us here, don't you think it would do some credit to our cover story if we were seen out together occasionally, doing normal things?'

Ember brushed the hair that clung to his brow aside then deposited the hammer on the bench this time. 'You're not going to drop this are you?' He was matter of fact.

Isyllia beamed, it was the first sign she knew she had won. 'No.'

'I'll need to wash.' He said.

'Fine.' She chirped, her smile widening.

Ember brushed the soot off his hands, the little difference it made, then nodded to the basket of clothes she was carrying. 'What exactly are you doing with those?' He asked, giving the impression it was less a question, his body as rigid as one of the objects he had crafted.

Isyllia ignored his reaction, 'Washing!' She chimed, a little more excited than she otherwise should have been.

'Let me see.' The scepticism on his face was palpable. He walked around his bench and out the shed; stopping in the small outdoor area where Isyllia had set up what she thought was her idea of a laundry yard. A small tub had been set on the floor, along with a larger tub. The larger tub had been half-filled with cold water, and clothes tossed in with no particular theme in mind and left. Ember doubled over in fits of laughter, holding his stomach for breath.

'What's so funny?' She asked, dumping her next basket on the floor, and crossing her arms.

'Let me help you. You are going to need some hot water first, can you light the kitchen fire and boil some water, and I'll fix this.' Isyllia took the smaller bucket and refilled it with water from the larger tub, slopping it again into the house. It took a few minutes to light the fire and then wait for the waiter to boil, so she used the opportunity to grumble under her breath, what did she know about washing clothes!

The steam interrupted her thoughts, heat billowed from the bucket and she gathered her makeshift apron into her hands, ready to collect it off the hook.

'Leave it, I'll get that.' Isyllia had not heard Ember come in, stepping aside as he grabbed for the bucket. 'Right, follow me.'

Isyllia did as he bid, dragging her feet somewhat behind her. Ember poured the hot water back into the larger tub, and then set it down on the ground. In her absence, he gathered a large jagged wooden board and placed it in the larger tub, along with a vial of strange liquid and a soap bar. 'What are all these for?'

'Right, kneel down in front of the board.' He indicated the jagged board sticking out of the now warm water. Isyllia kneeled, folding her dress under her knees as she did; Ember kneeled on the other side. 'Grab one of the garments and rub this on the stains.' He handed her the soap.

Isyllia frowned at the once white shirt and rubbed at the stubborn black stains until she had covered all the areas in a murky white sheen. 'Now what?'

300

'Now, rub it against that board until the stain lifts, and then if needed, add more soap. I have already put some Lye in the water, it will help.'

She considered the process for a moment, 'Like this?' She prodded the shirt down the board with such uncertainty it could have done a more effective job on its own. Not even the soap had lifted.

'Caros save me...' Ember moved behind her, placing his arms over hers, 'Like this.' And dug the shirt into the board, forcing it down and back.

Now Isyllia laughed.

Ember sat back, an amused expression on his face, 'What?'

It took a little bit for the gales of laughter to subside, but Isyllia found her voice again, holding her injured stomach in the process. 'I'm sorry; this is just not something I ever saw myself doing in a million years.'

Ember shook his head, but he was not annoyed, containing a smile to one side of his mouth as he sprung to his feet. 'Clearly not.' Then turned back to his shed.

'You injure me, come here and say that!' She said, containing a smile.

'Not a chance.'

Isyllia grabbed one of the wet shirts, balled it and hurled it in his direction.

The wet projectile made it halfway, its intended victim darting out of the way, then turning to catch the missile with one hand. For a moment, he smirked at the wet item, and then tossed it back, watching as it landed with a noisy flap against her dress. 'Careful with that.'

Isyllia had made no move to catch the returned item, her wits still on vacation. Ember rolled down his sleeves, and then continued to the shed, leaving her with an impish smile. It was some time until she could hear the rhythmic hammering begin again, leaving her to the task of laundering what was sure to be a year's worth of clothes. Any other time, Isyllia would have grumbled at the mammoth task in front of her, but not today, today she smiled and hummed to herself, revelling in the warm feeling that spread through her body. Today was a good day.

◁✳○✳

William, The Dale, City of Illingdale.

'That looks like it hurts?'

William took another swig from his dwindling whisky bottle, and then glanced in the woman's general direction, unsure if there were in fact two of her. He ignored a slight twinge from his bandaged shoulder, the alcohol had dulled the pain. 'Good thing I have my medicine then.' He finished the rest of the liquid then tossed the bottle aside.

The woman laughed, 'I could think of something a little more effective, if, you are interested?' She ran a finger down his arm, stopping on his inner thigh. 'Unless of course, there is someone else?'

William studied the woman's hand for a moment, a strong urge in him wanted to take the oblivion she offered. 'Another time.' He turned back to the bar, knowing that if he kept looking at the girl, he might change his mind. In truth, the pain troubled him little. But the demons swimming through his mind, replaying that moment over and over, and the dreadful secret Isyllia had hidden for so long still haunted him. So, he did his absolute best to deprive the Inn of as much whisky as possible. It was the only thing that helped.

The creek of the door opening interrupted his thoughts. It was Adella, and she didn't need to look around to spot her nephew; she knew where to find him. She sighed, and then walked over to the bar and sat down next to him. 'How much have you had tonight?'

'Not enough, he hasn't sold out yet.'

'Do you want to talk about it?'

'No, I don't!' William reached into his pocket and dropped more coins onto the bar, 'Another bottle.' The coins rolled in the general direction of the barman, who frowned but could not turn down a sale.

Adella would not be swayed. 'You didn't know she had powers?'

William took a swig from the new bottle, ignoring the glass that sat as clean as the one next to it. 'Want some?'

'No.' She pursed her lips, 'William?'

'What? No, of course I didn't know. Though if you want me to *stop* drinking, this is not the topic I would have picked.'

'I'm sorry Will; I know how much she meant to you.'

He ignored the sympathy, 'Why are you here? If you're not going to drink with me?'

She stared at the bar for a moment, then rifled in a pocket, producing a small stoppered bottle. 'This.'

'I tried that, thanks, Whisky is more effective.'

Her eyes narrowed, 'Take the bottle William.'

He turned back to the bar, 'Take it yourself.'

Adella slammed the tiny bottle on the bar and grabbed the larger whisky, depositing it back down on the opposite side of her, just out of his reach. 'How long do you think the King is going to tolerate your drunken behaviour? If you keep this up, you can forget his offer of clemency! Or is that what you want? ...'

William looked down at his lap.

'Take the fucking tonic and get a grip on yourself, they were my family too.'

He swore, stuffing the bottle into the pocket of his jacket.

'There's a good boy, now, the King wishes to see you, I suggest you straighten yourself up.'

'Tell his majesty I will arrive presently.' He over articulated the words, swinging the empty bottle grandly, and then taking a last swig only to find it was in fact the empty one, tossing it on the floor in disgust.

Adella shook her head and then thrust her stool back, indicating the barman took the whisky he had forgotten about. Then, taking one last look at her broken nephew, she slid out the door again. William had not returned to his family home since his mother had been found dead. Preferring instead to stay in a small lodging he rented on the poorer side of town. His soldier's income did not provide much, but then he did not need much, or nothing he could have anyway.

The walk to the castle took a little longer than he had anticipated. He was drunker than usual and a few times he found himself lost, unable to make out where he was going in the dark. When he did arrive, he stumbled up the main staircase leading to the king's rooms. Judging that was where he would be, and as luck would have it, an unsteady rap at the door later, he found himself faced with the new King's bodyguard, wishing he was a little more sober.

'Enter.' The voice came from deep within the chambers. William nodded to the guard, then walked into the room, acutely aware of each step he took toward the direction the voice had come from. Gelraen sat in an armchair, he did not look up as William approached, for which he was grateful.

'Majesty.' William bowed. 'You requested an audience?'

The new King sat for a moment, his face impassive. 'How are you finding your new lodgings?'

William shrugged. 'They serve their purpose; I do not need much sire.'

'And you still have no desire to return to your family estate?'

'Too many memories, sire.' He clenched his teeth, withholding his grief.

The king nodded. 'Ah, yes.' He was silent for a moment. 'I cannot pretend to understand the motive behind the events unfolding…Isyllia's condemnation was, with reluctance. But as king, I must uphold our laws… sometimes, those with power, are the biggest slaves of all.' He looked up 'Please, sit.'

William moved into the chair, grateful to be off his feet. 'What is your plan sire?' Even as the words left his mouth, a knot of tension began to form in his stomach that had nothing to do with the drink. He knew the penalty for being Malagara was death.

'She must be apprehended. I cannot make allowances because she was royalty, especially because she was royalty, she was to be my wife…'

He swallowed the surge of anger that bubbled up his throat, leaving the little ball of acid to fight heatedly with the knot that sat in his stomach. 'Her deception has shocked us all sire. But she has chosen her path; we that are left behind must carry on and do our duty.'

The king nodded, and William wondered if his words had been for the King, or for himself.

'Tomorrow I will hold court to announce our intentions, but I asked you here tonight, to ensure you are ready.'

'Sire?'

'I want to make good on my promise. Can I still count on your loyalty?'

William swallowed hard, the question weighing on him. The pains of the events were still raw, and he knew, should he say yes, it would be him who would undoubtedly be charged to hunt Isyllia down and bring her to justice. But could he do that? Was he angry enough to see her killed? 'Of course, Majesty. I intend to prove my loyalty to the crown in any way you desire.'

'Good. May I suggest you get some sleep; my guard will see you to a chamber. Court convenes early.'

'Sire' William rose and gave a long bow, desperate to hide the conflicted emotions coursing through his body.

When he left the room, he took a sigh of relief, finding himself tireder than he had been in days, and struggling to keep up with the guard walking in front of him, then waving a bleary dismissal as he stumbled through the door and collapsed onto the bed. For a while, he lay there, fighting sleep with thoughts. Why had she not trusted him with her secret? He could have tried to understand, things could have been different. But she had not. The moment played through his mind like it was yesterday. Isyllia's voice screaming from behind a bush. The soldier had been aiming for Ember's chest, and somehow, she had made the sword grow unnaturally, spearing the man with his own weapon. Isyllia had shown herself to a man she barely knew. And even as the memory of the pain piercing him in the shoulder seemed to reverberate through his body, somehow the recollection that she had not come to his aid, she had left him there to die. That was the worst pain of all. William lay there, more alone than he had ever felt, finally allowing himself to cry from the pain of the illusion of her he had held onto for so long, and finally fell asleep from exhaustion in the small hours of the morning.

He was woken short hours later by an insistent knock at the door. 'Lord Mallory.'

William sat up, placing his palm on the side of his face to hold his throbbing head from falling apart. He had fallen asleep in his clothes, but he was sure the king would be annoyed if he turned up stinking of alcohol. 'Enter, I'm up.'

The servant entered looking harried, his face beetroot red. 'Sir I bring fresh attire and breakfast. I am also advised you are required to attend court in 20 minutes.' He said, throwing the words out faster than he could say them. It was evident he wanted to be elsewhere.

'Fine, I can take care of myself.' William held the door open, his eyes still half closed with sleep, hoping the man would pick up on the hint.

He did, moving from the room without further encouragement.

'Have some hot water sent up.' He said, closing the door before a reply could be heard and turning to the food. His stomach growled in protest; he knew it was a bad idea to eat when his stomach was tender. 'Far worse not to, however.' He sat down and began taking small bites of the bread roll, while sniffing the honey porridge with his nose scrunched up in accusation. He had never been fond of porridge but knew better than to complain and ate the food without further protest. It was hot and the honey was sweet, a pleasant mask to the bland flavour it would otherwise present. Another knock at the door interrupted his eating, a younger servant, carrying a bucket of hot water and washing linen stepped into the room, nervous of spilling the contents.

'Just put it there.' He said, indicating to a free spot in the small room.

The boy placed the bucket and linen down with a heavy thud, remaining bent over the bucket for a moment. Then recovering his composure, he stood and ruffled his shoulders. 'Can I do anything else sir?' He seemed eager.

'Yes, take these, I am finished with them.' He indicated the food, where sat a mostly empty bowl and randomly bitten loaf of bread. The cheese lay untouched.

'Of course, sir.' The boy took his plate and left the room, not quite shutting the door all the way, and then pushing it closed a second time, this time until hearing the click. William set to washing and dressing, aware that he should already have been making his way to the council chambers. His attire was simple, a light blue doublet with golden buttons, no embroidery with simple tan coloured hose. He looked in the small mirror and retied his long blonde hair then shrugged, leaving the room without caring if he returned for the clothes he left behind. He seldom cared about much anymore.

The council chamber was already filled. Low murmurs came from all directions of the room as people chatted, all killing time until the king arrived. They did not have to wait long. It had been no more than five minutes when the guards called for silence. William shifted in his seat, aware his nerves were making him look uncomfortable, but he tried to block out the people that had noticed him.

The king strolled to the throne at the top of the room, staring at the golden chair for a moment, then sitting in the chair to the left. 'Lords of the council. I bring you here today to discuss our future. Many long years, we have been a proud country of victory. We are a people of strength and courage... but today, those values are challenged. Plots against the crown have sought to weaken us, but we will rise against them. Our own Queen has betrayed us, but we will have justice. Today, I present Duke Randal of Godswall for questioning. He has been accused of harbouring our denounced Queen.' Surprised voices filled the room, but the king was patient, waiting for the chatter to die down. 'Duke Randal has presented himself for questioning.' The king signalled to the door guard. Duke Randal walked in accompanied by two guards, but he was not chained. He held his head high, striding to the throne like he was accepting an invitation to a grand ball, bowing before the king. William frowned; he had not expected the Duke to be arrested.

'Duke Randal, welcome back to the city.'

'Thank you, sire.' He said, emphasising the last word with a cordial bow.

Gelraen clenched his teeth, 'Are you aware of the reason you have been asked to the council?'

Randal looked at the floor for a moment, then back at the King. He stood tall, with his hands clasped leisurely behind his back. Any other situation and you would think he was having an afternoon conversation with friends. 'I believe sire, you suspect an allegiance with my denounced niece.'

Gelraen did not however share his candour. He continued to stare at the Duke, a look of intensity on his face. 'Reports have reached my ears that you harboured her and a stranger. I am sure I need not remind you, harbouring a traitor, especially a Malagara, is a serious crime?'

The Duke moved his head to the side, squinting his eyes to remember, 'I did see my niece sire, but I was unaware at the time that she was Malagara. I was simply advised she was being taken from the city for protection. Her father had just been assassinated.'

'Did you not think to notify the crown?' The question was more of a challenge.

'I beg your forgiveness, but to my knowledge at the time, the crown was sitting in my dining room.'

Gelraen raised his lips to a snigger, 'Who was she travelling with, you mentioned she had company, was there others, how many?

'Just one other, a man.'

'And what was his name?' Gelraen sat forward in his seat.

'I believe he went by Ember sire, a serious young man but at the time I thought him of no consequence.' The Duke squinted. For a moment William thought he saw a flicker of a grin on the man's face.

Gelraen's jaw clenched hard, if William did not know better, he would say Gelraen too had picked up on the moment. 'Can you provide the crown any information on where she was headed?'

The Duke seemed to think again. 'They were searching for something…now what was it…a weapon I believe, but that is all I know, they did not say anything else.' To a casual onlooker, Randal seemed like the man of cooperation, but his eyes never left Gelraen, William could see as plain as day, he was baiting the man.

Gelraen paled until his face could have been mistaken for one of the marble statues that stood either side of the throne. 'What kind of weapon?oes the Malagara intend to strike the city? Speak?' The last order was shouted. He was losing his composure now.

'It was not my place to question my Queen, however in light of events, I would be happy to provide soldiers in aid of her search. Perhaps we can find this, *weapon*, together.' The word was emphasised, and Gelraen did not react to it well.

William shook his tender head, which did not appreciate the gesture at all. Whatever game was being played, Randal was winning, and Gelraen was turning red with anger.

Gelraen slammed his fist down hard on the bench, 'Guards take him to the dungeon. Make him talk.'

The guards hurried forward, not having to wait for Duke Randal, who had already turned and begun to stroll out alongside the guards.

William looked to the king. He sat, watching the man leave with loathing in his eyes. The king knew far more than he was saying.

'First our General, now Duke Randal, how many more allies of the throne will you condemn, sire.' The portly councillor spat the last word with contempt.

Gelraen's glare was as hard as diamond, 'Hold your incessantly wagging tongue, or I might begin to suspect you next.'

The portly councillor sat, but the look in his eye said he was far from done.

Now Gelraen spoke to the entire room. 'The city needs answers. Duke Randal is one of the crown's most trusted allies; and it must be remembered, Balor sent Isyllia to Randal for protection, knowing her condition. I refuse to believe our former Queen told him nothing. He will be questioned, and once he has provided a location, I will send forth a company of soldiers to take care of this situation for the last time.'

William shifted in his chair.

The king somehow seemed to sense it, looking him deep in the eyes. 'Rise, and approach, William Mallory.'

Murmurs began to travel through the room again, William ignored them, focusing his attention ahead.

'Are you aware of the crimes your father committed against the crown?'

'I am sire.'

'Do you stand here today, before the honoured people of Illingdale, before your king, and pledge your loyalty to the crown?'

'I do.'

'Kneel and repeat the oath.'

William kneeled. 'I pledge to serve the crown with honour and courage. I pledge to protect the royal family, as my own, and I pledge love and kindness to the people of the city, as I would my own child.' He hated where the last left his thoughts.

'Good. You may rise. Our law dictates regicide should stain your blood for eternity. But I am offering you a second chance, to prove your loyalty, and earn your family name back, do you accept this honour I offer.'

'Thank you sire, I will not let you down.'

'I believe you. You may be seated.' He turned back to the council, he seemed satisfied. 'Let it be known here today, William Mallory is a knight of Illingdale, and any crime committed against him, will be dealt with harshly. I will now take my leave.' He said, launching from his chair and sweeping from the room with a trail of questions fanning out behind him like Autumn leaves. William remained seated for a moment, trying to digest the turn of events. So, they had reached the Duchy, and she had been with *him*. The thought made him bubble with anger again. He needed another drink.

The rest of the afternoon swam by on a cloud of spirits. William had consumed another half a bottle of whisky when he rattled in his pocket, finding lint. 'Shit!'

'Ad to appen sometiym.' The nearly toothless man sighed on his behalf, forlorn over the potential loss of his best customer.

William scrunched up his nose in anger and stumbled out the bar as steady as his disagreeing legs would carry him. He considered going back and asking for credit, but another lurch in his stomach told him otherwise. Instead, he wavered his way back home, stopping to vomit in the gutter on the way. Drinking on an empty stomach had been a bad idea.

A few minutes later he found his way to the front door. It was not locked, he had nothing worth losing and so pushed his way through furniture until he found the little sofa sitting in the corner of the room. He slumped down, his body already half asleep by the time his eyes were closed, and he stayed that way long into the night. It was the sound of a bottle chinking against the floor that woke him. He looked down, his eyes still hazy, it was the bottle he had been given by Adella some hours earlier. It must have fallen from his pocket, making its escape under a nearby sofa. A strong part of him knew he should throw the bottle away, but he didn't, couldn't. '*It would make the pain go away.*' That is what she had said. And as he held the tiny bottle, the longing for the promised silence began to grow. He had nothing left to lose, nobody to miss him anymore. And without a moment's hesitation, he unstoppered the tiny bottle and threw the cork to the floor with the rest of the rubbish that lay forgotten, drinking the contents dry.

◁ ✳ ○ ✳

Randal, City Jail, Illingdale

'Randal ... Nemethiiniia be merciful.' The portly man stepped through the jail cell door, handing some golden coins to the jailer, who nodded, then left them alone.

The Duke of Godswall tried to stand, he was covered in blood from head to toe and he was weak, stumbling hard back to the floor.

'Don't stand, save your strength.'

He did not argue. 'Under the circumstances, it is good to see you, Imaar.'

The man nodded. 'I had hoped to find you in better spirits.'

'All is well.' Randal reassured.

There was silence for a moment. Imaar turned and looked out the bars, making sure they were alone, then turned back to

318

Randal, concern giving way to urgency. 'I don't believe the charges against Balor, or the Queen. I watched you in that room, you know something…'

Randal was silent for a moment, thinking how to approach the question. He had known Imaar a long time, he was a loyal servant of the royal family, and a secret follower of the old ways. 'Balor tried to warn the king, but he did not listen.'

'Then you think he was set up?' Imaar asked.

Randal was silent again. 'It's complicated.'

Imaar frowned, throwing his hand up in exasperation, 'The king is dead, our Queen is fleeing her own country and a madman sits on the throne, if I am to help you, I need to know something.'

Randal nodded. 'I need to know what you know… about the Queen?'

'Imaar sucked in a breath, thinking, then allowed it all to exhale at once. 'Lord Pennerly is saying she is Malagara, but it makes no sense. How could she hide that all these years, something doesn't add up!'

Randal nodded. 'She is not Malagara, she is chosen.'

Imaar paled. 'Chosen! There have been no Chosen for thousands of years … how do you know this?'

Randal ignored the question. 'I need you to listen. Malagara are escaping the Isle.'

Imaar began to mop sweat off his brow. 'Yes, Balor came to the king about this, he dismissed it, and said the reports were false.'

'They were not.' Randal was frank, knowing they did not have much time.

'Then why has Mespar not done anything?' Imaar asked, frustrated.

'I believe, they do not know about it. I sent Duke Preston to investigate in secret. I wanted to be sure when I approached the king, but I lost contact with him a while ago.'

Imaar shook his head, trying to keep up. 'I don't understand, any reports that come from the Isle, go straight to Mespar, how could they not know?'

Randal nodded. 'Normally, but our spies were able to confirm that nothing had been sent to the citadel.'

Imaar seemed nervous, fidgeting with the collar of his robes. 'Spies? Why do you have spies, do you suspect Mespar is letting them out?'

Randal ignored his discomfort. 'No. Gelraen was behind, Nemellia's death, she carried something he wanted.'

'I thought she went back to Mespar for political reasons?'

Randal scoffed, 'Nemellia was not concerned about her daughter being recognised as Mesparian royalty. That was a cover!'

'Did the king know?'

'No, and, Gelraen did not get what he sought so, since then, I have had spies watching, I knew someday he would try again.'

'And, Balor tried to warn the king?' Imaar finished.

'It is as I said, the King wouldn't listen... Gelraen was making a play for the throne, I couldn't risk him getting to Isyllia, too much is at stake.' Randal held his breath.

Imaar paled as the reality dawned. For a moment he clutched on the cell for support, then finding his composure again, he stood, his face remaining red. 'Nemethiiniia help us. Randal what have you done?'

'Balor did not kill the King, I did' There, it was said.

Imaar lost what little colour remained in his cheeks. 'Does she know?'

'No, she is safe, but she must not know I killed her father, she would never understand.'

Imaar's face turned a slight shade of red. 'I am not sure that *I* understand, Randal.'

Randal knew the jailer could not let them have much more time; he had to get through to Imaar. 'The king was going to announce a betrothal...The chosen are born for a reason Imaar, If Gelraen gets control of Isyllia we will lose any chance of finding out what that reason is, this is bigger than the king, bigger than me, and bigger than Balor, he knew that. He allowed his own life to be sacrificed because he knew that.'

Imaar walked over to the small window hole in the cell. People were walking past in the distance, a reminder to those that ended up there that life, went on without them. 'What do you need me to do?' Imaar seemed resigned.

Randal let out a sigh of relief. 'I have a plan, but I need you to get word to her, tell her I am compromised.' He paused for a minute. 'I also need you to keep an eye on, Gelraen; he will try to lure her into the city to save me. If you are to help her, you must condemn me and stand beside the king. If she does as I expect her to, she will come, and she will need your help.'

'Are you expecting her to attack the city?' Imaar waited; obviously he had not expected this.

'Yes, but not alone.' Randal's tone was set.

'What precisely are you hoping she will do?' Imaar looked worried but did not press. 'You know I cannot send a bird through Wentworth addressed to Isyllia, I'll end up right next to you.'

Randal ignored the question, 'Send it New Eddinsford addressed to, Thomas O'Brien.'

Imaar searched mentally, mouthing the name as if it would help make the man's identity clearer. 'I don't know that name.'

'No, but he's an ally.' Randal relaxed, trying to ignore the niggling feeling that he was forgetting something.

Imaar turned to leave; he looked confused, but willing.

'Wait, one more thing. Make sure you support, Gelraen's policies, you have already risked too much coming here at all.'

Imaar nodded apprehensively. 'I'll be more careful.' Signalling to the jailer to let him out.

Randal leant back against the wall, at least the Queen would be safe. That was all he ever wanted, to fulfill his promise to the gods, to her. Every inch of his body hurt from the hours of torture that still throbbed its way around on self-guided tour. Then it hit him, promise. 'Wait!'

Imaar half turned back, signalling for the jailer to halt.

'There is another letter I need to send.'

CHAPTER TWELVE

Isyllia, O'Brien Residence, New Eddinsford.

The shed stunk of sweat and hot metal, which at first burned her nostrils and often threatened to make her revisit the day's quinine of fish. But as time pressed on, she found herself becoming more accustomed to it, even now as she stood, she barely noticed it anymore, or so she told herself. 'It's been weeks. That thing is still unpredictable.'

'Thomas knows what he is doing.' Ember didn't stop working.

'Sorry, I know you're probably right, he seems dependable, I'm just anxious. I don't like sitting around... I was planning to go to the festival tonight, to take my mind off things.'

Ember stopped hammering abruptly. 'No.' His disapproving blue eyes used all their power to put a swift end to the discussion, but she was not buying it today.

325

'I was not asking for permission. We have taken other identities, Ember, what is the point if I am going to sit in the house all day.' Her eyes narrowed in challenge.

He looked up now, but he did not stop hammering, determined to be just as stubborn. 'I tolerate you visiting the markets, but the festival will be too crowded, too many chances for someone to recognise you.'

'Or, the perfect opportunity to blend in.' Isyllia knew it was a stupid argument. 'I'm going, Ember, if you're so bothered, you'll just have to tag along.' She did not wait for a reply, turning on her heels and storming out. She had agreed to listen to him, to learn from him, but she drew the line at him controlling her life, or what was left of it anyway.

Isyllia barely noticed the day pass anymore as she moved about the house, preparing the evening meals and cleaning from the previous night. She also surprised herself how quickly she picked up the knack for tidying, supposing it must have been from watching her maids' bustle about her rooms, or there were no complaints in any case. But today the sun seemed to stall on the horizon, mocking her. She had spent the last hour staring arms crossed at the table, occasionally glancing moodily out the window. It was all she could do to keep her impatience from bursting out of her skin and running off without her. But even time could not stand still, and eventually twilight began to creep in through the windows, shooing the afternoon sun away for the evening. Isyllia stood and walked into her assigned room for the next week. Thomas had decided it best she stay where she was, since his father was not due back for at least another week. Isyllia was just grateful for the privacy; she looked at the clothes she had laid out carefully to get the wrinkles out, wishing she had paid more attention to how her household staff seemed to do it. Wool and more wool, except one. She picked up the blue dress Ember had left. She knew he would be furious if she wore it, but she was tired of dressing in ugly, itchy wool. Tonight, she just wanted to smile, and feel good about herself, forgetting for a few minutes, that the last few weeks had happened at all, and *he had* chosen it.

Needing no further encouragement, she stripped the clothes she had on and discarded them on the floor, she would deal with them later, and began to put on the dress. It had not been long, but she had begun to feel accustomed to the idea of dressing herself, and even at times considered the idea of another carrying out the task utter stupidity. Happy with her efforts, she walked up to the meagre mirror that sat off to the side of the room and appraised her appearance. The dress fit well, there was a bit of room around her stomach where she had lost some weight, but overall, it looked good. A few weeks ago, she would have turned her nose up at something so simple, but now, the electric blue shimmered happily over the silk, elegant as a coronation gown. Isyllia breathed in the feeling of calm that the simple garment brought, deciding to wear her hair down. It had been a while since she had felt the length of her hair dance freely on her back. She looked out the window, finally the sun had set, and she could hear movement around the house. Heavy footsteps moved casually past her door; Ember had left the shed finally. Remembering she had already left him hot water, she waited until he had disappeared into his room, then opened the door. Deciding to serve the vegetable stew she had been simmering. She pulled out two bowls, knowing the butterflies dancing in her stomach would evaporate her hunger completely so there was no point in serving herself any.

'What is the occasion?'

Isyllia jumped slightly, putting down the ladle and glancing terrifyingly at her dress, making sure she had not spilt any, then turned to Thomas. 'I wanted to see the festival, and I am sick of dressing in wool.'

Thomas chuckled, grabbing a bowel and sitting down to eat. He sniffed the contents. 'No fish?'

'No!' Isyllia reminded herself not to sound too relieved. 'I wanted to try a dish I loved from home, if that is acceptable?'

Thomas took another spoonful, chewing his appraisal and then nodding in and it's nice, but I wish it had fish kind of way, then taking another spoon. 'I had forgotten about the festival … does Ember know your plans for this evening?' He chanced at nonchalance, but Isyllia could hear the scepticism. He knew as well as her how Ember felt about taking unnecessary risks.

She sat down heavily, and exhaled, remembering the conversation they had had earlier, wondering if he was going to insist on accompanying her. 'He was not pleased, but I made it clear I was going. I just need one night where I can smile and dance and be around people who don't know who I am. Two weeks ago, I was Queen, now I am cooking someone's supper. Tonight, I just want to be me, or figure out who that is now.'

Thomas seemed concerned, but sympathetic. 'I understand, I do.' He looked up, 'Ah, there you are, come, sit. Isyllia has made some Illingdalean cuisine.' Thomas Smiled wryly to himself. 'No fish!'

Isyllia stood, shifting from one foot to the other in order to hide her rapid breathing. Ember stood in the doorway, dressed in a simple white shirt and hose, his hair wet and tousled despite being brushed.

'I thought we had been over this?' He said through measured breaths, his voice soft and his eyes never leaving the dress.

'And I have also said; come if you must, but I am going... I'll wear a cloak if it will make you feel better.' She added.

Thomas shifted uncomfortably. 'It's usually just townsfolk there, most of which will be drunk.'

If Thomas thought he was helping, he wasn't. Ember continued to stand in the doorway with his jaw clenched stubbornly.

'Are you going to eat?' Isyllia indicated the bowl on the table, hoping food would put him in a better mood.

'No. I'll wait out front.' He turned and walked off, not saying another word.

Isyllia withheld the impulse to kick her chair and instead excused herself, storming out to her room. She swiped at the cloak, and fastened it around her shoulders angrily, he was determined to ruin everything, she was sure. The cloak covered most of the dress, dampening a considerable amount of her previous excitement. Isyllia knew it was a small thing to get upset about, a dress was no way to base one's identity, but she had lost so much, and it had given her something to look forward to. Deciding to try and make the best of the situation, she sighed, and then moved to face her surly companion who would assuredly be waiting out front as promised. It was on her way back through the bedroom door, she noticed the dagger Ember had given her sitting on the cupboard. Not wishing to antagonise him further, she grabbed it and stuffed it into the hidden pocket in the cloak, conceding compromise was the best approach and walked out the front to where he was waiting, feeling a little brighter within herself.

Music could be heard in the distance, and firelight danced through the night sky in all directions, the promise of its warmth beckoning. 'I am ready.' Ember reluctantly offered his arm, his expression unreadable.

Isyllia stood stunned for a moment, not sure whether to oblige or refuse. Then, remembering they had adopted a cover as man and wife. She took his arm, smiling politely. 'Thank you.' They walked for a time in silence, passing through streets and greeting returning festival goers as they went. It was Isyllia who decided to break the silence. 'Have you come here often, aside from, Thomas? You know your way around here well?'

He was silent for a moment, reflecting on her question. 'I have come here a few times. I used to walk to the beach to clear my head ... Thomas is a good friend.' He went quiet again, not finishing his thoughts aloud.

'I never asked how you met him?'

He shrugged. 'Chance. I was coming back from Mespar to find you; I felt your calling.'

'Calling?'

He nodded 'It's what we call it when the gods call you fourth to your purpose, when you receive your powers... I needed to know the finer points behind Illingdalean law, if I was going to have to live there. Thomas was recommended.'

'He's a kind man, I'm glad you brought us here.'

'He is.'

'How long did you live in Illingdale?'

'Only since your powers awoke.'

'I'm sorry you had to do that, live in hiding when in your own land you are celebrated.'

He looked off into the distance. 'It wasn't so bad; I prefer the quiet.'

She smiled. 'I used to escape, when I couldn't stand it anymore. I used to hide in the rose hedges and some nights I used to fall asleep looking at the stars... the guards would always find me, saying my father was in a panic. He had a horrible temper.' She laughed at the memory. She had always hated his outbursts, but now, somehow, it seemed so pointless.

The music reached them and rounding the last corner Isyllia could see merrymakers dancing to the tunes being played out in the firelight, stalls lined the streets giving away mead and various cuisines of fish to tempt the appetite. The people were happy here, unlike in Illingdale, there was a peace about the city, like this was the place you came to live for now. It did not take long for the smell of fish to waft up her nose, threatening to ruin her revere, but she flared her nostrils in defiance, banishing the smell. Nothing would ruin her evening. She instead returned her attention to the hot mead stalls, imagining the taste for a moment. Ember's face was tense; no doubt he was scanning the area for anyone that recognised her. She ignored it and let go of his arm, allowing the tantalising aroma to carry her over.

'Lovely lass, can I temp ye?'

'Two please.'

The vendor smiled wide with approval. 'Dat's da spirit lass.'

Isyllia chuckled and moved the few steps to where Ember stood rigid and out of place. 'Here.' She handed it over tentatively, unsure what his reaction would be.

Ember frowned at the goblet but took it. 'What did you want to do?' He looked at the dancers, frowning harder, if it were at all possible.

She smiled. 'I used to love to dance, and I thought I wanted to more … shall we just walk.'

Ember motioned for her to lead the way, taking a sip from his Goblet, and then wincing.

'Don't like mead?' She asked slightly amused.

'I prefer Ale.'

'Should I see if they have ale?'

He shook his head. 'No, thank you.' They were silent for a moment.

'I have never been to a gathering like this, not outside anyway. It is different here, people are so friendly, I thought I would miss home more, but I don't... is that wrong?' She took a swig from her goblet. The mead was warm and tasted strongly of honey and hot wine, it was delicious and welcoming all the way down to her stomach.

'It's not wrong. You are vivacious, Illingdalean's are not generally known for their sense of humour so it is understandable that you would feel happy here.'

She blushed. 'Vivacious. I am sure my father would have used a different term.'

He seemed to sense her sudden melancholy. 'You can be, yes, but your father died never knowing who you are. If he could see you now, and I believe he can, he would see that you are courageous, kind, and selfless. You put your own life and suffering aside; to follow a stranger into a world you know nothing about. That takes strength of soul; that I doubt many possess.' He paused for a moment. 'You might not have wanted to be Queen, but you would have made a good one, and your father would know that.'

Isyllia took his arm again, holding the goblet in her other hand. 'Thank you. Life is so precious, you never know when it can be gone forever, how many more moons we get to see, or if we will ever have someone to share them with... some of these people.' She looked around at the dancing strangers 'They don't know it now, but they will never be here again!'

They strolled for a time in companionable silence until they reached the half-sized wall looking out over the ocean. It was quieter here, most of the people were gathering around the festival bonfires for warmth. Ember seemed calm and more relaxed despite himself. Most of the time she had known him he had been angry, mostly with her. For the first time, she felt like she saw him as he must truly be without all the frustration he held onto. His eyes were a startling blue even in the moonlight and his face was wise beyond his years. The kind of face that told many stories, not least of which was the pride he took in his appearance, his square jaw perfectly framed by a barely visible van dyke. Not for the first time she noticed that he was breathtaking to look at, and blushing, she turned her focus down to her goblet, draining the rest of the contents as if the alcohol could soak away evidence of the moment. Then placing it on the wall, she decided to concentrate on something else. 'Do you miss home?'

He did not look over but continued to stare out to the horizon, there seemed to be something about the ocean that relaxed him. His face was peaceful, like he had finally flung the various things bothering him over the wall where they belonged. 'Sometimes. Mostly I miss my mother, and my brother Marcos.'

'What are they like?'

335

He smiled. 'My mother is beautiful, and strong. She used to spend hours teaching me to read and to write. And when I was afraid to leave, she gave me strength.' The moonlight caught his unassuming smile, 'I was the youngest so my two brothers would often play tricks on me.' At this point he started to chuckle, 'They would say I was called Ember because I was so small, and when I would start to cry they would both pick me up and tell me from a small ember I would one day become a raging fire.'

It took a moment for Isyllia to respond, realising she truly was seeing him for the first time. 'How did they feel about you being chosen?'

'My mother was happy … my brothers accepted it. They knew I had to leave some day; they just didn't understand why. Marcos rode with me for miles when I left. Had it not been for our father, I think he would have insisted on coming with me.'

'What about your father?' It was hard to ask another about their father, knowing how much she missed hers, and the little moments she would never have again.

'My father.' His shoulders dropped, pulling his face down to stare at his hands sitting despondent on the wall. It was unlike the burdens she had seen him carry, and it leapt over to her like a cat meowing for its supper. 'My father could never accept that I was chosen by Caros.' He deflated further. Isyllia placed her hand in his, hoping he would not reject the comfort.

'If I could take one lesson from my father and one alone, it is that love has *many* weights.'

Ember looked down to her hand clutched in his and closed his eyes. His breathing turned deep and ragged. 'It can make you feel like you're drowning.' He did not let go. Instead, he turned to face her, yearning and uncertainty battling together in his eyes. Something deep within had clawed its way to the surface and taken hold. Isyllia breathed deep, drawing her fingers along the length of his arm, slow and deliberate. He was warm, and he smelled of musk and steel, his smell. Isyllia felt her stomach clench with longing, ready to pull him into her when his temple creased with alarm. For a moment, his eyes darted to the side, focusing on some object behind him, then he shot around.

Over in the distance, a familiar face leaned against a pole and scoffed, his tied back blonde hair resting on his shoulder. Isyllia's mouth dropped open with shock, her stomach doing somersaults. It couldn't be. 'William?' The man tossed his goblet onto the ground, and then hurried away, disappearing back into the crowd without answering.

Isyllia began to panic. 'Wait William, wait!' She raced ahead, not waiting for Ember, pushing through startled merry makers, looking frantically for any sign of the direction he had taken. 'William!' She shouted it into the crowd, not caring who stared, he had to hear her, he had to.

Ember grabbed her by the arms; restraining her. 'It's not William.'

'Let me go, it was, I know his face.'

Ember was quieter now; he turned her to face him effortlessly, sadness almost speaking for him. 'Isyllia, he's gone.' She knew what he meant, and tears began to sting as the memory of him being pierced by the arrow replayed in her mind, the look of horror on his face as he closed his eyes. The man looked so like him. She looked around, people were beginning to stop, some pointing in their direction.

Ember paled. 'We have to go, now. Are you all right?'

'She nodded.' The last thing she needed in her humiliation was for him to have to carry her home.

Ember grabbed her by the hand firmly, all tenderness in his eyes gone, replaced with absolute concentration. 'This way.' They strode through some backstreets until they reached the little house they had been staying in. Ember threw open the door, latching it carefully behind him. 'Thomas.' They did not have to wait long. Thomas ran into the room, his face red from panic. Both parties stopped and waited. Thomas spoke first.

'I received a letter while you were gone.' He handed the letter to Ember, 'I thought it would be from the Duke of Godswall, who else would know you are here?'

Ember scoured the letter. 'It's in code.' He read aloud.

Dear Sunny

We have planted new crops this year. I am surprised to report however it has not been as fruitful as the year prior. Pests have been rife and destroyed most of the growth. The worst part is I cannot find them. They disappear without a trace. I am currently sourcing the seller that I used for last year's produce; however, I wonder if I will just encounter the same problem.

His wife has told me he is detained elsewhere, but I wonder, aside from casual mention of opening a market in Mespar, which he never seemed passionate about, I am not sure what could otherwise keep him. Everyone knows Mesparian's are not farmers. I will wait for more word in any case, and I will notify you if I find anything. Take care, and thank you for everything, I know I can at least count on you.

Long live the king,

Your friend

Imaar.

'We are going to need to go through this, but first, a townsman made us, it's too dangerous to stay now.' Ember was worried, his temple still creased with concern.

'I took the liberty of packing our bags, and the weapon, all that's left is to ready the horses.'

'Our bags?' Ember looked at Thomas questioningly. 'What do you mean *our* bags?'

Thomas raised his palm, then switched to one finger. 'Hear me out! When you left, I had a breakthrough, and I know where the Stone of Abashiina is!'

'Thomas!' Ember clapped him on the back, sending him forward a few steps, the wind in his lungs remaining behind.

'I don't believe it, where would we be without you!' Isyllia said, beaming.

Thomas jiggled his head happily, pleased with his own efforts. 'I concur.'

Ember interrupted him with a hard stare. 'Thomas.'

He seemed to get the general hint. 'I can't leave you to do this alone, you need my help.' His face was set; there was no arguing with him, not even Ember.

'What about the shop?' Isyllia felt guilty and it suddenly dawned on her, Thomas was willing to put his life aside to assist them. He had presented Isyllia with a level of kindness she had never known. She had been told so many stories about Eddinsford. About the wars, and none of it was true. Her whole life was a lie. A lump sank to the bottom of her stomach, how could she have been so blind in so many ways. 'Thomas, you cannot leave your life behind, our journey could be dangerous. You have been so kind; if something happened to you, I could never forgive myself.' She glanced at Ember; his look was approving.

'She's right, Tom, you're all your father has left.'

Thomas smiled at them, tucking the letter away in the pocket of his crimson jacket. 'Thank you, truly, but my mind is made up…I've spent my life studying the past and trying to tinker a better future, *this* is my chance. I can't sit here and waste away behind the counter of a shop, it's not me, I was made for more… I'm coming.'

Ember smiled at him. 'I'll ready the horses. Isyllia, since we only have two and we need to get away quickly, you will need to ride with me.'

She nodded, still caught in her own personal devastation. If Ember could sense her thoughts, he knew there was no time to question now, and so he left the room without another word.

Thomas sat next to her, taking her hand. 'It will be alright, you'll see.'

Isyllia smiled, hiding her emotions. 'We had best get ready…wait, what about the ra-Mr Fennly?'

Thomas chuckled. 'He's informing my father; he will know where to find me. They can follow a smell for miles.'

'Wait, he's flying?' Her eyes lit up with surprise, she had never actually thought the little rodent was capable of the task but hadn't the heart to tell Thomas.

'It has been a busy evening.' He smiled and then picked up their packs, motioning toward the door with his free hand. They waited outside with the bags in silence, the night had taken a dark turn and shivering, Isyllia looked up at the twinkling sky, wishing she had time to change. Thomas had taken more than either of them, but they managed to fit everything on once Ember returned, not burdening the horses too greatly. Niimorea however, was not happy with the extra weight and snorted grumpily at any available opportunity.

'I'll need you to ride behind, in case we are pursued.' Ember said, arranging Perrins reins in his hands.

Thomas nodded; his lips pursed with concentration.

Ember reached into his sleeve for a dagger. 'Do you have a weapon?'

Thomas waved him off midway. 'I'm more likely to hurt myself with that thing than the enemy!'

Ember shrugged, and then sheathed the small blade. She waited for him to climb up on Perrin first, and then when he was settled, took his hand, fitting her foot into the stirrup and swinging up onto Perrins back. Her dress tore in several places over the short journey, making her cringe with annoyance. But she resolved to hold tight to his waist, drawing on his natural warmth to compensate for the air holes her ruined dress now contained.

They crept through the quiet streets with caution, trying not to draw suspicion. It had not taken long to gather their things and leave the house, but guards would almost certainly be on alert. It was not until they reached the city exit that they noticed two such guards, craning their heads back and forth in the darkness, searching for them. Ember put up his palm for Thomas to stop, indicating he move in beside them. He leaned over, keeping his voice low. 'Just swordsmen, we could outrun them.'

Thomas nodded, his eyes on the guards. 'Most will be stationed at the festival still, I can't see them being trouble, it's tomorrow that I am more worried about.'

Ember nodded then moved back to an upright position.

'Tomorrow?' She almost regretted asking the question, there could be no good answer.

Thomas nodded again, leaning over to whisper. 'The council chambers will send a bird to Illingdale, by tomorrow every soldier in the area will know we are here.'

Isyllia blanched.

'First, we will get to safety, then we will discuss a plan, stay behind me Thomas, follow my lead.' Ember signalled Perrin into a run. Isyllia held on tighter, her stomach tingling in response. She ignored the feeling and tried to concentrate on remaining calm. It took the soldiers a few moments to notice the two horses coming toward them. One guard blew his whistle repeatedly in panic, while the second drew his blade, he meant to cut them down. Ember signalled to Perrin again, the horse changed course, instead of running past the man, he turned toward the man, plummeting straight for him. The ploy worked, the soldier, seeing the giant war horse speeding straight for him, hesitated and with seconds to spare, was forced to abandon his stance and dive out of the way. Ember stroked Perrin on the neck. 'Good boy, keep going.' There was nothing left for the guards to do but stare as the two horses fled into the distance. They had made it out of the city, but how far they would get was another matter. Pursuit would stalk their minds long into the night. Isyllia did not look back, refusing to say goodbye to another home, and the feeling of contentment she felt slipping away with each stride Perrin made forward. Instead she looked ahead, with the bland hope that the darkness was carrying them somewhere, wherever that somewhere was.

'We will stop here; horses need to rest.' Ember reined Perrin in by the river, leaving him to graze. Niimorea walked up beside Perrin, nosing him out the way of a lush tuft of grass, not caring to wait until Thomas had dismounted. Isyllia smiled at the horse, she was a spirited creature, and it had been a long week without her.

Isyllia stretched, her body ached from sitting and the shock to her muscles sent unhappy spasms up her spine in complaint, not to mention she would need to change. 'I am cold, I need to change.' She pointed to the pack.

Thomas, still battling Niimorea for his bags, did not hear and so she looked to Ember.

He nodded, but he did not turn around. 'Stay close.'

'Of course.' She said, sighed, and took a change of clothes. Light from the dawn still peaked over the horizon, in no clear hurry to offer its light for the day, so she did not need to go far to be out of view. It felt good to be warm again and at the same time, Isyllia found herself lamenting slightly the loss of another of life's pleasures, a desire for lavish clothes. She carried the feeling back to camp with the torn dress, knowing Ember would no doubt send her back to retrieve it if she tried to leave it behind again.

'You said you had found the stone?' The question drew her attention, so she picked up her pace slightly, her curiosity ever the undefeated enemy. Ember rifled through the packs, coming out with a water skin and some bread, Isyllia's stomach jolted with longing and sank just as quickly when she saw the smoked fish

Thomas had packed. Ember eyed Isyllia, he knew she hated fish. 'Not hungry?'

She balked. 'Just some bread, thanks.'

He tore off a portion of the loaf and tossed it over, shaking his head slightly, then offering the same to Thomas who took the fish gratefully.

'I did some reading earlier this evening, or...' He turned to look at the now fast rising sun, they had ridden through the night 'Last evening, and I think I finally made out that passage. It was not *Ĭćaiiṇ oiij Itriial* like I thought, it says *Ĭćaje oiij üutriial*. Cave of trials.'

'I have not heard of the cave of trials?' Ember took a bite of his fish.

Isyllia tried to hold her breath, the smell faint though it was, still weaving its way into her nostrils and down into her stomach, threatening to make its meagre contents scatter back out her mouth again, she would never get used to the smell, never.

'You probably know it as the Cave of lost Souls.'

Ember nodded in understanding then turned to Isyllia to explain. 'Storytellers say the cave is haunted with the ghosts of those the guild needs silenced. They are thrown into the cavern, their bodies never found.'

Thomas nodded. 'I think there is some truth to the story. Only, I think the bodies, or some at least, are treasure hunters who have tried and never returned. I think that is where the Stone of Abashiina lies.'

Ember seemed to consider the idea. 'Makes sense… There is a little over a week between us and the Cave. We will need to stop at Ravenswood Tavern and re supply.'

'Wait, if we could get the weapon of Nemethiiniia, why hasn't Gelraen tried to get mine?'

Ember heaved a long sigh, no doubt tossing the idea around in his head. 'Gelraen is not stupid, he knows a little more than the average Illingdalean … having said that though he has well and truly tied himself to the city so he cannot go himself, and he can't exactly send someone else to get it. No, I highly doubt he will cause any trouble, and if by chance I am wrong, I will know anyway.'

Isyllia gave a frustrated sigh. 'Well we still don't have any Tinderfordean money. I have coin from home, but I don't know if I can use it there.' Her attention on the stack of gold Dales sitting at the bottom of her sack.

Ember seemed sceptical. 'Dales?'

'I brought 15 gold dales, it's not much but I thought it might come in handy.'

The men chuckled.

Isyllia folded her arms, 'What's funny?'

Thomas explained. 'That's more money than most people have in a lifetime. It's best we don't use them, anywhere we traded them would be like lighting a beacon to our position.'

Ember Interjected, 'I have been building a stash of coins for years. It was one of the main reasons I opened the smithy in Docktown. We will have enough for what we *need*.' He gave her a stern look.

She did not miss his meaning, opting not to reply and instead walking over to the nearest tree to rest, a sour expression on her face. Thomas and Ember continued to talk for a few minutes, the faint murmur of their voices could be heard in the distance, but she chose to ignore them. The hours of riding had wearied her enough that even the daylight that began to shine overheard was not enough to deter her from falling into a troubled sleep.

It was some hours later that she felt a hand on her shoulder shaking her. She opened her eyes to find Ember, and he did not look rested. He crouched near her, and he was worried. 'Soldiers, up, now.'

Isyllia sat wide eyed, trying to ignore the protests from her back at the sudden movement. 'Who's?'

'Eddinsford.'

Isyllia looked over to Thomas, shoving his bags hurriedly back onto the horse, his face white as a sheet.

'Thomas, get clear, if they see you, they could recognise you.' Ember turned back to Isyllia 'There are three men, once Thomas spurs his horse off, they will hear and come in this direction. They are mounted so we will need to get them off their horses if we are going to kill them.'

'Kill them?' She regretted the alarm in her voice.

He nodded. 'We cannot risk them following us; we will kill them then hide their bodies in the bushes, which will buy us some time. Do you still have your stone?'

Isyllia nodded trying to calm her nerves. 'Yes, but shouldn't I use a blade?'

'I don't have time to teach you to wield a blade, you will need to use your power again. Just do as I say. When they come into the clearing, I need you to force them off their horses.'

'How?' She looked over to Thomas again, who had begun to climb up onto Niimorea, a light pang awoke in her stomach, but she turned away from them. She needed to focus.

'Make the ground shake!'

'With the stone, I can't!' She replied incredulously.

'The stone is to help you focus for now. You can do this, it's just like with the fire, and the sword, and the stone.' Ember cupped his hand around her fist and his voice softened. 'Focus your energy into the earth, will the rocks deep underground to vibrate. That should be enough to unsteady them into getting off their horses.'

'But.'

He cut her off, placing his hand over her mouth and signalling for Thomas to go. Thomas nodded back and spurred the horses forward. They took the bait. Within moments voices could be heard yelling. 'Over that way, quick.'

Ember crept over to the direction the men approached then turned back to where Isyllia stood and nodded.

Isyllia knelt down, placing her hands on the ground, nerves causing her body to shake, but she ignored that, instead she closed her eyes and thought of William, thought of the blade piercing his body, thought of the horror in his eyes, how it was her fault he was dead. Within moments she felt the familiar heat burn through her body and into her mind, the anger and resentment bursting to get out. She pushed on the ground, forcing the anger into the earth with her mind, small ripples began to spread underneath her. She focused on them, forcing them to spread.

'Go send word.'

Isyllia looked up, one of the riders turned back into the clearing. The other two, feeling the tremors, dismounted from their horses and began to approach on foot, it had worked. But her relief was short-lived. One of the men, sword drawn, began to walk her way. Isyllia's face drained of the little colour it had left. To her right she could hear clanging of swords as Ember fought, but she dared not look. Slowly, the man crept closer, occasionally glancing at his captain to ensure he was in no immediate danger. 'Come quietly now, I don't want to hurt you lass.'

Isyllia took a step backwards, drawing her dagger with a shaking hand. He may not be her subject but killing the man was still the last thing she wanted. It was best not to talk. Instead, she concentrated on the weapon, urging it to spin. Slowly, she relaxed her grip, taking a slow step back from it. Seeing her intentions, the soldier growled and lunged forward, the shock of the sudden movement causing her to break her concentration, the dagger dropping to the ground. She closed her eyes, knowing she would never pick her weapon up in time, knowing she could do nothing to save herself in time, except close her eyes. She heard a clang then a choking sound, was that her making that sound? Had he stuck her already? She had thought dying would be more painful.

Isyllia opened her eyes. The soldier had never made it to her. Ember stood protectively to her right; his left hand outstretched; exhibiting a fury so intense it could almost drip from him. He had blocked the man's strike with his own blade,

351

and then with his free hand plunged a dagger of his own into the man's neck. A few more moments and the soldier tumbled to the floor, as dead as his captain. Then grabbing her hand tightly, he ran in the other direction toward the men's horses. Isyllia did not protest, her mind still unconvinced for the moment, that she was not dead.

They had not gone far, trained to stay near their masters. Ember dropped her hand and approached slowly, careful not to startle them. Once he had reached them, he secured their reins and came back to where she stood. 'Can you ride?'

The question snapped her back to the present. 'Yes, I'm fine. I'll be fine.' She took his hand, scrambling onto the horse then looked down, he had made no move toward his own.

'Thomas won't be too far ahead, catch up with him.'

Her heart stopped in alarm. 'Catch up, what about you, what if there are more soldiers?'

'There isn't yet, the other one has a way to go to get help, and I need to hide the bodies.'

'I'll help.' She made to dismount.

'No, go.' Ember spurred her horse forward with a slap on the rump.

Isyllia looked over her shoulder, watching Ember's figure disappear behind the trees. Not understanding why, a panic began to settle in the pit of her stomach. It had been nearly a month since her father died. Nearly a month since Ember had rescued her from the castle that night, saving her from a repeat of the torment Gelraen had planned. She had begun to depend on him without realising. *'Concentrate, find Thomas.'* She forced herself to focus and look for a sign, how far could he have gotten?

No sooner had she thought it, two horses with one figure could be made just ahead. Thomas still sat on Niimorea, holding Perrin's reins in a free hand. He had stopped in a clearing, his face still white with alarm. 'Thomas!'

The sight of Isyllia saw him relax a little, until he saw that she was alone. 'Where is Ember?'

'Hiding the bodies. He insisted I ride ahead.' She took deep breaths, she needed to remain calm, for Thomas.

'I see.' His face had turned a slight shade of green.

'You've never seen someone die, have you?'

He shook his head. 'You have?' Almost instantly he closed his eyes in regret. 'I'm sorry, forgive me.'

Isyllia smiled weakly. 'In Illingdale, I was forced to watch executions. Father believed that if you did not have the stomach to see your decisions through, you were unworthy to rule. I watched so many criminals die. Burned, hung, beheaded, dismembered. I never wanted to know their names. I didn't want to know what they had done. How could their crimes be worse than my existence? Each breath I took was treason. I was never afraid of death, never afraid for myself. I guess I always thought one day it would be my turn. But it's different now. Now, for the first time, I feel like I have something to live for. Something more. Now, I am afraid.'

Thomas looked sympathetic; his unease forgotten. 'I can't imagine what it must have been like.'

Isyllia was quiet for a moment, memories of her old life playing through her mind. 'I had more money than sense, ladies to serve my desires, but I never knew hunger, I have never been left in the cold. Everything I lived was meaningless. I have never made my own decision beyond what dress I wanted to wear. I guess that's what I saw in William, he offered the only thing I ever wanted.'

'Freedom.' Thomas finished.

She nodded.

'Would you have married him, if you had been given the chance?'

Isyllia seemed to think for a while. 'I asked myself the same question… many times. I should have wanted to, we were so close, we did everything together, but it just wasn't there for me, that …thing. A part of me will always miss him, and the good times we had together. He was my light, in so many ways… But he never truly knew me, and I guess I always knew somewhere deep inside he could never accept what I was...'

'Given time, things might have been different!'

Isyllia's mind went back to that day, that last moment. The look of horror. 'I spent many more days contemplating that, but no. As much as we mean to each other, and as much as I need him, I don't think he could ever get past that, and since I can't give him what he wants, would it be fair to make him?' She stopped short and looked around; there was still no sign of Ember. 'He should be here by now?' The thought brought back the anxiety in her stomach. Thomas looked around, the worry on his face matching hers. It was another half an hour until a silhouetted figure emerged, stepping calmly through the undergrowth. It was Ember. Isyllia felt herself sigh with relief, her gut relaxing against the tension she had not realised she was cradling. 'Where is the other horse?'

Ember whistled to Perrin. 'Travelling in a different direction, I have hidden our trail and left a false one with him. It should buy us time.'

'Good thinking' Thomas seemed to have relaxed also, the colour returned to his cheeks. 'Now, which direction did you want to take?

'We will cross through the wetlands, it will be harder to track us that way. If we ride straight, we will reach there by nightfall.'

Thomas' expression was unreadable.

Isyllia blanched, the thought of trekking through miles of festering muck repulsed her. But she knew better than to argue.

'I do have to ask though; do you think we could swap horses? This one seems to hate me, and I am not altogether convinced the feeling isn't mutual.' Thomas frowned at Niimorea, who ignored him.

Isyllia on the other hand laughed heartily, 'I'd be delighted.' It took a few minutes to swap over but once they had finally settled, Thomas rode ahead and Niimorea gave a gentle whinny. 'I missed you too... I promise I won't tell Perrin.' She looked over to Ember, he rode quietly next to her, smiling ever so slightly, but he did not look over, instead concentrating on the road ahead.

The afternoon seemed to go by quickly, they had not run into any more soldiers and the smell of stale water ahead told them they had indeed reached the wetlands. Ember jumped down from his horse.

'We will want to dismount.'

'I'm sure we don't.' She kept the thought to herself, knowing better by now than to tempt Ember's mood and jumped down from Niimorea, trying to ignore the loud mud slapping sound

that launched reeking droplets in all directions. The stench did not take long to overwhelm. Seeping into her pores, as she squelched forward, each step leaving her feeling of hot sweat and filth, clinging to places of her body she did not know filth could cling to. Again, she found herself focused on the sack of dales in her pack, knowing she would give all of them for a hot bath. The idea made her smile but threatened to make the smell worse. 'How far do the Wetlands extend?'

Ember wiped his face with a square of cloth, the shared look of disgust clear. 'Two days, maybe three.'

Her heart stopped. 'Three days! You cannot be serious.'

'We only need to make it to the Ravenswood Tavern, that's about a day ahead.'

Isyllia balked. 'Who would run a tavern in this waste?'

'The tavern is not in the wetlands, it's on the outskirts of Tinderford!'

The thought comforted her. Only a day, then she could bathe. She looked down at the grimy wool dress; she would need to discard it. The thought made her curse, that's two dresses now; she would have nothing left to wear at this rate.

The hours droned on slower than she thought possible, even the normally comforting array of stars above offered no solace from the miles and miles of dead trees that silhouetted in the moonlight. The situation might have been more tolerable had there been some distraction. But each time she opened her mouth to talk, she felt the thick and slimy air vault down her throat, threatening to make her heave what was left of the small portion of food she had eaten earlier that day. They walked on in a shared miserable silence for what felt like another two hours when Ember stopped. We need to rest and eat. If you want to sleep, sleep.'

Isyllia frowned. 'What about you? When was the last time you slept?'

'I'm fine.'

Even in the small amount of light they had she could see the creases under his eyes. 'You're no use to anyone dead on your feet, you should sleep first.'

'She's right, it'll be fine, and we can keep watch.'

He frowned. She could tell he was unhappy with the idea. She watched as he trudged off to a tree a small distance away and settled down to close his eyes. She shook her head, letting Niimorea wander over to Perrin grumpily. Thomas had reached into his pack and retrieved the book of Odriid and settled down to read on a small patch of dry earth, chewing a portion of dried fish. For once, the smell was not the worst thing she could imagine. And so, she moved happily to sit next to him, relieved that at least, it did not make things worse. 'How can you read in this light.'

He looked up. 'I can't. But trying takes my mind off the smell.' He took another bite. 'Shoot, I should have offered.' He pointed to the pack. 'Are you hungry?'

Isyllia smiled. 'Not tonight, no.' She looked over to Ember again, his chest rose and fell with a slow gentle rhythm, he was asleep. 'I'll never understand him...' She said it almost absently, shaking her head then turning back to Thomas. 'Most of the time I feel like he despises me, others ...' Her mind set on the previous night at the fair, the longing in his eyes making her stomach tingle even now.

Thomas seemed to smile, but there was sadness to it. 'He does not hate you.'

She looked at the floor. 'He gives a good impression!'

'You said it yourself, he takes his calling seriously.' Thomas looked over to Ember, his expression unreadable. 'He gives the illusion that he is confident, in control... but in secret he doubts himself more than anyone I've met.'

'He said his father couldn't forgive him for who he was?'

Thomas nodded. 'Sometimes I don't think he ever left there. It would be easy to think he was arrogant or a control freak, but that's what he wants people to see. Underneath, I think he carries the weight of his father's disapproval everywhere he goes. It's one of the reasons he struggles with people so much, letting people in is just another chance to be hurt.'

'You see him so deeply.'

Thomas blushed. 'He's dedicated his life to the service of others, the least I can do is be a friend.'

Isyllia decided to change the subject, not entirely convinced Ember couldn't sense when people were talking about him! 'I should feed the horses; Niimorea gets grumpy when she's hungry.'

Thomas scowled. 'When she's hungry!'

Isyllia smiled. 'She'll warm up to you; you should try feeding her sometime.'

'Perhaps.' He took another bite of his dried fish, and then settled back down to read. Isyllia walked over to the packs and rummaged through, at last putting her hands on a dwindling sack of grain. It was not enough, she knew, but it was all they had left. Careful not to wake Ember, she stepped delicately to where the horses stood, miserably searching for even a single blade of grass. 'Niim, Perrin, come.' They did not need to be told twice, the sound of the strings on the sack told them it was food. Isyllia held some grain in her hand awkwardly, wishing she had something to put it in. 'Ah don't fight. Niim, you'll get some too, let Perrin eat first.' She stroked the dirty white horse's nose gently. It did not take long for them to empty the last of the contents in the bag, both animals sniffing forlornly for some hidden portion they had not been told about. 'I am sorry, that's all I have.' Isyllia walked back to the packs and put the empty bag in, feeling guilty. She refastened the ties tightly, knowing if she did not Niimorea would most likely come to investigate when she was not looking, then decided to look around herself. The Wetlands, another place she had read about at the castle. But once again, she found herself annoyed at her tutors' staggering loss of details. He had never once mentioned the smell, like a hundred dead bodies scattered around and left to decompose in the open air, all wafting into each other like some elaborate gathering of oxygenated bile. Green sludge grew in the wetter parts of the ground, the last remnants of the great river that stretched all the way down from Godswall Mountains. Greater, in words, but not strong enough to make it all the way to the ocean. It split up into smaller tendrils, like tree branches, stretching for miles across the landscapes of Eddinsford and Tinderford. There was no life out here; save for bugs. There was plenty of bugs. Isyllia walked around the area, swatting mosquitoes automatically as she went. After a few hours, she looked back at Thomas. He had finally given up trying to read and lay with his head on a pack, asleep. She sighed, looking back to Ember, he was still asleep. She was the only one still awake, watching as the moon disappeared over the horizon. Soon she would not be able to see and decided to find a place to sit while she still could. Instead relying on her senses.

Nothingness, except for the sound of Thomas snores. If someone were trying to sneak up on them, his noises would surely call to them like a beacon. Deciding there was nothing she could do, save wake him, she reached into the pocket of her cloak and pulled out the smooth stone Ember had given her and placed it on the ground. The stone may have been miles away for all she could see, but knowing she had nothing better to do, she set her mind to the task, willing it to rise, then slowly lowering it to the ground again. For a while nothing happened, but slowly, she began to feel the stone touch the top of her outstretched hand, then just as slowly descended back down again. Isyllia smiled at herself contentedly, when a streak of red caught her eye, Sunrise had cut the horizon in the distance. She had made it through her second watch. Picking up the now slightly visible stone she stowed it back in her cloak and decided it was time to wake Ember. Her back protested as she edged to her feet, hours of sitting in the same position again causing further riot. Isyllia placed her hand on his shoulder and shook tentatively at first, he stirred, breathing in deep and letting out a sleepy yawn.

'It's time to go.' She said.

He nodded, and then rose to his feet quietly.

Thomas shot up mid snore. 'I was just resting my eyes!'

She grinned. 'Vehemently.'

The morning wore on slow and teasing, the sun sauntering across the sky as they made their way through the sludge. It was near noon when the river at last started to fold back in and dry ground began to replace the mud, indicating they were nearing the edge of the swamp lands.

'We will reach the Ravens head by afternoon; we should clean up first. The less questions people ask, the better.' Ember said, not turning back to see if they objected.

'Wont people know you in these parts?' Isyllia asked, just realising they must have crossed into his homeland by now.

'My family are in the next town over, about a day's ride. People around here don't exactly travel much, only the guild knows everyone. It should be fine as long as we stick to the story.'

'I put the documents I made for you two in Ember's satchel. I will say I am on business for my father.'

Ember squinted, thinking. 'Good, I will say we travelled here to shop steel suppliers, and ran into you?'

'So, we use the false names here too?' It was Isyllia; the changing stories were threatening to leave her with a headache.

Ember shook his head. 'Not here. If we use names that are unfamiliar to the guild, it could raise more questions than we need.'

Isyllia paled. 'Won't Gelraen find us if we use our names!'

Ember shook his head again. 'Not here, no. He would not dare send soldiers into Tinderford, and anyone who agreed to spy for him would end up at the bottom of the nearest chasm.'

She gave a look of disgust. 'Sounds like a lovely country.'

He shrugged. 'It is what it is.'

'Do you think people will ask?' Although she had never travelled to Tinderford, it was hard to forget how quickly people had recognised her at the fair in Eddinsford, and Tinderford.

'I don't know, best to be prepared though.' Ember sat atop Perrin now, finally the ground was dry enough to ride. Isyllia needed no further prompting; her feet blistered from walking and so it felt

blissful to be riding again.

They continued to follow the river up to a point where it looked suitable enough to stop. Ember was the first to make for the river, a fresh change of clothes in hand.

'Take a minute to wash. Then we will approach the tavern.'

Isyllia got down, pulling out the second to last of the cleaner outfits in her pack and found a section of river that was far enough away from the other two, then washed off as best as she could. The water was freezing but it was clean, and shivering she scrubbed away some of the dirt that hugged her skin like a blanket then put on the outfit, again not bothered by the itch, simply happy to be clean and warm. When she walked back, Ember and Thomas waited. Both eating the last of the supplies. Isyllia looked down to a portion that had been laid aside, stale bread and dried fish. Her stomach growled, causing her heart to drop down from its chamber and sulk with the rest of her. Knowing there was no way she could refuse a third time, for fear of passing out.

'You'll have to eat and ride if you want to make it to the tavern for supper.' Isyllia looked at Ember, there was a hint of amusement on his face. Scowling inwardly she took the food, then retreated back to Niimorea and ate as swiftly as she could, the day could not go fast enough, and this was the last portion of fish she would ever suffer herself to eat, of that she was certain.

▽⚹○✳

Ember, Ravenswood Tavern, Tinderford.

The sun had begun to set as they rode into the first of the mining towns of Tinderford. The people were different to Eddinsford, instead of bakers, and fish sellers smiling and going about their business happily, Tinderfordean were a tougher folk. Families worked the earth together here, all clustered in little towns at the seat of the Godswall Mountains. The mountain housed all the richest mineral deposits on their continent. Towns were situated around mines and families worked those mines, ultimately lining the pockets of the guild, who took a cut of all profits. People that could not pay their share, disappeared. People of the world generally feared Tinderfordean's, misunderstood at best. But that never bothered Ember, it was who he was, it was home.

'So, this is where you grew up?'

'Mm-hmm.' Ember did not look back to see what the other two were laughing about, he needed to concentrate. Finally, they arrived at a stable next to the tavern. He closed his eyes for a moment, sensing the area around them for any sign of soldiers. He knew inwardly he was wasting his time, but it could never hurt to be sure. Except when it took a lot of his strength, but he ignored the tiredness creeping over him, pushing further into the town. After a few minutes, he was satisfied there was no immediate danger, and breathed a sigh of relief signalling them to move forward. The stables were small, housing mostly customers of the Inn. But Ember didn't mind, the less traffic, the better for them.

An elderly man approached, nodding to Ember who he assumed was the leader of their party 'You look like you'll be needing a stall?'

Ember jumped down. 'Three horses.'

The man seemed to chew his lip for a minute, looking the horses over. 'Eight coppers a day, they will need extra feeding, been running them dry!'

Ember nodded, and then handed over the reins, motioning for the others to do the same.

The man seemed confused. 'You ain't going to barter? You look like you're from around here!' He pointed to Ember's tanned skin.

'That depends on the horses when I return.'

The man smiled then nodded his understanding, collecting the reins of the three hapless animals, and then led them away to the stalls. Niimorea trotted off toward a bundle of hay, clearly intent on helping herself. He shook his head. The duke had been right, that horse suited her perfectly.

The Ravenswood tavern had seen better days, bits of the building had given up here and there, and some spots had been half attempted at repairs then abandoned mid-way. The white paint was dusty and in desperate need of a fresh coat along with the faded sign, which creaked in the afternoon breeze as they walked through the door. Ember approached the bar, Isyllia stood close behind. It was warm, a fire burned brightly in the hearth to the back of the room where a singer sat playing her heart away to patrons as they laughed and spilled ale, nobody caring to listen to what she sang. Nobody looked around to see the newcomers as they stood waiting for the in-keeps wife to shuffle over, a welcoming smile on her face.

'Do you have rooms left?' Ember felt for his coin pouch.

'You've come at a good time, how many dear?'

'Two rooms?'

The woman nodded, 'I can do you two, single for the lady?'

Ember looked to Isyllia. 'My wife, single for our friend.' Motioning to Thomas, who smiled and waved to the lady then continued to take in the scenery.

The lady looked over to where Isyllia stood. 'Will you be requiring hot water?'

'Please!'

The lady repeated her question to Thomas, who nodded.

'Two silvers per night, to be paid in the mornings if you wish to stay.'

Ember nodded, handing over the coins.

'Two rooms top of the stairs on the left, Pert will show you.' The woman pointed to a small boy who hopped to his mother's side. 'Supper will be served in an hour.'

Ember nodded his thanks then turned to follow pert. 'Is that a sword? Can I see it? Can I kill a bird with it?' He was young

368

and enthusiastic.

'Ah, no.' He smiled, a slight alarm on his face. Isyllia resisted the urge to laugh.

'I like killing birds!'

'Pert! Just show them to their rooms, I need help in the kitchen.' He did not ask any more questions along the way, politely pointing to two doors then hopping back down the stairs. Thomas excused himself to his room, closing the door behind him. Ember opened the door slowly, suddenly wishing he had given Isyllia the other room. They walked in, throwing their packs to the floor. It was small, but clean. A window sat opposite the door, overlooking the forest. A single lavatory pot sat in the corner with a towel draped over it, next to a large bed. The only other furniture was a small table and chair that sat next to the window. 'You can have the bed.'

Isyllia blushed. 'Thank you.' She sat down, avoiding his eyes. Ember removed his mail shirt, placing it on the back of the chair. He would wash later, when she was sleeping. For a moment he watched as she sorted through her belongings and what was left of her life and hummed gently to herself. She had changed so much already, from the first time he saw her, spoiled and wallowing in her own misery. Each day she grew a little more, blossoming like a delicate and beautiful flower. He watched, wishing he could forget the feel of her touch. The memory burned in him along with the doubts, knowing who they

were, and never able to forget, William. 'I am going for a drink.'
He made to leave.

'Should I follow?' She sounded disappointed.

'No!' He left, shutting the door a little harder than he had
intended, and stomped down the steps. The boy, Pert, was in the
kitchen with his mother, she had been scolding him for not
concentrating, a pot lay shattered on the floor. Ember looked
away, walking to the bar and motioning for the barman. 'Ale.'

The man nodded, seemingly a million miles away, snapped
into a kind of focus, and poured a tankard, almost throwing it on
the bar in his direction, then returning to his vacant state. Ember
hesitantly placed a copper on the bar, then left with the tankard
and took the drink to an empty table toward the fire. The warmth
was welcoming after the cold of the Wetlands, as was the drink.
He drained half in one gulp, sitting back in his chair, trying to
clear his mind. He was unsure how much time had passed when
Thomas came down the steps, first having a brief discussion with
the in-keep. He then ordered two more tankards, bringing them
over, seeming to sense Ember's mood from a distance. He was a
good friend.

'Where did you find the coin?' Ember asked.

'Exchange, luckily enough they find it useful to carry a little
of different currencies.' He took a sip of the Ale. 'It's not
Tinkerton's, but it will do, I daresay.' Thomas jiggled his head

slightly with amusement, stopping suddenly when he realised Ember was not sharing his mirth. He ignored it. Finishing the rest of the first tankard then reaching for the second. 'Thanks.'

'That bad huh?'

'Hm?' He looked up; unsure what Thomas was referring to.

'Have you talked to her?' Thomas had raised his eyebrows, like he didn't expect the answer to be favourable.

Ember looked to the fire, trying to empty his mind with the hypnotic flames. 'Bout what?'

'About what?' He sighed, squinting and pinching the top of his nose as if it would stop the frustration from getting worse. 'You come bursting into my house carrying some unconscious girl, beside yourself with worry, then spend the better half of the next weeks avoiding her completely. I have never seen you so cold to someone, and now I find you here trying to drain a keg by yourself.'

'Your point?' He took another gulp.

It wasn't often that Thomas was annoyed, but he was now, it was clear on his face. He pushed the mug away and shook his head. 'Are you aware she actually thinks you hate her?'

The words made his blood run cold, hate? Has it become that bad? 'I don't hate her.'

'I know.' Exasperation soaked his words. 'What you're doing is not good for you; it's not how life is meant to be.' He paused, 'Look at my father, look at me. Trust me, you don't want this!'

Ember sighed; there was no point in lying to Thomas. There was never any point in lying to Thomas. 'What do you *want* me to say, Thomas, that I love her? ... *Of course,* I love her! I need her so much, every minute I just want to scream...All my life I have prepared for who I am, and I was happy... Now ....'

'You're not, Semiir and she's not, Kathriin, you're not doomed to repeat their mistakes.'

Ember ignored him. 'And the stupid thing is, I almost gave in the other night... all she had to do was touch me, that was it, and I lost all control... that dress; I've never wanted anyone so much. But then she saw *him.*'

Thomas was silent for a moment, choosing his words. 'It's not what you think.'

'You didn't see her face light up; like the most beautiful sunrise.' Ember sighed. 'She loved him, she just doesn't realise it, and she would have done anything to get to him, if I had let her.' He drank deeply.

'He was her *friend*; she's grieving, give it a chance, Em... *talk* to her!'

'...I can't... Let her think I hate her, easier.' Ember knew his friend meant well, but he just didn't understand.

For a moment Thomas just shook his head slowly, then after a moment he pushed his chair back. 'Then, you're a fool.' He indicated toward the stairs, Isyllia had begun walking slowly down, one hand on the rail. 'Look at her.'

Ember never noticed Thomas get to his feet, his eyes were fixed on Isyllia. She had bathed and donned one of the wool garments she hated, her hair flowing silkily down her back. For a moment she looked around, searching. Ember held his breath, hoping she would not lock eyes with him. She did, breathing in deeply, then smiling at Thomas. She was breathtaking.

'Will your wife be eating too sir?' The in-keep had placed a plate of broth on the table with a hunk of bread next to it.

'Yes!' His tone was abrupt, and he felt a little ashamed, making a mental note to be more aware of it. 'Can I get some more ale please?' His voice softened.

The woman looked at the two empty tankards on the table then smiled. 'Right away.'

Ember looked at the plate of food, vegetable covered boar in a gravy sauce, Isyllia would be happy. He knew he should eat, but the burning warmth in his stomach made him slightly queasy. Deciding it best to ignore it, he began to take mouthfuls of the food, not looking up when Isyllia and Thomas re-joined the table.

The woman returned a moment later, carrying two more plates and the tankard Ember had asked for. 'And the lady?'

'Mead please?'

He gave the woman some coin and began to drink.

'These all yours?' It was Isyllia, and there was mocking in her voice.

'Mm-hm' He continued to eat, leaving the tankard aside for when he had finished. He could never eat and drink at the same time.

Isyllia turned to Thomas. 'And you, are you well Thomas? You look...' She seemed to struggle for the right words, 'Not... you!'

'Tired!' Thomas replied with a smirk. 'Unlike the chosen my dear, I do need to sleep... a bit more than a few hours.'

Ember could feel Thomas glaring at him, but he still did not look up, determined to finish his plate as quickly as would be polite.

'I don't know if I could ever not need to sleep.' Isyllia replied, oblivious to Thomas' frustration.

'History says of course that you do not need to, however, what else would one do with the evenings?' Ember felt his eyebrows furrow in annoyance, Thomas was being sly now. This was going to be impossible.

Isyllia chuckled, and then there was silence for a moment, just the sound of cutlery scraping and the general mull of the inn. Ember pushed his empty plate aside, now determined to return his focus on his ale and the warmth of the fire.

'What is she singing about, I can't hear her?'

Thomas sat forward, trying to hear. 'I'm not sure, I must confess I was not listening.'

'Time.'

They both looked at Ember, he did not return their gaze. 'The woman has lost her husband, and she sings about her favourite moments with him and what she would give to live them again.'

Thomas laughed, the irony in his voice unmistakable.

'Thomas! You're unkind, what's so funny!'

'Would be too hard to understand my dear, I daresay I barely do myself.'

Now Ember glared at Thomas, who eyed him defiantly.

'Nevertheless, it is a sad tale. I could never live a life without love.'

Ember shifted in his chair, not liking the direction the conversation was taking. 'Love only brings pain.'

'Only?' her voice was incredulous.

Ember looked at the door, wishing he could just stand and run, have any conversation but this one. 'There is fulfilment to be had in doing one's duty.' He looked up, they locked eyes.

'I had a duty; I promised my hand to Lord Pennerly. And every moment, however short, I wanted to die.' There were tears in her eyes. 'Nobody should live that way.'

'Some people don't have a choice.' He could stand it no longer, not waiting for her to reply he stood. 'I am going for a walk, don't wait for me.' Then putting one foot in front of the other he swung the door, not stopping to close it and just walked, on and on, not caring about direction, having no particular purpose other than the stillness he so longed for. He did not know how far he went or how long it had been; only that by the time he returned the moon was low in the sky. He opened the door to the tavern, a growling dog was tethered to the bar, it growled again, and deciding he was no threat lay back down to resume the important business of sleeping. Ember walked up the stairs, opening the door to the room as quietly as he could. Isyllia was asleep, her hair blanketing the pillows and her shoulder bare where her shift had slipped down. He watched her for a moment, wishing he could lie next to her, hold her, smell her hair, tell her it would be all right, but he couldn't, their purpose was too important, he could not fail Caros. Sighing, he walked over to the wash basin that had been left by the window hours earlier. He removed his clothes, dipping the cloth in the by now ice-cold water and washed his body, careful not to wake Isyllia. It felt good to scrub away the dirt, leaving him with a small sense of accomplishment, then putting a fresh shirt and hose on, he sat in the armchair. Something soft pressed into his back as he leant back. He sat forward and pulled out the item, a blanket had been placed on the chair. He looked back to Isyllia, she had turned over, her face towards the wall. She had given him her blanket, leaving herself with only a sheet. The impulse to go to her was overwhelming, like fire in his stomach. In his imagination, it was so easy to slip in next to her, touch her, kiss her, and feel her call his name instead of Williams. In his imagination he could tell her how much he needed her. But reality came back, always punctual, and sighing resolutely, he walked over to the bed and instead laid the blanket gently over her, watching as her chest rose and fell. For a moment he thought he saw her move but dismissed it as his imagination, then walked slowly back to the chair and sat down, grateful to close his eyes and forget for a few short hours.

A knock at the door started him awake. He rubbed his eyes glancing outside, the sun was bright in the sky, indicating they had overslept. He looked to the bed, Isyllia stirred, holding the blanket to cover herself. She did not meet his eyes, instead looking at his feet, embarrassed. 'Thank you for the blanket.'

He nodded. 'After breakfast we will get supplies in town then head out.'

'I will pack.' She was disappointed, he could tell.

He did not reply, wishing too that they could stay longer but he knew lingering anywhere put them at risk. 'I will see you downstairs.' He then moved out the door. Thomas had already dressed and sat at a table, papers were laid out over the surface, leaving no space for the food in which it was intended. Ember approached warily, 'Is there room at this table?'

Thomas looked up, then scurried to pack away some of the pages, the previous night blissfully forgotten. He waited patiently, taking the extended moment to appreciate his friend, Thomas never held a grudge. 'I was just going over the letter.'

Ember sat down, signalling the in-keep to bring food. He had found his appetite this morning and he was not disappointed, fresh hot bread and butter, eggs and cheese filled the plate, tendrils of delicious smelling steam wafting invitingly into his nose. He did not wait for invitation, gulping down the food while Thomas continued to go over the letter. 'What are your thoughts?' He answered through a mouthful of food.

Thomas frowned. 'Well, he has spelt sonny wrong, but I would think it obvious that was on purpose, my thought is that he is meaning almighty, queen, something like that.'

'Possibly.' He knew talking with his mouth full was rude, but he could not stop himself this morning.

'Then there is the rest of the letter… new crops.'

'King.' He had almost forgotten Isyllia was there, almost. Thomas jumped, spilling his drink down his front.

'I didn't mean to startle you, may I sit?'

Thomas motioned to the chair. 'Please, please, no it's fine I've had worse.'

'New crops, new King.' She turned and smiled at the innkeeper, who already prepared a plate of food. 'Thank you.'

Thomas looked excited. 'Yes, yes of course. New king, things going badly, that makes sense. Pests could be a reference to the Malagara, disappearing?'

'Makes sense.' Ember pushed his plate aside and sat back in his chair. 'Sourcing last year's produce seller, could be his way of saying we are in danger, if last year's crops are reference to Isyllia.'

'So Gelraen is king, things are going badly, he is after me still and Malagara are a problem. We know all this already.' She sounded slightly frustrated. 'We need *new* information, not the same thing over and over!'

'What about the last Half?' Ember nodded to Thomas, who read through it for a moment.

'He makes a point of saying his contact is detained... that could only mean arrested. I thought Duke Randal was the only one who knew where you were?'
Isyllia's face was pale with worry. 'He is.'

'So Gelraen has arrested Randal and somehow he has sent this Imaar to warn us.'

Thomas nodded. 'Then there is the last part, opening a market is Mespar, and he says something about at least being able to count on you.'

'Does Randal want us to go to Mespar, find out what is going on?' Isyllia shook her head, the thoughts flashing over her face remaining silent.

'Would be the wisest course of action.' Ember frowned, not altogether convinced of the resolution.

'Then the last part, I feel like he is trying to tell us there are enemies we are unaware of, but who?' Thomas looked to Isyllia.

She shook her head, stumped. 'No one that we don't already know about.'

They remained silent for a moment, no doubt digesting the news.

'I've been thinking.' She directed the thought at Ember pushing away the rest of her food, clearly still bothered.

Ember tensed automatically.

'I know we need to get to...our destination, but I think we should visit your family while we are so close.'

Ember resisted the urge to curse with great difficulty. 'No, we don't have time.'

'I'm not stupid Ember; I know it's dangerous right now, more so with Randal in custody. But isn't that just it? Any day could be our last. I would give anything for one more day with my father.' Her face was set.

He looked at Thomas, a map had been raised to cover his face. 'Thomas.'

'Hmm?' He pulled the map down, trying to pretend he had not been listening.

Ember glared.

'I don't know!' Thomas hated conflict. 'It couldn't hurt. Would be a reliable source of news at any rate, until Mr Fennly returns, we are still in the dark.'

Ember considered the last, agreeing after a while to a short visit.

Isyllia smiled contentedly, pushing back on her chair and rising to her feet. 'I will get the bags.'

Ember sighed. 'I will prepare the horses.' He did not wait for Thomas to reply, his mind on the days ahead. It had been a long time since he had seen his brothers, he had missed them. Even the strained relationship he had with Darin had passed over the years, and a part of him yearned to see his mother. Ember arrived at the stable sooner than he expected, looking up in surprise when the stable master greeted him. 'Want to look over the animals?'

Ember nodded. 'And collect.'

The man nodded. 'You will find them well rested, beauties all of them ... sept that one. Right temper on it that one.' The man pointed to Niimorea. Ember smirked; somehow, he had guessed she would be a handful. He waited while the man led the horses out, placing freshly cleaned saddles on their backs. Perrin whinnied happily when he saw Ember, trotting over and nuzzling him gently in the chest. A few more minutes and he paid the man, thanking him for the care and led them out. Thomas and Isyllia waited out the front of the Inn, bags in hand.

'I told the keep we were to be leaving.' Thomas walked over to his horse, careful to leave a wide berth between Niimorea and himself.

'Good.' Ember nodded, absentmindedly placing bags back on the horses. They spent the next hour refilling their supplies. And after quick calculations, Ember worked out that he had three quarters of the coin he had saved left. It was nearly noon by the time they were back on the road again, Ember taking the lead with Isyllia riding behind. They had been enjoying the morning ride when a squeaking sound high above cut through the silence. Mr Fennly had finally returned, flying lazily around Thomas, who spent a few good minutes chiding the animal for his tardiness.

'Where the devil did you go?'

'*Squeeeak.*'

'I don't care what you smelled; you should have been here yesterday.'

Ember chuckled, deciding it best to ignore them, and sure enough, after a while they had stopped their bickering, and looking around, he saw that Mr Fennly now sat comfortably on Thomas shoulder, their earlier quarrel forgotten.

The rest of the afternoon was quiet, events of the previous night still raw on their faces. It was not until they began to see houses in the distance that Ember felt a small pang of nerves. They had arrived. He put up his hand, motioning for a halt then closed his eyes and concentrated, searching. Part of him still wondered if Gelraen had set a trap. But after a few minutes, everything seemed clear still and he signalled they continue. It was another hour until they reached the first of the houses. Everything looked the same as he had left it all those years ago, except the people. Faces he had known, had grown older, children he did not know, ran the streets, as he had once with his brothers. For the first time Ember felt guilty about how much time had passed. And so, when they arrived at the place he used to call home, he found himself confused by the strange woman that walked out the door holding a basket of laundry and chiding a small boy to go play. Where were his brothers? He dismounted and approached the woman. 'Excuse me, I was looking for Marcos? He used to live here.'

The woman strained, clearly trying to put face to name. 'That would be my husband. But I am sorry, I don't know…'

Ember smiled. 'He is my brother.'

The woman blanched, dropping her basket, her eyes filling with tears. 'Ember?'

He nodded slowly.

The woman ran forward, embracing Ember, then stepping back suddenly embarrassed. 'I'm Mel, I'm sorry. He has told me so much, I wondered if I would ever meet you.'

Ember smiled. 'Is he home?'

She nodded, wiping her face. 'Yes, well, he's in smithy. Calen.' She called the small boy over. 'Calen, go get your father now, hurry?'

'What's wrong momma?'

'Nothing hon, nothing, just go get your father, be quick now.' The boy bounced off waving his toy in the air as he ran. Ember watched him go, he looked so much like Marcos.

'Who are your friends?'

Ember turned back, motioning for the others to join him. 'This is Marelle.' Isyllia approached, throwing a quizzical glance at Ember and then Kissing Mel on the cheek. He knew he had said she was to use her real name, but the fewer questions his family asked, the better. He continued. 'And this is Thomas?'

Mel smiled at Thomas. 'And who is your little friend there?'

Thomas stroked Mr Fennly on the chin. 'This, is Mr Fennly.'

'Nice to meet you all, come inside.' She was cut short, another voice, and older woman, determined but struggling on her way. 'I know that voice, is it...?' She came through the door, she had aged, her hair sporting thick wisps of grey, but she was the same.

'Momma' Ember beamed. His mother burst into tears, embracing her long-lost son. It was a few minutes until the ageing woman could gain her composure, too frightened to let him go. 'I thought I would never see you again.'

'I'm here.' He felt at peace for the first time in a while, they had been right to come.

'I'll take the horses.' Mel offered quietly, Ember did not look up, for once not caring.

'I'll help.' Thomas followed Mel to the stable leaving Ember with Isyllia and his mother. 'Mother, this is Marelle.'

Isyllia curtseyed, trying to hide the tears in her eyes.

'Marelle, this is my mother. Mary.' He tried to ignore the awkward sensation that suddenly flared in his stomach, shifting on his feet as if that would somehow dislodge it.

Mary walked forward placing a hand on Isyllia's face, 'Ah. What a beauty you are, my child…

Come.' Ember followed them inside, the house was much the same as he had always known it. Mary sat on a sofa, placing a blanket over her lap. More footsteps sounded on the hearth; this time heavier. Ember looked around to find his brother, Marcos. He had aged also, thin lines kissed his face in places and small hints of grey could be seen here and there in his short dark hair, but it was still him. Marcos bounded forward, embracing his brother deeply. 'It's been far too long brother, too long.' He laughed.

'You have a son!'

Marcos smiled, calling the boy over 'Just the one so far, we named him Calen, Calen Ember.'

Ember smiled for a moment, then just as quickly, his heart sank. Calen. 'Where is father? And Darin?'

This time it was Mary who spoke, and her voice was soft, too soft. 'Marcos, why don't you take Marelle and show her where she can freshen up.' Ember looked at Isyllia, her face echoing what he was feeling. Something was wrong, it was not good news coming.

◁✳○✳

Gelraen, Illingdale Castle.

'I have been sent to check on your progress. I must say, we expected you would fail, but not this spectacularly.' A man, advanced in age, stood with his back to Gelraen. He was dressed in black, looking out the window like a shadow that stood stock still against the glass, his walking cane held loosely in one hand, suggesting it was for effect only. Gelraen sucked in a breath, swallowing the oxygen hard, like it was made of granite. 'There is still one chance. Please, I beg you.'

At this, the man laughed, and turned to face the frightened king. There were lines on his face, suggesting the age he looked, but somehow, he was different, something ethereal emanated from this man. 'Why?' He did not wait for an answer. In a blink, the man had vanished, reappearing behind Gelraen. Gelraens eyes flew wide, turning to a scream as the man somehow extended his hand around Gelraens throat, and tightened. 'He bores of your incompetence.' The man eased his grip, causing Gelraen to fall forward, clutching at his throat and gasping for air. He took a few deep lungfuls and then turned, but the man was gone, a knock at the door standing in his stead. Gelraen rose, his face still red from struggle, 'What?'

A perplexed voice sounded from the other side, 'You called sire?' It was Lord Walton.

Gelraen took another deep breath, straightening his jerkin. 'Enter!' Lord Walton walked into the room, slightly nervous, whether sensing Gelraens tension, or from something else you couldn't tell. Gelraen stood tall, masking his panic as best he could. 'What news?'

Lord Walton hesitated, 'They were in Eddinsford Sire, someone spotted them at the annual fair.'

Gelraen held his breath, 'What do you mean, were?'

Lord Walton hesitated again, his nerves getting the better of him. 'They escaped sire; the guards were unable to stop them.' Gelraen chewed his lip for a moment, then threw a pot across the room, watching as it smashed into tiny shards, some of which fell into the fireplace. 'How can they have eluded you for this long, your incompetence is staggering.' He turned, glaring at Lord Walton.

Lord Walton bowed, sweat on his brow. 'She is Malagara sir, what can regular soldiers do against such evil.'

He took a deep breath. 'Did the report say which direction they were headed?'

'No sire, only that the soldiers went missing a day west of the Wetlands. There were large cracks in the ground where they were last seen, like an earthquake had struck.'

Gelraen stood, trying to digest the information. She was learning, if she got her hands on the stone, all would be lost. He paced the room for a bit, an idea forming in his head. 'Summon Adella to my chambers, now!'

General Walton bowed. 'Will that be all sire?'

Gelraen waved him off.

The Duke bowed again and left the room.

Gelraen moved over to a chair, he would need to be smart. If only he knew where the stone was, all history of the chosen had been burned in the uprising, all save the archives at Mespar. He knew writing to them for access to their records would be suspicious. No, his only chance was to draw her back into the city.

Adella's presence was announced twenty minutes later. 'Enter.' He said, his voice stoic.

Adella walked across the room, her face was passive, empty. 'How does William progress?'

Adella barely blinked, 'Badly. Had it not been for the bliss, I fear ...'? She did not finish. She did not need to.

Gelraen sighed. 'Continue giving it to him, but not too much, I need him coherent.'

Adella frowned, 'Sire?'

'Lord Walton is incompetent, I fear if I am to recapture Isyllia, and I must, I will have to take matters into my own hands.'

'I could go, William is not ready to hunt her, not yet. He needs more time.'

Gelraen shook his head, beginning to pace his thoughts out over the floorboards. 'We don't have that kind of time. No, I need to lure her here, and Randal is the only card I have left. I need to somehow get news of where they are.'

Adella nodded. 'They were last seen leaving Eddinsford, they have already fled Illingdale. That at least for the moment puts them in Tinderford.'

Gelraen looked puzzled, 'How?' Then remembering her profession, gave up on pursuing the answer. 'Good. I need you to send someone a letter for me, say that Randal is to be executed in one week. Make it sound like a public announcement, I want them to think they have a chance to save him.'

Adella nodded, 'I can do that. What is your plan?'

'I know Isyllia, Randal was like a second father to her, she would never let him die. She will try to come back and save him on her own. But if she is still with Ember, and I believe she is, he would never allow her to come alone. No, they will try to raise an army.'

'How is that a desired outcome?'

Gelraen paused, deciding whether to elaborate. He decided against it. 'Just make sure she is able to make it to the throne room. Keep Ember away if possible, but don't kill him. I want William here when she arrives. I only need to contain her.'

Adella frowned, not following the idea. 'As your majesty commands.'

'You are dismissed. 'Adella left without another word, leaving Gelraen to contemplate alone. *I should just tell them the stakes!* The thought sat for a moment, but no. They would never agree, this is the only way. He shook his head, ensuring the thought was completely gone and then downed another glass of whisky, knowing all he could do now, was wait.

◁✳ ○✳

Isyllia, Clae Residence, Tinderford.

The room was quiet, except for the playful noises of Calen in the corner. He had been stacking some blocks, then smashing them down again, repeating the process over and over.

'Does anyone know where he went?' It was Mel.

Mary took a deep breath, the sudden flight of her son had left her drained, and the stress was evident on her face. 'He shouldn't have found out this way. I said this would happen if he ever came back.' She had not heard the question.

'I don't suppose there's a smithy nearby?' Isyllia asked, already knowing exactly where he would be, if given the chance.

'Ours!' Marcos replied, looking at his mother with concern.

'That's where he is.' Isyllia let out a breath, not realising she had been holding it.

'I'll go!' Isyllia looked over to the source of the voice. Antonia and Darin had arrived shortly after Ember had left. Isyllia drew her breath back in sharply, Antonia.The memory of Ember's reaction to the name sending spikes of irrational anger down her spine. Antonia stood slowly, holding her heavily pregnant stomach as she rose. Darin sat straight, visibly gritting his teeth. If it were possible, Darin looked to be the more serious of the three brothers.

'No Antonia, you are too close to your time, stay, I'll go. Marelle, would you help me; these legs are not what they used to be.' They did not argue, watching as Mary got slowly to her feet, evidently in pain. Antonia sat back down, a hint of disappointment on her face.

Isyllia took his mother's arm, slowing her pace to match the ageing woman's.

'I have missed my son, my dear little heart... This is not how I wanted to see him again.'

Isyllia felt sorry for the woman, Ember was clearly her favourite. 'It must have been hard to let him go.'

She nodded, staring back at the memory, 'It was... I cried for many nights. He was so young, too young. But he was never mine to keep, Caros claimed him, as surely as he made this world.'

Isyllia stared ahead. 'How could he know the will of the gods?' Ember's words from the other night still playing over in her mind. *'Some of us have no choice.'* 'Surely they would wish the chosen to be happy too!'

Mary smiled knowingly. 'I could never tell him of course, but he is so much like his father, stubborn as mules, both... Calen was always kind. He would give his last meal to a starving babe, if it meant they could live another day.'

'Was Ember close to his father?'

Mary sighed. 'Calen loved Ember, and Ember craved that love. He saw so much of himself in the boy... It broke his heart when he saw the mark; he could never forgive Caros for taking his son. So, Calen pushed him away, too afraid to love him knowing he would be gone someday. Ember tried so hard to gain his father's approval, but stubborn Calen never gave in, not even the last time he saw the boy. He never said goodbye... I fear Ember carries his father's disapproval like a shadow. It makes him second guess himself. That is why he always closes himself in that tin shed, why he is so focused on his destiny; it's the only time he can feel in control, anything to avoid facing the real pain.'

Isyllia knew she had just met the woman an hour earlier, but there was something in her face, the same kindness she saw in Embers that made her feel like she could trust her. 'He's always so angry with me... I feel like I constantly disappoint him.'

'You terrify him, a mother sees these things.' Mary gave her a knowing smile, and the two continued in companionable silence for a moment, Isyllia treading a little uneasy, surely, she was not going to leave it there? Thankfully she did not. 'You make him question everything he believes in. So, he does the one thing his father taught him to do, he shuts you out.'

Isyllia felt her stomach drop, 'But why? What have I done to him!'

'My dear, isn't it obvious? Mary stopped and faced her, an amused cock to the side of her mouth that she recognised all too well.

Isyllia stared, but nothing came, except the tell-tale red stain of embarrassment. 'My dear, he is in love with you.'

The revelation hit her like a hammer, how had she not realised! 'I had no idea!'

'I see that.' Mary chuckled, 'Go my dear, comfort him, he needs you right now, even if the stubborn fool won't admit it.' Mary stroked Isyllia's cheek, then nodded to the shed that now sat beside them before turning to walk back alone. A half-faded sign hung above with the bold letters Clae Steel. Isyllia's stomach dropped further. Isyllia watched her for a moment, still reeling from the conversation, then took a deep breath and turned toward the small shop they had stopped at. She walked forward, spotting a patch of violet on her left. A small bush of flowers grew at the side, no doubt an effort to make it more inviting. Isyllia picked one of the blooms, then thinking it best not to announce herself, she walked in. What must have been a neat and orderly workshop, lay in ruin. It took a moment for him to realise she was standing there, his head down, staring through a hammer he held in his hand. He stood for a moment longer, and then dropped the tool, covering his face with his hands.

Isyllia's heart lurched, it had only been a few short weeks since she had lost her own father and the pain was still raw, she could feel it in her stomach. Isyllia dropped the flower and strode forward, wrapping her arms around his neck, holding him close, desperate to take away the pain. He did not protest, burying his face into her shoulder. 'I'm here.' She did not know how long she blew the words into his ear. Or when it was that he turned his head, his sad eyes locked on hers, and kissed her. Finally, everything was clear, all the times he had saved her, all the moments of panic and anger in his eyes. Now she could feel the overwhelming love that strangled him and the hunger that he kissed her with. Isyllia responded, feeling all the pain that she held sealed in her heart evaporate in his arms, at last realising she too had wanted this. She kissed him deeper, remembering the way his naked body shone in the night, when he had not realised, she was watching. Feeling him as he pressed himself into her, moving her gently against the bench, then pressing harder, making her groan from deep within as his hands began to wander.

Isyllia barely noticed as she began to remove his mail vest, discarding it on the ground and pulling him closer, tearing at his white shirt until the heat under her skin became uncontrollable, the furnace in the corner of the room igniting into flames, driving them out of the moment.

Ember turned, looking into the blaze, his shoulders sunk and his voice breathless. 'I'm sorry, I should not have done that.'

Isyllia placed one hand gently on his shoulder blade, unable to let go of what she had begun to feel. 'Ember...'

He lowered his head. 'We can't.' The pain in his voice was heartbreaking.

She stepped back, the rejection bringing tears to her eyes. 'Why? We are both human Ember, we are meant to love.'

Ember turned. 'But that's just it, we're not human, we're chosen. Isyllia, your powers could have killed us, then who would be there to protect the people? Can you honestly stand there and tell me we have a right to be selfish?'

Isyllia looked down, she could not let him see her cry, she had to hold it in. 'No. But I can't live like this either, Ember.'

'It's like I said, some people don't have a choice.' He turned back to the fire. 'Go, I'll clean up here.'

Isyllia did not need to be told twice, fleeing the shop and into the cold evening air. She walked back blindly, trying to come to grips with the gaping hole that now sat in her heart, more pieces of her soul stolen forever, for a destiny she didn't ask for. And as she neared the house, she stopped for a moment, straightening her skirts, even though she did not need to and took a deep breath. 'Keep it in. You are still a Bellamy, you can do this.' Words she had told herself many times, and even though she barely understood what they meant anymore, she steeled herself against her aching heart, and walked inside.

Mary had returned and was sitting on the couch; she looked up, taking in the situation. To others in the room, Isyllia looked like any other person, returning from an evening walk. But to Mary, it was clear exactly what had transcribed between the girl and her son, and Mary was heartbroken. Isyllia tried not to look at her, knowing she would lose her composure if she did. Instead she sat down; small talk was a good distraction. 'Ember will be along shortly.'

'How is he?' It was Marcos, of the two brothers, Marcos had seemed to be the one closest to Ember, and the concern still etched on his face confirmed as much. Darin still sat in the corner; his expression steeled against any emotion. What had happened between Ember and his eldest brother to cause such indifference? She tried not to think about that, or the pregnant woman sitting next to him and instead smiled at Marcos. 'He is well, he just needed some space, he has apologised for causing concern.' She looked at the floor.

'Well that is good news. Marcos, would you help Mel finish up the supper, I think it's time we all ate, no?' Mary cut in; leaving Isyllia with one more reason to be grateful to this kind woman she wished she could know better. Murmurs of agreement filled the room as everyone stood to prepare, where it was decided Darin and Marcos would eat on the couch, and Mel would eat hers after.

Ember finally returned as Mel was bringing out a heavy pot, followed dutifully by her husband and Calen doing his best to dance in the way of his mother. Isyllia looked to Ember, his expression was controlled, and the frown he wore so often sat back in its place, only now she could see so much more. Now she could see the aching need he fought against, now she could see how he struggled to hold her gaze. It sent fresh pangs of longing and despair through her stomach, and looking down, she wondered again how she had never noticed it!

'Ember.' It was Antonia, she stood, holding her stomach, waving off Darin's hand of support. 'My goodness! You have not changed at all!'

Ember smiled leaning in to kiss her on the cheek. 'I have a little ...congratulations.' He nodded to her stomach.

'Thank you, we have been trying for a while now. The gods finally saw fit to bless us.' She placed an arm around her husband, but something about the sparkle in her eye left the impression that he was not her first choice. The suspected rift between the two brothers was becoming clearer.

'Brother.' It was Darin, he seemed hesitant and his voice was stiff, but he stood beside his wife, hand outstretched.

Ember stared at it for a moment, then shook it, a weak smile spreading across his face.

Darin beamed, relief visibly floating through his body and without waiting a second longer, he embraced his brother.

'Congratulations Darin.'

'Thank you. I'm sorry you were not told about father.'

Ember stepped back, only nodding.

'How long are you planning to stay?' It was Antonia, the hope was unmistakable on her face. Isyllia resisted the urge to throw a plate at her, and at the same time, felt a little relieved to understand why she despised the woman so undeservedly.

'He's not going anywhere until I've fed him!' It was Mary; she placed one arm around her long-lost son and herded him to the table. 'Sit, you need a good meal, you look like a street urchin.' Isyllia looked at Mary, her jest not reaching her eyes. It was clear letting go of her son *any* day was too soon.

Thomas leant in, indicating Isyllia moved closer.

She held her breath, knowing that like Mary, he was not so easily fooled.

'I would ask what happened to his shirt, but I can see from the looks on your faces, you might rather not talk about it.' He smiled.

Isyllia bit her lip to avoid giggling despite herself; he always seemed to have a way of finding the humour in a situation. 'Indeed … later!' She looked down at her hands, Thomas squeezed her palm in comfort.

She smiled, grateful for the gesture. She had not known him for long, but in that time, he had become a good friend. If only she had met him long ago, things would have been easier with him around.

The rest of the evening sailed by as if a blur, as comforting times often do. Once the meal was done, Marcos and Darin took turns to tell stories about their childhood memories with Ember, and the various pranks they played on each other.

'Stole your clothes?' Isyllia looked incredulous.

Ember clenched his teeth. 'That was the worst one.'

'That was Darin.' Marcos lowered his face, eager to hide the red stain spreading across his cheeks.

'Bloody Liar, that was both of us.' Darin threw a napkin at his brother that resulted in gales of laughter.

'And what did you do about this?' It was Isyllia, relishing the embarrassment on Ember's face.

He shook his head; there was no dodging the question, but it was answered for him.

'He ran out after them and almost knocked me off my feet, that's what he did.' Antonia smiled. Darin looked to the floor.

'Yes, well. It was cold.' Ember didn't meet her eyes.

Isyllia looked at Thomas. He too had noticed the sudden temperature drop in the room.

'That's how we met, isn't that right, Ember? I remember it like yesterday; He was so embarrassed he could barely string a sentence together.' She pressed.

Everybody in the room was hoping someone would change the subject, but nobody wanted to be the one to do it.

'Yes, well I seem to remember a similar incident when you met Mel Marcos. As I recall it, you tried to sing to her when you were drunk, and fell into some manure?' Darin stole a look at Ember; there was apology in his eyes.

Ember grinned at his brother. The rift between them forgotten. 'Manure. An improvement I'm sure.'

Marcos' look was thunderous, but he laughed all the same.

'Oh, hush.' It was Mel, kissing her husband on the cheek. 'I thought he was adorable. I knew there was no one else for me.'

Isyllia looked at Ember, but he did not look over. Still, she could see the same thought of earlier flash across his face that shadowed her, still hanging in the air between them.

They talked for a time longer, and despite everything, Ember found it in himself to laugh. For one blissful moment he forgot himself and remembered easier times. At least until it came. A knock at the door sent the room into a collection of familiar frowns.

'Mel, would you?' Mary pointed to the door, but Mel was already on her feet. She was only away a moment when she came back looking puzzled.

'It's for Ember. But who would know you are here?'

Ember froze, as did Thomas.

Mary snatched the letter from Mel and ripped it open. The room waited in anticipation as she read the contents, her face took on the same puzzled expression as her daughter in law. 'Ember.' Then holding out the letter she passed it to her still frozen son.

He just stared at the object for a moment and then stole a glance at Isyllia as he read the contents. He swore, then handed the letter to Thomas, who blanched, then handed it to Isyllia.

Notice given to the Guild of Tinderford, with all due courtesy, to inform of the formal trial, addressing the charges of treason made against the honoured

Duke of Godswall of the Royal Kingdom of Illingdale. Sentence to be pronounced 2 weeks hence, execution to follow. We advise you in the interest of possible trade difficulties during this time.'

'What's the bloody letter say?' It was Marcos, his impatience getting the better of him.

Ember looked thunderous, like the last thing he wanted to do was be in a room full of people who he had to offer explanations to. 'It's time to go, that's what it said.' He rose to his feet.

'Wait, you've just returned, at least stay the night, it cannot be that important?' It was Marcos, he was hurt.

'I'm sorry, we cannot afford to delay too long anywhere.'

'You're sorry! You-.'

Mel tried to pull her husband away, but he wrenched his arm free, he would not be deterred.

'NO. You have been gone 15 years, not so much as a word to tell us you were ok, or that you were even alive. And all you care about is some damn destiny, but what about us? Never mind if we need you here.'

'Marcos!' It was Mel again, this time she was more insistent.

'I'm done.' He turned to walk away. 'If you have to go, go. But this time don't come back.' He walked out the door. Ember stood silent, trying to take in another pain he did not need to bear.

'We are leaving.' He set his jaw, locking more pain in the vault of sorrows he stored deep inside.

She nodded, knowing it was best not to say anything.

'What is the plan though.' Thomas said, his face turning red, no doubt knowing the question was not going to provoke a happy answer.

'We can discuss that out on the road.' Ember spoke through clenched teeth.

'We are your family Ember, what are you hiding from us?' It was Mary, she stood and held out her hand for the letter. 'Hand it over.' It was evident where the stubbornness and strength in the family came from.

Isyllia thought she might faint, her knees trying to bail on her. Both Mary and Ember gave her the same glare. In the end, she handed the letter over, deciding it could do no more harm, since Gelraen already knew they were here, and Mary had already read it.

Why would this concern you?' Ember and Isyllia looked at each other.

'My name isn't Marelle, It's Isyllia Bellamy. I'm the rightful queen of Illingdale, and Ember has been protecting me.' She blushed.

Mary had been looking from one to the other, resting on Ember. 'Is that true?'

'It is. She is chosen, like me. The letter is clearly a trap, designed to draw Isyllia back into the city.' Now he looked at Isyllia, 'We will be ignoring it.' Then back to his mother, 'But staying here any longer puts you in danger, we must go.'

'Let us talk about this for a minute though.' Darin had decided to chip in, Antonia sat beside him looking faint, her eyes on Isyllia. 'What exactly could the three of you do? This man is being held by a city full of soldiers, I'm assuming.' He looked to Isyllia for agreement.

Isyllia nodded. 'An army. Which is why I should go alone. It is me Gelraen wants!'

Ember stiffened.

'You said yourself, Kathriin took Illingdale on her own, so it's been done.'

Ember clenched his jaw so hard the bones could be seen under his skin, the first sign that his mind was made up. 'Two thousand years ago ... and she not only had the stone, she knew how to use her powers, and she was crazed. She killed Woman and children Isyllia, that is why she won. You still do not know how to use your powers. If you go back there, you will die. I know Gelraen, and he knows you'll try to rescue Randal. Why do you think he sent the letter here? He already knows exactly what we are going to do!'

'Then find a better way, because I am going.' If he could be stubborn, so could she.

'Do you have any allies you can call on, who are loyal to your family?' It was Darin, trying to be the voice of reason.

Thomas sat up, 'What about Imaar?'

Isyllia thought for a moment 'The Duke of Preston has always been father's best ally, but he was not at the Honour-Giving, no one has heard from him. Imaar is a councillor and could get us into the city if we wrote to him and arranged to meet, but we don't have that kind of time.'

'Well that's a start at least; can we see where he stands?' Thomas looked at Ember, shrinking back from the fury on his face.

'And even if Imaar is willing to get us inside the city, then what? How is he going to raise an army in time and then sneak it past Gelraen? You would doom him, and his men to death.'

Isyllia was silent for a moment, knowing he was right, knowing it left her only one option. 'Then I surrender; offer him what he wants in exchange for Randal's freedom.'

'No!' Ember was livid now. 'You're not sacrificing yourself; this is not what Abashiina chose you for.'

'Yes, it is! She chose me to protect the innocent, Randal is innocent. If I leave him to die, I am no better than Kathriin.'

Ember looked at the ground, his jaw still set. 'The life of one cannot replace the lives of many, I am not saying it is easy, but that is why we are chosen, to make the hard choices and put the people before our own wishes.'

Isyllia shook her head, he was arguing with himself, again. 'We don't know that. The Malagara are rumours, and even if they are escaping, why does that mean they are a danger? Why can't we consider that it's at least possible that they just blended into society. What if Gelraen is the threat we are meant to stop!'

Ember shook his head, his exasperation clear. 'I cannot stop you, so I will ask you one last time, don't do this, don't get yourself killed for nothing.' His expression had changed, she could see through the mask of stubbornness now; he was panicking, Ember did not like being in situations he could not control. They could all see it.

Isyllia lowered her voice to almost a whisper. 'You know I have to.'

'Wait.' Thomas' eyes had widened like saucers. 'What if Gelraen just thinks you are giving yourself up… as a diversion!'

Ember had lost none of the pained expression he nursed, but he was listening. 'Go on.'

'I will send Mr Fennly to the Duchy of Godswall, asking them to mobilise their men, to free the Duke. His Duchy is on the way, so if they prepare before we get there, we would not lose much time.'

'One duchy won't be enough to defeat an army.' Ember shot; his arms crossed in defiance again, you need to remember, they won't just have the city's men, they will have Gelraen's men. The Duke's men would be outnumbered and surrounded.'

Isyllia cut in. 'The Duke of Godswall is one faction of Illingdale's army, the city housing another, the city troops are spread out on all sides, we would have the advantage, and our numbers would be similar.'

Ember sighed, sitting back down heavily on the chair, like it would somehow discard the frustration that clung to him. It did not work. 'It's like I said, even if the Duchy can help us, they would have to march an army past Morliin to get to the city in time. The infantry would be swarmed on both sides by heavy cavalry, it would be a massacre. You would see hundreds of men slaughtered to save one man.

Ember's frustration had begun to spread to Isyllia, she crossed her arms in annoyance, there had to be a way. 'Randal is a smart man, I don't believe he would offer himself up to Gelraen without a plan, I have to trust that.'

Ember sat forward; his arms clasped together in front of him. 'All right, let's pretend for a minute that Randal has warned his men to be prepared, and they are willing to follow me, because let's be honest, an entire duchy is not going to march off to war with their own country for some merchant's son, sorry Thomas.'

Thomas waved him off.

'Nor would I put you at the helm since you cannot fight, have no military experience, and don't know how to use your powers. I am the best chance we have to get them to mobilise. And even if I can do that, and it's a big if, it could take days to get into the city, weeks.' Ember shook his head; they were not convincing him.

'What is your suggestion then?' It was Mary, she at least, was willing to humour the idea.

'We would have a better chance using the army as a distraction only, the real goal a smaller force to infiltrate the city, while the soldiers are focused on the army out front, but that does not change what I said, Gelraen is still the Duke of Morliin, and his troops will see us coming, that is the whole reason the duchies are where they are, to see an army coming.'

'Wait.' It was Thomas, a small spark of light flickered across his face. 'The powder.'

Ember glared at him, waiting for further explanation.

Thomas got the hint. 'A year ago, I found something. Long story short, it explodes when fire touches it.'

'I don't want to ask how you found that out' Isyllia could not help the hint of a smile from arresting her face.

'No.' Thomas however was strained, his nose crinkled like he was trying to restrain the uninvited memory from replaying.

'How does that help us.' Ember's patience was draining, the bigger surprise being that he had any left at all.

'I could go separately with a small company and destroy Morliin, and if I waited until they were a good distance out of the Duchy, it would take them time to again double back and protect the duchy, which should put them out of the equation at least.'

He frowned. 'It puts their cavalry out of the picture sure, but their infantry would continue marching to the city.'

Thomas scoffed with amusement. 'Well yes, but infantry are a lot slower, it still buys you a decent patch of time, and I don't exactly plan to stick around, all I need is archers to set the packages alight, and then we get out and make for the city, it's like you said. I am just a merchant's son! Nobody will notice me.'

Darin turned to Isyllia, 'Is there any other way to get into your city beside the two main gates?'

Isyllia thought for a moment. 'There is the water gate!'

'Water gate?' Thomas frowned.

'Yes, it's insignificant, tiny, just used to transport water from the stream, would be no good for an army, but we might be able to trick the guards into letting us in, if there were only a few of us.'

Ember seemed to be running an idea over in his head. 'Or if there is enough panic to confuse them … how much of this stuff do you have?' He turned back to Thomas.

'Enough to share.' Thomas seemed to follow his unspoken idea.

Ember stood and walked away to think. 'All right. Thomas, contact the duchy, we will begin riding tonight. You will go ahead to meet at the duchy, we will go to the cave, and come along after.'

'I'll write the letter and get the horses ready.' Thomas excused himself, walking some distance away. Mel followed, her face white as her undershirt.

'You have a plan?' Isyllia crossed over to where he stood on the other side of the room alone. She kept her voice low, the others busied themselves in discussion, no doubt about the turn of events all but Antonia, who sat staring ahead with her head cocked to the side, like she was listening. Isyllia ignored the pang of annoyance that followed and turned back to Ember. It was a moment before he responded, he seemed to be struggling with himself. His eyes widened, and he ran his hand through his hair. 'It is an ambitious plan, but if Godswall can give us what we need, it could work... you are going to go either way, this way I can at least protect you.'

Isyllia felt a pain rise in her chest, she reached out and touched his cheek, he was as warm and gentle as a sunrise. Ember closed his eyes, but did not move away, nor did he move forward. Isyllia felt the pangs of longing turn to guilt, and removed her hand, instead deciding to turn to the remaining members of Ember's family, each knowing it was time, and each hoping it was not.

'At least take some food, you don't eat enough.' It was Mary. Her voice was unsteady, but she kept her composure for her son's sake.

Ember hugged his mother. Isyllia didn't need to read his thoughts to know that leaving her, knowing that he may never see her again was torture. It was a short time later when Thomas and Mel returned with the horses. They both echoed the same thoughts on their face, both drawing their lips in sadness. Isyllia

413

turned to face Mel. 'I am sorry for the trouble.' She found herself unable to acknowledge Darin and Antonia. Especially Antonia, who did not look at all like she minded being forgotten.

'None of that.' Mel hugged her. 'Come; let me get you some things for the road.'

The farewells were short, Marcos, did not come to say goodbye.

'Have patience with him, he needs you, he will realise it eventually.' It was Mary.

Isyllia hugged the woman, tears stinging her eyes. She had never known her mother, and for a few hours, she had started to realise what it must feel like to have one.

'Be safe.' Mary let go, wiping her eyes.

'Thank you.' It was almost impossible to let go, but she did, climbing and sitting atop Niimorea, and then waiting for Ember's signal to ride. He said goodbye to his mother last, they exchanged some words that she did not hear, but she did not want to and instead turned her attention to tying the ropes on her sack, the new clothes Mel had given her struggling to fit in.

Finally, Ember remounted Perrin, kicking him into a trot. They rode through the town in silence, the cold evening air pushing them forward. At last Isyllia turned back, looking for the last time at the place Ember had called home, spotting in the distance, a figure. He sat atop a horse, but he did not come forward, instead, he turned and slowly rode away.

Marcos had come to say goodbye just as before, only this time, Ember would never know.

Chapter Thirteen

Isyllia, Ravenswood, Tinderford.

A day had passed since the incident, but still, an air of resentment trailed them like it had been five minutes. Ember barely spoke, always taking to riding ahead, then when it was time to rest, he sat by himself, offering the occasional one-worded answer, but never joining in the conversation. It was that afternoon, after staring at his sullen figure ahead Isyllia finally had to say something. 'He can't go on like this; one of us has to speak to him.'

Thomas sighed, swatting a fly from his arm. 'Sure, maybe he will increase his vocabulary to three words?' He asked, an air sarcasm following the comment.

'It's not funny, Thomas.'

He flicked it off his shoulder, not looking over. 'No, but I don't know what good you are hoping it will do.'

They rode in silence again for a time, the sun had begun to retreat on the horizon, leaving an evening chill in the air. Isyllia had never seen the mountains, they loomed overhead, overwhelming in their majesty. She craned her head, now barely able to see the top, they had to be close now.

'This is where I believe I leave you!' It was Thomas. 'Cave is just ahead.' He pointed stupidly.

Isyllia got down from her horse and walked over, Thomas doing the same.

'Take care, please.' Isyllia hugged him, feeling the tears sting her eyes. Saying goodbye to another friend, even for a short time, was not easy.

Thomas let go, his eyes not at all escaping the emotion. 'You too, be patient with him.' He nodded to Ember.

She cocked a smile, 'You sound like his mother.'

He returned the grin, 'Yes well.'

'See you soon.' He called over to Ember. Ember did not get down from his horse, but there was a deep respect in the smile that he returned to his friend. It was a fondness that no embrace could improve on. 'Be safe Thomas.'

Using that as his cue, Thomas returned to his horse, and clicked it on. 'I would be more worried if I was stuck with her.' He pointed to Niimorea, and then rode off into the distance, leaving the two to laugh at his retreating figure. After a while, Isyllia returned to Niimorea and looked ahead, a small cave opening could be seen in the distance. They had indeed found the Cave of lost souls. She stared ahead, a strange sensation coming over her, like an invisible hand pulled her forward, and kicking Niimorea into a trot, she flew forward toward the drumming. Unable to resist the calling.

'Isyllia!' She could hear his voice, but she could not stop. Just as she had at the Ruins of Eddinsford, she rode forward, steering Niimorea faster. The calling got stronger until she felt it pulse in her chest, like a heartbeat, only this time it felt much stronger, this time it felt right. This time, it was meant for her. Isyllia rode up to the cave mouth, leaving Niimorea at the entrance, only caring about getting inside. She ran in, hoof beats thundering in the distance, but she didn't care, running as fast as her feet would take her. Through darkness she ran, until at last she came to a chasm, stretching a mile wide. She would need light, looking around she searched for anything that could be used, a single torch sat against the wall, perhaps waiting for her? She moved to take it, nerves beginning to creep into her stomach. Closing her eyes, she drew heat around the torch until eventually it blazed with light. She took a sigh of relief, footsteps were getting closer, turning she moved back to the chasm.

'Isyllia stop.' It was Ember, fury and panic in his voice. She turned, just in time for him to grab her by the shoulders, his eyes afire in the glow of the torch. 'What in the name of the gods were you thinking?'

The thumping was getting louder, spreading through her body like a disease, 'The calling, it's so loud, I have to go.'

'I feel it too, but you have to resist, we need to think this through!' She wrenched free of his grip, searching for any way to cross the divide. Decayed rope ladders and various tools lay in ruin, evidence of previous treasure hunters trying to cross. Some of which never made it all the way, their skeletons lying crumpled below. She squinted, there had to be a way. Scanning the floor, she looked for a sign, anything she could use, perhaps she was meant to make the earth rise?

'That' Ember pointed absently to a tiny crystal protruding from the earth, 'But you can't just go blazing in, you have no idea what's in there. Think for a minute.'

'I still have to go in regardless, and I am not going to grow any wiser in the next five minutes with my powers. I don't believe if the…' She hesitated, 'Gods, wanted me to succeed, they would make me face a trial I have no hope of living through.'

Ember crossed his arms and clamped his jaw, 'Fine, but this time, I *am* coming.'

She turned to the stone, knowing there was no point in arguing. Then, focusing her will like she never had before, she pushed her energy into the crystal, feeding it, drawing from the

420

earth below it, willing it to grow and spread. The crystal began to move and spread across the chasm, like a bridge.

Once it was done, she sat forward, panting. It took a lot of energy. Ember grabbed her arm, 'Slowly. I'll start across in a bit.'

She obeyed, stepping onto the bridge warily. It wasn't until Ember stepped on that she heard the cracks. Her face lit up with alarm, just in time to see him vault back off again. 'RUN!'

She sprinted to the other side, making it by inches, the remnants of the bridge decorating the skeletons below. Isyllia looked back across the chasm; it may have been the other side of the world.

He had the same look in his eyes, 'Make another bridge.'

'Ember, I can't.'

'Try.' He searched around frantically, for anything that he could use.

She concentrated on the crystal again, trying to stretch her will across the divide, and create another bridge. But it was no use, already her energy was beginning to drain, and she did not know what was ahead. She had to leave him there. 'I'm not strong enough.' Her words were strained, like she had to force herself to utter them, to summon the strength to carry on, without him. As wide as the chasm stretched, she could still see the pain on his face, feel it as if he were burning into her. Taking a breath, she turned away and moved forward, ignoring his calls as she walked into the darkness alone. Corridor after corridor, she wound, not knowing if she was going the right way, stepping over more skeletons, the ones that had been lucky enough to make it through this far, but how?

After what felt like forever, finally she came to a block in the corridor, the next trial. A wall of ice. Isyllia approached, raising the torch to the frozen surface, looking for any hint at what was on the other side. The wall was solid, stretching for how long, she could not tell. She would have to use her will, to melt her way through. 'I can do this.' Stepping back, she raised the torch, again willing the heat around the fire to rise, pushing it forward until it touched the ice. Slowly, the ice began to melt, but it was not enough. As the ice slowly melted, new ice began to grow in its place, reshaping itself as if she had never been there. She stopped; she would need to push harder. Placing the torch down, she put her hands forward, touching the cold wall. Willing the ice to melt, feeding the heat from within her body, drawing from the torch that lay on the ground next to her. It was working, but she had to move forward, feeling the ice regrow behind her as she moved, until eventually, she was sealed in, she could not use the torch any longer. Terror began to grow in her stomach and her strength was beginning to fail her, she had never used her powers for anything like this. But she could not fail, she had to make it, people depended on her, what people she did not know, but that did not matter. She pushed harder, harder than she had pushed before, clenching her teeth for leverage against the utter cold darkness. The ice behind her had begun to grow back faster, bringing along her panic with it. Until; a tiny spark of light seemed to penetrate the massive wall. Almost there, her heart leapt, she could see more flickers of light, like tiny fireflies buzzing back and forth, calling her forward, calling her to safety.

Finally, she broke through, collapsing to the ground, a piece of her dress remaining trapped in the wall. She panted, looking up at where she had come to. Another hallway awaited, swarming with the tiny insects that now seemed to float and dance around her, urging her forward. Isyllia followed them, her eyes beginning to swim from the familiar dizzy spells. They wound through more corridors, her minute friends seeming to offer warmth somehow.

Isyllia followed them until she came to what seemed to be an antechamber, empty except for a single box. She stared, knowing it could not be that easy, but knowing she had to go forward. She took the first step, startling as the tiny lights flew away, leaving her alone, this could not be good. She stepped forward hesitantly, looking around for movement, would Odriid come again? She had made it halfway when movement could finally be heard; heavy footsteps thundered their way slowly in her direction. Her stomach filled with dread, she reached into her cloak for her dagger, remembering she had left it on the ground, days ago, when the soldier had tried to kill her. She was unarmed, except for a useless rock. All she could do was wait, fear enveloping her until her body began to shake. Slowly the footsteps got louder, until it felt as if they would burst her eardrums. She took a step back, unable to help herself.

Finally, a golden dragon rounded the corner, steam and jets of fire streaming from its nose. Isyllia stood frozen, was this it? Had she come this far just to die? The dragon walked to the centre of the room, showing no sign, it knew she was there, then stopped and turned, its eyes piercing hers. She took another step back, waiting for the moment to come, waiting for the dragon to open its mouth, and consume her with flame.
'Isyllia.' She turned away reluctantly to find Odriid again standing before her, only this time, he wore a stern expression on his face, 'Now, you must choose.'

She stared blankly. 'Choose what?'

'What your heart *truly* wants most.' He pointed behind her, toward the dragon.

Isyllia turned slowly, knowing she was going to find nothing good. The dragon had remained in the centre of the room, but this time, two figures stood in front of it, bound in ropes. She looked harder, On the left, stood Thomas, his face white with fear, unable to move through the ropes. On the right, a larger figure, bound and staring into her eyes, only he did not try to move, only shook his head sadly. It was Ember. 'NO!'

Odriid raised his voice, until it sounded like a growl. 'Abashiina chose you, as she chose Kathriin. One of them you will save, and one will be burned alive, prove that you are better than Kathriin.'

Isyllia cried, looking from Thomas to Ember, his sad eyes never leaving hers. She knew he wanted her to choose Thomas, but could she? Could she watch him die? 'This can't be the only way, I care for them both, I won't watch either of them burn!'

He didn't seem to be listening, 'The stone will pollute you, just as it polluted Kathriin. One of them will burn before you; just like Kathriin watched them burn.'

She felt the anger radiate with heat inside her, 'I am not Kathriin, don't make me do this, please I beg you, kill me instead.'

Odriid ignored her, the kind man she had met in Eddinsford was gone. The man before her was cold, unfeeling. 'You have five seconds, make your choice.'

Now she knew anything she said was pointless, but she tried nonetheless. 'He is chosen, you cannot kill him, you would be no better than Kathriin.'

Odriid laughed. '*I* am the chosen of Caros.'

Isyllia stared at Ember in horror. All thought left her mind except the impulse to run, and run she did, as fast as she had ever run in her life. The dragon sucked in a breath, preparing to exhale death. She threw herself, willing the air around her to create a

425

shield, protecting them from the fire. She did not watch as the fire came for her, hitting the shield where she cradled Thomas, who screamed in terror and confusion. Isyllia watched as the fire hit, watching as Ember fell to his knees, landing on the floor with a meaningless, soundless thud. Unable to save him, "Move. Damn you, get up!" She wanted to do something but knew the shield would break if she did, and then it would be for nothing. "Please stop. Ember, get up, please!" She focused her will, her energy beginning to run out, pushing against the fire in her rage until it burst forward, shocking the dragon backwards. It worked, the dragon stopped and slowly began to turn, moving back the way it had come. She needed no further encouragement, throwing herself forward to cradle the charred corpse that lay in Ember's place. Tears began to free themselves, and for once, she did not argue. "Please come back. Don't leave. Don't do this, please, I need you."

Ember did not respond, he was gone.

Isyllia felt herself begin to anger, breathing hard against the heat that bubbled under her skin, "Damn you. I can't do this alone. How dare you leave me, how dare you." The tears grew stronger and letting the shell that she cradled fall to the floor, she covered her face with her hands and cried broken hearted tears, "I hate you. I hate you so much!"

"Isyllia!" She looked up to find Thomas, his face also slack with grief. "The stone."

426

She turned to the floor, nothing mattered anymore, "I don't want it!"

Thomas grabbed her arm.

Isyllia shot up, her face turning whiter with shock, this was unlike Thomas.

"Take it, or he will have died for nothing at all." He let go.

"Fine." She looked around, her legs threatening to give way as she stood, a combination of weakness and terror. She moved toward the box, the lid opened, inside an ornate necklace of woven Chambrite sat, and in the centre a large oval stone, gleaming and swirling with incandescent light of every colour. She reached out her shaking hand to take the necklace, her fingers stopping short, unable to bear what it cost her.

'Isyllia.' It was Odriids voice again, only this time, he sounded calm, gentle, as he had the first time she had seen him. She turned, unable to stop the terror beginning to take her again. 'The stone is yours, take it, champion of Abashiina.' He said nothing more, bowing then disappearing as if he had never been there.

'Take the stone.' It was Thomas, tears distorting his words.

Isyllia did not need to be told twice, turning and placing a shaking hand over the stone, instantly the room began to quiver. She closed her eyes, the chain gripped tight in her hands. 'Isyllia.'

She opened her eyes, she was standing before the chasm, as if she had never crossed. Turning toward the voice, she saw Ember. But it couldn't be! She had seen him burn. She stepped back. 'No, I watched you burn! You're gone!' Tears streaming from her eyes. 'Odriid stop, I can't bear any more, please.'

'I'm right here!' Ember took a wary step forward, his hands stretched forward to calm her, but his attention on the stone.

'Get back; don't do this to me, please.'

Ember didn't listen. He continued to move closer, one step at a time. Until he was close enough to cup her face in his hands. 'I'm *here*.'

'... But you can't be!' She was less certain now, the warmth of his hands spreading through her cold, frightened skin.

He smiled reassuringly. 'Your safe. I'm here.'

Her whole body began to tremble, the terror and the joy overcoming her. Not caring if he protested, Isyllia threw her arms around him, feeling his heartbeat, and kissing his neck, his face, kissing every part of him that she could reach as she sobbed, for how long, she did not know. Ember held her, until at last the sobs began to give way, her eyes sore and empty. She moved back, looking to her hand, where the necklace was clutched between her fingers. Slowly, she raised her trembling fingers and fumbled the chain around her neck, feeling the stone pulse and filling her with energy, with warmth.

Closing her eyes, she willed the light to expand. She no longer felt the energy draw from her own strength, now, it drew from the stone. It almost took no effort, a dull blue glimmer shining off the walls, the hole inside her had begun to fill. She was complete. The part that she had never realised was missing.

'Can you walk?'

She nodded, looking into his eyes, wishing she didn't have to look away.

Slowly they made their way out the cave, the evening light of the moon was bright, offering comfort on any other evening. She willed the stone to retract the light, it flickered and faded into nothingness. Then looked for Niimorea, who stood not far off the side. The white horse nodded her head and swished her tail, the sudden appearance of her master distracting her to trot over dutifully. Isyllia gave her an affectionate rub on the nose, and then set herself on top, glad to ride long into the night, it was time to rest the horses. And setting them to graze and rest, they sat, grateful to be safe.

'Can you light the fire.' It was Ember, he indicated the ground before them.

Isyllia smiled, remembering the first time he had asked the same question, knowing this time it would be easier. She looked down, urging the wind to pull the wood that lay forgotten on the ground around them, until it lay in a neat pile before them. Then, build the heat, until a fire begins to burn softly.' She looked up. 'The energy comes from the Abashiina now. I still don't know how it all works, but it's much easier to control, especially things I have done before if that makes sense.'

He smiled. 'Good, in the meantime keep practicing with the rock, it will help.'

The flames were warm, filtering their heat into the stone, almost making her sleepy.

'What happened in the cave?' She knew he was going to ask, how could he not? But was she ready to relive the experience so soon? She was silent for a moment, thinking how best to continue.

'After I crossed the bridge in the cave, I followed a series of tunnels. Eventually I came to a wall of ice. The only way past was through, so I melted it.' She shook her head. 'I was terrified, it was pitch black, and the ice grew back around me, I almost didn't make it through.' She indicated the torn section of her dress, forever stuck in the wall.

Ember didn't speak, frowning with concentration. He kept his eyes down. Remaining as detached as possible.

'Then I came to the chamber.' She felt the tears begin to spill but wiped them away. 'I heard footsteps, they were so loud, like thunder. A dragon walked to the centre of the room and I heard Odriid speak again. He told me I had to choose, and when I turned back, I saw you, and Thomas. He said I could only save one of you, that one of you would burn, like Kathriin watched them burn. What my heart truly desires.' She looked at Ember, the tears had persisted, now streaming down her cheek. 'I chose Thomas. I watched as the dragon burned you, there was nothing left, nothing I could do, you were just, gone.' She could see Ember wanted to move, to comfort her. But he did not. He stayed where he was, his expression burned as brightly as the fire before them, suffocating himself in the flames that he would not give into. Isyllia breathed in deeply, then stood. She didn't look to see if he objected, instead deciding she was going to sit down beside him whether he wanted her to or not. He looked down to hide his face, severing the connection. 'I can't.'

She had known what he would say, but the hurt still clumped in her throat. 'I know.' She slowed her breathing, trying to ignore the overwhelming disappointment of rejection, reaching out again to touch his face, look into his eyes. Ember allowed her to lift his head. 'I love you, I knew

it in the cave, and I knew it when you kissed me.' Ember shook his head, still refusing to meet her eyes.

'I'm not asking you to change who you are, any more than I can be someone I'm not. All I am asking is that you hold me.'

431

'I can't.' Like even one word threatened to run away with the last of his composure. He had let her get in, and it was clearly tearing him apart.

She let the small amount of hope that had snuck up into her chest fall back down in the pit of her stomach. 'I understand.' She stood, knowing she would need to get moving, she could not let him see her disappointment. 'We should go; it's a long ride back to the Duchy.'

He nodded and then rose and walked over to Perrin. She waited for a moment, and doused the fire. Not sticking around to see where the ashes of her hopes landed. Instead, she rode into the night, as far away from the moment as Niimorea would carry her. Wondering if Mary had been wrong, wondering if she had seen only what she needed. Glad of the darkness, she fled to the Duchy of Godswall again. This time, running away from a different pain.

CHAPTER FOURTEEN

Isyllia, Duke of Godswall, Illingdale.

After a week and a half of riding, and then stopping barely to sleep before being hustled back onto the road again, they stood before the gates to the Duchy of Godswall hardly believing it was real. It was Ember that finally whistled for Perrin to move forward first, walking slowly toward the main gate. He had spoken little in the time that passed, falling back into his one worded answers and wordless commands. Isyllia ignored it, knowing now it was his way of dealing with the situation, it made it easier for him, and in a way, it was easier now for her to be patient.

They had reached most of the way when the gate began to open. Ember raised a fist, signalling them to halt. They did, waiting to see what lay on the other side. They had sent word ahead of their intentions and, as hoped, the Duke had left instructions with his commanding military officer to ready forces in case they were needed. A single guard rode out to greet them. He was partially dressed in armour, the undressed part accounted for by the harried expression he dragged along with him, 'Lord Clae, Majesty,' He hung on the last.

'Is Thomas here.' Isyllia asked hopefully. 'He rode ahead of us.'

The man nodded 'He is inside, please, follow me if you will.' The guard kicked his horse into a trot.

They were taken back to the main house, soldiers walked about on their own various errands; no Randal sprang forth this time to greet them. Isyllia sighed, and then followed silently, nursing the unease that had re asserted itself through the need to fidget with her dress. Finally, they came to what looked previously to be a large study, now a hurriedly scraped together war room with a large oak table sitting in the centre where couches had been hastily moved aside. It was Thomas who first noticed them enter. He sprang to his feet, the parchment he was reading thrown aside in haste. 'My word, at last!' He threw his arms around Isyllia, who returned the enthusiasm. She buried her face into his shoulder, knowing he would not ask questions, knowing she could count on him for comfort. When at last she did let go, his expression was pained. Somehow, he knew. And knew now was not the time to talk.

'Ember!' Knowing his friend would object, and clearly not caring in the slightest, Thomas wrapped his arms briefly around

Ember, who cocked an awkward smile, shaking his head as to remove the evidence that it had gotten to him. Several other men stood around the room awkwardly, arguing about tactics. It took a moment before the men noticed they had company, having completely missed the exchanges. Isyllia sighed again, knowing if she were home, this would normally be the part she would excuse herself to discover better ways to spend her time, usually with William. So much had changed. The guard that had walked them in stopped and saluted. 'Sir, May I introduce Her Majesty Queen Isyllia, Lord Clae, and Master Thomas, you know.'

Isyllia repressed a giggle, seeing Thomas blush with Mr Fennly sleeping on his shoulder was an unfairly amusing sight.

The men bowed, and then created a small gap for the newcomers.

'Gentlemen. Has the Duke left any word of his intentions?' It was Ember, immediately taking command of the situation, nobody argued.

The commanding officer stepped forward, inclining his head slightly then pointing to the map on the table, 'My Lord Clae. Only that we were to be ready to take the city at your command. Lord Randal is not one to share his intentions.'

Ember sighed, instead turning his focus to the scrambled together map. 'What is the situation?'

'There is one main entrance we can access, the main gate. There is no way we can get it down in the time we have, and not to mention archers will be firing down on us. We simply don't have enough time or men to pull it off and survive.' The commanding officer seemed tired; his eyes were heavy. He was a man well into his forties, sporting dark black hair and a thick beard. 'The problem is, the country has been designed to prevent an army sneaking up on the city, which is exactly what you are asking us to do.'

Ember nodded. 'I understand your frustration, but we have come up with a plan. How many men do you have Commander?'

He looked to one of the other officers, '500 infantry and cavalry 50.'

Ember continued. 'The infantry can approach through the plains.' He indicated the spot on the map.

One of the soldiers cut him off angrily. 'Preposterous! They would see us coming for miles; we would be slaughtered on both sides.'

Ember ignored him. 'Yes, Morliin will send troops to take our company from behind, the idea being to crush our infantry from both sides, as you stated.'

'Exactly' The officer seemed unwilling to give up on his annoyance.

'Thomas.' Ember indicated. 'Will take a small company to Morliin beforehand, where he will use his...devise, to blow it up, the cavalry will be forced to retreat back to protect the duchy.'

Now the commanding officer seemed to be catching the officer's scepticism, he crossed his arms and sniggered, 'Yes, he has mentioned this, but was reluctant to prove it until you arrived... No such device exists, I would know, and even if it did, what is to stop them splitting their forces?'

Ember persisted, undaunted by their scepticism, 'A commander will look to the bigger threat. A small company of infantry won't seem like a big threat when their entire duchy is smouldering behind them, not when there is already an army at the city to handle the situation. They will assume our plan is to break down the door, which even if achievable, will give them enough time to make it back to the fight anyway.'

Ember looked at Thomas and nodded.

He stood blankly for a moment, 'Right!' Then scurried over to a pack he had brought in with him, rifling through until he found a sizable pouch of what could only be powder. '... You might want to clear the map.' He unlaced the strings and waited for the soldiers to have everything cleared off. Isyllia walked a step closer, her curiosity getting the better of her. Thomas collected a small pinch of black powder in his fingers and placed it gently onto the table, then stepped back. 'I need a torch.' The commanding officer pointed to the wall, where one of the sconces held a flaming torch. Thomas took it and approached the table where he had placed the powder timidly, then dropping it down on the spot, he launched back just in time to avoid a loud crack which blew the torch over to the edge and finished the spectacle in a puff of smoke that rose slowly to the ceiling. It took a moment for the room to recover, men had jumped back in shock, and the commander stood in awe.

Ember was the only one who had not left his position. He stood patiently, waiting for the company to reassemble. 'That was just a small amount; imagine what the whole pouch could do?'

The Commander shook his head dumbly, 'I had no idea… where did you find this stuff.'

The pained expression returned, Thomas wrinkled his brow as if he had just swallowed something sharp, 'It's a long story.'

The commander nodded, not caring to push further. 'If Morliin's men could be taken out of the equation that would give us a small advantage, what then, Lord Clae?'

'I will take a small company and ride ahead of the army to infiltrate the city through the water gate. With the explosions from Morliin and the army out front to deal with, the city will be confused. We will use some powder to get in through the gate, and once we are in; our plan is to clear a path to the castle.'

The commander seemed to run the plan over in his head, 'It will certainly take them by surprise … there will be chaos in the city… this might just work!' His tired face lit up. 'How many men do you need?'

'20 would do fine, anymore and we take the risk of being spotted early.'

'You will have 20 of my best men.'

Ember nodded. 'Thank you!'

'How many will you need?' He turned his attention to Thomas.

'A few good archers and some men to protect me if needed… I can't fight.' He blushed again.

The commander nodded and then indicated to the side of the room, 'Speak with, Berrin.' He is our best archer, and incredibly good on a horse. He will set you up from there.'

Thomas bowed awkwardly, then walked to where indicated. The commander frowned slightly at the situation, 'There is still the matter of the Duke? What is your plan to free him?'

It was Isyllia who spoke this time. 'We plan to disable resistance from the inside, giving Gelraen no choice but to listen. Once he surrenders, the power of authority will fall to me again. I will free the Duke and then I intend to make some changes to our laws!'

The man paled visibly, 'Majesty, you can't possibly think of putting yourself in harm's way, you must remain here where you can be protected!'

Isyllia tried to smile reassuringly, 'I will be fine Commander, I can protect myself I assure you. I will not sit by and eat boar while Randal rots in a cell. It is no less than he would do for me.'

'I understand majesty, and I do not contest your will, but surely you are too important to risk over one man, the Duke would understand.'

'If I cannot protect my people when they need me, then I do not deserve my father's throne.'

He shook his head again, his arguments spent. 'We have 7 days until the deadline, and it will take us 6 to march infantry there, with minimal livestock; I suggest we move out as soon as possible.'

Ember nodded, 'Agreed. How soon can your men be ready?'

'A few hours. In the meantime, Tandus will see you rested.' His face took on an irked expression.

'Thank you, Commander.' She inclined her head, and then turned to find the familiar awkward servant already waiting behind, he stood uncomfortably close.

'This way.' He turned briskly and walked off, just as he had the last time they had been here, as if he had instantly forgotten their presence.

They followed until he stopped in front of a familiar door, inclining that Ember should enter.

'Master Clae.'

Ember seemed to hesitate, and then walked into the room, closing the door slowly. Isyllia made eye contact with him for a moment, until the oak barrier separated them, and then noticed with a small panic, that Tandus had already gotten some distance in front. She jogged to keep up, until Tandus stopped in front of the same room she had stayed in the last time she had been here. She inclined her head briefly as he held the door open for her. 'I shall send hot water shortly, majesty.' Tandus bowed briskly then walked off without ceremony. She shook her head; he made no more sense a second time round. Sighing, she walked into the room and sat on the bed removing her boots. It would be good to bathe. While she had become accustomed to the clothing, Isyllia found it harder still to suffer long periods without washing. And as promised, hot water came, along with a tub shortly after. She caught a momentary pang of guilt that fluttered up from her chest. So many men downstairs, tired and preparing for war, some would never return, and she was bathing.

'Your things majesty!' A shy maid stepped forward holding the sack from her horse. Isyllia put the invading guilt out of her mind and smiled at the girl. 'Thank you, on the bed if you please.'

The girl curtseyed, and then took the bag to where indicated. The commander has asked for a modest dinner to be put together for your majesty, and I am to see you dressed after your bath.'

Isyllia felt her mind go blank, the repeated turn of events robbing her of her ubiety.

'Majesty?'

'Sorry!' She shook the fog clouds out of her head and turned back to the girl, 'I thank you, but I think it best I wear my own clothes. There are some in my pack, perhaps you could see them laundered?'

The girl curtseyed. 'At once.'

With the parade of servants gone, Isyllia began to undress, the steam from the tub almost seeming to coil around her and drag her near.

'Allow me, majesty.' The small maid scurried over, mortified at seeing the queen remove her own clothes.

'No need, I have led a peculiar life of late and I am somewhat used to it now.' She smiled reassuringly at the girl who curtseyed again and then left with the clothes. Isyllia felt the fog clouds sneaking back in, but this time made no move to dispel them. There was a peace in emptiness, a clarity of its own. She was almost annoyed when a knock sounded at the door; how could she be done already? Isyllia sat back up perplexed at the speed in which time seemed to evaporate under her nose. The maid had in fact returned and walked over to linen laid out on one of the sitting chairs. Sighing, Isyllia stepped out of the now steam-less water, still not altogether convinced that she had gotten in that long ago, and took the sheet, wrapping it around her.

'Your clothes are being prepared now majesty, I laid this out for you before. Shall I dress you?'

Isyllia smiled again. 'No thank you, I will be fine.' And she giggled despite herself. Less than two months ago she had never once dressed herself and would not have considered touching the garment she held, let alone wear it. Now, she found herself content, and dare she say it, warm.

'How would you like to wear your hair?'

She began to feel guilty, she had denied all the girl's offers of help and so decided to concede this one small thing to her. 'I should like it up, something simple please.'

The small maid glowed with happiness, doing the hair of the Queen was an incredible honour and her small hands worked with passion and speed, in no way betraying her innately shy demeanour. When she was done, she stepped back. Isyllia turned her head to and fro, admiring the girl's work. Her hair had been placed into a bun, and it seemed simple, but at the back it seemed to curl into itself, like it spiralled in forever. 'You have done a beautiful job; you are wasted here with Randall!'

The maid continued to glow to herself, 'Shall I tell him you are ready?'

Isyllia started slightly 'Him?'

The girl nodded 'Lord Clae waits to escort you to dinner, he insisted majesty.' The girl blushed slightly.

Isyllia felt her heart skip a few beats, no doubt fluttering over the sudden temperature change within her body. 'No need, I will see myself out. Thank you for your help.' The girl curtseyed. Isyllia smiled, and then walked to the door slowly, ignoring the girl's happy humming as she cleared things away. Ember stood with his back to the door, his arms crossed in concentration. A creak made him turn around; it was a moment before he said 'I thought I would find you ... different.'

She tightened her lips against the urge to smile, 'I considered it, but it seems you were right after all. These garments are more suitable, if not only warmer.'

He smiled; his face was beautiful when he smiled. Her heart leapt as she looked into his eyes, what she would give for him to reach out and touch her again, to give in as he had only so few days ago. The thought seemed to reflect on her face, as he looked down, locking away his emotions then turned away slightly. 'We should go down.'

'Thank you.' She swallowed her disappointment, it swam around in her stomach like a bowl of thick soup, and so she decided it best she said no more as they walked through the halls, instead focusing her attention again on the tapestries that stretched the length of the walls. Occupants arranged in various moments of history seemed to follow her with their gaze, one after the other, like a gallery of spectators all privy to her lingering moment of despair. It almost took too long to reach the dining room. The Commander had already arrived, taking no time to change. He stood off toward the fire, his face quickly giving way to confusion as he took in their arrival. 'Majesty, I asked the maids to see you dressed, did they not assist you? I apologise…'

She interrupted, waving a hand at him, 'I thank you, Commander; and I feel the lovely girl would have wrapped me in gold silk had I allowed her. I am, however, content with my attire. We need to be on the road again as you are aware, so I feel it is best to be prepared.'

He bowed, offering no further objection, and then nodding to the table. A modest feast had been laid out. She needed no further prompting, the intoxicating smell of the boar wafted over, torturing her stomach. Thomas made most of the conversation, he was the last one to arrive, his talk with Berrin had been productive, and they had decided to hide the powder in small wooden boxes, currently being feverishly sawed by the local carpenter. Once they reached the duchy, the boxes would be coated in oil, then planted at the base of the wall, each a few meters apart. It would then be up to Berrin, and his company to light the boxes in unison, bringing down the wall in one giant explosion.

'And you are sure we will see it from the city?' It was the commander, though the effectiveness of the powder had been proven, his soldiers mind reeled in the unfamiliar territory.

'Absolutely. If we are lucky, it could scare away all the Grolls plaguing Cyndershire.'

The commander frowned in confusion; he was unused to Thomas' sense of humour. Ember interrupted the inevitable clarification the Commander was visibly itching to ask, 'Good job, Thomas.' Then turned back to the commander, 'When will the army begin their march?'

The commander dabbed his lips with a handkerchief, then sat back in his chair. 'Everything seems to be in place, I see no reason why we cannot begin the march tonight.'

Ember nodded, 'We will wait till morning to give you a decent start then we will make for the city. Thomas, you will need to follow in another day. If I am right, we should all arrive at our destinations at the same time, weather permitting.'

'We will make sure Morliin sees us, but there will be little time before they arrive in the city. I won't give the orders to engage until the explosion from Morliin goes off; we want to make sure that the soldiers have turned back, otherwise I risk them ignoring the blast.'

Ember finished the commander's thought, 'Leaving us to sneak into the city when everything is in chaos.'

The commander scratched his beard. 'We are cutting it fine. If your device doesn't go off, my army is going to be swarmed from two sides.'

Thomas made his best effort at being reassuring, 'It will go off, I promise.'

The commander did not seem reassured, but nodded all the same, 'It's the best plan we have in any case.' He turned to Ember. 'I have ordered 20 of my best men to stay behind. They will wait for you to brief them.'

Ember nodded, 'Thank you.'

'Are you sure 20 men will be enough to infiltrate the city and protect the queen?'

It was subtle, but Isyllia noticed Ember clench his jaw, though the others had not. 'Plenty, most of the soldiers will be occupied by the army out front, we should have minimal resistance.'

Isyllia's stomach dropped, he was right, but the army was trained to expect anything, it would not be easy, people would die. 'I can protect myself commander, I will be fine.' She glanced at the shimmering stone on her neck, glad she sounded more confident than she felt.

The commander seemed to nod wordlessly, 'We are as prepared as we can be under the time restraints.' He stood reluctantly. 'I must prepare the army to march.' They made to stand also, but the Commander waved his hand in objection, 'No please, take in what little comfort you can. I wish you all good luck.' He bowed to Isyllia curtly, and then swept from the room.

Thomas put down his glass. 'I should go see the carpenter.' He stood, apology on his face, 'We don't have time for him to get confused.' Isyllia stood and embraced her new friend.

It was Thomas who pulled away first, 'Are you sure you want to do this?' Tears lined his eyes.

Isyllia turned to face him, marvelling at the man before her. 'Thomas, you know I have to.'

'Do-not see Gelraen alone, so much could go wrong.' The reality was beginning to sink in, and he was frightened.

Isyllia placed a hand over his heart. 'We will see each other again, I promise.' It felt empty, could she truly promise anything? Any one of them could die; this could be the last time they would all be here together. The two embraced again, tears streaming from their eyes. In such a short time, he had become a good friend, she had grown to depend on him, and saying goodbye was almost more than she could bear. But she had to, pulling away and wiping her eyes. 'Mr Fennly.' She curtseyed.

Mr Fennly reached into a tiny pocket, producing a single grape, holding it up to her sadly. Isyllia took the grape with a watery laugh, placing it in her pocket. 'Take care of him!' She nodded to Thomas. The Fennel squeaked importantly, and then nuzzled back down to sleep.

'Ember.' He turned and shook his friend's hand. 'It will work, you will see!' It was clear Ember's confidence had taken temporary leave, though as usual, he tried to hide it.

'You have never given me good reason to doubt you... stay safe.' He tried to smile.

'And with a last nod, Thomas left through the same door as the Commander, leaving her alone with Ember. For a moment she contemplated sitting back down, and draining the rest of her glass, anything to drown the nerves that tried to claw their way up.

'I should speak with the men; there won't be time in the morning.' He turned to leave, his shoulders were slumped by the invisible weight he carried everywhere like a pet, his ever-faithful companion.

'Ember.' Isyllia swallowed against the panic that was growing stronger despite the wine. He turned, there were so many emotions written on his face, she knew it would take a night to understand them all. She wanted to tell him to stay; she wanted to wrap her arms around him. Instead she looked at the floor to hide her face, suffocating on the overpowering need she could feel between them. 'Thank you.'

'For what.' His voice was tender but short. Isyllia didn't look up; she couldn't bear to make his burden worse. To let him see her suffering.

'For everything. I just wanted you to know, in case things don't go as planned.' There was a long silence. Eventually she did look up. Ember's eyes were down and his face set. He nodded slightly then turned and fled through the doors, leaving her alone with the crackling fire. Isyllia poured another glass of the rich red wine and retired to a chair by the fire. She had no desire to sleep, so instead sat by the fire in contemplation. What if Ember never changed his mind, could she spend her life this way? And then, was there any other choice? Isyllia sighed, the illusion of control finally giving up the charade and leaving her with an almost unbearable reality, that her life had never been her own, and never would be.

She had no idea how much time had passed when she decided to get some rest and with reluctance, she stood and walked back to her room. A fire burned low on the hearth, leaving a thick warmth to comfort against the night chill. She crawled onto the bed, not bothering to remove her clothes or pull the blankets down, instead staring at the ceiling and trying to block her mind from wanting. From imagining him taking her in his arms as he had. From feeling his hands on her, needing her. She felt the fire in her stomach strengthen, the low growl of longing making her breathe deeper. Isyllia touched the stone, begging herself to find some calm, but the stone remained cool against her skin. Nothing could stop her mind from longing for the door to open but knowing it would not. Eventually she fell into a troubled sleep, her hand still clutching the stone.

It was barely dawn when the maid of the night before came in carrying a hot tray laden with food. It was the scent of fresh honey cakes that woke her.

'Breakfast majesty. Lord Clae says they will be ready to leave within the hour.'

Isyllia sat up, waiting a moment for consciousness to catch up with her body, then shuffled to the table on the side of the room and ate the food. It would be a long journey back to the city, and if the last few weeks were any indication, this would be the last decent meal she would eat in a while, perhaps ever. The thought threatened to make her sick, but she ignored it, and continued to eat, until there was nothing but an empty tray to contemplate.' She smiled up at the maid who waited patiently, 'I am done.'

'Wonderful, majesty. Shall I dress you?'

451

Isyllia knew the maid would be horrified, but it hardly mattered. 'No thank you, I will wear what I am in, you may go.' As predicted, the maids face drained slightly of colour, but she offered no further comment, collecting the tray and retreating from the room. Isyllia stood for a moment, gathering her wits, and picking up the solitary bag that contained everything she had left in her life, deciding to unfasten the buckle and look through. There was not much worth taking, the pendent she carried of her mothers, she placed around her neck with the stone of Abashiina, the ring of the king she put on her index finger, the sack of dales she left at the bottom, and lastly, the ring of the general, Balor's ring, Williams legacy stolen too soon. She placed it on her other hand, tracing the symbols with her fingers. Slowly she stood and made to re-fasten the buckle when a tiny slip of paper caught her eye, frowning, she picked it up, it was the message written by the Quill, and she had forgotten she had it. Opening the fold, she looked at the tiny message scrawled in perfect grace across the middle of the page *'So long as it is pure, love is always the right answer.'* Her eyes watered and she placed the message from Nemethiiniia into her dress, knowing it was not her, who needed to be convinced.

It took another twenty minutes for Isyllia to collect herself and stand ready at the front door, looking around the small company that readied themselves for Ember. He stood off to the side, checking the ties on Perrin. Isyllia fought against the pang that greeted her, and instead continued to look for Niimorea.

A stable boy stood, just managing to prevent her from knocking him aside.

Isyllia smiled, making her way to her beloved horse.

Niimorea whinnied, and walked forward, oblivious to the stable hand being dragged along behind her.

Isyllia laughed. 'Oh girl. Are you ready for another journey?'

The horse pawed the ground, as if in anticipation.

'Of course, you are, you were not made for these tiny boxes, were you.' She nuzzled the horse lovingly, and then looked over to Ember.

He sat atop Perrin, all trace of emotion on his face was gone, replaced by the frown that he so often hid behind. He spoke to the company.

'Mount up quick; we need to cover a lot of ground to make our mark on time.' One of the soldiers spoke up, 'Does the queen need a side saddle?' Isyllia looked to the soldiers, she could tell they were all thinking the same thing the maid had been, what on earth was she wearing?

She opened her mouth to speak but was cut off. 'She will manage, let's move.' Isyllia took a deep breath, and swung up onto Niimorea, wearing her pack on her back for the time being, she would tie it down later.

The day went by without much event. Stopping was brief, because they were a much larger party now and moved slower, so could manage shorter breaks. Ember used the time to survey their surroundings, ensuring they did not run into soldiers. Their passage had to remain secret, if word reached Morliin before the army arrived the game would be up. It wasn't until evening that Ember finally consented to the men to get a little sleep, insisting they do so without a campfire. 'We won't be here long enough.'

Isyllia shook her head and sat beside a tree on her own, chewing absently on some bread and cheese. Rations were worse than normal, each man had taken provisions of his own, but a small pack had been prepared for the Queen, some loaves of bread, salted meat and cheese. Isyllia couldn't watch as the men chewed miserably on their meat, and in the end, insisted the cheese be shared among them all. They had come to risk their lives for her; the least she could do was share her cheese. Ember barely ate as normal and didn't sleep. Instead he sat rigid as a board, focusing from behind his eyelids.

'Majesty.' Isyllia snapped her head up, surprised how unused she had become to being addressed by her former title.

'Can I offer you some refreshment?'

Isyllia smiled at the soldier, he was young, no more than 25, and there was a kindness in his eyes that would suggest any other profession to soldiering. 'Please.' She took the skin, 'Sit.'

The soldier seemed to hesitate, and then obeyed.

Isyllia took a drink then handed the skin back. 'What is your name?'

He tied the skin back to his belt 'Kevin, majesty.'

'Please just, Isyllia.'

Kevin blushed, clearly unprepared for the favour he was seemingly being shown.

'You don't have the look of a soldier!'

He cocked the side of his mouth in agreement, 'My father served, and his father before him, there was no choice for me.'

Isyllia nodded, understanding all too well the suffocating pressure of family expectations, 'What would you do, if it was up to you?'

He looked off into the distance for a moment, swept away on a cloud of dreams. 'I have always wanted to be a tailor. I love to make things... but.'

'Being a soldier was more appropriate.' She offered a knowing smile, he nodded. 'I had a friend like you... Sometimes I wonder if he had done something else with his life, would things have been different for him.'

Kevin shifted uncomfortably, perhaps knowing who she was referring to.

'Thank you for the drink, Kevin.'

Kevin smiled then rose to his feet, re-joining the other sleeping men. Isyllia could feel Ember's eyes on her but chose not to look over. She had to keep her mind clear, even if it was only for one night. Instead she pulled out the stone that she kept in her pocket, and held it in her outstretched palm, watching as it sat still and resolute in its insipidity. The darkness was absolute, but for the light of the moon above. Isyllia focused on the stone, feeling the pendant around her neck tingle. Slowly the stone rose up, and when it reached her eye level, she lowered it gently, repeating the cycle over and over. Each time trying to make it a little quicker. It was much easier now, the action no longer drained her strength, but Isyllia still did not know how her powers worked. The slightest break in her concentration, and the stone tumbled to the dusty floor, forcing her to fumble around until she found it. At first, she had felt nervous of how the men would react, but then realised it was better they were introduced to the idea now, and not during battle. The image of William swimming into her mind, waiting as if on cue, always there. Some that were awake stared, mixed with looks of curiosity and fear. Always fear.

'You can't control how people feel, just focus on what is in front of you.' Ember sat against the same tree and stared blankly at the floor, but she could still see the bags forming under his eyes.

Isyllia let the stone drop back into her palm and pocketed it. 'You should get some rest, you said it yourself, there is a long journey ahead.'

Ember leaned back against a tree. Over the weeks she had become accustomed to his many moods, but this was a new one. He seemed sad, like his spirit had been deflated; his shoulders were hunched, where normally he stood tall and confident. Then it came to her; it had only been a short time since they left Tinderford, and there had been no time to process the events that had taken place, namely the fight with his brother, and the loss of his father. 'Marcos was upset Ember; he didn't mean what he said.' The words came out without meaning too. She cursed inwardly, knowing he would no doubt dodge the conversation.

Ember looked up surprised, scratching his nose then leaning his head further against the tree 'It doesn't matter.'

'It matters to you.' She could see him growing uncomfortable already, noticing the worry lines that kissed his beautiful face. 'Ember, if Caros had wanted a statue, he could have made one.'

He smirked despite himself, and then found his sorrow again, which was never far away. 'We should not have gone back there.'

'Yes, we should have. I'm not going to pretend I know everything about you Ember, because I don't. But I know you take things too seriously. At some point, you need to remember to live too, otherwise what's the damn point?'

His eyes narrowed, 'Don't lecture me.'

Isyllia set her jaw, tired of his stubbornness, tired of him running away from his feelings, from her. Deep down she knew she was overreacting, but she couldn't help it, her temper was scorching her from within… she didn't want to let it out, she *had* to let it out, 'I will lecture you, someone has to. You care so much about your brother, but you didn't speak to him for 15 years! You're so stubborn about your stupid mission you shut out everyone around you, and damned if anyone tries to tell you otherwise, damned how anyone else feels. I might be reckless, Ember, but you're selfish.' Isyllia didn't wait for him to reply, carrying the rest of her anger into the forest and away from the awkward stares of the men, some of which were no longer sleeping. The stone around her neck glowed, and normally by now she would have begun to feel faint but, she didn't. Her hands were hot, but she was in control for the first time. The stone buzzed away gently, like it was feeding on her anger. Isyllia took a deep breath, allowing it to flow out of her and into the stone. She waited a few more minutes before deciding to make her way back. She had not gone far, but it still took a while to find the path in the dark. Eventually familiar shapes came into view, and Niimorea who had tried to follow nudged her in the side, almost sending Isyllia off her feet. 'Sorry girl, I needed some air.' Although she had not been gone long, the men had all woken in the time, and most had mounted their horses ready to continue through the night. Isyllia chose to ignore the overly large berth they seemed to give her, and instead used the excuse to ride behind the company where she could brood in peace. In fact, she continued like that until the next rest stop. They had been riding through the night and into the morning. The sun was high in the sky but leant none of the warmth it teased, and some of the horses had taken to grazing on the journey, oblivious to their passenger's shivers. It was not until Niimorea abandoned the need to follow the others altogether and instead find a suitable grazing spot that Ember finally called for a stop. 'We will rest here for a few hours; I need two men to scout!' Two men stepped forward; 'Good.' He nodded the men off. 'I also need a couple of volunteers to refill the water-skins.' Two more men stepped down from their horses, and began to collect skins from all the soldiers, careful not to drop any lest they must put them all down to pick the offending item up. 'The rest of you eat and get some rest, I will take over the watch in a couple of hours.' The men all began to dismount their horses, leading them off into different directions, but none too far away. Ember stroked Perrin and set him to graze. Isyllia dismounted and let Niimorea focus on her task, knowing she had little claim in the matter anyway, and settled to eat some rations. 'Lord Clae, we should not linger this close to Morliin!' It was one of the soldiers who had stood by awkwardly, no doubt trying to muster the courage to speak.

Ember seemed to take a deep breath, 'I am not comfortable with the idea either, but the men need to rest.'

'I am not tired sir; I'd be happy to help keep watch!'

Ember nodded, grateful. 'Just make sure you eat.'

The man bowed slightly, and then retreated to his assignment. Isyllia found it deeply amusing to see Ember's reaction when people bowed. To anyone else, he could have simply caught wind of something rancid. But Isyllia knew differently, and it took a good deal of willpower to stop her from chuckling despite herself. She had been mid biting her lip when he looked over, his uncomfortable moment giving way to a momentarily visible anger and hurt. He stared for a moment, and then once the men were taken care of, he slumped out of view. Isyllia sighed. A part of her knew she should apologise, and another knew she should not. 'What should I do girl?' She addressed Niimorea's rump, which was just as responsive as her front, jaws clamping down grumpily on grass. 'Your right, I should be kind… I am so glad you were here to help me.' Niimorea walked further away, not even trying to give the illusion that she was listening. Isyllia got to her feet and brushed the debris that clung eagerly to her skirt, making all the difference to her day's worn outfit. She was nervous but walked purposely in the direction that he had disappeared. Some soldiers stepped aside to let her through, she ignored the bows and murmurs', determined to concentrate on one thing at a time. Ember was sitting back against a tree; his face was peaceful. Isyllia stopped, he had finally decided to sleep and waking him from it would not be kind. She sighed, and then turned to walk back to her spot. 'What is it?'

She stopped, pivoting around slowly. 'Can I sit?'

He motioned to a spot opposite, but his eyes held a different response, they usually did. Isyllia decided to ignore it, and sit where he had indicated, folding her dress in as she sat, like it would somehow prevent more dirt from clinging. They sat for a moment while she thought of what to say. She had come over with the brave intention of apologising, and then had not at all planned what to say.

'You should get some sleep, there are soldiers keeping watch, it is going to be hard over the next couple of days.'

Isyllia nodded, looking at her fingers which were suddenly bursting with interest, 'I will... Ember I'm sorry for what I said!'

'Don't.' The uncomfortable shoulder slump was edging its way back, no doubt encouraged by the assumed invitation.

'I know you don't like to talk about things, and I don't mean to seem like I am forcing you, I just thought you should know I was wrong. I was angry and I took it out on you, I'm sorry for that. You have done nothing but help me; you don't deserve to be treated like that. I am the one who is selfish, I've always-'

He interjected 'Isyllia, it's all right. You weren't wrong.' He smiled at her sadly and began to untie a small pouch he had been holding, removing a small portion of food, and putting it aside to retie the pouch. 'I should have kept in touch; I should have gone to see Marcos. I'm the chosen of Caros, I'm meant to have the answers, but I don't. In truth, I don't know what, Caros wants from me.' He bit into his salted meat and chewed slowly, looking at the ground.

Isyllia's stomach plummeted under the weight of guilt, had she made him feel this bad? Ember was always confident, strong. She had seldom seen him vulnerable, and it worried her. She cursed inwardly, Thomas would know the right thing to say, he always knew the right thing to say. 'That's not true. I would have died so many times if you had not been there. I just think maybe we spend too much time thinking about what they want from us, maybe we just need to be who we are; maybe that is exactly what they want. If, Odriid's way had worked so well, wouldn't he still be here?'

Ember gave her a quizzical look, his mouth quirked slightly, 'You have an interesting way of looking at things.'

She shrugged, 'I've always tried to dream my life away, now I just want to be happy with who I am.'

'I can't help the people and live my own life. The people must come first, I owe that much to Caros.'

'But why? How can you help others, if you cannot help yourself?'

He sighed. 'You should get some rest; we need to be alert when we reach the city.'

She waited for a moment, and then decided it best to let him change the subject and stood. 'Yes, as long as Niim doesn't try to eat *me* when she runs out of grass.' Ember shook his head, laughing despite himself. Isyllia turned to go, satisfied with the talk until a thought struck her. 'Ember.' He looked up tiredly, 'My father used to say; a happy man serves you twice... Just something to contemplate.' He smiled tenderly and settled back against the tree, ready to sleep. She hoped some of it would sink in, as she trudged her way back to the spot near the grazing Niimorea. She had never thought there would be a day she would quote her father. If he could see her now.

As usual, a few hours masqueraded as mere minutes, interrupting her doze when one of the soldiers blundered their way over. She opened her eyes and waved him off. 'I'll wake Ember, ready the men.' She stood and walked slowly over to where he slept peacefully. For a moment she watched him, wishing she could leave him for a little longer, but the sounds of growing movement behind her, told her that was not going to happen. She crouched down next to him, touching him on the face with her hand, snatching any moment he could not shoo her away. And he didn't. Slowly one hand reached up through his sleep, cupping softly over hers, pulling it closer. 'Ember...' He stirred, then opened his eyes. To her surprise, he did not pull away, he held her gaze sleepily, making the most of the blissful moment before inhibitions realised, he was awake. Isyllia could feel the movements of men growing behind her, but she refused to move, she refused to so much as inhale, lest the moment be cut short. It was another voice altogether that broke them out of the moment. A yelp of pain coming from some yards away. Ember sprang to his feet, drawing his sword on his way over to the source of the voice. Isyllia followed, her heart thumping grumpily from within. A soldier, trying to be kind, had thought to lead Niimorea back to the rest of the party for the queen. What he had not counted on, was the reaction he would be greeted with from the angry mare that had clearly been waiting to express her dissatisfaction with someone, and bit him hard on the arm. The soldier had yelped, and stepped back, covering the bite with one hand. 'Stupid animal!'

Isyllia pushed past Ember, who had stopped to sheath his sword. She took one look at his arm and narrowed her eyes at the horse. 'You are not the only one who is hungry Niim, biting won't improve your circumstances.' The horse snorted, and then walked off back to where she had been, before being rudely interrupted. Isyllia approached her cautiously, hoping she would not get the same reaction. She placed her hands on one of the reins; Niim snorted again and threw her head in the air angrily. Isyllia tightened her grip, 'Enough. I'm getting on, don't you dare throw me off.' She took a tentative step forward, placing one foot in the stirrup. When the horse didn't react, she took tighter hold, then swung her weight over and settled into the saddle. Niimorea threw her head again but didn't protest further. 'I'm glad that's settled then.' She looked down to the soldier that still stood by covering his arm. 'It's best that nobody approaches her but me, she is not as humble about being starved as the others.' The soldier bowed awkwardly, then retreated to find his own horse. Ember followed suit, nodding to Isyllia, then moving to find Perrin. It was going to be one of those days.

By noon they were crossing the river in single file. It had started to drizzle and Isyllia cursed inwardly, wishing she had the fortitude to shoo the clouds. Dark and promising worse, they sat above happily dumping their load casually on all who dared to walk under. Despite the dank weather, they had made it most of the way past Morliin without being seen. Ember had taken to stopping frequently and checking to make sure the coast was clear. But it was clear to her after hours of this and little sleep as usual, his strength had started to wane, and he called for more men to ride out off to the side and ahead of the congregation to scout the conventional way. It was some hours later before one of the men returned, dust was approaching through the suffocatingly close trees and he seemed to have a smile on his face. He steered his horse awkwardly to one side and saluted Ember, 'Lord Clae.'

'What news?'

'The army is crossing the river on the East side; they should make it to the city within a day.'

'Good work. And Morliin?'
'Still no activity sir, we made it through unnoticed.'

'It will be for nothing if this rain doesn't stop.' He looked up to the sky, frowning as rain fell defiantly into his eyes. 'Thank you soldier, continue, we will camp for the evening West of Preston, then decide in the morning how to proceed.'

The soldier nodded, then steered his grumpy horse off back where it had come from. The rest continued for some distance before they finally had to stop. The sun had finally tagged way to moonlight, and it sat half above, shining its tiny amount of light through the even smaller gaps in the trees above. It was on stubbing another toe, that Isyllia decided this time, she would light a campfire. Although the drizzle had finally stopped, the leftover moisture clung to everything they found. Isyllia focused on calling on stone, willing heat to erupt on the painfully wet logs. She felt the moisture fight with the flame, causing her to concentrate harder. Tiny tufts of smoke began to crackle their way off into the world above, leaving Isyllia to take a sigh of relief, she had not realised she was holding her breath.

'Thank you, majesty.' One of the soldiers was wary but he did not step away. He nodded simply, and then moved to the warmth. Isyllia looked around for Ember in the darkness. Perrin stood grazing near Niimorea, each nudging the other away from a particularly plump patch of grass. She looked back to the fire, it was now surrounded inch by inch with men, all sitting as close as they could muster without getting burned. Isyllia thought for a moment, and then turned into the darkness in search of Ember. She did not have to go far before she reached the stream. The moonlight sparkled gently on the soft ripples of water as they flowed slowly away, into a life unknown. She watched for a moment relaxing, and almost forgot her reason for venturing out when she noticed the ripples were not all being made by the tug of water's natural journey. A figure moved out of the water slowly. Isyllia crouched behind one of the bushes, suddenly embarrassed. She had decided to turn back and creep in the opposite direction, when she noticed the figure in the moonlight. He had begun to return his hose, but water still clung to him, the moon reflecting off his sun-tanned skin. He stood still for a moment, and then lifted his head, his back suddenly rigid; he knew she was there. Isyllia felt her cheek redden further, she would have to reveal herself. Clutching the stone for a confidence it could not give her, she took a deep breath and then stood, walking shyly over to where he waited still holding his shirt in one hand. He was still a statue, the only sign that he was real, the slow movement of his back as he breathed. 'Why did you follow me?' His voice was low.

'Do you not know?' Isyllia waited as what was left of her courage threatened to desert her.

Ember continued to stand with his back to her, giving no indication of movement, until he spoke. 'Every moment you're near me, I forget how to breathe. Your presence is suffocating, I can't escape it anywhere I go, you are always there.'

Isyllia closed her eyes in a bid to trap inevitable the tears, but they found a way out, treacherous and defiant to the last, they always found a way out. 'I'm sorry.' She half turned to leave, but something stopped her midway and she spun back around, 'Actually.' Ember said nothing, so she pressed on. 'I followed you, because I love you, and I'm not ashamed of that.' She waited for a moment before continuing, hoping he would turn, hoping he would move at all. But he didn't. Ember continued to stare out to the river, giving nothing else away. 'Ember, I know you think it's selfish, and you know what, maybe it is... But *I* know what it feels like when it's too late... and it's unbearable.' Her voice broke but she ignored it, along with the impending panic that walked beside it. 'I watched you burn in that cave. I saw you turn into nothingness. And the searing blackness that swept through my chest, gods it was like fire... because I chose Thomas. I did my duty to the gods, and when you disappeared, I wanted to die with you, because there is no purpose without you.

I would rather be here, knowing you don't love me, than spend another moment of my life without you...'

There was barely time for another heartbeat to pass. Ember turned, crossing the distance between them like a lost soul at last finding a light through the darkness. He stopped and cradled her face in his hands, watching for a moment as the tears streamed down her porcelain skin with adoration, 'I do know how it feels.' For once he did not try to hide the longing that tore at him, 'Caros save me I know.' He kissed her, pulling her to him like a desperate man in pieces, knowing only she could put him together again. Isyllia responded, filling the memory of emptiness with the taste of his lips, and the warmth of his beating heart. He was real, and he was here, kissing her into the deep of the night. It was unclear how much time had passed when he pulled away, but the frown had found its home again.

'What's wrong?' She asked almost absently, placing her hand on his chest lovingly, soaking in the warmth that spread into her stomach, almost as if it was passing from his body to hers.

'We need to get back to the men.'

She leant up and kissed his chin, 'Just a minute longer.' Moving over to his neck, and then his ear.

Isyllia could feel him groan from deep within, it was clear he did not want to stop. 'We can't.'

Isyllia shivered as he dislodged himself decisively. 'Please don't shut me out again, not now.' The familiar distance crept between them.

Ember said nothing, but his eyes answered what his mouth could clearly not say. A bottomless sadness pierced its way to her, resting somewhere deep in her throat. 'Let's just get through tomorrow, and then we can talk.'

Isyllia felt her heart sink, but she agreed, knowing there was no other choice, 'Tomorrow.'

Ember drank in every detail of her face until at last he leant forward and kissed her tenderly, and then walked away not looking back as he gathered his discarded shirt and disappeared back toward the camp. She was alone.

It was some time before she finally gathered herself and found the men, still sitting by the fire, some seeming impatient for the night to be over. Not many were sleeping, Ember included. He looked up briefly as she passed, his feelings carefully masked. Isyllia did the same, locking away her aching heart and the part of her that just wanted to run to him and nuzzle into his chest. Instead she sat down near a sturdy looking tree, determined to get some sleep before dawn arrived with the uncertain future, they all faced with it.

CHAPTER FIFTEEN

Gelraen, Illingdale Castle.

'Sire?' The cell guard sprang to his feet, offering a clumsy bow in his haste. Gelraen took little notice.

'Open the door and leave.' The guard seemed confused for a minute, still gathering his scattered whits, then obliged, fumbling with the keys and then stepping aside so the king could enter the filthy cell. Gelraen waited as the jailor closed the door behind him and left the room, looking back a couple of times, perhaps uncertain that it was wise to leave him there alone. Randal on the other hand, sat up weakly, a grin spreading across his face. 'To what do I owe the pleasure, my king.' The last word was said in mocking, which Gelraen did not miss. 'I would stand, but as you can see.' He pointed to the dried blood that seemed to coat his body. 'I have been robbed of that pleasure.'

Gelraen shook his head, 'You brought this on yourself Randal, all I wanted was the bow, my birthright. I didn't ask for any of this, I wasn't given a choice. You never gave me a chance.'

Randal scoffed, then spat on the ground next to him. 'You lost your chance the day you murdered my queen.'

'She wasn't meant to die.' Gelraen looked pained, his brows creased as the long-lost guilt stabbed at him. 'My men were only meant to steal the bow, I never intended for her to die.'

Randal shook his head, clearly taken by the confession. 'Why steal it at all, why not come to me, face your trials.'

Now Gelraen shook his head, his anger getting the better of him. 'I tried, but you had already made up your mind about me. Your stubbornness has driven us to this moment. The true king has been murdered, causing his daughter to flee. All I wanted to do was protect her from Nethershire, and for what?' He sat on the filthy floor, no longer caring about his pride.

Randal sat up, stunned. 'We all make mistakes Gelraen, it is what makes us human. It's what we do next that truly counts.'

Gelraen rested his head against the cell wall, his mind carrying him off to some distant place, anywhere but his current reality. 'What mistakes have you made?'

Randal sucked in a breath. 'I killed the king. I ordered Williams death.' Gelraens head shot back up with alarm. 'Yes, me. I did it. I forced Isyllia onto her path, to find who she was. Set her free from these bonds.' He looked around the filthy cell.

'You made me kill an innocent man.' The look on Gelraens face was beyond anger, a deep disappointment took what was left of his will. For a long time, the two were silent. In the end, it was Gelraen who broke the silence. 'Do you know what the stupid thing is. I don't even want it anymore. I don't want any of this. All I ever wanted was her.'

Randal furrowed his brows, 'Isyllia?'

Gelraen laughed, 'No. We would kill each other in a day.' At that they both laughed, 'No. There was a girl once. She was married, but I loved her, and she loved me. I would have done anything for her. But Ember was right, our duty is greater. It must come first.'

Randal shook his head, barely able to comprehend what he was hearing. 'Why did you never tell me this?'

He looked Randal in the eyes, 'You never asked.'

Randal looked at the floor, defeated. Like his world was crumbling around him. 'It's not too late. Stop all this, go to Mespar, claim your weapon.'

Gelraen shook his head sadly. 'You don't understand, it's too late. I've done everything I can to stop them. You were my last chance. If Isyllia does not submit, they will come.'

'The Malagara?'

'Worse. After I left Ember I went to the Isle of the forgotten alone. I went too far. They want to destroy everything, my only chance to stop them was to neutralise Isyllia. Then, they would leave Illingdale alone. My country would live.'

'What about the others? Why not stand with your companions and fight, trust them?'

Gelraen shook his head, tears had begun to make his eyes go red. 'We cannot defeat them. This was the only way.' City horns broke the moment. People had begun to run back and forth in the city. Gelraen rose to his feet.

Randal grabbed his leg, pain shot across his face. 'It's not too late, survive, get your weapon and stand together, it's what you were born for.'

Gelraen dislodged himself, shaking his head. 'It's too late for that. There is only one thing left that I can do, and I hope the gods understand.' The horns sounded again, and Gelraen banged on the cell door.

'Gelraen.' Randal shouted, but he didn't listen, walking into the chaos alone, ready to accept whatever fate the gods handed him.

'Sire!' It was William, he was half dressed in armour. 'The guards said you came here, the army is outside, you need to barricade yourself in the castle.'

Gelraen smiled weakly. 'Come, William. Let's go and await our guest.'

◁ ✳ ○ ✳

Isyllia, Gates of Illingdale.

'What's the plan?'

Ember seemed to purse his lips in concentration, scratching his chin as if to dislodge hidden thoughts. He looked up at one of the men who had been scouting. 'You said the army is in position?'

He nodded, 'Almost, sir, if we head now, we should arrive at the same time. It's just up to the other men, sir.'

'Thomas.' He rested his arms on his crouching thighs, 'Let's get ready. We need to get through the gate, Isyllia' He looked around.

Isyllia stepped forward. 'Yes?'

He was all business. 'Can you blow the gate on my signal?'

Her eyes widened and she touched the stone instinctually, 'I'm not sure.'

He produced a small package he had been carrying in his pack, 'You won't need to use your powers that much, just blow this. I want you to try to get through the gate, make a scene and plant the package. When the men shoo you away, come back, and use your power to ignite the box, the black powder will do the rest.'

She nodded slowly, 'I should be able to do that.'

'Good.' He turned back and addressed the men 'Once the door is down, our goal is to clear a path to the citadel for the Queen. Gelraen is arrogant, but he is not stupid, and he will barricade himself in there.'

'What if there are too many men?' Some of the other soldiers nodded in assent, feeling the holes in the plan.

Ember nodded, his face one of confidence, 'I know there are risks, but I also know Thomas, if he says he can bring the wall down, I believe him. Once he does that Illingdale will have no backup and will need all their men to focus on the army out front, our small party will seem inconsequential.'

Isyllia spoke up, desperate to help ease their tensions in some way. 'It is protocol as you know in a time of crisis, to protect the royal family, most of the soldiers left behind will be surrounding the castle. Once we get inside, we will have him.'

Some of the men nodded at this, 'And what about the, Duke?'

Isyllia answered again. 'Once we have Gelraen I will formally take power again and release the Duke.'

Ember seemed to look at the floor for a moment, 'Are there any other questions?'

The air was quiet. 'Let's move then, and remember, no one moves until my command.' There was a nod of agreement as people began to look to their horses, gathering what armour and weaponry they could take on foot.

Isyllia moved to Niimorea, the mare waited patiently, pawing the ground in anxiety. Isyllia moved around to face her, stroking her muzzle. Niimorea nuzzled into her, closing her eyes. 'Oh, Niim, I can't take you this time girl.' The mare bucked her head as if in disagreement. 'I need you to protect, Perrin.' Niimorea snorted, pushing at her arm again. Isyllia laughed, 'Behave.' She stroked the horse again, taking in the feel of her fur against her skin. In such a short time, Niimorea had begun to mean so much to her. It hurt to leave her behind. 'Thanks for being my friend.' She kissed the horse, and then walked away, determined not to cry and refusing to look back as she walked toward the castle, past the soldiers who waited nervously, past Ember who stood at the front, waiting, the mask of concentration. She nodded to him once, he did the same. It was all she had the courage to do and settled on placing one foot in front of the other. It was not a long walk, but it felt like forever, all the while painfully aware of the tiny box that swung gently in her pocket as she walked. After a while the water gate came into view, and she picked up her pace, slamming into it with all the strength she could muster. 'Help. Please open the gate.' A soldier approached.

'Orders are that the gates are sealed; an army nears.'

'Please, I don't want to die!' She continued to slam against the door.

'Wench, move back now or you'll feel the butt of my sword.' He held it up to the hole in the gate.

Isyllia cried, carefully dropping the package against the door out of sight, then running back into the forest, where Ember and the others waited. He smiled at her encouragingly, Isyllia ignored it, wiping the tears away, knowing they were not for the door she was about to explode.

'Now, wait.' Some time passed before it happened, soldiers were running back and forth organising their wall defence against the army that loomed outside. The men had been listening, and they had been present when Thomas had set his demonstration. But if they had come up with any idea what a larger version of this demonstration would sound like, they were wrong.

'Dhoom' The ground seemed to shake, one explosion after another, a sound like nothing they had ever heard. The soldiers paled, shaking visibly, Isyllia took hold of a tree to keep herself steady, hoping desperately that Thomas was safe. Ember stared

ahead, not breaking his concentration for a moment. 'Isyllia, Now! Blow the gate.'

Isyllia closed her eyes, stretching her hand out, imagining herself touching the box, brushing flames onto it.

Ember concentrated. 'It's lit!'

She took a sigh of relief, waiting for the moment when the explosion would sound. They did not have to wait long; the package had been prepared to burn quickly, the gate, and a sizable portion of the wall discarding themselves in a thousand different directions. Some soldiers ran, the ones that had not been hit, and Ember gave the call, 'Now, watch for archers!' The men ran forward to the now open hole in the wall.

'Isyllia!' It was Ember, he pointed, some archers remained on the wall, shooting down in desperation, managing to catch two of their men and killing them on contact.

She concentrated, stopping the arrows on their flight, sending them back. The men barely had time to scream. Isyllia felt another tear slide down. They had been her father's men.

'Concentrate.' It was Ember again, his voice a growl.

Isyllia snapped out of it, passing through the door with the men, trying to stand out of the way as they fought to clear a path. Isyllia could see the castle in the distance. It wasn't too far, if she made a run for it, perhaps she could end all this before more people died. Her mind set, she hitched up her skirts, and ran, ignoring the men's screams as she plummeted forward. She knew the city better than them, better than the soldiers, better than anyone. It was her city. Isyllia weaved in and out of buildings, determined to lose any pursuers, desperate to blend in with the crowd running in every direction, using their fear to move her closer to the castle unseen. And moving closer, she could see soldiers posted on the steps, brandishing spears at anyone who approached. Isyllia slowed to a walk, placing her hand on the stone. The men raised a spear; they did not recognise her in the outfit. 'I believe Lord Gelraen is expecting me.'

The soldier sneered at her. 'Unlikely, move on or I'll spear you.'

Isyllia smiled. 'Don't you know how I am?' She moved her hand from the stone. Watching as the soldier studied her face for a moment, and then paled and moved back, allowing her to pass. She took the chance, hurling through the doors and toward the throne room, she knew where he would be in a moment like this, knew he would be expecting her.

It was a few minutes before the familiar oak doors sat before her, she took a deep breath and swung them open, she was not alone. The room could have been cold and as lifeless as the statues that surrounded it, councillors looked down from both sides, regarding her with hate. They had been waiting. She looked to her father's chair. It would always be his chair. 'I see you made it.' Gelraen hid a sneer, barely.

She nodded, noticing the crown, he was cunning, she could give him that. Isyllia refused to bow. 'That was the intention, was it not?'

He chuckled, 'You have not lost your humour I see… and you have been, busy.' He eyed the necklace and tensed.

She followed his gaze, 'You're referring to this?' She touched the stone, watching as he flinched. 'Indeed yes, it's a remarkable thing, amazing what you can find lying around.'

'So that was you making all that… noise?'

Isyllia smiled. 'Me? No, I brought friends.'

He bared his teeth, 'Did you!'

She shook her head, pitying him, 'I'm not afraid of you anymore, Gelraen.' The doors opened revealing a line of soldiers, each lining the outsides. If Isyllia had intended to leave, it was not going to happen now, he was taking no chances. One soldier arrayed in a full suit of armour walked slowly to the front. The man held the hilt of his sword, never taking his eyes of Isyllia. He stopped next to Gelraen, and stood, not breaking his stare.

They waited for the room to settle, she could hear the whispers, *'Malagara'* sounding from all corners of the room. They feared her, she could feel it.

'Isyllia Bellamy.' It was Gelraen, he paused, 'Former, Queen of Illingdale, have you come to answer to the charges of treason against you.'

Isyllia pushed out her chest; she had to remain confident. 'I have come to discuss charges of treason, not against myself however, since I have committed no crimes.'

'You are, Malagara; your existence is treason to your people.'

She shook her head, careful to look him in the eye. 'I am no different to you, Gelraen.'

He paled slightly but did not answer; she could see his throat working under his elaborate doublet.

She continued, 'It has come to my attention that a Duke of the realm has been wrongfully imprisoned, and I have come to ensure he is released at once.'

Gelraen seemed recovered but he kept his thoughts carefully screened. 'You refer to, Duke Randal of Godswall. He is currently waiting to stand trial for treason, for aiding you.'

'Duke Randal is innocent, and I want him released.'

Gelraen chuckled, some of the councillors on the sides joined in.

Isyllia's face remained serious, continuing to stare into his eyes.

'I think you misunderstand your position here, you see, you are no longer a Queen, Malagara.'

'I am not, Malagara, I am chosen.' She concentrated on the stone again, making it glow. 'Just like you.' She whispered, urging the wind to push the words to his ears. She had no idea if it would work and for a moment, she stood waiting, with her breath halted in her throat. For a moment he met her gaze, and then Isyllia knew the moment reality had dawned, watching as a red stain spread up his cheeks, forcing him to stumble back and onto the throne momentarily.

'Guards!' He screamed the words, pointing to the men that lined the walls. Isyllia turned, concentrating on the advancing soldiers, and trying to still her rising panic. She did not want to hurt her people, she could not be Kathriin, but she had to do something, and calling more wind from the stone, then magnifying it she let it surround herself like a shield. The men stopped their advance, baffled as the force field seemed to swirl around her. Then, she concentrated again, pushing. The field sprung out, throwing the men in all directions, most fell unconscious, others seemed too afraid to advance a second time. Isyllia turned back to Gelraen, he had begun to sweat. 'Don't be foolish, Gelraen you know you cannot stop me. I do not wish *my* people to die, and so, I have come to offer you a trade. Duke Randal of Godswall is to be freed of all charges and restored to his rightful place as Duke of the realm. In return, I will submit myself to the justice of my people. This is my offer.' She stood silent, waiting with bated breath. Isyllia knew she had to find a way to incriminate Gelraen in the eyes of the people, otherwise they would see her as nothing more than a murderer.'

Gelraen looked at his hands, 'I must say, I am a little disappointed.' His tone was dismissive, almost as if he had forgotten the situation at hand, he was playing.

Isyllia narrowed her eyes. 'I would apologise, but I deplore insincerity.' She heard the guard next to him snigger, Isyllia frowned, who was he? And why was he the only one with a helmet on?'

'I hear you keep interesting company nowadays?' He looked up; his tone was unchanged. 'I had thought he would be with you?'

Isyllia smiled winningly, 'He had more important engagements, next time perhaps?' If he wanted to play, she would play too.

The door burst open, a messenger running in red faced, 'Sire, Sire, men have made it into the city, they approach the citadel.'

Isyllia stood frozen, how had they caught up so quickly? 'Ember.' She had barely whispered his name, but the soldier flinched again, making Isyllia look up, and this time Gelraen noticed.

'Ah yes, how rude of me, I should introduce my faithful servant here.' Gelraen motioned to the soldier who stood rigid, like he could almost be made of stone. 'Though I believe you are already more than well acquainted.'

Isyllia stood puzzled, what was he talking about? She did not have to wait long. The man bent his head down, gently removing the helmet, a tuft of tied back blonde hair falling out.

'No!'

Now, Gelraen smiled. 'Oh yes. I do believe you know, Lord Mallory already.'

'William? No, I saw him die!'

'I heard you had a bit more to do with it than that. Pity you couldn't stick around, but then you have always been selfish.'

She snarled. 'It was Adella who stabbed him.' It suddenly made sense. 'You planned all of this.' She was losing control; she could feel it, feel the tears sliding down.

'You did this yourself.' It was William's turn to speak; his voice was hollow and cold.

Isyllia stared, unable to speak. William stared back, his eyes swimming with hatred and an emptiness that made her heart drop. He was alive, but he was no longer her friend, his face was the same yet somehow unrecognisable.

'I await your command my, king.' He placed his hand tighter on the hilt of his sword; there was no sign of hesitation.

Isyllia's heart pounded, sounds were beginning to filter in from outside, Ember was approaching already, she had to do something.

'What have you done to him?' She was angry.

'Me?' Gelraen feigned a look of hurt. 'I gave him a new life; I gave him purpose again. It was you who left him to die; it was you who lied, you who led his father to betrayal.'

'That is not.' But it was, and she knew it. She had betrayed her friend. Isyllia's gaze once again fell to the floor, unable to contain the joy and the misery that tugged her almost in two.

For a moment Gelraen seemed to turn pale, his gaze focused on the back of the room. Isyllia frowned, wanted to turn and see what he looked at, but not able to take her eyes off William. 'Seize her by any means necessary.' William drew his sword.

'I won't fight you.' She took a step back, eyeing his weapon.

William advanced slowly, his face set.

Gelraen smiled, this is what he had counted on.

Isyllia swore inwardly, she had to get through to him. Outside the sounds grew louder, closer. 'William, you don't have to do this, I know you are angry, but this is not you, you are not his pawn.'

William ignored her, striking his sword across her stomach, she moved back just in time, the sword slicing through her hand raised in defence. Isyllia screamed, her pain piercing the air while her eyes shot open in alarm, feeling the warm blood run down her arm, his blow had meant to kill her. Tears began to fall, how could this happen, how could it end this way. 'I loved you like a brother, I grieved for you, how could that mean nothing to you.' He continued to advance forward, but his hand was shaking. 'Will' She cried, barely able to control her devastation, he was here, and he was alive. Her memories flashed to grief-stricken days where she would have given anything to have him back, but now, not like this. 'Please!' She summoned what was left of her strength and looked at him. 'I need you.'

William hesitated, a mixture of anger and confusion flashing across his face.

'Kill her!' Gelraen spat the words.

The door burst open, revealing two soldiers falling to the floor with a thud. Ember burst in like thunder, his eyes searching, and then filling with relief. Isyllia cried out, her legs automatically carrying her toward him, whispering his name softly while he drew closer, at last making it to her side. He looked at her hand then at William's blood-soaked sword.

Isyllia tried to block his way, placing a hand on his chest. 'Ember, no!'

Ember clenched his teeth, the atmosphere around him almost seeming to darken because a mutual hatred carried the two men closer together. 'Ember don't hurt him… please …it's not his fault.' She said, and it was a mistake. William moved forward, swinging his sword viciously at Isyllia. Ember darted in front, his body shaking with rage but still he blocked the attack, his movements fluid and precise.

'Ember.' Gelraen said, his arms outstretched in mock warmth.

Ember raised his sword warningly toward a retreating William, cradling Isyllia behind him protectively.

Gelraen laughed. 'Well, isn't this ironic, I honestly never took you for a hypocrite.' There was coldness behind his words, a meaning Ember understood deep inside. He tightened his grip on Isyllia absently.

Gelraen turned to the council. 'Council I present Ember Clae of Tinderford, Malagara.'

'Enough! This isn't your purpose. Release the duke and stand down.' Ember was not one for games.

Gelraen stood and paced for a moment then turned and smiled slightly, 'For whom? A harlot and a Malagara!' He shook his head, 'No, no, you see, it wasn't enough for her to use this poor boy and leave him heartbroken.' Gelraen turned to indicate to William. 'But now she has used you for her schemes. Isyllia knowingly accepted my hand in marriage, a duty I accepted out of love for her father, a man who I have given not only my life too, but the services of my men also, and how did she repay that kindness? She leaves me to do her job, not caring about her city or what would happen to its citizens, only to return with an army, and a clear intent to kill her *own people*' He shook his head.

Isyllia balled her good fist in frustration.

'Tell them the truth, Gelraen.' Ember's glare was cold, the air thickening with his disgust.

Gelraen ignored Ember, 'And here she is. He pointed to Isyllia; standing clutched now in Ember's protective arms, her latest victim, fighting her battles for her. Council, this woman is an abomination, and she is not worthy to sit on her father's throne.' The council nodded their agreement; she now knew she had lost them.

'It doesn't matter what you say to us Gelraen, or them. It never has. Menethon is the one who hears you, and you will never have his bow.' Ember stood tall, his confidence imposing.

'You know what Ember, I don't care! Guards, take care of him, Mallory, kill the traitor.'

With reluctance, William moved his focus back to Isyllia, all traces of hesitation gone.

Ember let go, growling at William, 'Touch her again and I *will* kill you.' He said, spitting the barbed warning while shifting his focus to the remaining guards that had started to move in from both sides.

William sneered at Isyllia, moving forward slowly, like a cat stalking a mouse.

Isyllia stepped back with terror, watching her friend advance with his sword half raised. She moved back further, ducking while he swung, a pew taking the blow and spraying the air with splinters of wood. 'William, he is a liar, listen to your gut.' She had to delay him.

'Too late.' He spat the words.

'No, I'll never give up on you, I won't leave you again.' Isyllia looked at him, his eyes were red, and he smelled of alcohol. An empty vessel without a soul. He was a man broken, 'What have they done to you.'

'You did this!' He swung again. Isyllia ducked, using the stone to propel her forward. She glanced at Ember, he fought like a dervish, slashing seemingly in all places at once, but he was in no danger.

She stopped retreating. 'I did, you are right, and I'm so sorry. I should have trusted you, but I was so frightened, every day was like a nightmare. I couldn't bear to lose you, so I lied to you, so you wouldn't be frightened of me and leave me alone. These weeks have been torture thinking you were dead, thinking I would never see you again… And it was my fault, it was all because of me.' She didn't try to stop the tears, knowing there was no use, let him see them. 'Don't you get it; I would rather die than lose you again.'

William flinched, and his voice seemed strained. 'You told *him.*'

Isyllia cried harder, knowing what he meant, knowing she could not lie again, not if she wanted his trust. 'He's like me.'

William stopped, he was barely listening now, stuck on his own train of thought, she could see it on his face, 'You love him.'

She felt defeated, if she said yes, she knew she would lose him again, if she said no, she would lose Ember. Isyllia looked at Ember, fighting the last of the men, his movements were fast and aggressive, fighting his way to her. She looked back to what was left of her friend; there were tears in his eyes now. 'I'm so sorry.'

William lowered his blade, stumbling back.

Isyllia stood, willing her mind to think of something to say, but she was interrupted by the door being thrown open, the last of the men finally making it inside. They spread out on both sides, flanking Isyllia. Some of the councillors finally decided their fear was greater than their loyalty and fled from the room. 'Let them go.' It was Ember, removing his blade from the last soldier, and sweat blanketed his brow, but he wasted no moment, placing himself protectively between Isyllia and William again, she knew it would be the final nail in the coffin.

William stared, like he had lost the ability to think, and it hurt more than the wound she was clutching. William dropped his sword, and fell to his knees, defeated. She leant into Ember, the pain in hand was growing worse; she could feel the warm blood spill down onto the front of her dress.

'Will.'

Most of the room had cleared in the panic, most, but not all. Still sitting next to the throne, Gelraen slowly rose to his feet. His expression was unreadable while he drew his sword and walked down slowly to where they stood. 'So, this is it then.' But he spoke to the floor.

Ember stepped forward, forcing Isyllia back. 'Guard the doors.' His men obeyed, taking position on either side of its oaken frame, ready to strike anyone who entered.

Gelraen raised his sword, glaring at Ember, like a Lion waiting to take his prey.

'Is there no end to your perversion? Menethon chose you to give the people hope, to be their champion, why would you choose this path?' He said the words quiet and in control, always in control.

'You're a sentimental fool, Ember; It doesn't surprise me that you miss the bigger picture.' Gelraen swung his sword with an anger that could have penetrated the heavens. Ember stepped neatly out of its way, quickly moving his dagger towards Gelraen's shoulder. It should have dug in, but instead it merely grazed him. Gelraen recovered quickly, swinging back around barely missing Ember's stomach, the near miss making him laugh. 'What's the matter, forgotten how to fight or has love made you soft?' He didn't wait for Ember to reply, he had used the moment to reveal his own dagger, but he did not use it on Ember. In one fluid movement, he flung the dagger straight towards Isyllia, leaving another neat slice across her cheek. Gelraen realised his mistake the moment the dagger had left his hand. Ember's face darkened, his strikes would no longer be aiming to miss.

'You coward.' Ember snarled at him.

'Coward, am I?' The men circled each other slowly, 'I've done more for these people than you *boy*. Or your useless little harlot over there.'

Isyllia took a deep breath, trying to cool her anger; she could not distract Ember this time.

'You've brought death Gelraen, that is all you have done.' This time Ember moved first, rushing at Gelraen, then instead of aiming for his sword, he slid down, slashing Gelraen across the calves from behind. Gelraen grunted in pain, turning to aim his sword towards Ember's chest, but Ember spun quickly, launching to his feet and meeting the angry man in the middle again. They fought hard, each man swinging to kill. Both danced with skill, but Ember was better, more agile. Anticipating his moves before Gelraen swung, parrying them with ease. They fought, until at last, Ember threw him back, then kicking the sword out of Gelraen's hand he raised his sword to strike, but something happened, and Ember pulled himself back.

Gelraen laughed, 'Just kill me.' Ember paled, turning his gaze to the back of the room. The place Gelraen had been gazing. An elderly man stood, dressed all in black. He smiled darkly, cocking his head slightly before vanishing into thin air. Ember dropped his sword, swinging around in alarm. But he did not have to wait long. The man reappeared behind Gelraen, and without waiting a moment longer, stabbed him with his own sword. Ember barely made it in time to stop Gelraens fall. All that remained of the old man, was the bodiless laughter he left behind. He had disappeared again. Only this time, he did not come back.

'Didn't think it would end this way, did you?' He spluttered at his own joke, flecks of blood spraying from his mouth. Ember closed his eyes, there was nothing to be done.

'Why did you do this, why?'

'Gelraen shook his head. I'm sorry, I'm so sorry, I was frightened. I tried to do it by myself, I thought.' He started to trail off, his strength leaving him.

'No, not yet!'

Gelraen winced. 'I could protect everyone. But I failed, and now they will come. All of them.'

'Who, who is coming?'

Gelraen had begun to pale considerably, his end was drawing nearer by the second, and both men knew it. 'Neuridian Empire.' He winced again. 'Isyllia, where is Isyllia?'

Isyllia took measured steps, one at a time, overcome with the man's impending mortality. 'I am here.'

He seemed satisfied, 'Your mother. Find her. Bow must pass on.'

Isyllia fell onto a chair in shock, could he be serious? Her mother was alive? Alive all this time, and she never once reached out. Pain and happiness flooded her weak body. It couldn't be.

'Let me go friend, I want to see her again.'

Ember nodded, tears in his eyes. 'I'm sorry.'

Gelraen smiled weakly, his head falling to the side with the last effort. For a long time, Ember stared at Gelraen, his face desolate, no longer having any interest in what was going on around them.

Isyllia looked around, searching for one person. He was gone. The place he had been was empty. Her eyes widened with alarm, 'Wait!' She called, trying to follow, the sudden movement sending her head into a violent spin, and driving her hand back to the chair for support. She took several deep breaths, regaining her balance, and when she looked, she could see men approaching, swimming back and forth in her blurred vision. 'Here! In here! They have slain the king.' The soldiers advanced, only to halt before the waiting men, promising more bloodshed.

Enough death, 'I am the rightful ruler of this country, you will stand down.' Isyllia knew that would not stop them, but empty words were all she had left, even now she could feel the last of her strength ebbing away.

'You are a convicted traitor who has slain our legally appointed ruler.' It was one of the councillors, most had fled, but a few remained, previously cowing in the back of the room, and now finding their voices again. 'Your claim to the throne became invalid the moment you revealed yourself to be, Malagara.'

'But not mine.' A new voice entered the room, striding in from behind the guards. 'Stand down men!' They obeyed; it was the Duke of Preston. Isyllia wanted to cry out, but wanning strength would now allow it. The man turned, he was tall, and his presence was imposing, but kind. 'Call your men off.' He waited while Ember signalled to his men to stand down. They sheathed their swords but remained ready. 'Because I am Kin to the slain king, I claim my right to his throne.' No one could dispute his claim, and they knew it. 'You.' He pointed to the councillor who had spoken out, 'Bring physicians at once, and Duke Randal is to be released immediately, stop looking at the other councillors, do it now!' The once vocal man had now lost all his composure and scurried from the room. 'And you, step forward.' A soldier obeyed; it was impossible to ignore the command in his voice. 'Tell the armies to stand down at once, the war is over.'

A small part of Isyllia felt relieved, but it was small. 'Where have you been, father needed you … I needed you... and how did you get through the army outside.' She looked down, suddenly ashamed of her weakness.

'I got in through the Watergate; you weren't exactly subtle.'

She nodded, trying to keep herself upright.

His shoulders fell, but he pressed on, 'I *am* sorry child, my errand was too important to ignore. I mourned Cailem.'

Isyllia looked away, 'What errand?' The dizziness was getting worse.

'It is not the Malagara that are coming child, it's the Neuridian Empire. Gelraen struck a deal with them; kill you, and in exchange they would leave Illingdale in peace... Now...' He looked at Gelraen lying dead on the floor, pierced with his own sword. 'Now, they will kill everyone.' His face was pale.

Isyllia barely heard the words, her brain reeling, deciding enough was enough and plummeting her into blackness, bringing with it the dire statement and the dreams that were certain to plague her.

It was some hours later that she woke, the sound of snoring vibrating the walls around her. Isyllia sat, holding her hand for a moment and examining the bandages that restricted it, then turning to look at her friend, sitting slumped, fast asleep.

'Thomas!' She touched his face with her good hand, startling him awake. Thomas smiled, throwing his arms around her and barrelling into her bandaged cheek in his haste.

'Ouch.'

He jumped back in alarm, falling back into the chair he had just launched out of.

'How long have I been asleep?' She felt stiff, like she had been lying for an exceedingly long time.

'Three days. The physicians said you lost a lot of blood, but you should recover, you just need bed rest.'

Isyllia nodded, 'How is Randal?'

'The Duke was released not long after you collapsed. He was tortured badly, but I am told he is resting comfortably, the new King has given him the best accommodations.'

Isyllia sighed, 'New King.'

'Were you disappointed?'

Isyllia started. 'That Duke Preston took the throne, no. I never wanted the responsibility and that has not changed. I guess with my powers I knew deep down it was not what I was meant for. No, he is a good man; he will lead the people well... How many died, and what happened to Adella?' Her lip curled with distaste at the last, she chewed on the repugnance for a moment, then discarded it with a shudder.

Now it was Thomas turn to sigh, 'More than aught, a hundred or so they believe, a Duke Walton among them. Adella disappeared, no one seems to know where she went. Her, or her nephew.'

'How did Duke Walton die?' She leaned back against the bed.

'His head was crushed. He was near the Watergate at the time.' Isyllia nodded. She had never liked the man, but if she had thought about what fate he deserved, that was not it.

She shook her head, 'So much needless death.' Then she remembered, 'Your explosions, Thomas, it was like it shook the entire world!' Not for the first time was she in awe of his brilliance.

He blushed, jiggling his head slightly to dodge the compliment. 'It was nothing.'

Isyllia laughed, 'You would say that!'

He frowned. 'What about you though, how are you taking everything?'

Isyllia sat back again, 'Which part?'

'William, your mother, the Neuridian Empire...' He seemed to leave something unsaid.

Isyllia sighed. 'Everything is such a mess … I have no idea what we are we going to do.'

Thomas leaned forward, clasping her good hand for comfort, 'Things will turn out, you will see.'

She smiled back at him, grateful for the comfort, and then looked around the room, her old room. It had only just occurred to her that aside from Thomas, it was empty. Her stomach dropped. 'Where is Ember?'

His face fell and it was a moment before he replied, perhaps trying to find a way to sum up the last few days. 'I've never seen him so ...' He broke off and scratched the back of his head awkwardly; there was something he didn't want to say.

'So, What?'

He seemed to stumble over himself internally, at last coming to the right word, 'Heartbroken.'

Isyllia closed her eyes against the emotions probing at her, *'No more tears.'*

'What happened?' Thomas waited. He did not speak, offering no judgement, he just listened, the picture of perfect goodness. Isyllia poured her heart out, she told him about the night by the river, and about what had happened in the fight, about William, staring at the future scar she knew would mark that moment for the rest of her days. Thomas sat for a long while after, placing the pieces of information together in his mind. 'He wouldn't leave your side, you know, just sat there the whole time.' Thomas pointed to a spot by the bed. '... But when you said, William's name...' Thomas looked sad, like he had gained ten years in mere moments.

Isyllia closed her eyes, 'It's not what you think, he's my friend and he is suffering, suffering I caused him!'

Thomas measured his words. '*I* know that…but.'

'Ember.' She looked to the window, 'He has gone, hasn't he?'

Thomas exhaled. 'I tried to talk some sense into him, but…' He looked down. 'You know how he is. His mind was made up.'

'I understand.' Her voice shook, but she refused to cry.

'Will you go after him?'

She looked up again, taking a deep breath. 'I want to.' She was silent for a moment, collecting herself. 'But no… I am needed here. I cannot abandon the people for love. It hurts, but he has not left me with a choice.'

'What will you do?'

Isyllia Exhaled, 'I will train, I will dedicate myself to Abashiina, and I will fight to save our people, whether they want to be saved or not. I will find my mother, and I will save my friend. He will find his way; I know he will.' She touched the stone, reassured by its soft hum.

Thomas stood, nursing a contented smile, 'On that note, I should see the cook about some food for you, I know a great recipe, have you strong in no time!'

It took a moment for Isyllia to process the two opposite reactions that assaulted her at once. Thomas did not notice, rifling into his pocket for something and eventually finding a slip of paper. 'He left this.' Thomas placed it on the bed, and then backed away to the door.

Isyllia took it, unfolding it awkwardly. 'Thomas?'

He turned back.

'Thank you.'

He smiled, then turned again to leave.

'Oh, and Thomas, can you see that someone finds, Niimorea? I left her in the forest, she cannot be too far.' He left, closing the door quietly behind, but not before visibly trying to suppress a guilty shudder, that he no doubt carried down the hallway with him.

She turned her attention to the note. Unlike Ember's usual standard it was not short.

Isyllia,

Forgive me for not having the courage to face you in person. I knew if I had been there to watch you wake, I would never have found the strength to leave. For so long, I have wanted to tell you that each time I pushed you away I wanted to hold you. Each time I made you feel less than you are, it was because I couldn't breathe and for the first time, I feel afraid. The thought of not seeing you each day when I wake is more than I can bear. But I must leave, and wherever Caros takes me, whatever I face, know that I will carry your voice in my heart, until I see you again. I know I pretended that it didn't matter, and our mission came first. It has been so hard to see you with William, and see your eyes light up like sunrise when he was near. It pained me to hear you say his name just now, because I would have given anything for you to say mine. I don't know what the gods have planned for us, or if when I return you will still want me. All I know is I am lost, and I must trust in Caros to guide me. I love you.

Isyllia pushed back the covers to swing her feet out, resting them dubiously on the ground. Then, leaning on the cupboard for support, she rose, her body adjusting badly to the sudden task of standing. She waited for a moment, letting the dizzy spells fade, and then when it was decidedly safe, walked slowly to the window, looking to the horizon, her eyes locked on the mountains, and the destiny she was finally ready to live.

EPILOGUE

Kershen, [4]Ĩkiĩŋdom iife theii Ĩgodii, Ĩmespar.

'Pick your stance, never take your eyes off your enemy.' Kershen studied the soldiers before her; she had argued with the king about training poor men to fight, but in the end, she had lost. Then insisting she at least be the one to do it. Someone had to train them properly! 'Never attack first, now is your time to study your opponent. Identify his weaknesses, anticipate his attack ... Strike!' She shouted the words, cursing because men floundered and fell over their own feet. This would take years. 'Take a break, and if you're not back in five minutes, I'll run you through myself.' The men ran, she was clearly not someone to cross. Kershen took a swig from her water skin, and then threw it to the ground in annoyance.

'Mistress, Kershen.'

---

[4] Translation: Kingdom of the gods, Mespar.

505

She turned, glowering at the messenger. 'What!'

He blushed. 'The King asks for you.'

She sighed; waving him off and running her fingers over her long tied black hair. Arthiin was a patient man, but she knew it would not do to keep him waiting, and so she sheathed her sword, and turned toward the castle.

She had walked a few steps when it happened. At first, she tried to ignore it, but the pain began to build, to sear, like it was burning her alive. Gritting her teeth, she fumbled with the straps on her armour, removing the chest and throwing it to the ground, not caring who was staring. The pain was becoming unbearable and with panic, she ripped at her sleeve, tearing it away, looking for the source of the pain. A mark had been burned into her flesh. Kershen stared at it in disbelief, tears falling from her eyes in shock. She had been chosen, the mark Menethon, sitting proudly on her arm.

INDEX

Gods, Chosen, and Weapons

There were 4 gods. They created the earth and lived in the holy city of light in Cyndershire. The Temple of the gods is the very place the gods left the weapons of the chosen, right before disappearing.

Goddess Abashiina - Mother of the earth

Goddess Nemethiiniia - Mother to all living things

God Caros - Father to all living things

God Menethon - Father of the earth

In the beginning, when the gods walked earth, they created all things. But no matter how beautiful, Nemethiiniia remained sad. It is said the earth's lakes and rivers are the remainder of Nemethiiniia tears. She longed for sons and daughters, and Caros out of love for his Nemethiiniia, created the animals and presented them each to his beloved, but still, she shook her head, and cried. It wasn't until Caros, the father of all living things, created man and woman, in their very image that Nemethiiniia smiled once more. Next, Nemethiiniia gave man and woman powers of their own, so that they might protect their new home. But man was flawed and abused the power they were given. Caros, tried to remove the magic bestowed on them but did not get it all. They decided after a while, that it was time they left their children to live in the home they had given them. They each

507

appointed a champion, and gave them a weapon, chosen to protect man from themselves, while they were away, should the magic that was banished ever rise up again.

Abashiina created the stone of Elements

Menethon Created the Bow of Power

Caros created the sphere of Knowledge and Wisdom

Nemethüniia created the Quill of love and worship

The Stone of Abashiina was created to aid the chosen in using their power to bend the elements to help stave against famine for the people. It does not create the power in one without the ability already. But will make them better in certain areas. Consequence of using it is, you must take to get. So, if you want to kill someone, it requires a life in place, create fire it takes the elements required from around it, etc. if Isyllia is in a room of people, using the stone becomes takes careful consideration, she needs to know its requirements well if she is to avoid accidents.

The stone is a combination of the 4 main elements, to create a super element. The god element. The stone is big enough to sit comfortably in your palm. It is a bright iridescent white light with what appears to have wispy white flames gently burning off it. Another way to describe it is clear, mist like energy.

When Kathryn had this stone, she had it made into a pendant with a heavy gold chain. The stone was shaped to fashion by her; this stone is unable to be cut by conventional methods. Anyone who might behold the stone would know it is not an ordinary stone but of immense value, but as all records of the chosen and their objects was lost, not many would be able to identify it, Legend hunters would struggle, but stand a chance, few though they be.

The Bow of Menethon was created to enhance strength and power, to assist in battle with prowess and stamina. The stone of power was created to help the chosen to lead the people. When wielded by its chosen guardian, it radiates strength and stamina in those around it. Its consequence is eventual corruption by the power. It's designed this way so that you don't use and rely on it all the time, only when needed.

The bow of Menethon was entrusted to Odriid in the death of the chosen, to ensure it got handed down and given to the next chosen who was to see it to its guardian. The gods entrusted Odriid with this task knowing he was the best one to ensure its safety and hoping the great responsibility over generations would ensure when it came time for the correct chosen to take the bow, it would be ensured history did not repeat itself.

The bow is made of polished mahogany with golden patterns woven throughout. To the naked eye, this might be the bow of royalty, but not of any immense importance. It was deliberately fashioned to look ordinary to avert attention to it.

The Sphere of Caros arguably the most important of all, if not always the most desired, was meant to help its user make better decisions; it increases intelligence and helps the user see things others overlook. Used correctly, this sphere can be invaluable. When used by its chosen guardian, in addition to the above this sphere has the ability to see people over great distance and also on occasion see through time.

None know of the potential of the Sphere except the chosen wielders. The consequence of using the sphere is the pain of prophecy and future death of loved ones. Images come unbidden, sometimes happy sometimes painful, but wisdom and tolerance are the requirement of using it.

The Sphere was hidden within a telescope fashioned be Odriid the wise. Coupling his love of astronomy, he thought a small hand-held telescope would not only be a great way to disguise the object from unfriendly eyes, but also made it much easier to wield and stow. When looking in the telescope, all his focus was directed through the lens, which also increased the power between him and the sphere, in getting the result he needed. Any who looked in the telescope, and did not know what object they held, would think it broken due to its inability to function as a normal scope does, the sphere interferes with normal telescopic focus and magnification. Objects always appear off focus.

The telescope is made of rich leather and gold brass. It is attractive to look at and like the bow of Menethon, would be thought to any untrained eye, to be an object belonging to royalty.

The Quill of Nemethiiniia was created to give the people a sense of hope, when hopelessness was a bay, the chosen would have the power to wash the people with love and obedience, so that they may help them. Used incorrectly it can be used as a tool to control people. It is used telepathically, not wielded. The physical connection with the weapon is enough to give the wielder the boost to their power they need. The consequence of long use is eventual degradation of the wielders sanity in place of what was given.

The Quill was created, as the embodiment of love and hope that can be represented by nothing more perfect than a feather. It was at the urging of Odriid that the object be disguised as a quill. This also gave the object a practical use.

The Quill is white and seems to shimmer. When used for writing, it is the easiest of the four objects to distinguish as it contains no ink stains. Even when used with the blackest of inks, the quill always remains clean. It remains ever sharp and is UN breakable, as with the other objects.

The first chosen. A history.

The gods each created one object, a weapon as a representation of themselves to leave behind while they were gone. Each we weapon entrusted to a chosen guardian as an aid

511

to help them protect the people. The chosen were also given abilities above others and the opportunity to be long living. The chosen do not age as normal mortals, but life and experience age them. The structure and longevity of their life is entirely in their hands. They are naturally immune to sickness and pestilence.

When the gods left the world, they left the weapons in a shrine temple created in their honour; the guardians protected the weapons until they decided it was too risky for them to be in one place. They were taken to various places through the world,

The First disciples of the gods, the chosen.

Kathriin Oriin, Wielder of the stone of Elements

Semiir Tamworth, Wielder of the Bow of Power

Odriid Fenn, Wielder of the Sphere of Knowledge

Luron Dale, Wielder of the Quill of Love

For many years worked together in harmony. Each in turn doing their duty to the people and ensuring the earth the gods created flourished. But as time went on, greed, lust, power begun to corrupt the chosen and slowly, one by one, their hearts turned to selfish ends. Odriid the wise, wielder of the Sphere of Caros, was the only one that remained uncorrupted by his powers.

Semiir and Kathryn, lovers, returned to Illingdale to work together, and for many years the people looked up to them for guidance, even worshiped them. But as the years went on and their guidance turned to rule, and rule turned to tyranny the people sought a new ruler, King Medeus I, denounced the chosen as heretics, and in the year 1439 Semiir, was tortured and burned. Kathryn, able to wield much stronger powers was unable to be caught and, in her grief, destroyed much of the city. It wasn't until Odriid came that she finally stowed her wrath and began to see what she had done. She gave Semiirs bow, and her stone to Odriid and after she had said her goodbyes, she begged forgiveness of the gods, and gave herself to King Medeus, to face her crimes. Kathryn was also burned at the stake, and thus began the outlaw of magic and the gods. They were hence referred to as 'Malagara' meaning evil ones. Every reference to the gods was seized and burned.

Tandus, second son of Medeus, disagreed with his father's crusade against the gods, and left to establish his own kingdom of the Isle of Mespar. A couple of years later, as he was low on supplies, he struck an agreement with his father. Mespar sent all of Illingdale's Malagara, as well as their own, under 10 to the Isle of the forgotten. Mespar would escort them to the other side and establish a guard so that none could cross back over. Any Malagara that used their power on the guards were killed. The great culling of witches was a dark time in Illingdale history, many innocent citizens were burned. Accused out of vengeance by others, and eagerly burned in King Medeus' desire to make an example. Once the burning ceased, citizens of Illingdale quickly became afraid of magic, temples to the gods were pulled down, and life went on without the chosen.

Odriid, travelled to the forgotten lands beyond Mespar to see Luron who had gone to the Isle in his desire to guide the Malagara, as was their charge from the gods. Over the years, rumours reached Odriid that he had locked himself in a tower, taken with madness. Odriid, desperate not to fail the last of the guardians, set to convince Luron to return to Cyndershire to find another way to serve the gods. When Odriid arrived, the tower was empty. Luron had disappeared, except for a note with hastily written scrawl saying the following.

Odriid

I have failed my brother; I leave it for you.

Do not find me.

Live well

All four objects now in his possession, with a heavy heart, Odriid, travelled back to Cyndershire and beseeched the gods to banish the objects so their power could never corrupt another. The gods instead bade him take 3 of the objects, The stone of Abashiina, the Sphere of Caros, and the Quill of Nemethiiniia and secure them for the coming of the next guardians. The gods told Odriid the next ones would need the objects, but it was up to Odriid to ensure that the objects were secured so that their wielders would have to prove worthy to possess them. Odriid was granted the power of all the chosen, until his task was done.

Odriid decided to take each of the objects to a different place and set a test that their intended wielder would overcome.

THE STONE OF ABASHIINA

Was taken to a cave in Ravenswood, later named the cave of lost souls, for many had died trying to get to the end.

1. The chosen must prove their ability to overcome problems. To prove this, they must find a way over the great divide where no way seems obvious. Odriid made a tiny crystal grow from the ground that to any ordinary person would be overlooked. But to a chosen, it would be clear the intent.

2. The ability to overcome boundaries. This must be demonstrated by removing a giant wall of ice, which is extremely thick and dense, so cannot be cut through by conventional methods safely, and as the ice is not meant to be removed this way, it instantly grows back. Mortals who have tried remaining trapped forever in the wall where they were unable to get out before it froze back over.

3. Show courage in the face of danger. This must be demonstrated by using their ability to safely retract the stalactites and stalagmites without getting impaled. A couple of mortals were able to make it through the wall

of ice, but none made it through this section and bones can be found, where their victims still lay impaled.

4. The final test that must be passed, the champion falls into an illusion and much choose between duty and their greatest desire.

QUILL OF NEMETHIINIIA

Was taken to the ruins of Eddinsford and buried at the heart of the great city. With the help of Nemethiiniia, Odriid placed a powerful enchantment on the Quill that anyone seeking the Quill would be faced with the cries and anguish of all the lost souls of the Great War. The guardian could then learn humility and the importance of remembering the people first.

THE SPHERE OF CAROS

Was left in the city of light at the temple of the gods. Hidden underneath the statue of Caros by Odriid. It was decided that the only way to test a guardian, was for Caros himself to consider the heart of the intended.

BOW OF MENETHON

As a reward for his benevolence, Odriid was awarded the honour of being the guardian of the bow of Menethon. It was decided Odriid would retire as a chosen and return to the world to live out his life. He was to marry, then hand down the bow through his generations until the coming of the next chosen, and his descendent could endure the bow made it to the next guardian.

He was instructed to make sure his descendants knew to test the guardian when they should come, to make sure they were worthy of the bow.

Once the correct guardian was ready to take the bow, they were to be tested for their courage and lust for power. It was said an enchantment was placed on the bow that none other than the guardian could awaken. With their touch if their heart were not pure the bow would weaken them to the point of death. If their heart were pure, it would belong to them, as intended, having proved worthy.

With his task completed, Odriid travelled to the troubled Illingdale to start a new life. There he married and had a daughter, Faeliin. Stricken with grief at the loss of his wife, Odriid finally died in the year 1489 and having kept his promise handed the bow of Menethon to his daughter to start the line of bearers.

THE CHOSEN

The chosen are born into the world, when they are needed. They are marked at birth with a distinctive mark. The mark can appear anywhere on their body, and in appearance looks to be like the symbol of the god weapon they are chosen for.

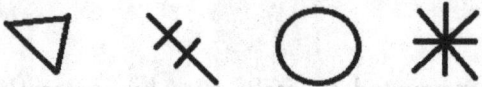

The chosen wait until the 'calling of the gods. When they get this calling, it is an urge within them to travel through the forbidden mountains. The chosen of Caros, if he is close enough, is able to feel their calling and it is his job to guide them safely. The chosen one can think of nothing else. Currently the chosen are.

- Ember Samuel Clae

- Isyllia Mae Bellamy

- Gelraen Pennerly, Kershen Thwaite

- Luron Dale

- Ember: was called at age 15

- Isyllia: did not received calling

- Gelraen: was called at age 18

- Kershen Thwaite: did not receive calling due to later-in-life transfer of power from Gelraen to Kershen.

- Luron: Chosen specifically by the gods in person.

Due to circumstances, Isyllia never feels the calling like the others as Ember finds her before she is ready.

Their abilities are as follows.

EMBER SAMUEL CLAE:

- Ability to see anyone's location in his mind's eye *(target must be within close proximity unless wielding Sphere)*

- Ability to sense danger

- Ability to see things others miss. When in possession of the sphere, this ability is instinctual and extraordinarily strong.

LORD GELRAEN PENNERLY

- Unusually gifted in battle when in possession of the bow.

- Unusually gifted with battle tactics

- Instil courage in people. Gelraen manipulates his powers to work more like mind control. Without the bow, this ability does not work to full effect.

LURON DALE

- Ability to communicate telepathically

- Ability to calm others, tranquil type effect. Can only be used person to person without the Quill.

- Can still rage and restore reason when in possession of the Quill.

ISYLLIA MAE BELLAMY:

- Control and bend all elements to her desire, magnitude greatly weakened without Stone of Elements.

- Control significantly hindered without the stone

- On use of her ability without the stone, energy is drained in place.

The chosen are immune to worldly sickness. They have the gift of long life, how long is determined by the worldly stresses they endure, but they do not age as normal people do. Given the right circumstances, a chosen can have the ability to live for hundreds, even thousands of years.

The chosen are able to reproduce like normal people, but this does not mean that their children will be chosen. That is something only the gods determine.

Rites of the Dead Ceremony – Illingdale

LUTHERAN ROOTS:

Death goes against what is naturally intended for us by the gods. It is thought that because of humankind's rebellion against the gods, death was created as a punishment.

Illingdalean believe that in death, the spirit is reunited with the gods. But as they have built their society on the belief that the gods were evil, they burn their dead. Once the body is destroyed, the spirit ceases to exist, forever robbing the gods of the ability to claim the dead and use the spirits in their evil deeds, some believe also avoiding further punishment for their rebellion. It is the belief of Illingdalean that the spirit is destroyed when the body is, and the ashes of the honoured are given back to the earth.

Overview of the ceremony; Family members (children, spouses etc.) wash and dress the deceased in their best garb and bare them to a temple of honour wrapped in a shroud of their station. The shroud covers the eyes as they believe that if the eyes are covered, the spirit is blind and cannot see its fate. The body is then placed in a large crypt like hollow at the alter where it is cleansed by fire.

Ceremonial Language:

Curator Says:

"You may now come forward, and make your offers of farewell"

Matriarch to the Deceased:

I have washed you and clad you with honour. May you now face the darkness with the love of your kin, the strength of your people, and the wisdom of your years.

Curator says:

With this fire, you protect your people once more.

Everyone says:

Gods never take thee, gods never prosper.

CHAMBRITE (*CAMELIION*)

Chambrite, also known as *Ćameliioṇ* in Old Dalliian is a type of mineral found mostly in the Tinderfordean mountains. Most of the properties of this compound are unknown, but upon ancient study it was found to have high quantities of Palladium *(Pd)*. This is most likely one of the key elements that make it 'reactive' to storm fire (*electricity*), and able to 'mend' itself and seemingly change its shape, as Palladium is known to have a low melting point.

Chambrite despite its inclusion of Palladium is incredibly dense in its dormant state. It becomes un-mineable unless large bolts of storm fire are pulsed through it, exciting the atom structure, and causing it to move about. This activates its 'transformatory' state and allows generic tools to cut through it.

There are no known images of Chambrite in its native state, due to its ability to adapt to its surroundings, Chambrite more often than not, will 'blend' to hide within its surroundings, thus earning its name. It's more famous characteristics and seemingly alive nature are attributes from its mysterious properties, and as such it is considered not only quite rare and hard to find, but incredibly lucrative.

Common uses for Chambrite included Armor and weapons.

HISTORY

Chambrite was first discovered in 1406 by a travelling Illingdale scientist, Īrałd Briightoṇ. His party were journeying back to the city when a storm hit, forcing them to seek shelter in a nearby cave. Ancient writings left by Īrałd say the metal appeared to glimmer and shine to the naked eye like nothing else. He took a sample of the mineral back to Illingdale, recording its strange behaviour on the way.

'The strange mineral, that only days before seemed to shine and dance before the eye, now lies resolute as any other in its insipidity'

The mineral was studied for some years with no success, but it was on conversation with Odriid Fenn, where it was suggested to the scientist to recreate the settings of the evening it was found. It was there that storm fire (electricity) was discovered to be the key component, and he was able to make it reactive once more. From this point mining and smithing was done at great risk and few knew how to successfully smith the mineral without risk of death.

In 1445 all use and knowledge of Chambrite was forbidden by Medeus in the uprising. Few documents survived the great purge and the art of mining the incredible mineral was lost with time. Few still know of its very existence. Armor and weapons created (though few could afford it) were seized, and unable to be destroyed hidden, and lost with time.

MINING

Chambrite was mined at great risk. Large metal rods were crafted and inserted into the ground surrounding the Mineral. The miner would then have to wait until an electrical storm formed. Once enough storm fire (electricity) had hit the prepared rods and filtered into the mineral, the miner would have a few hours at the most before the stone would return to its dormant state, and once again become un mineable and un-malleable. Miners were required to wear specialised suits to protect them from shock

SCIENTIFIC DATA

Chambrite is classified as a partially unstable isotope.

PhaseTransitionary

Melting Point$P = 100 \times 10^3$ A x 100 x 10^3 V

$= 10,000$ x 10^6VA or Watts

$= 1$ x 10^{10} Watts

Recall that 10^{10}Watts is 10,000,000,000 or 10 billion Watts.

10,000,000,000 watt $= 5,2752792631$ degree Fahrenheit hour/Btu (IT)

5,2752792631 degree Fahrenheit hour/Btu (IT) $=$ 29307106999.4444 degree Celsius.

DENSITY UNKNOWN

Due to its fluctuating nature, it is hard to accurately measure the native density of Chambrite. But unlike other minerals, Chambrite is almost impenetrable in its dormant state, and manages to retain a lighter weight than most other minerals. Minimal study was done or retained on the mineral due to the uprising, but it is known to reduce its overall density with the application of storm fire.

FENNEL

PHYSICAL CHARACTERISTICS

The Fennel carries many physical characteristics of the common rat. Two notable differences are the absence of a tail, and its fluffy feathery coat in place of fur. The most common colours of this species are dark grey and soft black, making it easy for the creature to camouflage at night. Variations of soft white and brown coats can be found though considered rarer as they have a harder time with camouflage

INTELLIGENCE

The Fennel has an amazing ability to remember people's faces and when in captivity grows overly attached to its primary owner. Metacognition, high problem-solving skills, decision making, and self-awareness are the most dominant attributes of this species.

The exact depth of a Fennel's intelligence is still largely unknown. Captive Fennels that have been studied were reported to have little difficulty overcoming tasks that were presented, however the flaw lies in the Fennels strong sense of independence, making it near impossible to get the creature to cooperate.

BEHAVIOUR / BREEDING

Fennels are naturally wary of others, especially humans. They can be trained quite easily however through persistence and kindness. Their natural intelligence sees they pick things up very quickly, and the easiest way to tame a wild fennel is through regular feeding and patience.

While in captivity fennels are considered quite clean and are most comfortable when provided somewhere warm to burrow into. They can possess quite an assertive, independent, and lively personality set.

Fennels are non-aggressive and experts at evading capture.

Fennels have some of the most complicated breeding rituals in the animal kingdom. When a female senses her time is right for conception, she creates a trail for her potential mate to follow, that deliberately leads past dangerous predators and waits to see who makes it through her deadly gauntlet, this dangerous method of mating, and currently the leading theory for their relatively low numbers in the wild, is believed to be their way of ensuring only the most resourceful mate makes it through to the end.

DIET

Fennels are herbivores surviving largely on fruits and leafy greens. It has been noted however Fennels have a strange fondness for worms and will go to great lengths to acquire them.

Fennels often hoard food and where competition stands before their objective have been known to offer their idea of a trade. A captive fennel was once known for leaving single grapes as currency exchange for items he pinched.

STRUCTURE OF BIRDERIES

Birds are trained mostly to fly back to their post. Transports are in constant operation to take birds to various points for commission. Upon payment, a message is carried back to its home base and delivered via messenger. Turnaround for urgent messages is approximately half a day.

Establishments try to stagger the release of birds, ensuring there is always enough waiting before the next lot arrive.

Transport agents are careful not to travel birds to often to bring on unnecessary stress to the bird. Breeding grounds are run in the company's main establishment, as well as training young birds.

Birds leave according to schedule and are able to carry a certain load. This enables them to monitor travel times and use of birds.

Companies have a main base of operation, each message is received and documented unless secrecy is paid for, these messages are carried via owl overnight and are not documented, a much higher price is put on these messages due to their usual risk factor.

MAYOR'S OFFICE BIRDERIE

New Eddinsford, 1 bird point.

New Eddinsford is a small town, set on the coast of a broken monarchy. The birderie is controlled by the town's mayor.

When the monarchy fell, in the Great War, and the beginning of the Age of Menethon, the survivors retreated to the coast lands. The nobles, formed a council, now known as the local government culminating in the mayor, elected by the local council. It was decided the local government would control the bird point in New Eddinsford to avoid any surprises, never wishing to be overthrown again.

News is delivered from other cities generally without handling fee, in exchange for food and rest for the delivering bird. Both Clydesdale and Wentworth offer great sums of money to purchase holding within New Eddinsford, but each time this is proposed, it is refused.

At one time, they sought to force compliance, by sabotaging some of the birds, but the mayor's office was able to thwart the attempt before it was made, ending the debate.

There is only 1 bird point in New Eddinsford.

ANTONIO'S FAMILY BIRDERIES

Isle of the Forgotten, 2 bird point.

The Antonio's family birderies are a military family originally from Mespar but agreed to run the management operation on the Isle of the Forgotten. The Wentworth's have never approached the Antonio's family for holding due to location. Living in close proximity to magic ones is generally accepted to be high risk, and were it not for the military backing provided, they would not have agreed to take up the post.

News mainly passes for the benefit of Mespar. News of other regions generally does not come though unless specifically requested.

Sophia Antonio's – mother

Mario's Antonio's – Father, monarch

Puerto Antonio's – Son

WENTWORTH FAMILY BIRDERIES

Illingdale, 1 bird point.

Mariin Wentworth first ran his birderies 200 years ago. Clydesdale birderies sought to assassinate him in order to take over the market. The plot was discovered by spies that Mariin had watching the Clydesdales. Wentworth knew the attempt was done in order to make him leave so Clydesdale could have total hold over Tinderford. Birderies were widely known to be exceptionally reliable for fast / confidential information, and as such, can make a lot of money.

The Wentworth family used to hold a bird point in Tinderford, making them the largest bird family. That was until the Clydesdale family, a powerful Tinderfordean family decided to increase their holding. They staged an assassination attempt on the Wentworth family birderie which was foiled. This began a war between the two families, until finally the guild of Tinderford interceded giving the Wentworth holdings to Clydesdale. Mariin retreated back to Illingdale but animosity has remained between these families ever since.

The Wentworth family hold 6 bird points. 4 in Mespar and surrounding country, 1 at dock town, and 1 Illingdale city.

Mariin Wentworth - father, monarch

Gwenda Wentworth – Mother – resides in Mespar.

Chet Wentworth – Son, eldest Illingdale

Dale Wentworth – son, middle – Mespar surrounding country

Cousin Wentworth – Mespar surrounding country

Cousin Wentworth - Mespar surrounding country

CLYDESDALE FAMILY BIRDERIES

Tinderford, 4 bird points.

The Clydesdale family now own all the bird points in Tinderford. They were always a wealthy family that saw early on the profit to be made in owning bird points. They decided to take over the market, and to do so, paid for an assassination attempt on their main rivals, the Wentworth family monarch. The attempt was discovered, and this started a war between the two families. The power struggle went on for months, until the economy started to suffer with the lack of communications, the guild got involved. The Clydesdales paid off the guild to be granted all the holdings, and the guild, wishing to end the trouble now and thwart any future issues, agreed. The Wentworth's left Tinderford.

Since that time, there has always been tension between these two families.

Perta Clydesdale – Mother

Sim Clydesdale – Father, Monarch

Rian Clydesdale – Daughter

Phillip Clydesdale – Son.

ACKNOWLEDGEMENTS

If you had told me when I was young that these characters that I had in my mind would one day become a story, I most likely would have told you, you are bonkers! But here I am, and like all good stories, many contribute to the journey along the way who must be thanked. First and foremost, I would like to say a big thank you to my editor, Amber Withers. Thank you for making your way through my own personal version of war and peace. It would be remiss of my to not thank this same girl for my beautiful cover design, multi-talented is she!

Secondly, I would like to thank my husband, who gave me little suggestions along the way, some of which raised more eyebrows than I own. Thank you for putting up with me writing instead of making dinner, and the many other tasks you had to do so I could do this instead. Thank you for being you. Thank you to my reader, Danielle Clark. Your enthusiasm was a joy for me, you are a wonderful woman, and I am so incredibly blessed to have you in my life, now and always.

Thank you to Morten Benning, Author in his own right. Thank you for helping me begin the editing, for helping me with advice and coaching. You are an amazing guy, and it will always be my pleasure to discuss many things with you, not forgetting your wonderful figures.

Thank you to my dad, for paying for my editor, for reading my book and encouraging me to move forward and get it done. Your support and blessing were important to me, and I cannot thank you enough for it.

Thank you, Tarina Marcinkowski. You are an inspirational woman, with an incredible story of your own. Your advice was a life saver in so many ways, I will be forever grateful.

Thank you, Ryan Carr, my grammar man and best friend, life isn't doable without you.

Thank you to my mum and stepdad upstairs, I love you both for your support of my life in general.

Thank you to my father-in-law, Max for not tearing your hair out when I asked you to look at my Chambrite formula and making it through my grammar mistakes. You are a wonderful, and patient man.

Thank you to my guides for inspiring me, even at 2am, to write. You really did take those requests very seriously. You are a credit.

Last but not least, thank you to the great father. There are many words for you, for which I know you already know. I will conclude my thank you's then to you with a simple, I love you. For what else can be said.

www.ingramcontent.com/pod-product-compliance
Lightning Source LLC
Chambersburg PA
CBHW010253100726
47904CB00011B/2575

* 9 7 8 0 6 4 5 0 3 7 7 8 4 *